THE HALLIE LAWRENCE STORY

T H E

HALLIE

LAWRENCE

S T O R Y

A NOVEL BY

J o y c e W a l t e r

ST. MARTIN'S PRESS   NEW YORK

Design by Glen M. Edelstein

Library of Congress Cataloging-in-Publication Data

Walter, Joyce.
  The Hallie Lawrence story: a novel/Joyce Wal-
ter.
    p. cm.
  ISBN 0-312-04959-5
  I. Title.
PS3573.A4722835H35   1991
813'.54—dc20   90-49231
                                             CIP

First Edition: February 1991
10 9 8 7 6 5 4 3 2 1

To Marjorie Weil, for those childhood days when you talked to me about books with so much love and enthusiasm that I decided one day I would write one for you.

To Lee Lacy, for his years of unfailing support. I'm sorry I had to do this alone but unfortunately you taught me how.

To Courtney Walter, my excellent daughter, because I'm so proud of you and I wanted to put it in writing.

And, to my hero, my husband, Mr. David Schiff.

THE

HALLIE
LAWRENCE

STORY

1

THE HORROR OF THE HALLIE LAW-
rence story was that it happened to
Hallie Lawrence. People who met him
knew one thing: they wanted to do
business with him. Any kind of business. As a result, he had a very successful law career, and the laundry never
lost his shirts. It wasn't just that he was
smart and charming, which he was, it
was that he also seemed incongruously
shy, a shyness no one expected from
someone of his illustrious background.
When he engaged someone in conversation, it was with a certain intimacy
that suggested it was the first time that
he had ever spoken with intimacy to
anyone before. That he never disclosed anything personal, despite his
confidential manner, went unnoticed.
People were far too distracted by the
flattery.

Of course, had he truly never disclosed anything personal, he would have been a weirdo with no friends, which wasn't the case. There was Kip Courtland, whom Hallie had first met at prep school nearly twenty years ago. After knowing someone that long, even Hallie developed a sense of trust. But with most people, Hallie calculated just how much personal disclosure was necessary to keep things warm, without ever spending an emotional nickel. It was a very elegant talent.

That ability was by no means the result of instinct, but rather came from having spent most of his childhood in psychoanalysis. It was his mother's idea of preventive medicine. As a result, Hallie was in control of himself and of others, but in the most attractive sort of way.

And Hallie Lawrence was an attractive young man. He had an aristocratic carriage and moved with the slender strength of a great thoroughbred, albeit a Jewish one. There was a beautiful assemblage to his face, a warmth to his mouth, even a sensuousness to it, a delicate if long nose, and the brown eyes that held people's attention at once. Sharp eyes. He wore a pretty deadpan expression most of the time, but his eyes went a million miles a minute.

You would think with a personality like that, and the sellable good looks, Hallie would have gone into politics, but he wasn't two-dimensional enough. And he didn't smile nearly enough for any kind of relationship with cameras. He didn't like cameras.

He was educated at Collegiate, Exeter, Harvard, and Harvard Law, as one might expect from the son of the dynamic Lawrences. And while his schooling was overseen by his mother, Lily, elegant German-American Jewish socialite, his father, Alfred, took him around the world, many times, to sit in darkened concert halls while the brilliant Alfred Lawrence guest-conducted symphony orchestras, or. toured with his own. Fortunately, Hallie liked classical music. It made great sense to him, the way math did. For Hallie, music was emotional math.

Then he discovered rock music and marijuana.

Adolescent rebellion held little joy for Hallie. Alfred and Lily were rebels in their own right, although as they aged, their eccentricities became the prerogatives of their station. When Hallie's stereo blasted rock 'n' roll, Alfred would come into his room and bellow, "That's not bad!" Then he'd want to sit around and analyze it, for Christ's sake. Lily thought the music made the house feel young. And when Lily found the bag of pot in Hallie's mini-Mosler safe, Alfred came in to have a talk with him, which began with the announcement that he, the great Alfred Lawrence, His Holiness Himself, had smoked the stuff all his life. Then they smoked a joint together, at Alfred's insistence and to Hallie's mortification. The evening ended with Alfred playing Bach on the piano until four in the morning while Hallie fell asleep underneath it.

The Hallie Lawrence story reminded people that the universe was, in fact, totally chaotic, no matter how much they had invented to convince themselves otherwise. It wreaked havoc with any sense of order. But it also filled people with longing.

Needless to say, the person most bothered by the Hallie Lawrence story was Hallie himself. He told himself it wasn't the worst thing that ever happened in the history of the world. But he often forgot that, at the time, he thought it was.

The story is best begun a few days before anything had really happened, on a very late afternoon in November. Hallie was in his office high up above Fifty-seventh Street, standing at the window, with his hands in his pockets. It was almost dark. He happened to be thinking about the very time he got stoned with his father and lay under the piano listening to him play Bach. But the Bach began to fade away as Hallie stared out the window at the Magnificent View.

Gazing from the heights of Hallie's office windows put you in the third dimension, not looking *at* the skyline, but aware that you were *in* it. On a clear day you could practically see the North Pole. The only things at eye level were the tops of other skyscrapers and the sky, which you realized wasn't being scraped at all. Below was Central Park, the Plaza Hotel looking like a miniature castle plucked from Liechtenstein, and billions of windows that one hoped had people behind them. That anything was happening at street level was completely forgotten.

There's the Magnificent View, he thought, with irony. Sometimes Hallie kept himself entertained with his own irony.

Every visitor to Hallie's office commented on the view, or rather, the Magnificent View. As soon as Hallie had begun detecting this, he started a log, in his head, to chart the consistency of the comments, and they were as consistent at the view itself. For a while, as an experiment, he had closed the curtains. But people would go over to them, pull them apart, and have a look anyway. It was a powerful view, in that sense. The problem for Hallie was, he had always grown up with a Magnificent View. So when people commented about it, he sort of felt embarrassed, for himself and for them.

But he was looking at it now because this was the only time of day when it actually was worth looking at; something was actually happening. The sky was black on top, turning to a wonderful sapphire as it poured west toward the horizon to meet with a ring of flaming orange that was itself topped with deep mauve. Darkness had almost replaced the day. Against all this, the artificial white lights were on in the billions of windows. It was good. It was comforting and it was reliable, as opposed to embarrassing and reliable.

At that moment, Lisa Norman came into his office. She knocked first, but came right in with the authority he liked her to have, so that she would feel like a trusted assistant. Lisa was efficient. She was very smart, and on top of that, a pretty girl. She had a fantastic amount of long black curls, which was stunning, and she knew it. She always wore very sleek simple clothes and high-heel pumps. She read a lot of fashion publications, this fine young woman with a master's from Yale.

"God, Hallie, I know you don't want to be disturbed, but it's getting late. I have a ton of messages for you." And efficiently she went to his desk and laid out papers for his review.

"You've got to call George Mason in Houston and tell him Herman can do two performances in February."

"He knows that. What does he really want?"

"Probably a deal for the two dates. He'll pretend he only budgeted for one performance but would love to have two."

"That's very good, Lisa." Hallie smiled.

"They don't have as much money in Houston as they used to."

She was always doing that, adding obvious information. Hallie never responded when she did, hoping in time it might cure her.

"You know I'm not a lawyer, really," said Hallie.

"What are you talking about? Of course you're a lawyer. You're the best lawyer in New York."

"I could have been the best, but I'm an agent, that's what I am. I should move over to Broadway and get a second-floor office with a view of a triple-feature porn theater. I could pick up a few clients who do bird calls. In fact, I might specialize in barnyard callers of all types—a guy who does a pig, a fat woman who does cows—"

"Bite your tongue," said Lisa, with the half-smile she used when she thought they were having a lighter moment. He figured it was something she'd picked up from watching too much television.

"The following people would like you to call them: Randolph Billings, Joe Epstein, Harriet at the *Times* . . ."

Hallie watched her red lips read off names from her pad. She had a nice body because she worked out a lot. Actually, she was a nice girl. Very bright. Very quick. He hated the red lipstick.

"Oh, and your mother called."

"My mother." Hallie repeated this in a monotone. He picked up one of the documents from his desk, but he imagined Lily twirling the phone line, talking to that "awfully-nice-girl, Lisa," making small talk for which Lily had very little patience but at which she was so good.

"She said to tell you, please, don't be late."

The way Lisa spoke the word "please," the way she paused over it just as Lily undoubtedly had, alerted Hallie that a mistake might be coming.

"Hallie, *please*," Lisa began, looking straight at him with the half-smile, "don't be late. Not for your mother."

Lisa had just assumed familiar tones. She had jumped over the border and acknowledged that not only did Hallie have a mother, but that she had some idea about their relationship. Only Kip, his best friend since prep school, could assume intimacy about Lily. Lisa, his assistant, pretending to know how Lily felt about lateness? The presumption was stupendous.

Hallie was a little bit touchy on the subject of his personal life.

However, that Lisa had dared to refer so boldly to Hallie's mother didn't come from some hallucinogen laced into her afternoon herbal tea. Hallie had recently asked Lisa to join him for the opening night of the opera season. It had meant going in the Lawrence party, sitting with the Lawrences, dining afterward with the Lawrences, and that was quite an inclusion.

It had started with a phone call from Lily.

"Who are you bringing?"

"No one."

Deadly silence, then: "Absolutely not."

That was all Lily needed to say. He'd bring someone. He got very few thrills anymore by annoying Lily. Hallie would ask Lisa and make it a business evening, which it was anyway. By escorting Lisa, he could demonstrate to the business dudes, who would no doubt be members of the party, his complete confidence in her. In turn, they would give her less hassle in the future when he wanted to get something done.

After accepting Hallie's invitation, Lisa went into such a state of shock; you had to wonder if some unseen part of her wasn't stuck in a socket.

Ah, the bolt of possibility.

Her first thoughts were, of course, what to wear. Lisa had seen many pictures of Lily Lawrence, a fashion empress of cosmic proportions, and the one thing she knew she must be was appropriate.

The night was full of festivity and sparkle. With a fortunate inclination toward the classical, Lisa wore a black velvet dress and white gloves. She looked good, kind of debutantish. And she wore no jewelry other than earrings, the diamond ones her father had given her when she turned twenty-one. They weren't spectacular or anything, just diamonds.

She was not nearly prepared for Lily Lawrence, and she was stunned.

Lily Lawrence had some magic circulating in her blood, radiating through her skin, and pulsing in her statuesque bone structure. She gave off a glow; that was the only way to describe it. She occupied space so elegantly that places seemed to shimmer after she'd left them. She had a way of embracing everyone she spoke to without ever touching them. She was stunning.

And mesmerizing. At dinner, at a table with well-chosen luminaries, Lily spent the appropriate amount of time complimenting Lisa's dress and those fabulous curls, and then proceeded to have a heated argument with Alfred about Berlioz, an argument that was becoming increasingly personal and nasty and less about the innocent-enough composer. Hallie joined the argument just long enough to guide them from Berlioz to Brahms, and the Lawrences were suddenly passionately agreeing.

The need for such intervention was what made these evenings one of Hallie's less favorite pastimes.

When the evening finally did end, he dropped his parents at their building and then went on in the Lawrences' car to take Lisa home. Hallie had walked her to the door of her building, joked with her about what a stink bomb the opera had been, and then said good night.

He went back to the car and got in. She waved and went into her building.

Lisa walked across her lobby toward the elevator without knowing how she was managing to move her feet. It had never occurred to her that Hallie wouldn't come up for a drink, that somehow, when the evening ended, it wouldn't find him in her apartment, noticing how nicely decorated it was, noticing her. She had even imagined them going off to work together in the morning and pretending he hadn't spent the night.

She couldn't believe it.

She got into the elevator and pressed her floor. She couldn't believe they weren't having the dialogue they were supposed to be having as they rode up in the elevator.

But by the time she had entered her apartment, she had a whole new scenario. She had entered her rationalization phase and it was fertile. It would be like a Spencer Tracy–Katharine Hepburn movie. One night they'd be working late and it would dawn on him that he had been blind all along to what a miracle of womanhood she was. She had to win him with her competency. Eventually he'd be overwhelmed by her competency.

Poor Lisa.

So there they were, on a late November day in his office, and Lisa had assumed familiar tones about his mother. And Hallie said, "I won't be late, you know how my mother is." He even grinned a little boyishly, appropriately embarrassed, turning on a little warmth, but keeping all the emotional nickels. He had revealed nothing, not even his annoyance.

"These three have to go out tonight," Lisa said, laying more papers in front of him. "If your mother's cocktail party is such torture, I'll go with you."

Oh, my God. She had to be stopped.

"You're a masochist?" asked Hallie. "I didn't know that about you, Lisa." Her response was the half-smile, with the addition of a slight arch of the lower back.

He wondered what kind of underpants she was wearing, and how worn in they were from being on her all day.

"Oh, you exaggerate about how terrible those parties are, and we might have fun," she said.

Exaggerate? Have fun? God, she was raving like a madwoman.

"I appreciate the offer, but I'm a nice guy. I wouldn't do that to you."

"Oh, Hallie," she said, "I was just kidding."

So obviously had she not been "just kidding" that she knocked a paper-clip box from Hallie's desk to the floor. But she took advantage of it by bending from the waist, demonstrating her well-worked-on flexibility. Unfortunately, it was lost on Hallie, who had, a few months earlier, broken off a long affair with a ballet dancer. But he looked at the legs revealed under the short, straight skirt and thought about fucking her.

The truth was, he already had. Many times, he had bent her over his desk, pulled up her skirts, and taken her from behind.

In his mind.

But if you fucked every girl you had a fantasy about, what would you think about while you were jerking off? That had been Hallie's consolation and motto for most of his life.

He signed the papers that had to go out that night, then put on his jacket and fixed his tie.

"Go home and do something nice for yourself," Hallie said.

"What do you mean?" she asked, the half-smile beaming.

"I don't know," Hallie said, putting on his overcoat. "What do girls do? Take a nice bath or something."

Needless to say, Lisa found his suggestion to be at least somewhat intriguing. He must be picturing her lying in a bath, she thought.

"Good idea, Hallie. That's just exactly what I'll do."

Hallie was pleased that his suggestion was so well accepted.

"A nice perfumy, oiled bath. That's a great idea."

"Good! One of us should have a pleasant evening. Now, if I don't leave this second, I'll be late. Can't be late, can I."

He smiled at her, one of his best smiles, saw in her eyes its effect, and knew he'd feel bad for a while. Lisa had a crush on him, or was certainly developing one, and it depressed him.

2

AS HALLIE CAME OUT OF THE BUILD-
ing, he was met with a full frontal
whack of cold air. It felt great, and any
further thought of Lisa blew off into
the night. There was no doubt about it,
winter was back. He tied his scarf
tighter around his neck but didn't
bother to button his coat, which was
flying behind him in the wind. And
then he heard the words: "You might
as well take the scarf and throw it in the
street if you're not going to button
your coat, Hallie." Those howling
gusts of caution were his mother's
words living forever in the winds of
winter.

Because, for all of her distance from
the shtetl, and it was considerable, the
fear of losing food, shelter, sleep, or
outer garments lived in Lily's genes. If
you didn't sleep or eat, you were at
risk of picking up leprosy. If you went

9

outside too often, eventually something would fall on you. And if you left your coat open in the winter, you died of pneumonia within the week. And a powerful suggestion it was, since Hallie got colds every winter until he went to prep school and met Kip.

Coat flying, scarf tied, Hallie arrived at his parents' building on Fifth Avenue. Pete, the depressing doorman, greeted him with delight and a curtsey. Pete liked to think of himself as a mere slip of a girl, although he was in his sixties with the build of a linebacker. Pete had worked the door since the days when Hallie would come shooting out of the lobby in a pedal car. Pete was depressing because he was one of the biggest snobs Hallie had ever met. He was always referring to "the wrong kind of people." These were all applicants to the building before they were approved, and certain kinds of guests. He took great pleasure in sending delivery men around the corner to the service entrance. During Hallie's prep-school days, the first time Kip Courtland came to New York to stay with the Lawrences, Pete had sent him to the service entrance. Kip had long hair at the time, and a tendency to wear clothes that looked as if he'd slept in them, on the beach, for maybe a year. He was delighted to use the service entrance. Kip Courtland came from one of the oldest and wealthiest families in the country, and the service entrance was cool.

"Young Mr. Lawrence!" exclaimed Pete as he saw Hallie. His cheeks were quickly acquiring their winter roses. He tipped his hat with the address of the building on it.

"How're ya doin', Pete," said Hallie, in his talk-to-the-doorman voice.

"Not bad for an old hag."

Pete had been using that line since Hallie's pedal-car days. It sort of summed him up. He would say "Not bad for an old hag" and clap his gloved hands together and you could really see the mere slip of a girl come alive.

"Mother's having a party," said Pete in a low voice, in case the wrong kind of people were listening behind the shrubs. He ceremoniously held the door for Hallie.

"Is that a fact!" Hallie said cheerfully. "You look great, Pete!" Hallie had told Pete what he wanted to hear most, and he entered the lobby.

Ah, the lobby smell. Sometimes lobbies smell of urine and cigarettes and rotten oranges and whiskey. Not this lobby.

This lobby had the mossy smell of oiled wood paneling, the cool smell of the marble floor, and something warm and buttery. The smell was maintenance. The seating areas were subdued by regal velvets and silk-shaded lamplight. A thick green damask tablecloth covered a central round table with an impeccable arrangement of flowers. It was one of New York's most aristocratic residential buildings. Even the floors were snobby and definitely gave you a dirty look when you crossed them. Lily liked to say what a miracle it was that they had ever been approved to live in such a conservative residence, what with the Lawrences in the arts. This was of course Lily's identification with Bohemia and had nothing to do with reality. The issue was the Lawrences in the synagogue. And that had been overlooked because Lily Oppenheim Lawrence, of the extremely important German-American Jewish Oppenheims, was acceptable to the building, and would have been the day it was built, had her grandfather not chosen to build a quiet mansion on Riverside Drive.

The elevator arrived and Hallie took off his scarf as he entered and rode up to the penthouse.

The Lawrence living room glowed with creamy light, intended to make everyone look beautiful. It was all in the calculated silk shades, the exactness of the dimmed chandelier, the strategically placed candles. It was light that sent sparkles to the serious jewelry worn by the women. It was light that made everybody's eyes shine.

The general decor had an inspired originality to it, featuring antique furnishings that had known creative singularity even in their own time. The tremendous subtlety of the colors and the fabrics reflected the choice of an artist, and that artist was Lily Lawrence. But art for art's sake was missing, except for a seriously important 1913 Léger hung over the mantel, and a pretty wonderful collage done before the twenties by Picasso. There was a reason for the lack of fancy paintings in an age of acquiring fancy paintings. The Oppenheim art collection had been extraordinary, accumulated by Lily's parents and grandparents. But when it passed to her generation, Lily had convinced her sisters that art should not be hoarded, that this was a mortifying sign of self-aggrandizement. No one is really worthy of having a great Matisse all to himself, and pretending you were was, to say the least, a dreadful faux pas. That was the Lily Lawrence philosophy of art. So she and her sisters had all chosen two things each and given the rest to museums. The paintings were hanging in galleries all over, with little signs next to them identifying the artist, title, and date, and the donor as Anonymous.

The Lawrence house made distinguished people feel good to be there, and others talk in soft voices.

Lily herself was still stationed fairly near the living-room entrance, greeting newly arriving guests. She was not only doing her usual embracing, she was actually offering hugs and kisses. But all the while, she surveyed the room. Lily was on duty; she was the commandant and the war games were on. A periscope had surfaced and no interchange of any sort between guests went unobserved for its appropriateness or potential intrigue.

The group was quite a distinguished one because Lily's sense of assembly was simply unrivaled. Basically, the guests fell into two categories: New Yorkers who had lots of money and contributed to the arts, and the crème de la crème from the arts that were contributed to. Being invited to a party at the Lawrences' marked a serious arrival, but no one asked exactly where it was they had arrived. They didn't want to know. Everybody loved the comfortable feeling of being so surrounded by beauty and by Lily's glow, except for a few hysterical women who always felt slightly faint from jealousy.

Lily located Alfred across the room. His thick white hair always stood out. He was as usual surrounded by a group of admirers, including a mezzo soprano who Lily knew Alfred thought was second-rate. But she had huge, amply revealed breasts, and was getting most of Alfred's attention. Alfred, in his once well-cut but now totally bagged-out gray velvet jacket, with a silk scarf tied around his neck instead of a tie, and in his crummy old velvet slippers with the little emblems on them, was enjoying himself. Lily didn't care a fig what Alfred wore, as long as he behaved himself and didn't disappear halfway through the evening, never to be seen again. Actually, on the subject of dressing for these soirees, Lily had once said, "If there is one pair of breasts left at the end of the evening that you haven't smothered, you can wear whatever the hell you want." To be sure, this handicap wasn't too difficult for Alfred; Lily would always invite one flat-chested female, and sometimes a backup. So there was always a pair he could claim he hadn't smothered at all. He didn't actually go around putting his face between orbs, he only thought about it. But his thoughts were loud and clear. He liked breasts. Lily accepted his flirtations, his ego, all of it. She knew he loved her and thought she had pretty great breasts of her own. And she still loved to arrange things so that Alfred had a good time. Bring on the 42 DD-cup mezzos.

Lily was approached by Noel Brandt, designer haute and de rigueur, a creation of whose Lily was actually wearing. Long-sleeved black cashmere on top, full black satin long skirt on the bottom. Her only jewelry was a simply magnificent pair of White Russian antique earrings. Her dark hair was pulled into a bun at the nape of her neck, allowing those eyes and those cheekbones and the fabulous Lily Lawrence smile to assume prominence.

Noel leaned toward her to kiss her cheek and feel her fragrance fill his senses. He whispered into her ear.

"You look sensational," he said, loving his importance in the matter. "I'd rather dress you than anyone else I know."

Obviously, Noel did what he did because he preferred to dress women rather than undress them.

"Noel, darling, I would be bedridden without you" came Lily's deadpan reply. Her voice was very distinctive, with a touch of gravel and rounded, perfectly pronounced vowels. A mellifluous voice.

Noel laughed and fluttered slightly, which he normally contained, adoring the compliment.

"I would hope so," he said.

Lily's watchful gaze saw Hallie entering the apartment.

Hallie knew that wherever she was, Lily would know when he'd arrived. So there was no possibility of going up to his old room for a while and looking around at his old stuff. He ignored the coat racks that were always put out for parties and went to the front-hall closet. When he opened it the light automatically went on, highlighting Lily's furs and Alfred's assortment of theatrical-looking outerwear. He put his coat on a hanger and breathed in the smell of Lily embedded in the furs. "Jicky" by Guerlain.

He crossed the entrance foyer, passing the George III mirror without a glance, but found himself running his hand through his hair anyway.

Which Lily noticed. She beamed as he walked toward her.

"Good evening, Mother," Hallie said with his usual mock formality.

"Oh, Hallie, you've come," she crooned in an intimate low voice. She kissed him. "You didn't have to, my darling!"

"Right," Hallie said.

"I never take for granted that you'll turn up just because I've asked you. It makes inviting you so exciting."

"I'm not late, Mom," Hallie said, getting to the real point.

"No, of course not. It's just I do want you to know that you're never obligated to come to my little parties . . ."

"Of course I am," said Hallie. "I value my life."

Lily took his arm.

"What's not to value," she said, very intimately now, with a hint of luxurious gefilte fish, and she allowed him to escort her through the room.

"I guess the truth is I always hope you'll come early so we can have a private chat before the masses show up."

"Why don't you just ask me to come early?" Hallie asked.

"Next time come early," said Lily, with a deep, meaningful smile and a sparkle in her brown eyes. She thought they had just had a no-bullshit exchange.

Not exactly.

That would mean Hallie having to tell her that the reason she wanted him to come early, before the masses, was to allow early-arriving guests to see that Hallie was such a good son, he got there before anyone else. And why? Because she was such a fabulous mother. Hallie-the-Slightly-Unavailable to most people, had given her full and exclusive access. She was that fabulous.

Hallie smiled back at his mother the way one does when a lunatic is trying to say hello to you on a bus.

He looked out over the guests, people madly thinking they were having a good time. Then he began to focus on who was there that he knew, and the first one he saw was Daniella.

"Ah, look who's among the masses," Hallie said.

"Yes, well, these things can't be avoided," said Lily, knowing instantly to whom he was referring.

"Yes, they can," Hallie said.

"My dearest Hallie." The well-rounded vowels were particularly pronounced when she was about to make a statement that was to be taken as undisputable. "I can't not invite Daniella. She knows everybody. And besides, she's having a sensational season. It wouldn't make any sense. You, my dearest, will simply handle it."

"Right," Hallie said. The Commandant had spoken. He removed her arm from his gallantly, squeezing her hand a little. He was about to leave her.

"Where are you going?"

"To handle it."

"Well, you don't have to do it this minute," Lily said. Only Hallie, and maybe Alfred if he were standing there, could have smelled the singe in her voice.

"I do. I like to dispense with good form as soon as possible."

"Don't start, Hallie."

They were near the French doors that led to the penthouse terrace, tall French doors with sweeping cream silk draperies tied with silk tassels. Lily opened one of the doors slightly. Her instinct, as commandant, was that the room was growing warm.

"I think you should know something," Lily said. "Allan Rupert wants to see her. He wants to ask her out."

"You mean he wants to fuck her."

"Hallie, please," Lily said, stiffening. There had to be some kind of obligatory reprimand, even if miles away from the smack he had gotten the first time he decided four-letter words were fun. "Allan's divorced now and why shouldn't he see Daniella? She's absolutely nothing like his ex-wife and half her age. He'll be very good to her."

"Well, then it's perfect!" They were discussing the ballet dancer, Daniella Landauer, with whom Hallie had had the affair. That Lily now felt no compunction about discussing Danny's suitableness for someone else signified how truly over it was, but it still made Hallie hostile that Lily had such know-it-all gall.

"It's perfect," he repeated.

"Well, I didn't say it was perfect—"

"Okay, it's not perfect, but I do have to say hello to her, since she's here. The longer I wait, the more it will become an issue. The more it becomes an issue, the more I'll want to torture you, Lil."

"Please," Lily said. Hallie smiled at her and moved off. "Be a good boy, Hallie."

Lily had never learned to stop saying that.

Daniella was standing in a group that included a stunning black fashion model who was very "happening." God, how Hallie hated that word, but that was how Daniella had once described her to him. As he approached, he saw Daniella catch him in her eyes. They quickly darted away, but a reddening blush was forming on her velvety, translucent cheeks. Everything about Daniellas was like velvet, actually. Her skin, her voice, her whole suppleness. Powdery. She had the proverbial ballet-dancer posture, turned out and delicate. Hallie was at her side.

"Well, hello, Danny," he said, trying to sound nonchalant.

He was thinking of adding "What are you doing here?" a line he noticed was always in Woody Allen movies.

But Daniella did this really pathetic thing. She looked at him and pretended she was totally surprised to see him, as if she hadn't noticed him approaching, as if she hadn't noticed him the minute he walked into the house.

"Hallie!" she exclaimed. "I didn't know you'd be here!"

"How've you been?" he said, and leaned down to kiss her cheek. She leaned toward him for a full body embrace, in which she was much more eager than he was, and they both knew it. It was one of those horrible moments.

"Oh, I'm just fine," she said, not a little sarcasm in her voice.

"Good," said Hallie, with not a little blindness feigned to the sarcasm. "You look great!"

She did actually. She was wearing a peach-colored dress that looked like scarves had landed all over her, and the nipples on her small breasts caught the diaphanous fabric on their protrusions. Her dark-blond hair was long and loose and not in the usual ballet dancer's bun.

"I don't think I look great," she said. "I've gotten very fat."

"You know that twelve-hundred-pound man in the news? I was thinking you looked just like him," he said, patting her shoulder. Daniella was composed of extraordinarily developed muscle, and where there wasn't muscle, there was bone.

But she smiled at his words.

At least he got a smile.

Get out, now.

So he turned the pat on the shoulder to an affectionate good-bye squeeze.

"I've got to say hello to Alfred, I haven't seen him yet."

"Okay. Can we talk later?" asked Daniella.

Oh no, thought Hallie. He looked into her large and very blue eyes where, to his horror, he saw that she wanted to discuss trying the relationship again. She actually looked hopeful.

Relationships. Hallie was convinced that talking about them was the real reason people got herpes.

That was how he was before anything had happened.

Hallie smiled and nodded and walked away from Daniella. Because he knew she'd be watching him, he figured he'd better head toward Alfred.

For a minute he remembered how limber Danny was in bed.

Even as he held court, Alfred saw Hallie from the corner of his eye and became even more animated for his guests.

"It's a question of the complexities in subjugating tone, and who does the subjugating is an issue."

Everyone laughed. Hallie knew he had missed something, but he smiled at coming upon Alfred in full swing.

Without looking at Hallie, while still laughing with his little audience (some hostile-takeover types and the mezzo with the big tits), Alfred opened his arms. Hallie went into them and received the embrace. There was nothing he could do about it.

"Ah, my lawyer is here! Just the man I want to see."

The day Hallie had graduated from law school, he ceased to be Alfred's son and became, instead, his lawyer.

Alfred, with his arm still around Hallie's shoulder, steered him away. Hallie kept his hands in his pockets, perhaps the single most preppy thing he was inclined to do. When Hallie was about fourteen, he had kept count, on paper, of the number of times "Take your hands out of your pockets, Hallie" was said to him by his parents on any given day. The record was thirteen times. While he was at prep school, they had a speech contest and he wrote his on the subject of what he did on his Christmas vacation, and it included the number of times his mother said "Take your hands out of your pockets, Hallie." He didn't win because he figured it made the faculty judges a little nervous to vote for someone making fun of his parents. But his speech was hands-down the favorite of the other boys. And that was the whole point.

As Alfred walked with Hallie through the guests, he not only kept his arm around Hallie's shoulder, he leaned on him. And he spoke in very intimate tones, behind one hand.

"Look at that one over there," said Alfred, indicating a tall, thin person who you could assume was a woman because she wore a dress. She was quite elegant but had an amazing amount of makeup on, with two sort of purple lines that were supposed to be shading her cheeks, and eyes black with kohl.

"Mrs. Angler?"

"I swear she's a drag queen," said Alfred.

Hallie actually laughed. He couldn't help it.

"Well, what does that make Dick Angler?"

"A big fancy pansy. I've been saying that for years," Alfred said. The Dick Angler mentioned happened to be a political analyst, considered, by those whose politics leaned to the right, an intellectual. Hallie had known him all his life and thought he was a boob, and felt it showed how desperate the right was to find intellectuals. But the idea of Mrs. Angler being a drag queen was pretty amusing.

His father was in a good mood, which was always a little bit of a relief. Hallie noticed Lily, across the room, smiling at them.

"You must be starving," said Alfred. "Let's go to the kitchen and get some real food. All these cockamamie hors d'oeuvres, the hell with them."

Alfred delighted in insulting Lily's food when beyond her earshot.

The kitchen was a large room with high ceilings, and row after row of cupboards with glass doors. On the wall were the original and impeccably maintained white tiles. Down the middle of the room ran a twenty-foot refectory table, now laden with food yet to be served by the bastions of men and women in black-and-white uniforms, Lily's foot soldiers. Being in the kitchen during one of Lily's parties was a little like going backstage.

The bustle was completely ignored by Alfred as he led his son to one of two large Sub-Zero refrigerators. He and Hallie peered over the contents like biblical scholars at work, frowning, searching for answers.

"What's in the bag?" Hallie asked, indicating a small brown parcel.

"Aha!" said Alfred. "You're a genius."

With glee Alfred took out the bag and opened it for Hallie to have a look. Inside were two halves of sandwiches from the Carnegie Delicatessen, Alfred's favorite place to have lunch in the world.

"Great," said Hallie.

"And look what else," said Alfred, reaching behind Lily's green health drinks. He produced two Dr. Brown's Cream Sodas.

They took their bounty to the breakfast nook, a banquette done in French blue-and-white-check fabric. Alfred noticed the slightly worried looks on the faces of the caterers.

"You fellas don't mind if we hide out in here for a minute?" boomed Alfred.

The catering staff in fact were finding it eccentric in the most titillating way. The great Alfred Lawrence had come to eat in the kitchen. He unwrapped the sandwich halves, one of corned beef and one of pastrami.

"Have the pastrami," Alfred said. "It's even worse for me than the corned beef."

"So I should eat it?"

"Eat while you're young," Alfred said. He picked up his sandwich in both hands, which were noticeably white and delicate. "The one thing I don't regret in my life is the pastrami sandwiches I've eaten. I have a client for you."

"We should put these in the microwave," said Hallie, but he knew they wouldn't.

"Nichola Mikhailovitch, the fiddle player."

Alfred referred to all violinists as fiddle players. All of them.

"She's the one you say is so good."

"Good?" Alfred ceased chewing for dramatic effect. "No, I never said good. Brilliant maybe, but good? Not Nikki. She's a genius!" Now he went into a sort of lamenting sway. "And still so young—she's what, twenty-eight, maybe?—but the depths of her playing, the richness, the contact she has . . . I can't . . ." His regard for her talent had become so intense he had to pause.

"What's the matter with her, is she dying?" Hallie asked, knowing of course that she wasn't. It couldn't be that simple. He watched Alfred take another mouthful of corned beef before continuing.

"It's not a question of death the way the average person understands death."

"I see." Hallie decided to avoid that one. "Isn't she a Russian defector?"

"Immigrant! Her family left—I don't know—maybe ten years ago? The Russians pretended they didn't know what they were letting out."

"And now they do, so she needs a lawyer."

"Not so fast—"

"The Russians are trying to kidnap her! A regular international caper. I'll take the case! After all, I'm an entertainment lawyer; afterward I can do an article, then a book, which I can sell to the movies—"

"It's worse than the Russians," said Alfred. "And bite your tongue because it *is* . . . Hollywood." Alfred said this in a whisper, as if he couldn't even bear to pronounce it aloud.

Hallie moved in his seat and reached for the mustard. He said nothing for several seconds, and he knew Alfred was studying him while he pulled a limp pickle from the bag.

"She doesn't have a lawyer?"

"She doesn't have you."

"Dad—"

"Don't be modest, Hallie, life's too short. They want to make some kind of facocktah film about a fiddle player and they want her to play the part because (a) she plays the fiddle, which they somehow noticed, and (b) because she happens to be some beauty. But she can't do this."

"Does she want to?"

"If she didn't want to, would she need a lawyer?"

"You want me to negotiate her contract? Well, that's simple enough."

Boy, did he know it couldn't be that simple.

Alfred sank back against the banquette, an affectation of exhaustion. Whenever Alfred was about to explain something he considered painfully obvious, Alfred would feign exhaustion first.

"Hallie, you've never heard her play?"

"I've heard her play."

"Well, for God's sake, playing like that comes a few times a century! Her musicianship is defiant. It doesn't seem to have limits. Unfortunately, neither does she." Alfred closed his eyes and shook his head, to emphasize the tragedy he could somehow foresee. Then he reached for his glass of Dr. Brown's. He needed a drink to continue. "Now, if she does this thing, if she appears in a movie, that makes her an actor! She'll never be taken seriously again in the real music world."

The real music world meant classical music to Alfred. Any other kind of music wasn't really music. It was something else. Go figure.

"Why not?" asked Hallie. He couldn't resist.

"Why not? Because dancers can be actors, who cares? Dancers are actors in the first place. The same for a singer. A singer is an actor. But a musician? A musician makes a movie, they end up playing fiddle on the 'Ed Sullivan Show.'"

"Ed Sullivan is dead, Dad, and I think the show was canceled, but I'm not sure." said Hallie to be annoying. "Well, if she wants to do it, what can you do?"

"Me, her mentor—you know when she was sixteen years old, she played with me at Tanglewood—I've tried everything. Nothing works. But you could do it."

Hallie thought it over. He watched Alfred's look of tragedy now turn slightly petulant. Alfred always resorted to petulance when he really wanted something. All of a sudden, Hallie felt bad.

"Okay, I see it," Hallie said. "You want me, as her lawyer, to somehow screw up her contract negotiations? Is that it?"

"Would I ask such a thing?"

"Not directly, no. Probably not."

"I'm shocked you would think I'd be asking you to throw away your integrity. Shocked! That would only be a last resort." Again, a petulant look.

"Right," said Hallie. He ate the last piece of rye-bread crust and crumpled up the wrapping. "You should always ask for extra pickles when you tell them to wrap up your sandwich."

"I'm asking you to take her as a client."

"I think if this Nichola Mickeymousekovitch wants to be in a movie, that's exactly what she should do, and good luck to her."

"This is exactly why you should become her lawyer! You think just the way she does!"

"Right. And at what point do I start thinking the way you do and talk her out of it, Alfred?"

"Oh, I leave that up to you."

Hallie watched Alfred pat a spot of mustard on his lip, using a paper napkin that had come in the bag. Hallie felt some kind of serum being released into his blood that definitely began to give encouragement to his patricidal feelings.

But he made a point of saying nothing. It was the only way to handle it.

"You'll meet her. Just meet her," said Alfred.

"I don't have a lot of time these days, Dad—"

"She's here! She's here tonight. You've got enough time to meet her tonight?"

"Fine," said Hallie pleasantly, and he left the kitchen. The years of therapy had taught him to leave the room before the patricidal feelings could be acted out, a validation of Lily's preventive medicine theory.

He was not going to meet with this Nikki girl, he was going to get out of the apartment before that could happen. But first Hallie took refuge on the terrace. He stood leaning on the balustrade, drinking a brandy and looking out over the expanse of park that appeared as if someone had taken a big eraser and rubbed out a black rectangle in the middle of the shimmering city. The terrace was a dead place this time of year. The potted mums were stalky and faded, and the evergreens hadn't been delivered yet. In the summer the garden was so lush and the garden furniture so cozy you might think you were in the middle of England or something. He used to camp out on the terrace sometimes, although not without a prophecy from Lily that he would somehow roll off, despite the stone balustrades.

Alfred still thought he could make Hallie do anything he wanted. He just couldn't be taught otherwise. Hallie no longer felt bad, he had moved on to feeling depressed. It wasn't some Russian fiddle player, it was the proverbial last thirty-two years of his life.

He took a deep breath and a swig of brandy. Then the terrace door opened and someone came out.

"Hallie Lawrence?"

No, you're mistaken. I'm somebody else.

"Alfred is looking everywhere, but I manage to find you!"

The voice was young, but it had the accent of an old woman, and it made Hallie turn around.

He was at once amused. In front of him was a girl with long red curly hair tossed high by the terrace wind, and a manner about her that could only be called feisty. Challenging. She spoke with her chin slightly thrust forward and she had the most devilish, daring eyes he'd ever seen. And the word "devilish" was not one that occurred to him often.

He knew at once who she was, and he was a little chagrined to find that already Alfred was right about one thing: she was some beauty and a really unique one at that.

"You must be Nichola Mikhailovitch," Hallie said.

"Of course," she said. "Nikki, you can call me, if you want." He realized that the old-woman sound to her voice was her Russian accent. His maternal grandfather, Carl Philip Oppenheim, third-generation venerable German-American Jew, had, in an eccentric moment, married a Russian girl, Hallie's grandmother. The family had been horrified until, as time went by, the little Russian girl became an arbiter of taste as she accumulated most of the remarkable art collection. She had had that accent. Hallie had always thought that his frail grandmother looked like a bird. When she died, he had told Lily she had flown away.

"How do you do?" said Hallie, shaking the hand of Nikki Mikhailovitch, and a strong little hand it was. Hallie looked down at that hand, at a ruby-and-rose-gold deco bracelet, at an arm tightly wrapped in green velvet, but only to make it less obvious when he

raised his eyes and took in the breasts as his eyes returned to hers.
The breasts were definitely interesting.

"Good," she said, approving of their handshake, then looking
out over the twinkling city. "Very nice view, don't you think? No,
don't tell me, you're used to it already. To you, this means nothing.
To me? I'd say it's . . . Rachmaninoff. No more, no less." Her eyes
crinkled and shot him one of her daring looks, while she looked as
if she was trying hard not to burst out laughing.

"Rachmaninoff? No, if anything it's Gershwin."

The truth was, she'd taken him off guard. He could usually
pre-guess someone trying to establish a rapport with him. But a
funny bell went off because calling something by the name of the
composer it would be if it were a composer, was something he had,
on occasion, done with Kip. For a moment of time too small to be
measured, Hallie felt a familiarity with Nikki.

"Oh, please, Gershwin. That's so obvious! So American!"

"Rachmaninoff and Gershwin are both corny" was all the comeback he could manage.

"I agree." She laughed easily. "You want to talk to me, don't
you!" It was definitely a statement, not a question. And Hallie
might actually have had some kind of momentary interest in talking
to her had he not absently put his fingers to his nose and smelled
the lingering essence of corned beef.

Talk to you? thought Hallie. I think I'd rather roll off the terrace.

"I'd be delighted to talk to you," he said, effortlessly dredging
up some charm. "Alfred tells me you've been asked to do a movie."

Her eyes really did sparkle, he noticed, as if they had extra liquid
in them or something. And in that sparkle was a dare.

"I know what Alfred thinks about that! And you? You think the
same, am I right?"

"You don't have any idea how I think," Hallie said.

A little frown knit into her brow as she looked at him slightly
askance, obviously sizing him up. "Maybe not," she said, and then
she laughed. "Okay! We talk. But we must go inside first, it's
fuckink freezink out here."

The way she said "fuckink freezink" was amusing.

Be a good boy, Hallie.

Back in the warmth of the glowing living room, where all the
guests really thought they were having a good time now, Hallie
returned with Nikki Mikhailovitch. They stood together chatting.
Hallie had edged back into his business posture, tall and a little
more poised. Nikki was focusing on him hard. When Hallie looked
at her red curls, he couldn't help thinking about her pubic hair.

"Don't misunderstand me," she said, reaching for a glass of

champagne from a circulating tray. "Your father is very important to me; I played with him my first time in America. He is a genius and we understand each other. Normally, we always get on very well."

We have an Ego Maniac here, thought Hallie, having not missed Nikki's implication that if Alfred was a genius, the only way for them to understand each other was that Nikki was a genius too, and this, he could tell by her tone, she understood to be a given . . .

"Who are the people who want you to do the film?" Hallie asked. Please. He didn't really want to hear about geniuses, not from a girl who might have red pubic hair that must smell from the exotic and urging fragrance she wore. He noticed that there was always the hint of a smile on her full and pretty lips. It accounted for her devilishness. It was cute, thought Hallie.

He sniffed the fingers that smelled of corned beef, this time intentionally.

She began to tell him about the project, and he heard her use the words "me" and "I" a lot, but his attention was taken now with Danny, who he could see was saying good night to Lily. He was relieved at first at the thought of getting out of having another conversation with her, but then he felt a little sad that Danny was leaving and thought that maybe he should go and say good night.

And all the while he appeared to be listening to Nikki.

He was just about to excuse himself and go to Danny when along came an interception: Bobby Josephson and his wife, Tracy. Bobby at a party at Lily's? Jesus Christ. He had known Bobby at Exeter, and on occasion, when totally desperate really, he had hung out with him. Bobby had become some kind of big-shot investment banker and he was riding the stairway to the stars. And one of those steps, naturally, was making contributions to the arts and going to Lily's parties.

Nikki was forced to stop mid-sentence.

"Hallie, old boy," said Bobby, trying to pretend they'd been best friends.

"Hey, Bobby."

They shook hands and then Tracy spoke up. Tracy was one of the girls whom Hallie had always known, through grade school, prep school, and college. She was a high-strung, tight-assed, neurotic snob of a girl, from a hyperprotective Upper East Side background, and she worked at Sotheby's with the rest of them.

"Hello, Hallie," she said with a studied coy smile and an awkward toss of her streaked-blond hair. Hallie remembered that he and Kip used to laugh a lot thinking about her being porked up the ass by an enormous gorilla. They'd felt sorry for the gorilla.

"Tracy!" said Hallie. "You're looking very swanksville."

She took that bit of sarcasm as a compliment. It amused Hallie for about half a second. He introduced Nikki, and then with the charm that made Hallie Lawrence who he was, he explained, almost sorrowfully, that he and Nikki had to finish up a business conversation.

As they moved off to a corner and leaned against the silk-covered walls, it was apparent that Nikki was pleased that Hallie had chosen to extricate them from what she considered an unwarranted distraction.

"I am happy to see you stick to business. Those are friends of yours?"

"Acquaintances," said Hallie, and in one shift of his posture they were totally dismissed. "Where were we?"

"Your father of course tells me you are genius lawyer and one day you will work on the Supreme Court or maybe you will be Attorney General, or both, maybe, at the same time. This is true?"

"Yes," said Hallie, quite deadpan.

"Well, if you agree with your father about that, you must agree with him that I shouldn't make a film!" Nikki laughed at her own quickness and saw that even Hallie had smiled. "I know who Hallie Lawrence is before your father told me."

She said this with such assurance it made Hallie want to ask, well then, come on, who is he? But instead he told her, "I think you should definitely consider the film. Why don't we leave it that way. If you want to talk to me, call me at the office."

"You're right. This is a social gathering. The hell with talking business."

Hallie thought it was weird talking to Nikki at all. There was something about her that made him uncomfortable and something that drew him to her at the same time. There was someone inside her he wanted to see but he felt compelled to step back.

At that point, it was important to cut the conversation off for two other reasons. He had fulfilled his obligation to meet her and that should have been sufficient, but he also detected that Nikki had shown some definite signs of Ego Maniac (all those "me's" and "I's"), and he knew that if you ever hope to have a chance in dealing with an E.M., even the non-world-class type, you have to be sparse with your availability early on. Lack of availability to an Ego Maniac triggers an instant dependence.

The notion of a wild-cossack fuck did occur to him, though: in a winter palace, on fur-covered pillows, with that exotic scent burning, coming from the copper-colored pubic hair, the jiggling breasts, as she screamed out desperate Russian encouragements. Then Alfred entered the Byzantine room. *"Aha!"*

"Give me a call tomorrow. I think I'm free for lunch, if you'd like to have lunch." He happened to know he had a lunch cancellation.

"I'll call you," she said, her eyes filled with new challenge.

"Um, I actually do have to leave," Hallie added with a fine, charming smile.

The air was thickening suddenly.

Across the room, Alfred was watching him talk to Nikki. Hallie could feel his chest tightening. The ceiling was lowering, chandelier and all. A waiter passed with a tray of hors d'oeuvres and Hallie looked to see if any of them had a tag that read "Eat Me" that would magically take him someplace else.

3

BUT EVEN WITHOUT MAGIC, HALLIE
managed to get out. It only took telling
Lily that he was tired, that he hadn't
been sleeping too well lately and he
felt as if he might be coming down
with something.

He didn't say good night to Alfred, though. He just didn't want the
hassle.

Walking over to Madison Avenue,
he went down a side street lined with
brownstone houses and lit by streetlights. The pavement was wet and
shiny. There was a time when he'd
walked down this street every day of
his life. And he'd always looked up at
one particular second-floor bay window where he could see warm light
and thick cozy curtains drawn aside.
The walls were dark green and on one
of them hung a painting of a rabbit.
People were probably happy in there,

26

he had always thought. They were probably just sitting around being normal.

At the corner he turned and walked up Madison, without so much as a glance at the opulent wares in the opulent shops. He was trying to forget about Alfred and Nikki.

Hallie lived between Madison and Park in a small prewar building that had a mural in the lobby depicting an English hunting scene. Hallie's own apartment was a little eccentric. All the walls were painted dark colors, and with bookshelves everywhere, you felt that you were in study hall. Lily had managed to find a lot of Mission furniture before anyone else even thought to look. There were quite a few pieces of pre-Columbian art displayed haphazardly, and a couple of terrific old oriental carpets covered the wood floors. The apartment made girls want to do it over with lots of cushiony sofas and flowery patterns. Hallie preferred study hall.

He took off his coat, his jacket, and his shoes, and picked up his mail and began sorting through it, thinking that what he'd like to do was take off all his clothes and maybe watch TV. He didn't feel like working tonight. But then the doorbell rang.

That was a little peculiar, because normally nobody could come up unless the doorman announced them over the intercom. Maybe it was a neighbor.

But it was Danny.

And the fact that she had been able to come up unannounced was not good.

"I told Tony you were expecting me," she said softly, Tony being the doorman who should have announced her.

He would have to talk to Tony about that. He would actually have to tell his doorman that the woman who used to stay with him so often, well, wasn't staying with him anymore. God, what a horrifying conversation.

"Come in, Danny," he said.

She entered, but stood in the foyer without moving as Hallie shut the door. She made no move to take off her coat, some kind of white fur.

"I know I shouldn't have come," she began.

"It's all right," said Hallie. He could tell how nervous she was and he felt sorry for her. "Want a drink?"

She seemed to be posing for something, a portrait of a madonna maybe, with her eyes lowered and her head held delicately high. Hallie tried to pretend he didn't notice.

"I know you would rather I wasn't here," she said quietly.

"Danny, for Chrissake, take off your coat. Have a drink!"

She allowed the coat to slip from her shoulders, and Hallie took it and hung it up. He noticed that her skin looked very soft and he commended himself for not touching it.

He fixed himself a brandy, and a Cointreau on the rocks for her. It was her favorite drink, which made sense to Hallie, who thought that if she had been a drink, that's the drink she would have been.

He brought the drinks to the sofa, where she sat very tall, her hands folded on her lap.

"I really wanted to talk to you tonight," she began. "Then I saw you were with Nikki Mikhailovitch."

"Yes," said Hallie. "We had a few things to discuss." He was naturally compelled to ambiguity.

"She's considered quite beautiful," said Danny.

"I thought you looked very good tonight," he said.

"You did?"

"Uh-huh." What the hell, it was true.

Danny slipped the crystal rim of her glass between her lips and sipped her Cointreau. She had great lips. They were full and pouty, quite a contrast to a face that was otherwise so finely chiseled.

"Do you like my dress?"

"It's very pretty," Hallie said. Hallie couldn't have lived in the same house with Lily and not acquired some education when it came to women's clothes. But the truth was, he had never cared that much how a girl was dressed. If you were crazy for a girl, you thought she always looked good. And if you weren't? Well, talk about the meaning of nothing helping. So he had learned to say things such as "It's very pretty" because Lily had warned him about compliments. "You give them," she had said with her Lily Lawrence finality. "Period."

Tears started pouring down Danny's cheeks.

"I bought this dress because I knew you'd be at the party. Is that pathetic, or what?"

"Danny, it's not pathetic."

"And tonight, a perfectly nice man, Allan something—Randolph or Rudolph?—asked if I wanted to have dinner with him after the party."

He decided not to correct her, the man's name was Rupert, not Randolph or Rudolph. Allan had certainly made a big impression, thought Hallie.

"I should have said yes," said Danny.

"Don't cry, Danny," Hallie said softly, reaching for the tissue box and offering her a few.

"I can't help it," she said, and she spoke the truth. Danny cried so much that she made up for maybe a hundred people who never cry at all.

"I should have said yes, but I didn't, because I thought that maybe if we talked, maybe if we— I was hoping we could go to dinner. I was hoping it would just happen."

"Danny, I'll go to dinner with you anytime you want. But, Danny, we're not going to get back together."

Could he have put it more clearly?

"Hallie, you don't know how much I've changed." She waited for him to say something.

"Well, good," said Hallie, and his voice cracked slightly, one of his most endearing preppy leftovers.

"I know I was always too concerned about dancing. I know I drove myself too hard, and you know something? I just— It just doesn't mean that much to me, suddenly. I'd rather have a life. I've had this whole new insight into things between us."

"You should have a life," he said amicably. "That's definitely something you should have, Danny." He simply ignored her last sentence.

But it didn't do any good.

"I know that my dancing came between us because I was always so exhausted. That just won't happen again."

Holy Christ.

"Dancers dance," Hallie said. "I never minded that, Danny."

The hysteria that resulted from her endless self-criticism was what he had minded.

"I've realized that the time I spend dancing is going to be so much shorter than the time I spend no longer dancing, that I'd better prepare for that, rather than put too much time into something that won't last."

This was so succinctly put, for Danny, that he knew she had rehearsed it.

"I know I was always criticizing you for things you didn't do for me, Hallie. I'm sorry."

This was her idea of great new insight? A revelation? What she was forgetting somehow was that they'd had this exact conversation about two hundred million times. God, it was amazing how many bullshit conversations people were willing to have.

"You were probably right, Danny. I probably didn't do enough for you."

The truth was, he had never really been in love with her. He had found her very charming for a while, even captivating at times, and in fact had loved watching her dance. Even though they had gone out for nearly a year, he had spent a good part of that time thinking he had to end it and never quite getting around to it. But as her hysterical outbursts became as regular as toast every morning, he had finally broken things off.

Sitting there, listening to her little speech, made him feel like a really hard-hearted bastard. The truth does that to people, especially when you can't let the other person in on it.

It was over because I didn't feel enough for you, Danny.

At least he got to say it to himself.

"But it wasn't you, you did a lot of nice things for me," said Danny. She slipped off her cream satin shoes with the pearls sewn on the toes and slid her legs underneath her, a sign that the Cointreau was easing her nerves. She looked fragile. It was that delicate way her head balanced on her neck. She took his hand.

He didn't know exactly why he did it, but Hallie leaned over and kissed her. The kiss felt semi-familiar, which was interesting. Though definitely a familiar kiss, it had the sweetness of distance from its last encounter. He knew it was a mistake, but he also knew that the moment he had taken off her coat he was going to end up going to bed with her.

He knew he would go to bed with her and he knew he was going to regret it.

But his hand was on her thigh, stroking it, the defined, taut muscles now straining slightly. She was wearing stockings and a garter belt. She always did. She lifted her dress and watched his hand against her silk underpants. Then she stood up and took off her dress.

Great body. Amazing muscle definition, those deltoids, those calves. And all covered in amazing skin, skin like powder.

"I want to make love," she said, in case taking off her dress hadn't implied that.

Hallie had a hard-on. When a girl like Danny Landauer comes into your living room and takes off her dress, it can do that to a man. The voices of warning were drowned out by the sloshing of his male hormones.

So he reached out and took off her underpants.

Before long they were in his bedroom, really going at it. Hallie watched her fantastic body as she performed for him, because that's what she did, perform. Not only with her lithe and performance-trained body, but with squeals and screams and shouts of his name so that he knew someone, somewhere, was hearing all this. Hallie was so painfully aware of her performing, he almost couldn't start fucking her harder each time she did it. But "almost" is the key.

Just as he shut his eyes for the finale, he suddenly imagined that it was Nikki beneath him. He both accepted the image and immediately dispelled it. Then the sex with Danny was over. The hormonal ragings had made a hasty retreat and made way for calm seas. And over them now slid the voice, loud and clear, saying, "Do you have any idea what kind of trouble this is going to be?"

She lay next to him, and he kept his arm around her for an appropriate amount of time, thanking God neither of them had spoken.

"That was the best it's ever been," Danny whispered.

"It was terrific," Hallie whispered back. He had to. Then he kissed her. "Now we have to go to sleep. I have an early meeting." He kissed her again. "Good night."

"Good night, Hallie," she said. He could hear the disappointment in her voice and knew that as they lay in silence she was still thinking of something to say. But Hallie felt sleep washing over him.

Obviously, the worst thing he could do was to go to sleep right then. It was bad form and he knew it.

Well, at least he had never once lied to her.

4

HALLIE AND DANNY CAME OUT OF his building the next morning to a splendid November day. The sun was shining and the sky was cloudless and brilliantly blue. The air was fresh and frosty and almost felt clean.

He was wearing business clothes, ready for work, and she was wearing the same peachy dress. It depressed him like crazy that she was wearing that dress. It had depressed him to come from his shower and find her wearing it as she handed him a cup of coffee. She always used to make him coffee while he was showering for work. She would be wearing his robe and she would stay in the apartment after he had left. So he had never seen her put on the same dress from the night before. But today, on this blindingly sunny day, she was wearing it.

And even worse, she was smiling a

lot and trying to be cheerful. She had the good sense somehow not to try and have a conversation with him about when they would see each other again or where they would go from here. In fact, he couldn't believe they had made it all the way to the street without having it.

Hallie went to the curb and hailed a cab.

"Will you call me later?"

"Yes," he said, kissing her cheek.

A kiss on the cheek after a night of lovemaking should say all that needs to be said, if you're willing to notice.

"I had a wonderful time, Hallie," she said.

"Me too."

As the cab drove away, Hallie stood watching it. He felt awful. He put his hands in his pockets and started walking.

Danny was going to take this very seriously. The last time he'd seen her, he had met her for a drink at a bar and the issue of sex had been a discussion about the fact that it wasn't going to happen again, a, needless to say, horrible discussion that now needed to be repeated.

Repeated, for God's sake.

Why did he ever let himself get that horny? Hallie made a note to go to a magazine store and buy a lot of porn magazines and jerk off more frequently.

That made him think of Kip. Kip loved to buy porn magazines. And he loved to ask for certain magazines in quite a public voice. "Excuse me, my good man, do you have the latest *Chunky Asses?*"

With this thought, Hallie managed to smile. He had to call Kip. Kip would cheer him up. As a matter of fact, what he had to do was see Kip. That thought made him feel a little bit better as he approached his office building, but he wished it were at least raining. All that sun was so silly.

As Hallie walked down the office corridor to his suite of offices, he could see Lisa at her desk. Her office also served as a private reception area, as it was quite large. And seated on the sofa, reading *The New York Times,* was Alfred.

The light from the window fell along one side of his father's face, which was tilted back despite a pair of reading glasses balanced on his nose. His prominent features, large eyes, long curled nose, absence of lips, were silhouetted. It was a touching sight, thought Hallie for a moment, before he put on his armor.

"Here he is," said Lisa brightly to Alfred, as she saw Hallie. "Your father's here," she said to Hallie. Obvious information or what?

Alfred lowered his head and looked over the top of his glasses.

"Well, well, well!" bellowed Alfred. "Here he is!" He made a big deal out of looking at his watch.

"It's nine-thirty," Hallie told him.

"I have nine thirty-five," said Alfred, telling his own time. "I didn't know when the hell you get in, but I wanted to catch you before you got busy."

"Usually I get in at eight," Hallie said.

"I thought that. That's what I thought," said Alfred.

"How long have you been here?" Hallie asked, picking up some unopened letters from Lisa's desk.

"Oh, about a goddamn hour."

"I thought that," said Hallie. "That's what I thought."

"Didn't mind a bit," Alfred said. "This girl knows how to take care of a man." He indicated a cup of coffee and a half-eaten Danish.

This girl knows how to take care of a man?

Alfred might as well have said, "Those darkies certainly do have rhythm." But then Hallie saw Lisa smiling proudly, like a nut-case Miss America contestant, so he realized the mortification was his own.

"Come in, I want to talk to you," said Alfred, bounding up from the sofa and walking toward Hallie's office.

He's inviting me into my own office, Hallie thought, following him.

Once inside, Alfred went right over and opened the drapes. Even Alfred had to look at the view, although at least he never commented on it. Then he went behind Hallie's desk, picked up Hallie's phone, and dialed.

"Alfred here," he said. "The rehearsal's going to start half an hour late this morning. I've been detained." As he listened, a big smile filled out his lips, followed by a laugh that might have made you think he'd just heard something funny, except you knew it couldn't be that funny. "Fantastic!" he bellowed. "Well, thanks so much. I'll see you later. In fact, I'll buy you lunch."

Alfred hung up the phone. Lisa had come in with a trayful of fresh coffee and Danish. She put it on a coffee table near the sofas.

"Fernheidt was killed in Paris!" Alfred said. Had it been death by murder, there would have been something lunatic about Alfred's delight, but it was murder by critics, of his oldest rival.

"Congratulations." Hallie said the appropriate thing. He reached for the single French cruller set between the Danish. He loved French crullers. He always used to stop and get one on his way to school. Lily considered heroin and sugar to be the same thing. Hallie always found that at times a French cruller was just the fix he needed.

The phone on Hallie's desk rang. Alfred was about to pick it up when he felt Hallie's gaze and allowed Hallie to answer his own phone. He smiled his petulant little grin, asking for forgiveness.

Hallie took the call.

"Nikki, hello," said Hallie. He didn't even have to look at him, so obvious was the rise in Alfred's attention. "You can? That's great. The Russian Tea Room, I was thinking. Oh, good, good. One o'clock. See you then."

"You're having lunch with Nikki? That's terrific!" boomed Alfred. He went over to the chesterfield sofas and sat down, patting the place next to him for Hallie. Hallie came over, but sat on the sofa opposite.

"Of course you left last night without saying anything to me, so I had no idea how anything went." Alfred paused and poured some coffee.

"I have my opinions, but I'm not ready to say," Hallie offered. "What I do want to know is, why are you so obsessed with her?"

"Who's obsessed?"

"You are."

"With Mahler you get obsessed, late Beethoven maybe, but—"

"Then why are you here?" Hallie asked with astonishing calm.

Alfred drew himself up slowly till seated at his full height.

"You think I'm here because of *Nikki?*" His eyes bulged a little. "Nonsense! Nikki? I've asked you to do a little favor for me. Whatever happens, at least I'm satisfied that the smartest person I know couldn't prevent it."

"Oh," said Hallie. "So you had no intention of asking me anything about her?"

"If her name came up, I would discuss her, of course. I'm here because the board would like you to co-chair the benefit. That's why I'm here, Mr. Chief Counsel."

With that, Alfred made a large gesture of sipping his coffee—picking up the cup and saucer, sipping, then putting it all back down again. He was giving Hallie a chance to let what he had just said sink in.

"As far as Nikki goes, as long as you're having lunch with her, why not come by to the rehearsal afterward?"

What a master he is, thought Hallie.

"I'll see how lunch goes. I'm not going to co-chair the benefit."

Alfred went into a new persona—responsible caretaker of a great symphony orchestra. While retired from the position of principal conductor, he was a member of the board.

"Jack's going to call you this morning, but I wanted to tell you first."

"No," said Hallie. "If I were you, I'd call Jack and suggest someone else."

"Go ahead," Alfred said, leaning back, folding his arms over his chest. He was wearing a well-worn tweed jacket and a red turtle-neck sweater. "Go ahead and say no. To me. But not to the board."

"It's a social position, Dad," said Hallie.

"So? So big deal! You're already in a social position," yelled Alfred. "Nothing can change that. As chief counsel and as a Law-rence, you're the obvious choice. It's an obligation, Hallie. It just means wearing another hat—"

"No hats!" said Hallie.

"It's an honor," said Alfred, suddenly weakened by what an honor it was.

"Honors I don't need, Dad," said Hallie.

"Maybe you'll meet some very nice girls," said Alfred.

The two of them locked eyes.

"Well, that's how she put it to me; what can I say." Alfred sighed and winked at his son over their shared understanding that those had been Lily's words.

"I'll purchase benefit tickets and send an additional five grand. But no chairman of anything."

"Hallie, please—"

"I'm serious."

"Five thousand? You couldn't manage a little more?"

"Five thousand, and tell Jack I'm not the man for the job. Don't make me tell him myself or I won't even show up at the benefit." Shocked at how quickly he had become ten years old again, Hallie blamed it on the cruller.

He got up and went to his desk and without hesitation began to look at his work, as if Alfred weren't there.

"Don't make threats, Hallie. I'll talk to Jack. Maybe someday you'll find a wife who can take care of obligations for you. But who knows? Maybe not. I don't know what I'd do without Lily."

Lisa had heard Alfred's pronouncement as she walked in, and she wore an idiotically sentimental smile.

"May I have my coat, darling?" asked Alfred, not without some petulance.

In a flash Lisa returned with his coat, cashmere with a mouton collar, and Alfred allowed her to drape it around his shoulders.

"Lisa, you are a perfect colt."

Lisa probably didn't notice it, she was so busy feeling somehow complimented by Alfred, but Hallie saw Alfred's eyes linger an extra moment over her breasts, in a sleek-fitting dress.

"Enjoy lunch and I'll see you at the rehearsal." Alfred swept out of the office. Hallie never remembered saying anything about going to the rehearsal.

"You don't have to put up with him," said Hallie to Lisa.

"I don't mind, I think I understand him."

"Right," said Hallie.

Another depressing thought, on a day with so many of them. When Lisa left the room, Hallie closed his door and called Kip.

Every time Hallie went to the Russian Tea Room, he would start feeling sleepy. It came from his childhood associations with the place. Taken there often late at night, after Alfred's concerts, he would end up lying on the banquette, looking at everybody's shoes under the table, before eventually falling asleep. So, to this day, he would start to feel sleepy every time he got to the Russian Tea Room. Another big point for Pavlov.

But any fears of somnambulance were dispelled by the presence of Nikki Mikhailovitch. Soon Hallie was eating blini and drinking vodka and listening to this very animated girl, passionate, you could say, prone to great gasps and gesturings. She spoke in a manner that invited a sense of intimacy or outrage, depending. But there was also a compelling sadness to her.

It was sexy.

"All I can remember—well, ever since I was four and started to play—is that people treated me differently. I was very privileged because of some gift I was born with, some gift to play violin that I didn't ask anybody to give me. And everyone I can remember was always telling me what to do. The only reason I played the violin was to shut them up. Okay, I'll practice. At least when I was practicing, no one was telling me what to do. I've been talking about myself the whole lunch."

That's true, thought Hallie, even though he hadn't really been bored.

"Tell me about you, Hallie. You too had a privileged childhood, no?"

"Yes, I did," said Hallie slowly, choosing the three words with care because he intended them to be his last three words on the subject. He remembered something about child prodigies. They were a little bit like freaks. Part of them was intensely adult and part of them had never progressed beyond kindergarten.

"I met you a couple of times, you know. You don't remember, that's okay, but I do." Nikki was looking right into his eyes now but she didn't seem flirtatious—just incredibly direct.

"I remember," said Hallie, wishing he did, trying to find the occasions of those meetings somewhere at the back of his brain.

"No, not like me. I remember. I was once having dinner at your parents' house and you came home. It was for Thanksgiving or something; you were coming home from Harvard College. That's where you went to school, right?"

"Yes."

"I thought you were so handsome I couldn't believe my eyes. All that year I hoped you would come whenever I played with Alfred, but you never did. I was heartbroken. I was also seventeen and a pathetic lovesick teenager."

Hallie Lawrence was embarrassed. Mortified, actually. He managed only to spurt, "Oh, well, I'm sorry. I never—"

"Don't worry about it, I got over it. I was so young." She flashed him a worldly little smile and had a sip of vodka. Then she began heaping red caviar and sour cream on her blini. "So tell me, did you ever hear me play when I didn't know about it? I always wanted to ask you that."

"I've heard you play," said Hallie, who was not a little confused by her. He thought that by bringing up her teenage feelings she had perhaps been flirting with him, but the way she said "Don't worry, I got over it" was so absolutely dismissive that it could be nothing but the truth. She had pulled him in and thrown him on his ass.

"Good. Then you know how I play."

"It's been a while—"

"It doesn't matter, you know how I play. It's nothing but a gift."

"So you keep saying," Hallie said pleasantly, taking a subtle but huge sip of his vodka.

"Look, it's a gift that's . . . attached to me—" She cupped both her breasts for emphasis. "From birth. Playing for me is like walking, like breathing. But it is separate from me, do you understand?" She frowned slightly. "Please, tell me you understand what I'm talking about."

"I understand. I can see that way of looking at it. It must be very lonely to be so detached."

Somehow this response seemed to please her. He noticed her take it in and smile. He also noticed she wore a light-gray suit that was beautifully cut and he could sense her exotic fragrance in the loose red curls.

"Lonely. Yes, I guess so." She stopped smiling. "Was it lonely being the son of Alfred Lawrence? Is that why you understand loneliness?"

"Well, I don't really think you're making an appropriate comparison," Hallie said with a charming smile. That was even more depressing than her intimate teen confession. And yet, here was a young woman who actually knew Alfred very well. He was her

mentor and she had been thoroughly exposed to the real Alfred
Lawrence, of that Hallie was sure. She struck Hallie as a curious
commodity that he simply wanted to get away from. He decided
to get back down to business, where things were safe.

"I think you see this movie project as a way of trying something
you're not so sure you can do."

"I can do it!"

"All right, you can do it. Let's just say it's challenging because
it's something you've never done before. And maybe it won't be
as easy as breathing."

"Maybe." Her eyes filled with sparks and her lips broadened into
a lovely smile. "So! You think I have the right to do it or not?"

"You certainly have the right to do whatever you want."

"You're not going to remind me about my responsibility to
music, blah blah blah?"

"You're responsible for everything you do, Nikki."

"How profound," she whispered to him with mischievous irony.

"You certainly have the right to do it."

"You believe in free will?"

"I think it's sort of basic, yes."

Nikki patted the table for emphasis and said, "There's no such
thing as free will."

"Is that some sort of Russian thing?" asked Hallie.

"You talk about responsibility and free will in one lunch. I like
you, Hallie Lawrence." Her Russian accent made her sound like an
old philosophy professor, so her conclusion at least didn't sound
ludicrous. "So, speaking as a lawyer, are you interested in me?"

"I'll look after you, if you like."

These were Hallie's special words for the Ego Maniac, who purrs
on hearing the words "look after." Normally, he would say something like "I'll take your case."

"I think I would like that," she purred. "I think you understand me."

"I think I do," said Hallie, knowing he wasn't sure at all that he
did, but what he could do for her was give protection against
Alfred. He almost felt like telling her that, but he figured it would
be too revealing about himself.

Nikki was staring out across the restaurant, leaning on one
elbow. Hallie looked at her face closely. He tried to convince
himself that she wasn't the "some beauty" Alfred had described.
The cossack fuck once again crossed his mind, with a little gypsy
music this time.

He got the check.

They walked out into the blaring afternoon sun and a blast of

winter cold. Lucky they had had the vodkas. Nikki put on a pair of
sunglasses, black with very dark lenses. She wore a black coat
bought in Paris, and a big green cashmere scarf. She was very
stylish. Hallie noted that she had thin but nice legs, in black stockings.

"Now I must go to rehearsal. Walk with me a little bit?"

"Okay," said Hallie.

She had a nice brisk walking pace, which Hallie naturally had
too, so they strode up Fifty-seventh Street quickly.

"Have you seen a script yet for this film?" said Hallie, resuming
a businesslike tone. The fresh air seemed to help.

"They said the writer is having problems, but soon it will be
ready."

"When they say the writer is having problems, it's usually a
euphemism for financing."

"They are prepared to make an offer of money. That's why I
need a lawyer, Hallie Lawrence."

"Aren't you curious to see a script first?"

"No, no, no, no, no." Five no's. "You must now call them and
ask them to send the script soon because I'm not interested, but
maybe if I read it, then I'll be interested." She shrugged her shoulders.

"If you're not interested, Nikki, you have to tell them. If you're
interested, then read a script."

"You are very smart, Hallie Lawrence. I was just testing you. I
was wondering how you were at doing the bullshit."

"I'm great at it. But why would I do it with you? You're the
client. Read the script."

"And you're what? Such a nice guy you would never bullshit
me?"

Hallie laughed, more at the way she said it than at the actual
words. There was a tough little creature in there.

When they were across from Lincoln Center, waiting for a light,
they saw the Whooping Crane Lady.

She was very ordinary-looking, an elderly woman in a regular
beige down coat and a lavender woolly hat trimmed in purple
angora. She wore ordinary elderly-lady shoes and carried a brown
purse, well worn but not extraordinarily so for an elderly lady. She
didn't stand out at all, and in fact had one of those nice faces that
could have been selling geriatric diapers on television. She stepped
out into the street and waited for the light to change.

All of a sudden, she let out three whooping noises, in a high
soprano register. Really loud. *Whoop, whoop, whoop.* And she went
right back to being a regular elderly lady.

It killed Hallie. He had seen her a couple of times before in the Lincoln Center area, and once again it struck him as one of the Great Moments. But usually when something absolutely stupendous like that happened he was alone, and he would forget about it; it was not worth repeating, you had to be there. But this time he happened to be with Nikki.

"Oh my God!" she gasped loudly. Nikki did not take a step back in horror, as a few other people did, she just gasped, "Oh my God!" Her eyes instantly went to Hallie's and he could see they were brimming with delight.

"I know just how she feels," whispered Nikki.

Hallie smiled. Who would have thought he would ever have a Great Moment with Nikki Mikhailovitch. Oddly, she seemed to appreciate it too.

He would see the Whooping Crane Lady again.

On the stage, musicians were tuning up, casually chatting, setting up music. Alfred was at the podium in his turtleneck, a scarf draped around his neck as if he had found it lying around somewhere and didn't want to lose it. He lit a cigar, puffed a few times up at the proscenium, and laid it in a big ashtray on a stool. He stared down at the score.

Hallie was sitting in the darkened house, near the back. He had decided not to let Alfred or Nikki know he was there and had, in fact, left Nikki at the door. Now he watched her come from the wings, carrying her violin under her arm. She took off her suit jacket as she spoke to Alfred for a minute. They both consulted the score. They looked, from Hallie's advantage, like toys.

Alfred tapped on the podium and brought the orchestra to attention. He took a puff on his cigar and said something, which Hallie couldn't hear, but which made the orchestra members chuckle as they prepared to play. They began the Brahms Violin Concerto, from the top.

And then Nikki began playing.

Hallie had been unconsciously tapping the beat to the piece that he knew so well, and equally unconsciously, he stopped.

He expected it would take more than a few bars to hear anything of Nikki's talent, but that wasn't the case. The sound she pulled from her violin was really extraordinary; a mellow clarity, incredibly rich, deep tones. And the more she played, the more he could hear her exquisite musicianship. You could feel her keep her emotional explosion handsomely controlled, but it was there and it was awesome.

Familiar passage after familiar passage flowed to Hallie in the darkness, and in a short while he knew the thing he had come to find out. Alfred was right.

So he got up and left.

He decided to walk back to his office through the park.

He found himself walking briskly, scarf tied around his neck, shoulders up, hands in his pockets. The trees were naked and scratchy-looking.

It had been a long time since he had felt this bad, and he found himself disengaging from it, which was the Hallie Lawrence thing to do.

Alfred was right, but that wasn't the thing that bothered him. He had been perfectly prepared to discover that his father's assessment of Nikki's talent would be accurate.

And Nikki was right. Her talent was something that had been attached to her. There was nothing about Nikki that even remotely suggested the incredible maturity of her musicianship.

The depressing part was dealing with what lay ahead. Maintaining neutrality took a lot of work under the most ordinary circumstances. This felt like the Olympics. The Maintaining Neutrality event.

When he tried to take his mind off Alfred and Nikki, he thought about Danny, not exactly a respite. He would have to call her when he got back to the office; it was the well-mannered thing to do. He couldn't not call her.

Then he thought about Kip, whom he had arranged to see the next day. What a stroke of genius it had been, calling Kip. Hallie had told him about Danny because Kip always wanted to know if Hallie had had any lately. Kip said Hallie should stock up on porn mags so it wouldn't happen again. Kip told him the new *Big Fucking Tits* was on the stands. Hallie laughed. He just wanted to sit around with Kip and talk.

As he walked toward his office through the chilled park, he was glad it was Friday.

It was the last Friday afternoon Hallie would ever be the same.

5

"I THINK IT'S SO GREAT THAT YOU always get here before I do."

"It's an accident, believe me. I don't do it intentionally."

"Sure you do. Just admit you're glad to see me, that's it's a real honor—could we get in the car? It's fucking freezing out here."

"Glad to see you? What are you, nuts? Why would I be that? The car is unlocked, asshole."

So Hallie opened the door and got into Kip's old Jeep Wagoneer. Their reunions always started with a lot of insults to cover up the real joy they felt but wouldn't think of expressing—not because they couldn't, but because it would have been sentimental.

Picking up Hallie at the station was part of the tradition of these weekends together. Kip would drive over from western Massachusetts and meet Hal-

lie's train from Grand Central at the Rhinebeck station, and together they would head up the Hudson River Valley. The Lawrences had a country house actually overlooking the Hudson River,
in the town of Darling, New York. Kip and Hallie used to come
up for Weekends with the Parents. They would wander off and find
the places along the river where you could look out and see no sign
of civilization, and think about old Henry Hudson seeing all this
for the first time. Well, first time for a white man. Kip would say
there was nothing left to do for the first time anymore, trying to
sound like Hemingway or F. Scott Fitzgerald or something. They
both had girls for the first time in the Hudson River Valley one
sweet, successful summer.

"Smoke a joint?" asked Kip.

"Sure," said Hallie. The question were redundant. They always
smoked a joint for the drive and would be doing so when they were
ninety-five.

Hallie felt relieved being with Kip again. He studied Kip's face.
It never seemed to change, although it must have since they were
fourteen. It was a fact that Kip was very handsome, wire-framed
glasses and all. All the girls thought Kip was *so* gorgeous, and it was
something Hallie had gotten used to. Lots of girls had, in the course
of the friendship, tried to get Hallie to introduce them to Kip. Not
that Hallie really had any trouble getting girls for himself, but
somehow not the same ones who would be crazy over Kip.

Kip was Episcopalian. The real Episcopalian, not the kind some
German Jews become, always a statement about those kinds of
German Jews. Hallie had known several of the latter, so when Kip
informed him of his religious affiliation in prep school, Hallie had
said, "No kidding," because he knew Kip was the real thing.

Kip, on the other hand, would have traded anything to be a Jew.
There was a mystery for him about Jews that drove him crazy. He
absolutely believed in the dominance of the Jewish male intellect.
Gentile males could be cuter, he knew, but when it came to brains,
the Jews had it all. That was his experience, and you know how one
can always find experiences that help prove a point.

Hallie was the only person in the whole world Kip felt really
close to, even though Kip was married now. He figured you could
reveal a lot more about how you felt to a Jew because Jews were
easier with their feelings. They weren't embarrassed about them or
anything. They could even tolerate hysteria. Remarkable. And so,
delighting in his self-made illuminations, Kip revealed a lot to
Hallie, had even gotten upset in front of him, and had once even
cried. Hallie was a prince and had never made fun of him once, not
even when he was drunk.

They didn't stop talking much for the early part of the drive. And their conversation was fragmented because there was so much to get out of the way—observations they'd made about things since they'd seen each other last, and sports. They always gave some time to the game.

The third Rachmaninoff Piano Concerto was playing on the tape deck. The ground outside was beginning to harden, and the sky was very white and heavy, maybe even with snow.

"Darling," said Hallie aloud, reading the highway sign indicating the town of Darling to be among the next exits.

"Yes, my dear?" answered Kip, as he always did whenever they passed the sign.

The tape reached the end and clicked off.

There was silence in the car.

"Who gives a shit?" said Kip, as they passed the sign that read "Darling."

"That's the spot," said Hallie, grinning.

The remark "Who gives a shit?" referred to the story of how Hallie convinced Kip to go to Harvard. It had happened as they had driven past that very sign. Kip had been having a running battle with his parents, which he had been enjoying immensely. He found it thrilling to mumble that he wasn't too interested in Harvard, alma mater to the men in his family since Harvard had opened up for business. The statement was met with silence and a change of subject. Translation: Episcopalian hysteria.

Then one day, Hallie had talked him into it. Boy, did Kip's parents ever start approving of Hallie Lawrence. They had never disapproved of him really; he was, after all, the right kind of Jew. But when they thought Hallie had managed to convince Kip how invaluable the Harvard experience would be, they were impressed.

They had been exiting the highway at Darling, two high school boys, seniors, shooting the breeze.

"If you don't come to Harvard, that's it between us."

"You got in because you're smart, Hallie."

"Oh, and I hang around with you because I like hanging around with idiots? Would I have a friend who couldn't get into Harvard? I ask you!"

"I got in because of the old boys. Period."

"Who gives a shit?" said Hallie.

Suddenly, Kip couldn't think of a possible person who would, and realized he was the only person who probably did. It was one of those moments you have when you're a senior and you're beginning to think you're the Dalai Lama every time you have a little insight. Kip decided that nothing could stop him from spending the next four years with Hallie.

"You know, 'Who gives a shit?' was very good advice."

"My good man, if it hadn't been good advice, I wouldn't have taken it," said Kip, deadpan. "I say we brew up at the inn."

"Yea, let's brew up," said Hallie.

Kip pulled his car into the parking lot of the Darling Inn. They were both crazy about the place because it was so corny. Part of the building dated from Revolutionary War times, and it was said that George Washington had used it for meetings on several occasions, and had even stayed overnight. Over the years this distinction had been expressed in various ways. Currently, the waitresses wore Revolutionary War outfits, with long skirts and bustier blouses, and if they had a big bosoms, well, those outfits were very complimentary.

Kip and Hallie got out of the car. They wore similar tweed jackets that they had purchased on their first trip to London together, before going off to Harvard. Hallie buttoned his now to ward off the frozen gray and white day. Not Kip. He had only one arm in a sleeve, which left him virtually wearing only his frayed blue oxford button-down shirt. He bent down into the car and started looking for something.

Look at him, thought Hallie. The bastard is never cold. Hallie paced as he waited.

"What are you doing?" he finally asked. "It's fucking freezing out here." Realizing he had used this phrase earlier, Hallie now recalled Nikki's slavic "fuckink freezink."

"I dropped my wallet," said Kip, standing up, wallet in hand. "You're cold? You think this is cold?"

They walked toward the inn.

"You're such a gentile," said Hallie.

"I am not," said Kip.

"You are. Look at you, you've got nothing on and you're not even cold."

"I'm freezing, what are you kidding? I'm freezing."

"You are not."

"I am too."

On that mature note, they entered the white clapboard building.

They told the hostess they were two for lunch. She wasn't wearing the Revolutionary War outfit, which was only for waitresses, although the purple clingy jersey dress she wore suggested how well she might have looked in one. On her breast was a plastic pin with an image of George Washington and the inn's claim, "George Washington Slept Here." It also read that the hostess's name was Nancy.

Nancy was smiling at them, amused and a little unsure.

"If there's a wait, we can go to the bar," Kip said, with charm.

"Do you guys have ties or anything?" Nancy asked, smiling, her dark eyes, with the touch of blue on the lids, squinting. She looked at them in their khakis and tattered jackets.

"These jackets happen to be antiques," said Hallie.

"This establishment surely has respect for the antique," said Kip.

"Come on," said Nancy. "The dress code only says you have to have jackets." She led them to a table. "You guys are fine."

"Thank you, m'am," said Kip.

They were seated near the restaurant's fireplace, whose mantel supported a collection of things made out of copper. The beams in the ceiling were wood, the floor was stone, and cheerful curtains covered a large mullioned window.

The first thing the men did was order a couple of beers from Sandy, their Revolutionary War Maiden waitress. Her plastic sign with the image of George Washington and the claim "George Washington Slept Here" was pinned to her bosom-revealing top, and seemed to indicate that perhaps it was with this very bosom he had indeed slept.

Or at least that's how it hit Kip and Hallie at the same time.

Kip was giving her his full attention, Hallie noted. His charm routine. Sandy looked a little as if it was her big dream in life to be a game-show hostess and that she probably got a bang out of wearing the uniform because it made her feel that she was in show business.

She went off to bring them beers.

Kip watched her go with that funny look in his eye. Boy, did Hallie know that look. It was understood that Kip could look at women as much as he liked. And express appreciation. It had nothing to do with Kate.

"How's Kate?" asked Hallie.

"She wants to have a baby."

Hallie burst out laughing. It was kind of thoughtless, but Hallie was unconsciously unsympathetic.

"You as somebody's dad. That's funny."

"You're not supposed to laugh, for Christ's sake. Jesus." But Kip smiled, always ready to revert back to prep-school retard. Hallie was the last person left who wouldn't give him a lecture about growing up.

"You always said Katie was your destiny. So go forth and multiply."

"Thank you, Rabbi," said Kip.

Everything about Kip's marriage to Kate had to do with being members of the same club, but Hallie didn't actually want to come right out and say it. Besides, Kip knew.

It had been okay for Kate to marry Kip, the notorious black sheep of the family, because she was a little bit arty herself. She wore black stockings and big earrings. She had a degree in ceramics, and believe it or not, had gone on to a career in that field, designing ceramic cups and things, with her signature, little farm animals, painted on them.

It drove Kip around the bend.

"You're happy with Kate, Kipper," said Hallie with finality.

"I'm not, you know. I'm really not."

Hallie just gave him a "Give me a break" look.

"I sold my first fifteen-thousand-dollar painting," said Kip suddenly.

Hallie started grinning like crazy, but he didn't say anything for a moment. It was a great announcement and certainly easier than the subject of fatherhood. "Congratulations! Well, congratulations indeed, old boy," said Hallie, assuming one of those phony repressed voices. "I must say, that was quick."

"Ten years? I've been painting for ten years," said Kip.

"Good! I hate a quitter."

"Thank you."

"B.P. is going to have to admit that his son is an artist. This could be good." Hallie was referring to Kip's father, Barnes Prescott Courtland.

" 'And what is young Kipper up to these days?' " came Kip's imitation of any of his father's friends. "Which means, 'With what firm is he, and to where has he advanced?' 'Oh, Kip paints.' 'Sorry, Barnes, old man. Uh, pity about that.' "

"If we had been a little older, you could have dodged the draft. If he had lived through that, he'd be used to you by now."

Sandy returned with the beers. She also took their lunch orders for the prime rib dinner and a fine Bordeaux. They were in a red-meat kind of mood.

"I think I've met a new Ego Maniac," Hallie began when Sandy left.

"Male or female?"

"Female."

"Arts or politics?"

"She plays violin, she's Russian, and Alfred is in full tilt to get me to talk her out of being in some movie."

"Sounds great!"

Hallie went on to fill Kip in on the highlights of recent Alfredisms, especially as they related to Nikki. Now, if there was anyone in the world who understood Alfred, it was Kip. Kip had been the one to nominate Alfred to the category of World-Class Ego Maniac in the first place. Once he had convinced Hallie that Ego Mania was, for the most part, what Alfred was all about, nothing ever seemed to hurt as much again.

Hallie remembered the night when Kip first coined the category.

He and Kip had come down from Harvard for the weekend. It was their freshman year. The first thing Lily did was inform them that they would be attending the orchestra's first night of the season, conducted by Alfred.

No problem.

In the Green Room afterward, Hallie and Kip were lolling against the wall, observing Alfred sponging up passionate kudos from his gushing fans. Alfred had removed his coat and was in his tux shirt, unbuttoned for the most part, and moist from his mayhem at the podium. He embraced people as if he weren't a sweatball, probably thinking people wanted to get close to his sweat, which had, after all, come from his inspiration and genius. Nobody seemed to mind, so it must've been the case, and he was embracing some pretty dolled-up women and elegant gents.

Hallie and Kip saw Alfred spot them and begin a labored and exhausted move through the crowd, as if whatever strength was left in him, after the genius display, he would summon to get to his son. It was impressive.

Hallie felt like dying.

"My son . . ." said Alfred, seeming on the verge of collapse, balanced only on the ecstasy the vision of his offspring inspired. And with this ecstasy, he opened his arms for Hallie. He knew anyone who was watching, which was everybody there, was witness to this touching moment.

But into Hallie's ear he whispered, "What are you slouching against the wall for, for Christ's sake. You look like a bum."

Kip heard it. He just happened to have been close enough to Hallie. They exchanged looks, Hallie from over Alfred's shoulder, locked in the embrace.

Then Hallie was free, as Alfred bellowed to the fans, "My biggest critic."

It was a pretty sensational moment because Hallie had grown up with hundreds of such moments, and Kip had gotten to see one firsthand.

Later, they went in the Lawrences' car to the restaurant where a small party was being held for Alfred's first night of the season. Kip and Hallie in their tuxedos, two freshmen from Harvard, made Lily especially radiant that night; it made her feel reminiscent.

Kip offered Lily his arm as they alighted from the car and made their way to the celebrations. He did it because it was cool, not because of his breeding. He was at the age when acting a little bit like Humphrey Bogart was appealing.

Hallie found himself waiting on the sidewalk for Alfred. He swayed back and forth for a few minutes, hands in his pockets, then looked into the dark car. Alfred was slouched deep into the seat, his head thrown back, his eyes closed. For a second, Hallie thought he was dead. Then Alfred let out an enormous breath of air.

"Are you all right?" asked Hallie.

"I was just elsewhere," said Alfred. "I'm ready now."

And he held his hand out for Hallie to help him.

Elsewhere? And where the fuck was that? thought Hallie. But one does not ask where geniuses go when they are holding their breath and pretending to be dead.

Hallie was used to Alfred, at that point in his life, but his father was really beginning to piss him off more and more.

"I wanted to go in just with you," Alfred said, putting his arm around Hallie as they walked toward the restaurant doors. "I was just detaining things so the others would go in first, and I could enter with you."

Hallie took a deep breath of night air. Alfred had just told him exactly where geniuses go when they're "elsewhere." They're refueling on bullshit.

Inside, various admiring big shots surrounded Alfred immediately, pumping his hand. Voices rose, laughter was heard, Alfred began making quips. Hallie had been left where the first hand-pumper had accosted them, near the entrance. And he stood there, not moving, as Alfred made his way through well-wishers toward the table where Lily and Kip were seated with some other celebrated types. He stood there thinking about how Alfred had just told him, "I want to enter with you," and decided that when you see someone forget his words that quickly, you get a major idea of how full of shit he really is.

Then he saw Kip get up from the table and come toward him. Kip had watched the whole thing.

"I got it all figured out," Kip said as he came to Hallie's side, taking out two cigars. "Alfred is a world-class, and I'm talking big-time, Ego Maniac. Possibly on the level with the pope. You've got nothing to worry about. You never had a chance."

That really made Hallie laugh. They lit up cigars and joined the family at the table.

Lily was furious with them for smoking cigars before dinner.

After telling Kip the Nikki-Alfred movie saga, Hallie found he couldn't take it very seriously anymore.

"Okay, so she makes the movie," said Kip, emptying the last drops of Bordeaux into his glass and slicing into his prime rib. "And then she's never accepted again as a classical musician. No, I like this. This is Dostoyevski, man."

Hallie laughed. He was feeling the wine. Now, the fact that he had ever felt anything but amusement about Alfred's manipulations astonished him.

"Okay. Get to the point. Is she good-looking?" asked Kip. He signaled for the return of Sandy and another bottle of wine.

Hallie thought for a moment.

"Oh, she's definitely good-looking. Red hair, medium tits; she's good-looking."

"You going to shtup her?" Kip loved Yiddish expressions.

"Shtupping her isn't the point," said Hallie. "I think that might be exactly what Lily and Alfred would like."

"Alfred," said Kip in a falsetto voice that was supposed to be Lily, "I think it would be simply marvelous if Hallie shtupped that darling little fiddle player."

"It's a possibility," said Hallie. "But I'm not supposed to shtup them, just marry them. No shtupping except for grandchildren."

"So you're not attracted?"

"To someone my mother wants me to shtup?"

"Good. Then should I meet her?"

Sandy had reappeared and was uncorking a second bottle of wine. The bottle was pressed against her breasts, the green glass touching the ivory orbs as she worked in the corkscrew. Hallie wasn't sure about more wine. Kip's eyes, behind the wire glasses, were sparkling with enough mischief already, watching the bottle and the breasts. Hallie wasn't sure they should drink any more.

"Another bottle?" asked Hallie the Semite.

"Should I meet her?" asked Kip again, lighting a cigar and savoring his once-again full glass.

"Will you give me a break! What about Kate?"

"You're right. Katie is great, always in charge of everything, always managing things, I love her. She's great. We're going to stay in Darling tonight, aren't we? Because I want to get drunk and smoke some more dope and talk all night long."

"Sounds good," said Hallie.

"I'll even drive you back to New York. Should I meet her?"

Hallie looked away. Kip was doing his annoying-pest routine. It often happened when he was starting to feel his alcohol. Fortunately, it usually passed.

And as Hallie looked away, half smiling, he noticed that at a nearby table three women were having lunch. Hallie hadn't been particularly aware of other diners; he and Kip had been totally absorbed with catching up with each other. But now he focused on these three. There was something about their faces that made him realize that they were sisters. It struck him as interesting how their faces were like variations on a theme. The youngest was maybe eighteen, the middle one looked to be in her mid-twenties, and the eldest, in her thirties. They were all very pretty.

They seemed to be having such a nice time together, although occasionally one would protest something said. The way in which they dealt with the protests made him think that it was more than physical resemblance that gave their relationship away.

"Could easily be friends of Kate's," said Kip, having followed Hallie's eye to the women.

Hallie smiled. He knew what Kip meant.

"Is something really wrong with you two?" Hallie asked, returning his attention to Kip.

"Not really. She wants to have a baby, that's all."

"So you said," Hallie said, a little more gently this time.

And then it happened.

She came into his line of view just before she reached the table with the sisters. He remembered hearing them reacting with various degrees of delight, then admonition, as if she was late. But mostly there were girlish noises and they all got up to hug her. Hallie stared openly, but it didn't matter.

Hallie had been struck down.

Something had happened to the earth. It had stopped moving for about fifteen seconds, and it would be fifteen seconds missing from the rest of Hallie's life.

He looked back at Kip with what he imagined was wild-eyed intensity, but was actually a very blank expression. He waited whatever the acceptable number of seconds were before looking back again.

Something about her made him think of white chocolate. He didn't particularly seek out white chocolate, but every time he had some he was surprised at the stupendous creamy taste. He just stared at her. She had dark-blond hair that must be made of silk, long hair parted on the side, with long bangs that topped off spectacular almond-shaped eyes. She had a wide mouth which broke into remarkable smiles as she held the attention of the others with an anecdote and extreme girlish secrecy. She had bone structure you find in one out of every two hundred million people. Hallie wanted to get up and kiss her.

"Jesus," said Kip, when Hallie looked back to him.

"Am I very pale? Do I look different?" asked Hallie, reaching for a glass of water.

"Like a ghost, Hal." Kip was a little amused. This kind of thing happened to Kip every day. "It'll pass, man."

"Wow," said Hallie.

"Humdinger," said Kip, the way they had said it hundreds of times, at school, in Europe, on the beaches of New England. And that was it. You get on with the conversation.

"I want to have a show," said Kip. "I want to sell more pictures."

"Sounds logical," said Hallie, trying desperately to focus on what Kip was saying. But Hallie was looking at her again, and, to his horror, the group seemed to be leaving. But in fact the white chocolate kissed them all and then sat back down at the table. Hallie thought that if she had left too, he might have killed himself, or at least embarrassed himself to death. She took out a folder tied with pink ribbon and began to look through some papers. Then she looked up.

She looked up, saw Hallie, and she smiled.

And worse, she didn't then just look away. She kept smiling as if she maybe knew him or something. He couldn't believe it. He felt himself sliding down something long and slippery.

"Maybe we should stay here at the inn," said Kip.

Hearing Kip's voice was a lifeline. He looked away from her and smiled rather nonchalantly at Kip, as if he didn't have stuffing coming out all over the place.

"Let's do that. Let's get a room," Hallie said, hoping his voice sounded like the regular old Hallie.

Kip stood up. "I'll take care of it. You talk to her. You might find out I'm not the roommate for you."

"Nothing's going to change between us because of this," Hallie said earnestly.

They looked at each other, equally aware of the psychosis of the statement, but both knowing it was not the time to discuss it.

With Kip off on the room mission, Hallie picked up his wineglass and finished off the last sip, as if he wasn't already spinning out, and not from the wine. Maybe she would look at him first. He wouldn't look over at her right away, but he would try to see if maybe somehow, from the corner of his eye, he could tell if she was looking at him. If she had looked at him first, he would talk to her. If not, he was leaving.

It happened spontaneously. Just as he couldn't stand it another second, he looked up just as she did. That sensuous, wide mouth smiled the most friendly smile he had ever seen. Then she sort of cocked her head. The silky hair fell to one side.

"Do I know you?" she asked, in a completely confident voice.

"Uh, no," said Hallie, amazed to find any voice at all.

"Oh. Well, you've been looking at me, so I thought maybe we'd met and I didn't remember you."

Thanks a whole lot.

"I was looking at you because you're so beautiful," Hallie said.

A rush went through him for having been so candid. It had seemed like the most logical thing to say. It had just fallen out.

"Oh!" she said, registering genuine surprise. She made a slight face as if to disavow his observation. It was so girlish he couldn't believe it. But she didn't say "No, I'm not" or start pointing out all her flaws.

Of course not. There weren't any.

"Thanks," she said softly. Such confidence.

"You're welcome."

Then came a pause. For all his years at Harvard, then Harvard Law School, for all his years of cleverly worded arguments during intricate negotiations, Hallie could not at that moment remember a single word in the English language. It was so extreme that he looked down and realized he had even forgotten the word for table, glass, spoon.

J'attend l'autobus avec ma grandmère. Really. That's all he could remember of language as a skill.

So his body took over and got him to stand up and start walking. He got no farther than her table, and she got up too.

"Are you leaving?" he asked, recalling the words, but not too sure what they meant.

"No, I work here."

God, she was tall. She was easily as tall as he was, which was nearly six feet.

"What do you do?" said Hallie. Another phrase came back to him. He had decided to go very slowly, putting one basic word in front of the other, as if he really were back in sixth-grade French.

They were walking together now, out of the restaurant, back to the lobby. There were a few people sitting on the sofas, having a drink, complaining about the weather, but Hallie didn't notice them and neither did she.

"I do the calligraphy for the menus. They're all hand-written? I do that. The calligraphy?"

She had stopped and they were very close to each other, their eyes practically at the same level, smiling like crazy.

"Isn't that interesting," said Hallie. Lucky for him, he had a naturally droll delivery or he would have sounded like a jerk.

"Isn't it?" she leveled back, smiling, without missing a beat. "Isn't that why you came here? For the calligraphy?"

"Absolutely. You don't see a good piece of calligraphy very

often," he said. "How long does a thing like that take, caligraphiz-
ing a menu?"

She laughed. He wondered if she was laughing to be polite, or
actually laughing for real, and if so, why?

She had brown eyes with little specks of gold in them. No, not
brown, honey-colored. Her eyes were the color of honey.

"Oh, I'll be here till late tonight. After I do the menus, I promised to help Mimi—she's the manager—with reservations. I have
to. She's my sister."

"Oh," said Hallie, beginning to lose grip on language skills again
as he allowed himself to look into her eyes.

She seemed to look right into him when she spoke, yet oddly,
at the same time, you couldn't be sure if it wasn't the way she talked
to everybody. She was so friendly. And so beautiful.

"Mimi was the oldest one at the table. I thought you might have
noticed," she said with a little tease. "I mean, you were staring
enough!"

She said this to him as if he were her brother, as if they had shared
a lifetime together and were welcome to say anything they wanted
to each other and not be offended.

"Not before you came," said Hallie. "I mean, nothing against
your sisters or anything."

"Are you sure we've never met?" she asked, smiling.

"Look. If we had met, let's just say, and you didn't remember me,
I'd be heartbroken. So be merciful and let me think we've never
met, okay? So, let's meet. What is your name?"

"Martha. Martha Housewright."

"Martha Housewright? That's actually your name? Martha
Housewright?" For some reason the name astonished him. It
sounded like the grossest fat girl you could imagine getting stuck
with at a dance.

She just gave him a look, playfully pissed off, waiting for him to
get over her name.

"Okay, what's your name?" she said.

Hallie's mind was off again. She looks like some kind of photograph, he thought. That's what it is. One of those mesmerizing
magazine photos that always made you wonder where are the girls
like that in the real world?

Name. She asked you your name.

"My name? Hallie. Hallie Lawrence."

"What kind of name is Hallie, for Jesus's sake? That's supposed
to be a name?" She practically poked him in the ribs with her joyful
eyes.

"It's short for Harold."

Wait a minute, he never told people that. What's going on?

"Harold, Hal—Prince Hal. Oh, I get it. Sort of Shakespearean," she said, still mocking him gleefully. "Well, Hallie Lawrence, that's a very nice name."

"Thank you, Martha."

She started to walk toward the reception area and Hallie uncontrollably followed her.

"Are you staying at the inn?" Martha asked.

"No—uh, yes! Yes, as a matter of fact," he stammered. "We stopped by for lunch but we thought we'd stay. My friend Kip, uh, went to get a room."

"He's very cute," she said.

No. Please, no, she didn't say that.

"Thank you," said Hallie with his deadpan irony. That was it. She was interested in Kip and only talking to Hallie to get an introduction. God, how many times had it happened to him in his life? He would have to go into his good-sport mode, and he already knew it was too late.

No. It just couldn't be.

"Want to have a drink later?" she asked. "Around ten-thirty?" He watched her go behind the front desk and find pens, ink, and blank menus from a supply cupboard. "I have to do menus for the whole week, or I'd have a drink with you now. I'd rather get this over with."

He was thinking about the drink, about sitting across a table from her and talking to her and taking her hand. But what if she expected him to bring Kip?

"Do you want to or not?" she said with feigned impatience.

"Of course I want to. You want me to come on my own?"

"No, I want you to wait and do it with me." She gave him the most playfully lascivious look anyone had ever given Hallie Lawrence. Then she giggled. "Whoops, I shouldn't have said that!"

It was too late; Hallie had a hard-on.

"Where will I find you?" he managed to ask.

"If I'm not here, ask whoever's at the desk, okay?"

"If you're not here, and they don't know where you are when I ask at the desk, I'll kill myself. Remember that."

He smiled and turned to go.

"Oh, you're not too dramatic or anything," she called after him. "What a nerd!"

"She called me a nerd," mumbled Hallie. He was squatting, with his back pressed against the wall. You could say he was in a little bit of a daze.

"Hey, what can I tell you?" said Kip, stoking up the fire. All the rooms had fireplaces and were tastefully decorated in Early American style. "Sounds like love at first sight."

"Do you have to minimize this? I think I'm sick. I actually think I'm sick."

Kip was seriously annoying him. It seemed to have skipped Hallie's mind that it was their regular behavior to tease one another when a new woman entered the picture.

Hallie watched Kip, who was in his socks, go back to a club chair and lounge deeply into it. A bottle of Rémy-Martin and some glasses were on the side table, courtesy of room service. In the ashtray were the remains of a joint and a recently lit cigar.

"Anywhere you go, you just consider home, don't you," said Hallie.

"No, I might not feel too homey in, say, a Turkish prison."

"You'd be fine in a Turkish prison. You're just the type who'd be fine."

"You're not sick," said Kip. He decided he would take Hallie seriously. "You haven't even had a real conversation with her yet. She might turn out to be an airhead."

Hallie looked over at Kip, so obviously comfortable with one leg draped over the arm of the chair, while he was rigid against the wall.

"She's not an airhead," said Hallie, again in a mumble. "Oh, I wish she were an airhead."

Kip puffed on his cigar, bringing it back to life. He flipped back the lock of hair that was always falling into his eyes. He studied Hallie.

"You're in big trouble, Hal."

"That's what I've been trying to tell you for the last hour and a half. I'm starting to get a little pissed off, frankly."

"I noticed. I just decided not to do anything for you."

"Thank you. Thank you very much."

"It's about time you got into trouble, my man."

Sometimes Kip would make a statement like that and it was supposed to be righteous in the old black jazz musician sense of the word. It occured to Hallie that what normally amused him was now extremely annoying.

The truth is, Hallie was scared.

He stared into the floral pattern on one of the twin bedspreads, following the entwining blue vines and flowers and birds. The entire room was blue and white, Hallie noticed for the first time. He began to feel the warmth of the fireplace and was drawn to it. Sliding down to the floor, he moved forward on his knees and realized that he was crawling toward it, and that Kip was watching him.

"I'm ruined," said Hallie. "I have never felt like this in my life. She might be one of those New England witches, you know. Just because we don't burn them anymore doesn't mean they're not out there."

"Hallie, you're being a little extreme here."

"You know what? You want to know what? It might even be *you* she likes! Yes! She might be trying to get to you!"

"Did she ask to have a drink with *me,* Hallie? Did she say, 'By the way, bring along your cute friend'?"

"She said that! She said you were cute!"

"That's like saying it's a nice day. Certain things are just facts."

This caught Hallie like a net. He had long ago learned, from being Kip's friend, that being what the girls called cute didn't give you any less heartache. He smiled, slowly, but he smiled.

"Have a cigar," said Kip.

Hallie forced himself to get up off his hands and knees. Kip handed him the cigar and some matches. Hallie paced back and forth a few times lighting up, and then sat on the bed.

"All right. Let's change the subject." Hallie decided it was an essential thing to do in order to deal with his blood pressure. "Tell me about your painting. Using much blue these days?"

"As a matter of fact—"

"Seriously. Talk to me about your painting. Tell me about having a show. Why don't you do it? Come on, tell me; I'll let you know if you start sounding like an asshole."

"I'm blocked. I haven't been able to paint since I sold my first painting."

Kip and Hallie had had a lengthy conversation about women, over a cold lamb and horseradish. Then Kip decided he needed some sleep. He needed a nap. Besides, it was time for Hallie to go down and find Martha. He was already a little late, and since no one is ever a little late for no reason (a lesson from the catechism of his psychoanalyzed childhood), he had to confront the fact that he was terrified of seeing her again. He had taken an extra ten minutes in the bathroom, staring into the mirror.

As he approached the front desk, he could see plainly that she wasn't there. A man who looked like the town librarian, which he was, sat reading behind the registry.

"Excuse me," said Hallie.

"Oh! Yes, what can I do for you?" asked the librarian, who didn't bother to take off his rather thick reading glasses with natty aviator frames. He was so friendly, thought Hallie.

"I'm uh—"The words froze. He was about to say her name. He

tried to recall the facial expression he had rehearsed for this moment in the bathroom mirror, before leaving the room. Where the fuck was it?

"I'm uh— Did Martha Housewright leave me a message?"

"If you're Mr. Lawrence, she left you a message."

"I am," Hallie said.

"She's in the bar," the librarian said.

The bar was a popular place to come on Saturday night in the town of Darling and its environs. Hallie looked around and on first pass he didn't see Martha. The room was filled with people who all seemed to be in a good mood. Women falling into little cliques as the men gathered in huddles. Everybody was drinking beer or gin and tonics. The scene was cheerful, if you find people socializing a cheerful notion. The air wasn't riddled with hostility and treachery the way it would be in New York. So Hallie started feeling like a Martian. But then he saw Martha coming toward him, and he felt himself turning into a pool of some kind, and found that he had preferred Martian.

He remembered the story of *Little Black Sambo,* who was accredited with turning a tiger into butter. At that moment, he too was turning into butter.

"Hi," she said. She had been wearing a tight-fitting brown crewneck sweater, and now, over it, she had a black jacket that made the silky long straight hair look even more blond and shiny.

"Hi," said Hallie, smiling like a perfect idiot.

"You're only ten minutes late," she said. "Not bad. I thought you might be much later."

"Well, I—"

"No, I'm delighted. It was sort of exciting, wondering if you'd even show up."

Wait a minute. Déjà fucking vu here. Hadn't he been in this conversation before—don't know where; don't know when; yes, I do?

Suddenly, he realized how noisy it was in the bar. How could she think this was a good way to have a drink? They would have to stand and yell at each other. But she took his hand and was leading him through the customers, out to the darkened restaurant, through to a patio enclosed in a glass conservatory that was removed for dining outdoors during the warmer months. Here, the noise of the bar was completely erased.

She went behind the bar, while Hallie looked over the tables, set for breakfast. Everything looked so ready for something. It gave him a little courage.

"Do you want some wine? There's a good bottle back here."

"Sure. I feel like a glass of wine," said Hallie, thinking that what he really felt like was a bowl of Jell-O. He put one hand in his pocket, trying to look casual.

"Take a table," she said with a laugh. He chose one right in the middle. She came over with wine and two glasses.

"You pour," she said, while she lit a match, then a candle in a brass holder. "Remind me to replace this if we burn it out, or Mims will kill me."

She had definitely given this rendezvous some thought. Maybe. Or maybe it was just some way she could talk to him without anybody seeing her talking to him. She was embarrassed to be seen with him. That was it. But he was Hallie Lawrence, for Christ's sake. Or at least he had been.

"Cheers," she said, clicking his glass. "Isn't this great? I mean, is this romantic, or what?"

"I was meaning to compliment you," said Hallie.

"I'm going to tell you everything," she said, looking off with those glittering honey-colored eyes for some kind of assurance. Then she looked right at Hallie. "You were here a few months ago, weren't you."

"That's possible, yes." He was intrigued.

"You were, because I saw you. That's why I asked you if we'd met, because I was hoping you had seen me, too."

"If I had seen you, I wouldn't have waited a few months before coming back."

"Oh, shut up," she said playfully. "So, this afternoon, when my sisters were having lunch, they saw you. Glenn called me and told me. Did you see her leave the table?"

"No, I hate to admit this, but I didn't actually notice your sisters until a minute before you came in."

"Well, my sisters noticed you," she said adorably.

"Wait a minute. You saw me a couple of months ago and so did your sisters?"

"I asked them if they had seen you. The cute Jewish guy. They had lunch here that day. They remembered."

All he heard, of course, was "cute Jewish guy."

"And now, here we are, having a glass of wine. It's weird, life doesn't usually work out this way."

God, is she beautiful, thought Hallie.

"I don't know what to say," said Hallie. The truth was, it was hard for all she had told him to sink in. She wanted to be here with him. This was her doing. It was dizzying. He began grinning, a sort of ecstatic lunatic grin, or so it felt. And he still couldn't speak.

She began to tell him about her life. She told him about her sisters, Mimi, Gin, and Glenna, telling him their ages, what they did, and how Gin, the youngest, had been "a mistake." Then she went on to tell him about her brothers. She had two brothers.

The Housewright family.

"What does your father do?" asked Hallie.

"He's retired. He used to coach college football, though. I mean, that's what he was known for. That's why it's so funny about Ham. Ham Housewright, the baseball player? He plays for the Mets? He's my brother."

Ham Housewright was her brother? Ham Housewright, pitcher for the New York Mets, who had had the greatest rookie season in the history of baseball? Seriously, the rookie with the all-time record-breaking year was her brother? Ham House-wright, who in the six years of Met baseball following that dazzler of a debut still had never gone less than twenty wins? And, get this: he hit home runs. No wonder "cute Jewish boy" was what she thought of Hallie.

Her other brother was an orthopedist specializing in sports injuries. Oh, boy.

Her lips looked so soft and full of life. She had such a big smile.

"What do you do?" she asked, putting those lips to the edge of the glass and sipping the wine.

"I'm a lawyer," said Hallie. "I'm a partner at an entertainment law firm. Most of our clients are in the classical-music world."

"Do you have any cellists? I play the cello."

God, to be that cello between those legs.

Suddenly he felt both her legs close on either side of his. She had read his mind. He got heart palpitations.

"So, you play the cello?" he said.

"No, not anymore. I sort of gave it up in the tenth grade. That's also the year I started."

She told him that she painted, that's what she liked best, but she also made clothes and loved to garden, and she was a terrific cook. He imagined how good she would look doing any of those things. Those legs remained against his. He took her hand. A fine hand, with short, square-cut nails and long fingers with rather large knuckles.

"You're a lawyer. A man of the law," she said, putting her hand on top of his.

"Yes, it's a respectable position for a cute Jewish guy."

"Oh, Hallie, don't be such a nerd. It doesn't matter one bit if you're Jewish. I wasn't brought up that way."

No? thought Hallie. But then he thought, it doesn't matter. She's sitting here with me right now, looking at me with those honey eyes, her hand on top of mine. It doesn't matter, he thought. Or even better, who gives a shit?

"Martha Housewright," he said and touched the silky hair.

He remembered that, at some point, a street lamp went out. He remembered because it isn't too often that you're actually looking at one and see it go out.

He remembered at one point that she took off her jacket and went off to the ladies' room, and he watched her walk. She was like a large and graceful cat, with great long legs.

Kip woke up suddenly, as if someone had called him. He began beating around for the bed lamp, knocked into it, and turned it on. He put on his glasses. It was 3:30 A.M. He got up and went into the bathroom, where he washed up, then put on his jacket and shoes, and left the room.

He found Hallie and Martha on the patio, but he stopped in the doorway, thinking it looked very pretty, the two of them surrounded by empty tables, the candlelight, the streetlights, shining gently and blue through the glass.

"Kip!" said Hallie, seeing him.

"Shhhh," giggled Martha. "It's—oh, my God, look, it's quarter to four!"

"Kip!" repeated Hallie, this time in a loud whisper.

"My man," said Kip, coming toward them, all black blues musician. "I just wanted to check and see if you were still alive."

"This is Martha," said Hallie.

She stretched out a long arm and shook hands with Kip. She smiled at him, but Hallie could plainly see it was not the same smile she had been aiming at him.

"Have a glass of wine," she said. "Pull up a chair."

"Are you crazy?" said Kip. "I was just checking on my boy here, I'll be going now."

"Sit down," said Hallie, although he was not without some trepidation.

Martha leaned close to Hallie and whispered into his ear.

"It's too bad we can't use your room."

What? thought Hallie. Sex? She thinks this is just about sex?

"Well, I don't know about you, but I thought there was more than that going on here," he whispered back.

"You sound like a girl," she said and laughed. She laughed right at him. Hallie wondered if he could even function sexually.

Kip pretended not to have heard any of the exchange, including the regrets expressed in Martha's whisper.

Kip was being charming. He told the story of their similar tweed jackets, of buying them on Jermyn Street, in London, and being tailored as if they were kings, or at least in the army. Hallie began to feel good that Kip had joined them, especially when Martha reached out and took Hallie's hand. Then he even started feeling good that Kip and Martha seemed to be enjoying each other.

Kip went on with his anecdote about their first trip to London together, and told about the time Hallie had slept on the floor, in the hall outside their room, so that Kip could have a girl.

Hallie wanted to kill him.

But Martha said, "Then you owe him one," and she smiled right at Kip.

"Well, that was kind of my point, but I didn't want to just come right out and say it."

"Oh, but I enjoyed the part about the jackets," she said. "There's only one problem," said Martha. You could see she was enjoying this. "He hasn't even kissed me yet."

"My man!" said Kip, feigning outrage, which was nothing like the outrage Hallie was feeling. This woman was negotiating for him. It was the most exciting thing he had ever experienced.

"You want me to kiss her?" said Hallie to Kip. "You want me to kiss you?" he said to Martha. He didn't wait for an answer. He leaned over to her and kissed her.

The minute his lips touched hers, a jolt went through him that nearly knocked him off his chair, or so it felt. When he looked at her again, he knew just what to do.

He stood up and took her hand.

"You can sleep in the hall," he said to Kip.

"Don't be silly," said Martha. What? Had he read this all wrong? "Kip doesn't have to give up his room." She gave Hallie a look that told him there were other rooms and that she had access to them all.

Kip got up and wished them good night and told them to feel free to join him, if they were in the mood.

When Kip walked off, Martha stood up. She stood very close to Hallie and then she began to kiss him, taking him in her arms.

Hallie was sure he had those big red blotches on his face that he used to get from hours of making out.

"What's going on here, Hallie?" she asked quietly, leaning against him as if she had been leaning against him all her life.

"I wish I knew," said Hallie. "I want you. Those are the only words I can think of. Give me time, I might be able to put it better, but right now? I want you, Martha."

She blew out the candle stub and led them out of the patio, through the restaurant and out to the lobby. The librarian was asleep; his head had fallen back and his book rested on his chest. His glasses magically remained in his hand.

"Shhh," said Martha as she led them past the sleeping night man. They went into the back office and closed the door. She opened another door that led to a small bedroom with a fireplace. It was also done in Early American style and featured a double bed, or at least that's all Hallie saw. Martha went to the fireplace and lit the fire expertly.

"Do you like my secret room?" she asked. "It's not mine really, but I stay here a lot. Mims doesn't rent this one unless it's the high season. It's sort of here for emergencies."

"Is this an emergency?" asked Hallie, coming to her and pulling her into his arms. He had to have another one of those kisses.

She took off her jacket, and then she took off her sweater. Underneath, she wore only a slip, no bra or anything. She kept her skirt on, but took off her shoes: a pair of Timberland hiking boots.

Hallie thought he was going to die. She had, he could tell, the best breasts he had ever seen. Much larger than he expected. Her hair hung down and touched the top of the white satin slip. He got such a hard-on that he thought he would faint.

She moved to the bed and then took off her skirt. She was wearing socks. Somewhere at the end of those legs that were about twenty miles long she was wearing socks. She sat on the bed, looking at him. She laughed, and flipped her long hair over her back.

Hallie fumbled around removing his jacket and shirt.

He came to the bed and sat next to her. He knew something she didn't. The hard-on had gone. And there was no way it was going to come back. He was just too terrified.

"Do we want to be here like this?" he asked, touching her face. "I don't know."

"You don't?"

"I mean, what about tomorrow, and the next day?"

" 'Tonight you're mine, completely,' " she sang softly, calling on the Shirelles. " 'But will you love me tomorrow?' "

"God, you're just so . . . beautiful. That face is some kind of miracle or something. And your body . . ."

He ran his hand over her leg and then leaned down and kissed her thigh. They rolled back together and began kissing and making out. Then she discovered what he knew and she didn't.

No hard-on.

"It doesn't mean anything," said Hallie nervously.

"I have my period," she said. "It's almost over, but I have it. So relax. We don't have to go all the way."

"I don't mind periods," said Hallie. Certainly not hers.

"You can't be nervous," she said softly. "You can't keep on being nervous."

She was touching him. There was something expert about her touch, but he didn't want to think about it. She was touching him and it was as if she were touching his arm.

Come on! he told himself. Will you just look at her? Look at this woman—oh, my God! She's taking off the slip. Nothing but breasts and panties, God, white cotton panties. God, look at those breasts. She's touching them. That could be me touching them. Come on, down there, boys, what the fuck are you doing, having a chess game?

He touched her breasts, he took the nipples into his mouth and felt them get hard and heard a little gasping noise coming from her. He thought he was beginning to feel the boys finish their chess game.

And then she took over.

"Take off your pants."

"Oh, God—"

"Just do it."

So he did. She lay on top of him, both of them naked now, and Hallie held her very close. He had the feeling that he never wanted her to leave him again. She began to move down his body, kissing him, his chest, his abdomen, and then—

His entire body was electrified. Stunned. Swimming in swollen waters, carrying him along, washing over him with ecstasy. There had never been anything like this before. He was in her mouth. Those lips were closed around him, moving so perfectly, and her hand was holding him, so perfectly. There was no chess game now. He heard his voice groan. He had never heard that before. He had never groaned before. Wait a minute, this was too—

When he came, he almost feared for his life. He felt himself slammed into the sky, as his heart slammed inside his chest. He heard her murmur, "Oh, Hallie," as she worked him to the end.

The room was silent except for his heart, which was beating so loudly he wondered if it might wake up some of the guests. She moved alongside him and he took her in his arms. He couldn't speak yet, he was too breathless.

"I love you," he gasped. "I love you."

And still he hadn't recovered from what she had done to him. It wasn't like any other time he had ever experienced. He hadn't even been that much of a fan of that particular practice before. But now he knew, as he lay in the dark, with Martha's breathing becoming more regular and sleepy, that he simply could no longer consider life without her.

"Hallie, can I ask you something?" she said softly.

"It was great," he whispered without a thought. "Will you marry me?"

She giggled softly.

"Oh, come on, don't laugh. I know it's crazy, but you don't have to laugh."

"I'm laughing because that's what I was going to ask you."

"Well, thank God I got it out first, you know what I mean? You keep a guy on his toes."

"Well, since you asked first, I get to say I'll think it over." She giggled.

Until the dark windows began to fade to deep blue, they talked and made love. It was pretty fabulous.

The next day, Hallie, Kip, and Martha hung around together. It felt comfortable, the three of them together. Martha was soon teasing Kip unmercifully, and Kip, who had two sisters, knew just how to tease her back. Martha showed them some local sights and they ended up having lunch together, a lunch that lasted till five in the afternoon. Then Hallie and Kip left for New York.

Hallie felt panic the minute the car pulled away. Kip talked him through things all the way home, and assured Hallie that no, he didn't feel disappointed about the weekend, how could he, he got to see Hallie get into deep trouble. He kept telling him how terrific Martha was, like some kind of dream come true.

Kip spent the night at Hallie's apartment, although they did go to sleep and didn't talk much. Hallie had a dream about falling through this large hole that he didn't even see and waking up on Orange Grove Avenue in Los Angeles, outside a funny stucco house he had never seen before. He was waiting for someone to come and put water in his pool. It felt like an emergency. Then he realized that there was a dead squirrel at the bottom and he got anxious that the pool man wouldn't take it out before putting in the water. Alfred was suddenly at the bottom of the pool, holding the dead squirrel and yelling at Hallie for being irresponsible. Then Martha was coming toward him. He didn't want her to see Alfred with the dead squirrel, but she said she was the pool man, and kept laughing.

The alarm woke him up.

After he and Kip had breakfast, Kip dropped Hallie at his office. They resolved to stay very close for a while, which both knew they would do.

Hallie worked very hard all day and was especially nice to Lisa. She was being particularly efficient that day and he told her several times how well she was doing. Lisa began to glow and offered to work late that night with him on a new contract. Hallie said they could knock that one off before quitting time, an expression she had never heard him use, and they did.

At seven fifty-eight, Hallie met the train at Grand Central Station. Sure, she could have taken a cab to his house, but he wouldn't hear of it.

He bought some pretty decent-looking roses from a man outside the station.

When Martha came walking down the platform, suitcase in hand, in a trench coat and a big woolly scarf, he ran to her. They hugged. She said it was like some corny commercial for the phone company, roses and everything.

He told her to shut up, and held on for his life.

6

THE NEXT DAY, TUESDAY, HALLIE didn't show up at work. In fact, he didn't even call in. And not only did he not answer his phone, he unplugged it from the wall. (Of course he had an answering service.)

Hallie just stayed at home with Martha.

Unlike any other time in his life when a woman had made her presence felt in his apartment, he delighted every time he found signs of her. Her toilet kit in his bathroom, her bottles of creams and lotions, he wanted to smell everything. The sight of her moving around his place as if she had come home was wringing some kind of fantastic chemical from his heart and pumping it through his veins. She had assumed immediate familiarity about everything, from the coffee maker to where he kept the toilet paper. It all seemed so natural, partly because of her teasing nature. She had asked him if toilet paper was something he believed in, since she couldn't find any in the bathroom. She said she didn't care if he didn't like to use it, she'd just get her own supply. He immediately wondered if she thought he smelled. She then had to convince him that he didn't. He showed her a hall closet that had a whole shelf of toilet paper, and marveled how she had said "we" had run out.

Hallie couldn't imagine how he had ever lived without her.

They spent most of the time talking, moving from the bedroom to the living room, from the sofa to the pillows in front of the fireplace. Not only did Hallie wish to reveal everything that had ever happened to him, he couldn't stand that there were things that he did not yet know about her. For example, what had she done with every minute of her life from birth until he had met her, forty-eight hours earlier? He wanted to get inside her and see it all.

He was crazy about her.

"So while you were growing up, your father's job was football coach?"

"Yup, oh yes. We were the daughters of Ham One. My mother made that up. Ham One was my father and Ham Two was my brother. She hated junior and senior. She said it made Dad sound old and it would make Ham Two feel like a junior member of something for the rest of his life."

He was just staring at her face, at the blush from the warmth of the fire.

"As opposed to just being number two," said Hallie, but his irony was lost on her own confident logic.

"Yes, number two just means you were Ham also. It isn't so bad as Ham Junior. My mother always said it's so weird to find yourself talking to some ninety-year-old guy and everyone's calling him Joe Junior, or something."

"This is so incredibly gentile." He smiled at her. She fended his remarks about gentiles very well. But that was very gentile of her. You can't exactly hurt a gentile's feelings because gentiles are not too touchy about what they are. They aren't subject to total genocide every few centuries. Somehow, they know in their bones what they are doing must be right.

"So we have Ham Two, pitcher, and Ham One, football coach— you know, you can't sit there like that, in that *thing*, that T-shirt, with your breasts bouncing and free and juicy, right underneath. Couldn't you put them in a bra? Don't you ever wear a bra?"

Martha tossed her hair over her shoulder. She was leaning back, legs extended for several miles in front of her. She was wearing small white panties, a tank-style undershirt, and a pair of socks. She got up and went to Hallie's wall of records, tapes, and CDs. Her hand held absently on to the back of a chair and Hallie wondered how he had ever existed without that hand on that chair. She began to scrutinize the recordings, twirling a length of hair, brushing it against her lips. "It's just an undershirt, Hallie. Sometimes I wear a bra."

"That's not an undershirt. That's some kind of prayer shawl that they drape over holy books. Look at them just standing around in there!"

"I love it when you get dramatic," said Martha, still looking over the sound collection. Hallie got up and lunged for her, holding her in his arms and smothering his face in her chest. She laughed. "You hardly have any music," she noted.

Hallie's face emerged from the breasts. "What? There's over two thousand recordings here."

"Yea, but it's all classical."

"No, it's not, there's jazz. There's even some blues somewhere."

"Sure, but what, three records out of two thousand?" She was teasing him in the nicest possible way, but she gave him a look that said she thought he was a dork. He knew there were lots of people who thought that if you listen only to classical music you must be some kind of dork. He had always dismissed them as morons, and felt perfectly content, but Martha was rattling all that now. Oh, Jesus, was he vulnerable to this girl.

"Oh, look, Muddy Waters. This is cool."

"I told you I had the blues."

"You have the blues, Hallie Lawrence?" Martha looked right at him and then began slowly to lift her T-shirt, while she sang in the softest voice, to the tune of "Bye Bye Blackbird": " 'Pack up all your cares and woes, let them go, in the snow'—I don't know the words—'Bye bye blackbird.' " Then she laughed and put on some Muddy Waters. "Do you realize it's practically dark? Look. We haven't been out all day," she said suddenly.

Sure enough, the room was growing dark. As Martha looked toward the window, Hallie looked at her profile—the slightly long, lifted nose, the curve of her upper lip, the cheekbone that held things in place so stupendously—and he found himself observing one of those moments when her face achieved numbing beauty. Maybe it was the expression. Maybe it was the light from the fireplace. But it was numbing. He wanted to reach out and touch that face, he wanted to have it near his own, he wanted to lick it off. But he just stood there staring at her until she looked at him, ran the palm of her hand gently along his cheek and smiled.

Then Martha began to organize dirty plates, empty coffee cups, wineglasses, but Hallie lay back down on the cushions near the fire.

"No, don't do that, talk to me more. Tell me about the coach. Tell me what was it like."

"No, it's time to clear up. We can talk over dinner, I'm starving!"

Hallie realized she was right, it was getting late. And it was getting dark. It was that time of day when you have to add artificial light of some kind or admit you're a weirdo. Or madly in love.

That time of day.

Then, for the first moment since she had arrived, Hallie left her for another thought. He was really going to have to call the office. He reached up for the phone and plugged it back into its outlet. Then he held it on his stomach for a moment. He reached out for the pillow he had earlier shoved under her ass. Suddenly, he wanted to do it again. He held on to himself.

He thought about the afternoon in flashes. Martha talking, telling him stories; Martha, eyes closed, breathing in her gaspy little breaths with each movement of her hips. And then there was the way she did to him that rocket-blasting enshrinement of him in her scabbard from the *Arabian Nights*, that mouth, oh, God, that mouth. It was so dumbfounding that it occurred to Hallie that inevitably there had to be a shortening of life for each time she did it, but it was completely worth it.

He lay there for a moment in the growing darkness, with the phone on his stomach. He was trying to recall the Hallie Lawrence who was about to call his office. Was it the same one who hadn't called in all day? It would be interesting to find out. He dialed the number.

"Hello?" he said to Lisa, once he was put through.

"Hallie? . . . Are you all right?" Lisa tried to sound very cool. She wasn't stupid, remember.

"Yes, oh, yes, I'm fine. I'm fine now, I was—" What the hell was he about to tell her? He sat up. Maybe sitting up would help. "I wasn't feeling myself, this morning," he said. Perfect. Not even a lie.

"Maybe you're exhausted, Hallie, you know? It's a good idea sometimes to just stay back and rest."

Profound, or what? thought Hallie.

"I agree with you, Lisa. Did anything earth-shattering happen today?"

"I don't think so. Your phone messages can really all wait till tomorrow. Oh, except your mother called, and Alfred, and Nikki Mikhailovitch."

The sound of that trilogy was chilling.

"I'll get back to them tomorrow, too. Well . . . everything okay with you?"

"Everything's fine, Hallie."

He could hear the half-smile right through the phone.

"Good. Then I'll see you in the morning."

As he hung up the phone, Martha appeared in the living-room doorway wearing jeans and shoes and pulling on her big trench coat.

"You're leaving me?" asked Hallie. Martha laughed. But Hallie was not a little bit terrified.

"I'm going to the market. We have no food. There's only so many tricks I have with cans of tuna fish, Hallie."

"So you're going to the market? In the dark? Do you realize it's dark out?"

"There's a market just down the block."

"The nearest market is in Kansas!" said Hallie.

The phone rang. The phone was ringing, not two minutes after he had replugged it. It was Lily's ring.

"Take your coat off," said Hallie. The phone rang a second time. "We'll go out. You don't have to go to the market now."

"What? We don't want to go out! I don't want to sit in some dumb restaurant and not be able to touch you. On second thought . . ." She gave him a look that shot him in both testicles.

The phone rang for a third time.

"Take off the coat," said Hallie. And he answered the phone.

It was Lily all right.

"Hi, Mom," said Hallie. Mom? He hadn't called her anything but Mother or Lily for years.

There was a silence on the other end. Not a long one, just long enough for it to be registered as a silence.

"You're alive. That's all I wanted to know. We don't have to stay on the phone." Oh, those mellifluous tones.

"I'm alive, Mother."

"The only reason I was concerned was, you did say we might do something on Sunday, Hallie, and then I just never heard a word. And when I didn't hear from you yesterday either, and then when I called today and they said you hadn't come in, well, I'm a mother, Hallie, I can't help it. You said we'd do something and then you vanished."

"That's the only reason you were concerned? Because I said we would do something? If I hadn't said that, you wouldn't have been concerned? Mother, I'm crushed."

"Oh, Hallie, stop." She crooned the admonition. It occurred to them both that it had been a while since he had teased her. It was a sign of affection and they both knew it. "I don't give a thought to what you're doing when you're not with me, my darling." That was Lily's idea of teasing him back. Actually, she was feeling a little giddy relief, the kind that comes from keeping an inner hysteria at bay for several days.

"I went up to Darling with Kip," he said.

"Oh, how is Kip?" said Lily, oozing the special enthusiasm that she genuinely felt for Kip. Hearing Kip's name made her feel somehow even more relieved.

"He's terrific."

Hallie looked over at Martha, who was sitting on the sofa reading a magazine, still wearing the trench coat, which was opened to reveal her long legs in the tight jeans. The sheer beauty of it all. He tuned out Lily's praises of Kip and pretty much whatever she was saying next, until he heard the following:

"So we'll have dinner afterward, okay with you?"

"Dinner after what?"

"You know, Hallie, you still have that god-awful habit of reading when you're on the phone with someone. You know, people always know. They always know when you're reading and not really listening."

"I wasn't reading. Dinner after what?" asked Hallie.

Martha looked up at Hallie, smiled, and wantonly spread apart her legs.

"The concert tonight? Alfred and Nikki doing the Brahms? I was led to believe you had to attend. Maybe I misread the situation."

They both knew damn well no situation had been misread. Hallie had forgotten all about it. "Right."

"And remember there's a little dinner organized for afterward." A "little dinner" was a euphemism if ever there was one. She made it sound so quaint and intimate and born of genuine affection, when she was only manipulating him to join what would undoubtedly be a crashing bore.

"Hallie? Are you bringing someone?"

"I will, actually," said Hallie. He hadn't expected that it would be happening so soon, the meeting of Lily and Alfred and Martha. It did not, however, terrify him. He felt brave, like a warrior with lots of armor and feathers in his helmet, so he repeated himself. "I will bring someone, okay?"

"Marvelous." It was kind of a flat marvelous, not readable.

"Then I'll see you later," said Hallie.

"Of course. Who are you bringing, my darling?"

"You'll see," said Hallie. He loved the way Lily just couldn't resist. It took another thirty seconds to conclude the conversation, as it always did, but then he hung up the phone.

"Get dressed, we're going out," said Hallie and he walked out of the room. Martha looked after him a little amused. That was an odd Hallie Lawrence, she thought, who just told her to get dressed and walked out of the room.

"Make me!" she called out playfully.

She jumped up, took off her trench coat, slipped the twenty-five-mile-long legs out of the jeans, took off her shirt, undershirt, and underpants, and, socks on, went to the bedroom.

"Did you say something?" asked Hallie, aware that she had come into the room, but with his back to her.

"I said, make me get dressed, Hallie Lawrence, Mr. Grumpo. 'Get dressed, we're going out,' " she mimicked.

Hallie turned at that point and was besotted by the bombshell that lay on his bed. Besotted. He wasn't in the least bit used to seeing her naked yet and it unplugged him; just the way he had unplugged the phone, he no longer felt a connection with the outside world. Without knowing how he got to the bed, he was kissing her calves, her thighs, her flat stomach, and then he was in her again, and he lay very still on top of her, with a cheek of her ass in either hand.

"Something wrong?" she asked.

"I just want to memorize this." He came about two seconds later.

They took a shower and his soapy hands washed every inch of her. Cleaning had never been so much fun. Then, wrapped in towels, they sat on the bed. She searched around in her large brown leather satchel and found a pack of Camels. She hadn't smoked all day.

"So should I be nervous, Hallie?" She gave him a teasing smile as she blew out the smoke.

"Well, no, of course not. I just wish I had more time to fill you in about my parents before you meet them. There won't be enough time now."

"How much more do I have to know? They're just parents."

"They're not just parents."

"Why don't you just let me think they are, and wing it," she said.

Hallie knew that one thing was sure, Martha had never met parents like his, but he decided that letting her wing it was all he could do.

Since he had never felt about anyone the way he did about Martha, he had no experience with how to deal with the introduction to his parents. Alfred would be dazzled by her. Lily? Lily would recognize the dazzling qualities, even appreciate them, but basically all she would see was the S-word, *shiksa*.

"What should I wear?" asked Martha. "What do you wear to a thing like this?"

"Well, it's a concert, you know. Just wear a nice dress."

"Well, don't act like I'm a retard, this isn't the kind of concert I'm used to going to, okay?" She wrinkled her nose at him affectionately. "Unless you just want me to wear a black leather bra and jeans."

"I think that would be fabulous," said Hallie.

"I'm not meeting your parents in a black leather bra and jeans."

She went to the closet he had cleared for her and surveyed her clothes while Hallie just stood there grinning and not saying anything.

He had a momentary flash of making her go completely naked, wearing only her coat. He could sit there all evening and imagine her nakedness, right under that coat, right in Avery Fisher Hall. Then he realized that no matter what she wore, her nakedness would be right there, right underneath.

That could be trouble.

"I'm wearing a suit and tie, if that helps," he said, noting a look of consternation coming to her eyes.

"Oh, I brought this! The good old reliable black dress. Good old Mom's philosophy of life: Never go anywhere without a basic black dress."

"Oh, that's fine. That's perfect."

She laid it out on the bed, pulled some black stockings, garter belt and bra from her drawer in the bureau, and laid them out with the dress. Then she went into the bathroom and twisted her wet hair up into a big loose knot and made it stay with a big tortoise-shell clothespin of some kind. Hallie came and stood in the doorway. "You told your parents you were staying for a week?"

"Yeah, with a friend—hey, you can't come in here and see all my beauty tricks, are you nuts? Scat, get out of here, you can't come in."

Hallie found this very amusing. There was a girl in his house. There was a girl living in his house, doing girl things that she didn't want him to see. It was fantastic.

He put on a somber dark-blue pin-striped suit with a blue-striped shirt and fine red paisley tie. He should have worn a white shirt, but he didn't feel like wearing a business uniform tonight.

"I'm going into the living room now. You can use the bedroom," he called out to her.

"Okay! Thanks," she called out from behind the door. Then he heard the hair dryer.

He went to the bed and picked up one of the stockings. He sniffed it, played with it between his fingers, then left the room.

About fifteen minutes later she emerged from the bedroom and even Hallie, expecting the world, was astonished. What had looked like an ordinary-enough black dress fit her like a glove; high-necked, long-sleeved, short, straight skirt. The black stockings looked fabulous on her long legs, and she wore simple high-heeled black suede pumps. The long silky hair perfectly framed her face and fell past her shoulders, shining and clean. The wispy bangs were a little puffier than they had been, and it was hard to tell if she had done anything to her face; that face, and that body in that dress, were simply breathtaking.

"You're unbelievable. How could any human being look that gorgeous?"

"You're sure? You're not just saying that? I want to look nice for your parents, Hallie."

"To me you look like the Queen of the Smut Goddesses, but to my parents you'll simply look . . . stunning. That's what they'll think. Both of them. They are going to be stunned, Martha. Stunned." Actually, the more he said the word, the more it rang true, but like a death knell. How was Lily going to handle the fact that Hallie had found his woman? How disgustingly gushing would Alfred be?

"Well, is that good or bad? I think maybe we'd better have a drink before we go."

He had to get up and kiss her. She had an overwhelming clean smell, and the air around her was freshened wherever she went.

"A Smut Goddess?" she said, breaking from the kiss and laughing out loud, her wonderfully abandoned girlish laugh. "Okay, then I'll just have to keep you hard all evening." She reached down and pressed her hand against his trousers exquisitely.

"No! God, no, Martha, I was kidding. You don't look like a Smut Goddess."

"I *like* Smut Goddess." She kissed him again. "Now, how about a little drink, to smooth our way into the night?"

"You'll need a drink," he said. God, he was taking her to meet Lily and Alfred. "I'll need a drink. A drink is a very good idea."

"I'll have a neat Jack Daniels."

He appreciated the heartiness of her taste and poured them each a shot.

"We should get there by seven forty-five. It's only six."

"Let's go out and walk a little bit. We haven't left the house all day." She chugged her shot, so Hallie followed suit. She immediately kissed him on the lips. "By the way, Hallie, I love you," she said.

They walked down Madison Avenue, which was quite busy with people coming home from work. It was freezing out and Hallie was very upset that all Martha had to wear was her trench coat. She kept saying she wasn't in the least bit cold, honestly, and he knew she wasn't lying because she was such a gentile, but Hallie just didn't like the idea that she wasn't dressed warm enough.

"Nobody wears only a trench coat in the middle of November."

It occurred to him several blocks ahead what he would do, so when they came to the furrier's, which was luckily open till seven that night, he simply steered her in.

"Pick a coat," he said. "Pick any coat."

"Get out of here," she said into his neck as the elderly salesman came toward them.

"Can I help you?" the salesman asked in a German accent.

"Hallie," said Martha with warning on her whisper.

"Pick a coat, and get it over with." He sat down on a gray silk sofa. Martha looked at him as if he were a babbling weirdo, not sure whether to humor him out of the store or do exactly what she had been told.

"I don't know what kind of coat to pick," she said. "They're all *fur*."

"Mink," said Hallie from the sofa. "They farm mink. Wearing mink is like eating chicken. Mink is warm."

The salesman, no dummy, took a good look at Martha, the beauty of her, the stature of her, and knew just what to bring. It made him feel a little nostalgia for the old days when gentlemen came in and ordered coats for women who looked like this. Now, mostly the women came in by themselves.

He slipped a beautifully cut coat around her and Martha took one look at herself in the mirror and smiled.

"God Almighty," she said. "I've only seen coats like this in magazines."

"It fits all right?" Hallie asked.

"Oh, yes," said the salesman. "It takes a tall person to wear this particular coat. So many women come in here and they swim in it. I have to talk them out of it, as politely as possible, of course."

"Of course," said Hallie. The salesman discreetly backed off, busying himself with an arrangement of fur hats. Hallie took the furry Martha in his arms. "Please let me buy you this coat. Please don't give me a hard time and say 'No, I can't let you, it's not right, it's too expensive.'"

"But it is, Hallie," she said, pushing a little curl from his forehead.

"You look sensational."

"Who wouldn't, wearing this?"

She broke from his arms and inspected herself in the mirror, turning, modeling it. She had a look of fascination in her face, like a small girl awestruck by the sight of herself in a party dress.

"We'll take it," Hallie said to the salesman.

"Hallie, no! I mean it!" she whispered to him. "Did you seriously see what this costs? I mean, you could buy a car!"

"I don't want a car! Look, aside from the fact that you will freeze to death without a warm coat, it sort of makes your outfit, know what I mean?"

"But there are people starving in Ethiopia."

"What they need in Ethiopia is food. They don't need fur, it's too warm there. In New York, you're going to find a lot of use for it. You'll probably be furious when you find out how much money I give away to fight things like starvation. It's the only thing I can do about it. I can't actually go there and feed people because they have these huge bugs in that part of the world—"

"Shut up, Lawrence!" She laughed.

"Uh, by the way, I love you too, Martha."

They started kissing, serious French kissing, and the salesman waited with the kind of patience that comes with a sale at hand, a sale of an extraordinary coat to a gentleman for such a beauty.

"We'll take the coat," said Hallie. "Could you send her other one over in the morning? She's going to wear this one."

The way Hallie solved the what-to-do-with-the-other-coat problem excited Martha and made her smile. She watched him present a credit card and thought that the Hallie Lawrence who had fascinated her in Darling was turning out to be some kind of magic prince after all.

Martha insisted that they walk all the way to Lincoln Center or it would be a waste of the coat. As they walked across Central Park South, Hallie filled her in a little bit about Nikki and Alfred, their relationship, the issue of the film, so if the subject came up at all during the evening, as it inevitably would, Martha wouldn't be in a total jungle. She listened with interest, as Hallie explained the dilemma of Nikki's doing the film or not.

"I'd say she was pretty lucky either way," said Martha, with the slightly ironic undertone, the tease, that was so often part of her inflection. "Some people go through their whole lives without being able to play the violin *or* being asked to be in a movie."

"They do?" he said. "You're kidding."

"Nerd," said Martha, and as they walked at their fast, long-legged pace, she bent her face toward his and kissed him. They walked right into a lamppost.

"Jesus!" yelped Hallie, who had taken the brunt of the post in the temple. "You're—my life isn't safe with you."

"What do you want to have a safe life for, asshole!" She giggled. "Oh, I'm sorry you banged your head. Here, let me rub it." She began stroking his head with her fingers.

Something about her proximity excited him, despite the stars he was seeing on account of the blow, despite the freezing night.

"I'm okay, really," he said, watching the stars fade, actually kind of embarrassed about the whole thing. He held her against him for a moment.

Then they assumed their fast pace. Her legs moved in time with his, as they were, if anything, even longer. Most girls took several steps to one of his and he always felt that he should slow down. Actually, he recalled, Nikki had a very fast pace for her size. But he didn't think about Nikki for very long.

Hallie couldn't get over how different things looked on this street, Central Park South, that he knew so well. His childhood dentist's office had been located there. They were passing Rumplemeyer's, where he was usually taken after the dentist to compensate for the nightmare and, ironically, to start the decay process going again with a butterscotch sundae. Now he saw Rumplemeyer's through the eyes of Martha, who stopped to admire all the stuffed animals to be seen from the windows. She said she would love an ice cream cone because she was starving and they wouldn't be eating until after the concert. She wanted an ice cream cone to go.

An ice cream cone before dinner? Outdoors? In the winter?

Would they make it to Lincoln Center before she collapsed in his arms like the Lady of the Camellias?

She chose chocolate. They walked along together, laughing. He said he really wasn't in the mood for ice cream, but she pushed the cone against his mouth until he opened it. This resulted in a good deal of chocolate ice cream on his upper lip. He smiled as he took the tissue she offered him and while she licked ice cream from his lips with her tongue, but Hallie Lawrence was terrified by her abandon.

To his amazement they arrived at Lincoln Center, cone consumed, without even getting a sore throat.

As they crossed the plaza and passed the fountain, Hallie's rapid walking pace slowed to such a degree that Martha actually lunged a step ahead of him.

"What's the matter?" she asked, stopping.

With the full blazing splendor of Avery Fisher Hall looming in front of them, Hallie realized that the giddy, horrified, mesmerized, consumed person who walked beside Martha was not the Hallie Lawrence he would become when he entered the theater.

His pace had suddenly slowed. He saw what he was about to become. He could only have described it as an out-of-body experience.

"This is Lincoln Center," said Hallie stupidly.

"Thanks a lot." Martha threw her hands up in a gesture of mock exasperation. "You think I've never been to Lincoln Center before? We used to come every year to see the *Nutcracker*. I loved the *Nutcracker*."

The giddiness flooded him again. What? She was one of those beautiful little girls he would see at the ballet and stare at during the boring parts? One of those little girls was now standing in front of him, with that mouth and all that she could do with it, and those legs wearing stockings?

Remarkable, Hallie thought.

"I realize you've been here before. It's just that we can't just—we were sort of running. We were walking very fast. We can slow down now."

"We were walking fine. We were being normal," she said. "You're just nervous because I'm going to meet your parents.

Now that she mentioned it, never had anyone been more accurate. He smiled at her and they continued walking, but at a much slower pace. They entered the concert hall.

Hallie knew the usher, a young Julliard soprano with whom he had once had a conversation, finding her the most interesting person to talk to during an intermission. He exchanged pleasantries with her as she escorted them to the seats.

The seats. Always the same seats, always four, eighth row, on the aisle. Hallie liked the aisle. If he couldn't sit on the aisle, he felt that he might suffocate and die.

The seats were empty. That meant that Lily and whomever she had invited to take the fourth seat at an Alfred concert (needless to say, a valued seat) were backstage.

"Nice seats," Martha whispered as he helped her off with the new coat. "I want it near me, around me for the whole show."

Show?

Show???

She called an Alfred concert a *show?*

Martha was a genius.

He stared at the way her upper lip sort of tilted up and he watched a smile spread as she leaned to him and whispered that she wished she had him in her mouth. The orchestra was tuning, and that sound was not a particularly erotic accompaniment for him, which he considered fortunate, for her words caused a terrific hard-on.

He realized he was going to have to keep his coat in his lap for the entire performance.

And then, without turning, he could smell the approach of Lily. His heart gave an enormous pound, and then settled down to a lot of little ones.

And he stood up to greet his mother.

7

LILY WAS RADIATING AT FULL
throttle, her head poised on the elegant neck, the smile poised on the lips,
and she seemed to be shining, despite
the shockingly appropriate, if severe,
black evening suit. Eyes were on her,
because there was only a very small
percentage of people seated in the
house who didn't know who Lily Lawrence was, so if they had happened to
notice her, eyes remained. She was in
full form; the old posture of Benevolence Bordered with Disdain (the
BBDs) gave her movements their excellent grace. She wore a pair of seriously important Cartier earrings from
the 1940s.

"Hallie, darling." She embraced
him. Hallie knew Lily had already
taken Martha in completely. "You
know Noel, don't you, darling?" She
smiled as the two men exchanged

greetings, then she looked right at Martha, who automatically rose. "And this is?"

"Mother, Martha Housewright. Martha, this is my mother, Lily Lawrence." He paused to allow them to shake hands.

"Martha," said Lily, showering her with a splash of Benevolence. Her eyes raised slightly as she took in Martha's height. Lily herself was nearly five feet seven, and she liked being taller than the average woman. But occasionally, along would come a truly tall woman and it always gave Lily a sense of instant admiration. She had wanted to grow to six feet as a girl, because it irritated her mother, who thought women should be small. So, taking in Martha's height, Lily was already prone toward admiration. But when she saw the face, glanced into it, sized it up, it was quite plain that she was indeed stunned, and there was nothing to do but increase her all-embracing but never tactile warmth.

"Martha. Aren't you beautiful," she said. This line was delivered with such cultivated directness that it could only be construed as a charming compliment.

Unless you were Hallie.

"It's so nice to meet you, Mrs. Lawrence," said Martha. "Hallie's told me so much about you."

"Has he?" said Lily with fabulous innocence. "Well, I hope he said *some* nice things." She paused for an adorable Lily moment. "Martha, have you met Noel Brandt? Noely, this is Martha Housewright."

With all that over, they took their seats. As if by magic, at that moment, the concert started. The orchestra slowly stopped tuning, the lights dimmed, and Alfred came onto the stage, doing his best Humble Act as he took the podium.

Hallie could smell Lily. He sat on the aisle, Martha next to him, next to Martha, Noel Brandt, and then, next to Noel, sat Lily. But Hallie could smell her. Martha pressed her leg against his and he felt a dizzying return of the warrior confidence. This is great, thought Hallie.

Alfred was conducting an all-Brahms evening. This was considered a hot ticket in the concert world because Alfred was perhaps the best conductor of Brahms in the world and would usually do only one all-Brahms evening a session. Conducting Brahms was too much of a religious experience for him, it left him too exhausted. But every season he would play an all-Brahms evening because, after all, he had to think of his public.

He opened with the *Academic Festival* Overture because he thought a light and giddy start was necessary to continue on to the consecrated Violin Concerto and then to the unutterable hallowed heights of the E Minor symphony. People who loved Brahms would finish the evening prostrate. There would be a swell in the sales of his Brahms recordings. But Alfred, oddly, didn't give a shit. In fact, Alfred loved Brahms and that's why he played him so well. He was, truly, a gifted Brahms man. He did have a first-rate side, but of course that was what had entered him into World Class in the ranks of Ego Maniacs in the first place.

Hallie knew the *Academic* too well, which was kind of annoying for him, so he wasn't thinking about the music. He knew that Lily, who had known the piece too well long before Hallie was born, would not be listening to the performance either. She would be picking from the air everything that she could about Martha, without actually looking at her, which, of course, would have been rude.

Hallie was astonished at how good it felt to be as confident as he was about Martha. He had spent the last thirty-two years of his life known as a confident young man, but now, for the first time, he knew how it *felt* to be confident.

It was really something.

He had spent a good deal of his life worrying about things that weren't important, that the rest of the world never suspected were wrong in the first place. Now he felt calm.

It was the calm before the storm.

He looked over at Martha and she smiled and inclined toward him, hugging his arm close to her. They held hands in his lap.

After an extended period of listening to the *Academic* and holding Martha's hand, Hallie began to notice that their hands had somehow worked themselves below his coat that he held on his lap for fear of just this very thing: she had cupped his private parts in her large hand with the long fingers, and he thought his pants might burst open. And worse, he felt pins in his cheeks that told him he was blushing. But how could he stop her?

He focused on the music, the crescendo of energy building as the piece moved toward the finale, but it didn't really help. When the cymbals crashed into the final theme, Hallie recited the words to "Gaudeamus Igateur" and it helped him through the final bars. Fortunately, the finale came and everyone had to applaud, including Martha, whose hand finally left him. He pictured a balloon and tried mentally to deflate it. Slowly.

Alfred took a modified bow, full of gratuity, but with measured control; after all, that was only the overture. He left the stage, only to return to new applause and retake the podium. Then, after a moment, out came Nikki Mikhailovitch.

"Is she the one?" Martha whispered in his ear as they applauded Nikki's entrance.

"Yes," said Hallie, composing himself, preparing to give his attention to the work at hand.

"That's a beautiful dress," said Martha.

Nikki wore a black velvet evening gown of magnificent simplicity. And the light hit her red curls, which were free floating around her. She's wearing unbound hair, thought Hallie casually to himself. It must be like performing in your pajamas.

Everything settled down, audience, orchestra, coughers, and Alfred lifted his baton. He looked up into the proscenium as if he were having a few personal words with God before he started. He seemed to have been given full endorsement of his genius and the music began.

It never failed to amuse Hallie, that old Look Up to God, the LUG, or LUGGING, as Hallie and Kip had so often observed. He wondered if Martha had taken note of it for discussion later. He looked at her. Her entire attention was focused on the stage. He realized Martha was looking at Alfred and seeing his father for the first time, which was probably what she was thinking about, and not what a colossal ham he was. She seemed a little mesmerized.

"That's so cool that he's your father," she whispered to him, and continued watching.

Pay attention to Nikki, he told himself.

Watch and listen and learn her, at least musically. Pay attention to her opening notes. But once again, Martha inclined toward him and slipped her hand magically under the coat.

No, thought Hallie, as he felt her hand on him again, just when his trousers were fitting more comfortably. Had his mother seen Martha tunnel her hand under the coat? Could she in fact see right through the coat to where Martha's hand lay? But he couldn't stop Martha. His arms were paralyzed. In fact, all but one part of him was paralyzed, and the remaining part was about to become ambulatory, run up onto the stage and shower the entire house.

Christ, he couldn't come in his pinstripes.

But Martha knew and she stopped, and let out the smallest, almost inaudible, little breath. She took her hand to her skirt hem and tugged it a little as she crossed her legs. His hand went immediately after hers. Resting it on her thighs, he felt her squeeze them together. Then she looked over at him and smiled, bit her lower lip, and shook her head.

Hallie couldn't afford to move one muscle for several seconds. He felt like he was in a pressure cooker, and that he was going to explode. He focused on the image of his theater seat, suddenly empty, except for a smoking little pile of what had once been a pin-striped suit with a man it it. Eventually the feeling passed, but he felt a little as if he had been on the verge of death.

Well, with that under control, Hallie refocused on the stage, where he realized that Nikki was already playing. He'd missed hearing her entrance into the piece. Normally, that would have infuriated him, because he loved to take particular notice of how a soloist played the very first notes. But Hallie wasn't in the least upset. He was grateful that he had remembered to listen at all.

Nikki Mikhailovitch gave a brilliant performance.

"We have to do this," Hallie whispered to Martha as they followed Lily and Noel Brandt through the crowds backstage and moved toward the Green Room, where Alfred would be receiving guests. Hallie was holding Martha's hand.

"I don't mind, Hallie," she said, smiling that pearly magnificent smile.

Hallie noticed now how many people stole glances at her. Men did double takes and triple takes and pretended they hadn't. But the women also stole glances, pretended they hadn't, and pulled in their stomachs. Martha walked beside him with her kicky athletic stride, holding his arm as if they were taking a walk in the country. And she did that in high heels. Nobody walked in high heels the way Martha did. They might as well have been Nike's.

She was a killer.

Once inside the Green Room, Hallie was greeted by various regulars in the life of the Lawrence family. There was always a number of the Money People who enjoyed hanging out with Alfred after a concert, and who, for the privilege, gave more and more money. They gave Hallie compliments about various recent legal achievements and Hallie complimented them back, always allowing them to think that they had had some play in whatever he had achieved. He had become Hallie Lawrence again in a big way. With Martha by his side, it was exhilarating.

"You're so popular," she whispered to him.

"Right," said Hallie.

"Hallie, you must come say hello to your father," said Lily, sweeping up to them.

As if he didn't know he had to say hello to his father. Apparently Lily had decided that it was the right moment to do it. So Lily, with perfect refinement, lent Martha her arm and laid one hand gently on Hallie's back, and the crowds parted as if she were Moses allowing her access to the Master.

Alfred was about to feast his eyes on Martha. For a second Hallie thought he felt nauseous.

"Aghh!" came the exhausted half-bellow from Alfred, seeing his son.

Hallie allowed for Alfred's embrace, plunging right into the sweaty, wet tux shirt, and then introduced Martha. Alfred took her in without shame and grinned his most goatish smile of approval.

"Martha! Well, how do you do, my dear."

"It's so nice to meet you, Mr. Lawrence. I really enjoyed the concert."

Thank God she had said concert and not show, thought Hallie.

"I hope you're all joining us tonight," said Alfred, taking both of Martha's hands in his and directing his question at her.

"Aren't we, Hallie?" She looked over at him.

A certain aura around Lily's lips, subtle as it was, announced her approval at the correctness of Martha's reply.

"We are," said Hallie.

"All right then! I'll go change!" said Alfred.

"Fabulous," said Lily in a low throaty voice that also said, Please do. Now.

But Hallie and Lily knew that it would take Alfred some time to wend his way to the dressing room, pausing for greetings and praises till he'd had his fill. They wouldn't be making a swift exit.

"Now, Martha, we're going to Brandolini's tonight for supper. I do so hope you're hungry, my dear, because the food is superb."

"I'm starving, Mrs. Lawrence."

"You're starving?" repeated Lily. "Really?" Young ladies don't starve, they get quite an appetite, or they get a little bit hungry, but they never starve. "Well, we can't have that, can we."

"There's always a food tray around here, isn't there, Mother?" asked Hallie to be annoying.

"With all those gross cheeses? Oh, don't do that."

"I can wait," said Martha. "I had an ice cream cone on the walk over, so I'm not really that hungry."

"An ice cream cone," pondered Lily.

Before dinner?

In the middle of winter?

Outdoors?

Did Hallie realize this girl was coming down with something?

"Well, hold out, the food is divine at Brandolini's." Lily smiled one of her good ones.

"Mrs. Lawrence, your earrings are so beautiful. Where did you ever get them?"

"These?" asked Lily. Her hand went up to them as if to remember which she had on. She also had to pause before responding, to acknowledge the question's incredible directness. Lily knew at once Martha had not been gauche. She realized the girl was simply comfortable with herself, and the ease with which she had asked a question no one readily asked Lily Lawrence spoke clearly of her confidence. It was worth repeating. "Where did I get them? Oh, I guess Alfred picked them up somewhere along the line. He's a great gift giver."

Hallie was enjoying it all. He knew as well that no one asked Lily Lawrence questions like that.

"So that's where you get it from," Martha said, with a teasing little edge.

"Has Hallie given you a present?" Lily asked, all innocence.

He wasn't quite ready for his mother to hear about the coat but he told her anyway, and for the life of him he couldn't figure out why.

"I gave her this coat," he said, indicating the mink Martha had draped over one arm. "I've got to go talk to Nikki." Changing the subject was a well-mannered thing to do because it saved Lily the embarrassment of having to react to the coat news. "I'm afraid there's going to be a little war between Alfred and me for a while."

A minor tension subtly gripped Lily's lips. Hallie had just said something about his father he would have said only to Lily, in private. Never with anyone else around.

"I certainly hope not," said Lily. "Are you referring to the situation with Nikki?"

"Nice guess, Mom. Really. How do you do it?" He teased her with his smile.

"You'll come in the car with us to Brandolini's?" Lily asked. Hallie was being so silly. Contemplating war with his father was hopeless, he so rarely won. And why would he bring this up in front of a girl he had obviously just met?

"Lil, I wouldn't travel any other way," said Hallie cutely. "I think I'd better say hello to Nikki."

Before Hallie and Martha could turn and leave her, Lily turned away first, to join Noel Brandt and a group delighted to see her.

But Lily watched Hallie and Martha, without anyone suspecting. She watched the way he was completely attached to her, never letting his hand leave her for a moment.

Martha *was* quite extraordinary.

Rather charming, nicely poised.

Absolutely gorgeous.

This shiksa.

Lily's intuition had been accurate. She had first had the feeling this was happening to Hallie when she hadn't heard from him during the weekend. Then, when he hadn't been at his office all day, a voice spoke to her, accompanied by a great gospel chorus, and told her something was happening to her son and it had to do with a girl. And now she'd met her. Hallie was in love. Oh my.

There was something about the way Martha looked at her son, something about the way her son looked at Martha, something Lily couldn't define, but she knew she had never seen it before. And it moved her. She was not a bad person.

A mink coat?

"We'll have my mother in small doses, thank you," said Hallie, plowing through the pool of admirers that surrounded Nikki. He held Martha's hand.

"God, your mom's so elegant, Hallie! She sounds like Audrey Hepburn, did you ever notice? She's so regal, does she have royal blood?"

"Are you kidding me?" asked Hallie. "She's a Jew."

"Well, Jews have royalty, don't they?"

What?

"I think the present Queen of England is a Jew, actually," Hallie said. "No. The answer is no, there is no Jewish royalty."

They stood very close, looking into each other's eyes with a lot of what you would have to call mirth.

"What about King Solomon and King David and all those guys?"

"Dead," said Hallie. Suddenly, whatever they were saying was beside the point. So he kissed her. "I've got to say hello to Nikki."

Nikki spotted Hallie making his way toward her and her face lit up.

"Well, finally, Mr. Lawrence, my lawyer, you come to see me! Well? So? What did you think?" Her eyes were shooting those daring sparks all over him. It made him smile. It no longer made him nervous.

"Well, I thought maybe in places it was a little heavy-handed—"

"What places?" she demanded, hands on her hips, pretending outrage.

"Eeze joke!" said Hallie, mimicking her accent.

She adored his teasing, clapped her hands together and laughed. Not because it was funny, but because she was delighted to see Hallie Lawrence so relaxed and making a joke at all. She threw her arms around his neck and saw Martha, standing just behind him.

The warm way Martha smiled at her gave Nikki the terrifying notion that she might be attached to Hallie.

No. It couldn't be.

It was. Nikki was introduced to her, and Nikki saw Hallie's hand on Martha's waist. How could he be with such a shiksa, though Nikki, in Russian. She found it completely annoying.

Finally Hallie received a signal from Lily that Alfred was on the verge of being ready to leave, having returned from his dressin

room, showered and changed into a crisp clean shirt and b
old blazer that had his initials embroidered on the pocket so
cately that it looked from a distance like some kind of crest. H
took the signal to lead Martha quickly from the Green Room to
corridor, where some people still lingered, chatted, and waited
say something to Alfred.

"Let's get out of here!" Hallie said with relief.

He led her along until they came to the stairs that took them
underground where Alfred's limousine waited. They walked fast,
Martha holding her new coat closed with one hand, not so much
for warmth but just to feel it touch her ears. With the other hand
she held on to Hallie hard, as he led her along.

"Why are you walking so fast?" she laughed. Her heels made
rapid clicks with each of her long strides. "Where are we going?"

Hallie stopped at the Lawrence limo and said an amiable good
evening to Victor, the driver, who opened the back door. Hallie
practically shoved Martha in.

They sank into the dark spacious interior of the car, with a lap
rug made of cashmere that smelled of Lily. Realizing they were
alone, they began to kiss each other madly, already breathless from
the rapid escape walk.

"Is this why you were walking so fast? So we could be alone?"

"Of course. I couldn't stand it another minute without kissing you."

"Don't ever leave me," she whispered.

"Oh, Martha," said Hallie.

"Well, you must tell me now: where and when did you two
meet?" Lily said, in response to the blatant fondling that was going
on between this girl and her son, as the car drove through the New
York night.

Hallie actually liked the way Lily asked the question. She
spoke with enthusiasm that broadcast both resignation and acceptance. Alfred could be caught beaming at Martha when he
wasn't staring out the window, pretending to suck inspiration
from everything he saw.

"We met in Darling," volunteered Hallie.

"Darling? No fooling! That's where you met? How about that,
Lil," said Alfred.

"Isn't that something," responded Lily.

While checking their coats at Brandolini's, Hallie had asked his
father if Nikki was joining them but Alfred said no.

During the dinner, at an intimate table for fourteen, Lily eventually directed her attention to Hallie and Martha, who were seated

next to her. She assumed a tone that fully acknowledged her perceptions about her son and this girl. The perceptions weren't too
difficult because the heat coming from them could have set the
tablecloth on fire. Lily told herself that at least Hallie and his Martha
were incredibly handsome together.

Lily was feeling quite relaxed that evening, for God only knows
what reason, so her acceptance of the situation came fairly easily.
She was enjoying her Bordeaux and the warm, safe feeling of being
at Brandolini's, with the dark-paneled walls and the velvet-covered
chairs. It certainly surprised Hallie to see her so relaxed but he
figured she was doing her Relaxed Act, and he remained on guard
for some Lily sarcasm that only he would get. And eventually the
moment came.

Lily slowly lifted the wineglass to her moist lips and allowed some
of the ruby drink to slip into her mouth and down her throat. Then
she said, "So, you actually grew up in Darling, Martha."

Okay, there it was. She was confirming that Martha was a local.
While there was absolutely nothing wrong with that, Darling was
a very first-rate town, well, locals were locals and people were
people. No judgment intended, just a statement of fact.

"That's where I grew up all right. Hallie told me about your
house, Mrs. Lawrence—"

"Oh, why don't you call me Lily" came the refined soft voice
used for that conferral.

"Okay, thank you, Lily. Um, thank you." Martha smiled and
looked beautiful. "Well, we used to bike down that road all the
time, and I loved looking at the houses. Yours was my favorite one.
The one with the weather vane? And the perfect porch, and a
carport and a circular drive. And perfectly proportioned windows."

It occurred to Lily that perhaps she had been tracking down the
owners, found out they had a son, and that now she was after that
son. It also occurred to Lily that Martha obviously had good taste
in houses.

"I can't believe I wasn't looking out the window just one of those
times that you rode by," Hallie said, smiling at his girl.

"What were you doing indoors, jerk-o," teased Martha, turning
her head toward him. When they looked at each other, everyone
else was eliminated from the planet, Lily observed. Her son was
going to learn something from this girl. It had been a long time
since Hallie had been open to instruction. A mother's job was to
stand back and allow knowledge to come to her son. This was once
in the Torah, but about forty-two-hundred years ago some vandals
scratched it out. It was known by only a few well-connected Jewesses.

"I love that house, too," said Lily, bringing them back. "It was my grandfather's house. He built it in 1888 and then gave it to my parents because he never went there. I spent most of my childhood weekends in that house."

"It's so beautiful, I'd love to see the inside," said Martha, her face filled with her unconcealed admiration.

"Well, I'm sure you will, my dear," said Lily, with her ever-polished smile. Hallie decided that Martha was right, Lily did sound like Audrey Hepburn, but with a few more smoke scars on the larynx. Lily was doing her Extending Herself Graciously Act.

Martha leaned toward Lily, as if what she was about to say was meant just for the two of them. It was one of her natural, girlish gestures, that little incline to indicate intimacy, and Lily found it endearing.

"I have to go to the ladies' room, do you know where it is?" That was what Martha had to say. Then she excused herself and left the table.

Alfred, in the middle of some anecdote or other, revealed a subtle look of horror that Martha was leaving the table while he was telling a story. But he didn't stop talking.

"What do you think?" Hallie said quietly to his mother.

"Quite captivating."

"Do you see what I see?"

"She's very sexy, yes," said Lily, each *s* afforded a little hiss. She reached for her little black evening purse and removed a cigarette from a cigarette case. Lily was one of the few people who still used one, because she didn't smoke very often, or so she claimed. She allowed Hallie to light it. "I think she's stunning. Does she model, dear?"

"She's not a model, mother."

"Hallie, you seem quite serious about her."

"Definitely."

"Serious for someone you only just met this weekend. That's a very serious coat."

"She looks good in it."

"However . . ." Lily paused for thought. "When these things happen, they often happen very quickly."

He was almost touched by this remark. Almost.

"You're right about that. I'm going to marry her."

Lily's dark eyes bore into Hallie's for a deadly moment.

"Not that quickly" came the deep-throated whisper, accompanied with a "Don't fuck with me, I know what I'm talking about" look. It was pure Lily Lawrence.

Whoa.

Hallie tried to feel all the armor he had on before he left the house, but he seemed to have lost it somewhere, and he felt remarkably exposed. It was the kind of vulnerability one can feel only toward a mother.

Time to go, and they hadn't even been served the main course. Where was Martha? God, he needed her.

"I'm going to marry her, Mom. Excuse me, I think I'll go to the bathroom myself."

He got up and left the table and went to the back of the restaurant where the rest rooms were. Martha was just coming out of the ladies' room. He stopped her and leaned her up against the wood-paneled wall, next to a pay phone.

"Listen, I've got to ask you something."

"What's the matter?" she asked, amused by the look of panic in Hallie's eyes.

"It's completely crazy. But it's not, you know what I mean? It really isn't, but I've got to ask you now. Um—will you marry me, Martha?"

The expression on her face, ready to tease him, suddenly melted slightly. He wished he could have recorded that face at that moment to keep forever, so touched was she, so intensely moved.

"Hallie," she said softly.

Oh, no. She's going to say no.

"Please, Martha? I'll buy you a ring, I'll do the whole bit. Don't get logical and say no. You've had plenty of time to think it over."

"Of course I'll marry you, Hallie Lawrence," she said, taking him in her arms. "God, I thought you'd never ask."

They French-kissed passionately, groped each other madly, and then returned to the table.

Hallie felt armed for life.

8

THE NEXT DAY HALLIE WAS IN HIS office at his usual early time, which was no small accomplishment, considering the fact that when he woke up, Martha Housewright was in his bed. But she said they would have to wait a few more hours before they made love again because she was feeling as if she couldn't walk, let alone make love again. So she made him some boiled eggs and toast, and said she wanted to go out and buy some groceries. He told her she should go out and buy anything her heart desired because as long as she was going to be his wife and stay with him for the rest of her life, she would probably need more than groceries and what little she had brought in her suitcase.

She said she could think of a few things she would need.

Hallie gave her his cash card and

told her the code and said he would get her credit cards with her name on them. She said she wanted it to say Martha Housewright Lawrence.

So Hallie left his apartment for the office the same way he had done every day before Martha happened to him. He went down in the elevator, crossed the lobby, headed out into a wonderfully gray day, and started walking. He was glad he couldn't tap-dance because he would've tap-danced all the way.

Lisa looked very happy to see him and was a little unprepared for his good spirits. She knew they had nothing to do with her. She tried to tell herself that he was refreshed from his day off, but her mind skimmed across what she considered the unthinkable, that this mood was the result of another female.

"Good morning!" exclaimed Hallie as she came into his office.

"You're back!" she said through smiling red lips.

"Absolutely. Back to the craziness. Thank you for covering for me, you deserve a medal."

Lisa knew she did; she had put off more than one needy client the previous day and she had done it skillfully. And now Hallie had noticed. That was progress.

"Did a script come for Nikki?" he asked.

"Yes, here it is." She pulled it from the pile of mail she carried. "Do you want me to read it?"

"How else will I know if it's any good? Of course I want you to read it. But can I read it first? I'm having lunch with her today."

Lisa smiled and shuddered a little, it felt so good.

"Do you want a French cruller?"

"No, I had a big fat breakfast at home this morning, thanks. By the way, that's a nice dress. I like that dress. It's cheerful."

Great big half-smile. She had hoped he'd like the raspberry-colored dress. "Cheerful" may not have been what she had in mind, but he had noticed.

"Thanks," she said. She left the office feeling, for lack of any other description, breezy.

He spent the next forty minutes reading the script about the Russian fiddle player, and thought it wasn't as bad as he had expected it to be. A certain amount of intelligence was evident in it, but if it wasn't handled by a skillful director, it could be pretty sappy. Hallie had been a fanatic film buff at one time and had seen close to every movie ever made and read a great many screenplays. He never talked about how much he knew about films, and it rarely came up in the course of his everyday life, except perhaps when some asshole at one of Lily's gatherings invited him to trade opinions about a particular current film. Hallie had very astute opinions.

The script helped him decide what he would tell Nikki to do.

He sat back in his chair, then turned it to face the view. Nikki should have whatever she wanted, he thought. The hell with Alfred.

Suddenly, it was just that simple.

He buzzed Lisa and told her to call Nikki and confirm lunch.

Then he called Martha to make sure she was still alive.

Hallie and Nikki met at a Japanese restaurant. She was late and Hallie reread parts of the script as he drank a Perrier. He looked up to see Nikki sweep up to the table in an enormous sable coat.

"My darling," she said, her Russian voice a little hoarse. She was a bit breathless, indicating that she had been walking briskly. "I did so much talking last night I have lost my voice." She kissed Hallie on both cheeks.

He thought of making a dumb joke and saying, "Well, I hope you find it," but he didn't get the chance.

"I had a few friends over after the concert. What do you think of my new coat?" She took a step back and posed, hands on hips. "Very glamorous, no?"

"You look like a movie star."

She gathered her height and gave him the subtlest of Clara Bow stares. Then she smiled and sat down.

"You're being sarcastic, Hallie?"

"Not at all!"

Nikki peeled off a pair of green leather gloves and slipped out of the coat. She was dressed rather dramatically, all in black. Even her jewelry was black. The red curls were tied with a black velvet ribbon. She smiled one of her daring smiles.

"I'm glad you think I look like a movie star. Now we can talk."

"You were brilliant last night," said Hallie.

"What, you were surprised?"

"No. To give credit to Alfred, he's usually never wrong about things like musical brilliance. I never doubted your ability to play the fiddle, Nikki."

She looked at him playfully. "You know, I was going to invite you to come to my apartment last night and join me and my friends."

"Good Lord!" said Hallie. "Maybe some other time."

"You left before I could ask. I saw you had a date." She put a little mischievous emphasis on the word "date." "I figured you were busy. That was some cute date you had, Hallie."

Oh, Christ.

"So, I read the script. It's not bad."

"Not bad? It happens to be a wonderful script. What we have to worry about is whether you help me or whether you help Alfred. That's the issue."

"I know the issue, Nikki." He put an edge of finality to his voice. Nikki couldn't have cared less about the finality.

"The issue is that, according to Alfred, I will lose credibility with my peers. My peers! Phlagh! And you, you agree with him. No?"

"I think you should do the film, Nikki. We've already discussed that. I'm here to help you negotiate contracts. That's why you hired me. That's what I do. Have they said anything about the director?"

Before she could say anything, a Japanese waitress who looked about fourteen came and took their orders. They ordered sashimi and sushi à la carte and Perriers. Then Nikki said the hell with it, and asked for a sake martini with onions, so Hallie did too.

"So, you are for real, then. You are going to help me. Just making sure, Hallie Lawrence. Just testing!" The child in her, which usually makes up about eighty percent of any serious talent, found that funny.

"Your success depends very much on who directs this thing," said Hallie, immediately resuming their dialogue.

"Malcolm Ferrari. They told me, Malcolm Ferrari."

"Is that so," said Hallie.

"You know him? He's English, even though he sounds like a sports car."

"I've heard of him," said Hallie.

"I think you've met him. Once, oh, about a year ago, he came backstage after a performance. Big praises, full of compliments. And then he shows up at a party at Alfred and Lily's. You were there, I remember that!"

The last thing Hallie wanted to think about was trying to distinguish one asshole from another at a party at Lily's.

"I remember that was the night I think to myself, every time I see you over the years, I always feel like we have never been introduced and have to go through it all over again, the way we did the other night."

"It won't happen again," said the ever-charming Prince Hal.

"I think maybe when you go to your parents' house everybody there becomes one person. All the guests you think of as one big fat guest, no?"

"Could be," said Hallie and he smiled boyishly to hear his thoughts pronounced by someone else. "They told you they've signed Malcolm Ferrari?"

"How do I know who signed what? That's what they told me, that he's the director. I assumed he's signed. Christ!"

"That's fantastic," said Hallie.

"Do you really think so, Hallie?" Her green eyes narrowed slightly. There really was something amazing about her eyes, thought Hallie. They seemed to grab light and hold it fast and shimmering. Other people didn't have that light.

"Absolutely. I think it's exciting, Nikki. Some people never get to be a brilliant violinist and be asked to be in a movie directed by Malcolm Ferrari."

"You're joking me, I never knew that! I thought everybody was having this experience. No!"

Hallie thought that Nikki always seemed as if any minute she might get up and dance, as if she were hearing music all the time and on the verge of not being able to control a little jig. It was actually kind of tantalizing. It was Energy.

"The people at the studio asked me if I would like to have an agent in Los Angeles. They would be very happy to get me anybody I want."

"Jack's your agent."

"Jack manages my violin playing. He knows bupkis about movies."

"Hardly bupkis," said Hallie. He was amused by the Russian pronunciation of this Yiddish word. It came out sort of "boobkis" and sounded more like a pastry. "There isn't an agent in Hollywood who wouldn't take you now, Nikki. Agents love people who already have work. You don't need an agent just to do legal work. For this, you have your own legal department. You have me."

"I told them. I told them, 'Talk to Hallie Lawrence, he's my lawyer!' I think they were very impressed." She sipped her drink the minute the Japanese waitress who looked fourteen put it down.

"I doubt that," said Hallie.

Over the years, he had met several of the members of the Hollywood community. He knew they didn't feel comfortable with him but he wasn't sure why. The fact was Hallie Lawrence made them realize the truth about themselves, and this did unsettling things to their peculiar egos. As far as Hallie was concerned, they were a bunch of minor leaguers, none of whom he knew from school.

"You will get a telephone call from Andy Werdlow," said Nikki, deftly chop-sticking a slice of smoked mackerel. "He is in charge of this project for the studio."

"I think I've heard of Andy Werdlow. I think he's actually got some power. Well, good, they put someone important on the project, it obviously means a lot to them. What's your performance schedule, Nikki?" he asked.

"Boston this weekend, with Alfred to do the Brahms again. Then

we go to Dallas, I think. I am playing two more times this week,
I don't know where. Then I am free for two weeks."

"Okay. Good. I'll call you after I've spoken to Werdlow."

As far as Hallie was concerned, lunch was over. They finished off
their meal, ordered green-tea ice cream and talked about ballet,
mostly the Prokofiev *Romeo and Juliet.*

Outside, the afternoon sky was heavily overcast. The clouds were
white and there were no shadows, which was why Hallie preferred
overcast days. Nikki walked along with him, and while he felt that
he wasn't going to be able to get rid of her, he also found that he
didn't mind, the way he might have with someone else.

"So, it's too bad you couldn't come to my gathering last night.
It would have been better than spending the evening with Alfred
and Lily, no?"

"I'm sure it would have." Wait a minute, thought Hallie. Why
did it seem so natural for him to share an intimate criticism of his
parents with Nikki? Yet it seemed natural, as if they both shared
some kind of inside information. Peculiar.

"You could have brought your date. That cute date you had last
night."

"So you said, Nikki." Although perfectly pleasant about it, Hallie was slightly admonishing. "My cute date is called Martha Housewright."

"Martha Housewright," repeated Nikki. She was intent on being
playful. "I see. So, she was a serious date?"

"Yes. I'm going to marry that particular date."

"Really! That's wonderful for you! That's really wonderful. Oh,
Hallie."

She kissed him impulsively on both cheeks and seemed to Hallie
to be genuinely delighted for him. He was glad.

"Thanks, Nikki. Want to walk a little?"

"No, I must get to rehearsal. Oh, look— Taxi! I will talk to you
later . . . Congratulations, Hallie Lawrence." Nikki rushed off to
catch a vacant cab.

Nikki is so nice, thought Hallie. Then he went to Cartier's.

The ring Hallie bought Martha fit her perfectly. He had memo-
rized her hands and fingers, and he had been born with Lily's eye
for detail, although he tried to keep this buried. But there was no
denying the genetics involved in helping him choose the exquisite
emerald-cut diamond with baguettes.

Martha cried.

She just broke down and cried, sobbing uncontrollably.

"You want to tell me what's wrong?" Hallie despaired as Martha sobbed and blew her nose and stole glances at the ring, which would start the crying all over again.

"I can't talk about it," sniffled Martha.

"What do you mean, you can't talk about it?" demanded the exasperated Hallie.

Wait a minute, he thought. Of course she can't, this is just general shiksacity, idiot.

"Okay, you don't have to talk; I'll guess. You don't like it. It's not something you'd wear. Okay! So—"

"No!" said Martha. He waited, but she gave no further hint. Then she started sobbing all over again, and opened her arms for him. He went into her embrace, grateful for it, but wary. Certainly she couldn't have changed her mind about marrying him. Christ! Last night she had been so happy. "We'll have to give it a lot of thought," Lily had said to Martha, "we'll have to give a lot of thought to this wedding." And Martha had thought that Lily was the Queen of the Solar System.

But now he had given her a ring and Martha couldn't stop crying. This had not exactly been the desired effect. Martha reached to the bed table for another tissue. She blew her nose and dabbed at her eyes, which were quite red and heavy-lidded. She seemed to have drawn herself together for a moment, but as soon as she said, "I can't believe any of this is happening to me," she began crying all over again. She kept talking, but it was a little hard to understand what she was saying because she was doing some serious sobbing. But Hallie listened closely.

"My mom used to say wonderful things would happen to me when I grew up. She said, more than any of the other girls in the family, she just had that feeling about me. So I grew up. And nothing happened. The wonderful things just never happened— well, no, some things happened that at first I thought might be wonderful, but it turned out they weren't and it was awful. And then, all of a sudden, you. I met you. My mom was right. You just came riding into town like"—her face assumed a full-blown crying expression—"like a knight on a white horse, just like my mother always said—"

It was too much for her. She collapsed into his arms.

"It's okay," Hallie whispered. He was very touched by what Martha had said, even though he was always a little wary when people got sentimental. "How can you tell that you grew up when you're such a crybaby?"

"What? Aw, Hallie, don't be a tease right now, okay?" Then she broke from the embrace and glared at him with the early signs of a smile. "I never cry, Hallie Lawrence. Never! I even have a reputation for never crying.

"Could have fooled me," he said calmly.

"How dare you call me a crybaby when I finally do cry! That's *so* mean!"

"Oh, God, Marth!" He grabbed her to him and held on to her. "I didn't mean it that way at all. You can cry. Maybe I'll cry too, would that help?"

Then they were hugging and rolling around on the floor, telling how much they loved each other, and would forever, and deciding to get married the following week.

"I want to wear a bride's dress," said Martha. "A real one, with a train and a veil. The whole bit."

"So wear a bride's dress," said Hallie. She began to cry all over again, as if she had just burst out crying for the first time. "Please don't cry, Martha. Please. We're running out of Kleenex."

She stopped and just looked at him with a serious expression. Then she kissed him. "Want some dinner? I made a stew."

"You made a *stew?* That's the cutest thing I've ever heard."

"I love you so much, Hallie Lawrence."

They ate their stew, sitting at the mission dining table that Martha had set with great style by simply using things Hallie had around the house. His irreplaceable collection of small pre-Columbian pots now had little arrangements of flowers in them and were set in a circle around a plant she had found in the kitchen.

The plant had been given to him by Danny. Seeing it reminded him that she had called his office and left a message, which he had forgotten to return.

Martha had used the china Lily had given Hallie, despite his protests that he rarely ate in and had no need for Lily's great-aunt's Limoges. The Limoges that had belonged to Lily's grandmother was used by Lily alternately with six other "important sets."

Martha had laid the silverware, heavily patterned with grapes and ivy (another outcast service of Lily's), and set out the wineglasses that Hallie had bought himself. Four lighted candles in ornate silver holders made it very pretty, even though Hallie was a little uncertain about actually using the pre-Columbian pots for flowers.

And he was also a little uncertain about the music playing in the background. He thought maybe it was the Eagles, but since he didn't even know why he thought it was the Eagles, he didn't say anything.

As they dined on what could only be called the most delicious and most gentile lamb stew he had ever eaten, Hallie got a whiff of what it was going to be like to be content. Martha talked about her day, which had included a trip to Tower Records for some great CDs that she couldn't *live* without. Her long legs reached out to

him under the table and he was thrilled that she had bought the CDs
if it meant she would continue living there. He had the feeling that
he himself might not have bought exactly the same CDs, but he was
pleased if Martha's was pleased.

"I'll have to go to L.A. soon," he said. "Want to come?"

"Really?" said Martha.

"Get some L.A. clothes tomorrow. Something to wear to dinner
in L.A. Want some coffee? I'll make it."

Hallie left the table and went into the kitchen.

Martha simply nodded, and looked down at her ring.

"My sister Glenna is going to just die when she sees this ring,"
Martha called out to Hallie. "She'll pretend she thinks it's really
gorgeous but then, you'll see, she'll do something like borrow a
sweater of mine and return it ripped and say 'Oh, it was an accident,
I'll get you a new one.' You know, Glenna owes me about twenty
sweaters."

"Don't show her the ring, or she might burn your whole ward-
robe." Hallie came back with mugs of coffee in his New York Mets
cups.

"Hallie, God! You have New York Mets mugs? What a riot! So
does Hammie. He's really corny like that, having all the parapher-
nalia. He gets a kick out of it, even though he actually is a Met and
everything. He says he knows it's corny, but he doesn't care. He's
kind of shy."

"He's the guy who had the best rookie year in the history of
baseball and you're telling me he's shy? Boy, I wouldn't be shy."

"Oh, I can't wait for you to meet Hammie!" she interrupted with
great girlish mirth.

"It's gonna be great! I am a complete, seriously fanatic Met fan.
I love the Mets! I was bred to be a Yankee fan, I am genetically an
American League, NFL man, if that makes any sense. It is an act of
total crossover for me to be a Met fan."

Martha laughed. She knew exactly what he meant. "And not only
that, now you're marrying a Protestant! Hallie Lawrence, you are
wild in the streets." She laughed again, then got up and hugged
him. She kissed him on the lips and then laughed. He kissed her,
and didn't laugh.

The doorbell rang.

Martha popped out to the kitchen and returned with a strawberry
shortcake. Hallie had made no move to answer the door.

"Look at that cake. You made that cake? Look at that. What
are you doing to me, fattening me up so no other woman will
look at me?"

The doorbell rang again.

"How'd you guess?" said Martha. "Aren't you going to answer the door?" She licked whipped cream from her finger.

"Who could it be? They didn't ring up from the desk." Hallie was hoping that whoever it was would be whisked off to Mars.

"Maybe it's your neighbor or something."

The bell rang again, and this time Hallie heard his name spoken in none other than Danny's voice.

"Oh, God, it's a girl!" Martha's smile was horrifyingly mischievous.

"How can you tell that? You can't tell that necessarily."

"I bet it's one of your girlfriends, Hallie Lawrence. You didn't tell me you had girlfriends!" Martha was overflowing with delight.

"I don't have girlfriends. I haven't gone out with her in months. I just ran into her last week and then she showed up here, just like this!"

Danny said his name again, from outside the door, and then rang the bell.

"What are you going to do?" asked Martha, intrigued. She looked as if she was planning to tease him to death about this. "Did you sleep with her last week, when she showed up?"

"Martha, we have to be civilized about this, okay? Can you do this for me, let me handle this? She's going to have to come in. I can't just go to the door and tell her to go home. Just be nice, okay? Your kindness will be handsomely rewarded, I promise."

"Of course I'll be nice, you nerd. I'm the winner!" Then she added in a whisper, "I can't believe you slept with her if you didn't care about her! God, boys are such creeps."

Hallie headed creepily for the door, but stopped and turned back to look at her. "I'm sorry, Marth," he said.

Hallie opened the door to Danny, whose expression wore a slight veil of desperation. Hallie knew in that instant that it was exactly that look of desperation that had kept him from going any further in a relationship with Danny.

She came in and stood in the middle of the foyer, just as she had done the time before.

"Danny, it's a mistake for you to come over here," said Hallie right off the bat.

"I know," said Danny, not without drama, before Hallie could continue. "I haven't heard from you since last week. I know how busy you are, Hallie, I understand you can't always return my calls immediately. I always understood that when we were together."

What she didn't understand was that Hallie would henceforth order Martha's calls put through no matter to whom he was speaking, or meeting with.

"I would have called you back, Danny."

"I danced *Giselle* tonight. That always reminds me of you. You always said you liked seeing me do it." There was a blush on the velvet cheekbones. "Anyway, when I finished the performance tonight, I just had this mad urge to see you. I know it's kind of illogical, but I just decided to come over here."

Illogical? Try certifiable.

"I still like seeing you dance *Giselle,* " he said, not able to control the Hallie Lawrence who just had to make people feel good.

"Can I take off my coat?"

"Danny, it's kind of late . . ."

She looked away, into the living room, and saw the mission table with the candles that had been set for a dinner for two. Then she saw Martha.

Martha was slicing strawberry shortcake.

You could practically hear the tingles of embarrassment and mortification break out across her forehead.

"You have somebody here, Hallie. God, I'm sorry."

"I do, actually," said Hallie, with a sort of thank-you-for-under-standing smile.

"You should have said something. I'm so embarrassed," said Danny, with a smile of her own. Her eyes darted back to the dining table. The pause was short but heavy. "I'd better go."

"I'll call you tomorrow, I promise," Hallie said, thinking maybe it wasn't going to be so bad after all.

Wrong.

"Who is she?" asked Danny.

"No one you know," Hallie answered awkwardly.

"You could have told me you were seeing someone else the other night."

"I hadn't met her yet," Hallie said. It seemed logical to be honest with her, but it was equally obvious that it was impractical. There was no need for him to reveal anything, and yet he had.

"Oh, so it's someone you just met." Danny's eyes went to the living room again, and this time looked around boldly. "You might as well introduce us. Or is she too temporary to bother with that?" Sarcasm was not Danny's forte, as it was the first indication of impending hysteria. Hallie said nothing. "If she's someone new in your life, we'll meet eventually."

"Let's leave it till then," said Hallie. How else could he put it?

But this only confirmed for Danny that it was not someone temporary. Her soft cupid lips trembled almost imperceptibly and her cheeks were flushed a bright rose color. She pulled her coat close.

"Then I guess I'll just go," she said.

Hallie could actually feel the heat given off from her burning cheeks. That could have been what made him say what he said.

"You don't have to. You could stay for a drink."

He couldn't believe it! What corner of his brain had that come from? She was just leaving! He held his breath and waited for her refusal.

"All right," said Danny. "Why not?"

If she had been a clever girl, she would have questioned why Hallie was willing to have this confrontation, but she wasn't clever really, once she stepped out of her toe shoes.

But the question certainly hit Hallie, as he realized she had agreed to stay. Why had he suggested the confrontation? He knew why and it made him feel like an asshole. He knew once Danny saw Martha, she would understand and probably never call him again. Oh, the cowardliness of it, he thought. He detected a possible headache playing behind his eyes.

But why Danny would want to stay posed a problem more terrible than even cowardliness. Watching her go into the living room was a little like watching someone in the act of self-flagellation. Totally embarrassing.

Hallie turned on a lamp as Martha came toward them, illuminated now, and Danny could really see her. An "Oh my God" look revealed that what Danny certainly didn't want to see in Hallie Lawrence's home, dressed in tight jeans and some kind of undershirt, was a beauty like Martha, coming toward her, smiling like the nicest person in the world. The whip was raised.

Hallie introduced them. He told Martha that Danny was a ballet dancer. Martha was properly impressed. Martha was unthreatened the way few people are unthreatened and Danny knew this at once.

"Want some strawberry shortcake?" asked Martha.

"No, thank you, I can't eat dessert."

"No, God, if you're a ballet dancer I guess not, but don't you burn up thousands of calories just dancing?" said Martha, the total girl at all times.

"You have to stay very light," said Danny. But she took the iced Cointreau Hallie was offering and got to say, "Thank you, Hallie, you knew exactly what I wanted."

"I love the ballet," said Martha, sitting on the floor, hugging her knees, oblivious to Danny's attempts to claim intimacy with Hallie. "It must be such hard work."

All Danny could think about was that Martha was gorgeous. Martha was flawless—her skin, the wide, interesting mouth, perfect nose, the eyes that were not only exactly the eyes Danny had always wished she had, but were friendly and warm and full of confidence. The ease with which Martha complimented her, the way she was openly and unabashedly impressed with who Danny was and what Danny did, made Danny miserable. It was a nightmare.

Danny also found that she had nothing to say. Oh, she was talking, answering Martha's question about how many hours of day she rehearsed and took class, but she found herself speaking like a very stupid person, inarticulate on the one subject she really knew anything about.

Hallie noticed this, but his only concern, and please don't be too hard on him, was that Martha would be upset by Danny's impetuous appearance. To his relief, Martha was being the nicest person in the world.

"What did you dance tonight?" asked Hallie, considering this a pithy entrance to the conversation.

Danny looked at him before answering.

"I told you. I danced *Giselle.*"

"Oh, I've seen that one," said Martha. "That's the one about the girl who goes crazy, right?"

"I guess that's as good a way of describing it as any," said Danny, her neck quivering slightly like a swan.

"Did they throw roses at the stage?" asked Martha, her hands pressed together dreamily. "God, that must be a wonderful feeling."

"Well, yes, there are usually roses." Danny's line of vision fell on Martha's ring. She focused there for a moment, Hallie noticed.

Christ, she's going to compliment the ring and Martha's going to tell her where she got it. He prepared himself. But that's not what happened. Danny's face suddenly relaxed completely and a small little smile crossed her puffed lips.

It had occurred to Danny that Martha was obviously engaged to be married, and as Hallie had only just met her, it had to be to someone other than him. In fact, she might already be married, and what Danny had discovered here tonight was not only temporary, but clandestine, and that's why Hallie had been so weird at the door. He would call her tomorrow and explain how much he needed her discretion. It would make them closer. Eventually, Danny imagined, Martha's marital status would prove too much of a burden for either of them, and Hallie would lose interest. Meanwhile, there would be Danny, who had been his closest confidante.

Danny managed to join in the conversation with her articulation nearly fully recovered, all because of her nice false sense of relief. Embarrassing, or what?

Then somehow the gathering came to an end, and somehow it had been Martha's doing. She ceased asking her chatty questions

and withdrew, still smiling, still present, but leaving only one conclusion: that the encounter was over.

They all said good night, and Hallie walked Danny to the elevator. Hallie saw the pink in Danny's cheeks turn to red. God, he
wished you couldn't read everything about Danny in her blush.
How horrible to have been cursed with such a physical deformity.

But helping her out was all he wanted to do.

"Danny," he began slowly, "I'm sorry if this has been awkward."

"No, it's okay. Martha's very nice. She's married, isn't she?"

"Not yet."

"She's having one last fling?" She gave him some kind of look
that Hallie couldn't understand. It was a "Your secret's safe with
me" look.

"Not exactly . . . I'm the one she's marrying," said Hallie.
"Sometimes when these things happen, they happen very fast." He
couldn't think of anything else to say.

The elevator arrived and Danny quickly got in and, believe it or
not, she said, "Call me" as the doors slid closed.

He couldn't believe that, after all that, she had still asked him to
call her.

Women.

The dining room table was cleared away and as neat as a pin.
Hallie went into the bedroom and saw Martha in the bathroom,
pinning her hair up, about to wash her face.

Hallie came and sat on the edge of the tub.

"I'm sorry, Marth. I never mentioned Danny because—"

"Shhh. It's amazing how girls do that, come over to a guy's house
and never get that maybe the guy doesn't want them there. There's
no encouragement at all from the guy, but the girl comes over
anyway. Then the guy sleeps with her and she think it means
something. Well, we've all done it, I guess; it's just Girl."

"I'm sorry, Martha. Believe me, I know I shouldn't have slept
with her."

Martha laughed. "Why are you apologizing? It's not like you
were cheating on me, asshole, we hadn't even met yet." She
reached over and rumpled Hallie's hair.

"Wait a minute, what do you mean it's something we've all
done? You did that?"

"Well," said Martha, with a bratty little look that told him she
was not about to reveal a thing. "Maybe and maybe not."

He reached his hand out for her denim-wrapped leg.

"I don't want to know," he said. He actually found the idea
profoundly disturbing, but this disturbance still lay buried many
miles deep.

"Anyway, stop acting so guilty about the whole thing because you weren't cheating on me. But if I ever do catch you cheating on me, I'll have your ass. Now leave so I can cream my face."

Hallie got up and started to leave the bathroom, but first he licked her cheek with his whole tongue.

Then he went into the bedroom and lay down on the bed. He thought it was kind of erotic, the way Martha had threatened him, erotic and fabulous. But he found himself forced to think that while there had been many Dannys in his life, Martha, too, had previous experience. It made him feel sick.

Martha came back and began to make love to him and Hallie realized she was taking things somehow to a new level. She had been eroticized, as if she had spent the day plugged into a recharging socket and was on overload. The look on her face during the whole thing seemed to be telling him that it wasn't possible for him to think of anyone else ever again, that nobody did it better.

It was stunning.

When it finally came to a conclusion, all Hallie could think about was that, once again, he had made it through alive.

9

THE NEXT DAY, HALLIE GOT A CALL from Andy Werdlow in Hollywood. Hallie engaged in brief pleasantries and got down to business, which seemed to throw Andy Werdlow off. Pleasantries are engaged in for longer periods out in Hollywood.

Hallie asked him for a tentative completion date for the film, in order to foresee the resumption of Nikki's concert schedule. It was a small thing, really.

"Hal, you can't always be exact about when a picture is going to wrap. It's give and take. You have to give and take."

Hal? He called him Hal?

"Well, in this case, we're going to have to take, Andy. We have to determine her future availability before any of this even starts. If she's booked with a symphony, she has to show up."

"Actors have to get on to other pictures. I know about completion, Hal." Again he called him Hal. And with an "I can get serious
too" voice, which was a little pathetic. "We can work that out, I'm
sure," continued Andy.

"Good!" enthused Hallie in his "You bet your ass we can"
voice.

"We need to arrange a screen test. It's a usual thing for someone
who's never been on film before."

"When would you like to do that?"

"How about next week? Could she come out next week?"

Hallie looked over Nikki's performance schedule for the next
year that Lisa had written out on a legal pad.

"Yes," Hallie said. "How's Tuesday?"

"I can't see why Tuesday couldn't work," Andy said. "Tuesday
is great. We'll know in a day about the test because there's really
no one here who doubts that she'll be terrific. It's just a formality."

"Good. Then I'll come out with her, and if the test works out,
we can work out the deal."

When Andy heard the expedience in Hallie's voice, the no-
nonsense, I-have-other-work-to-do sound, he felt the very thing
intended, unimportant. Hallie was gearing up for negotiation.

"That sounds very positive," Andy said proudly. "Come on out
here. We'll arrange everything. We'll put you guys up at the Beverly Hills, if that's okay—"

"Oh, I'll make all the arrangements," said Hallie. "We'll have
dinner."

"You got it," said Andy.

"Wonderful. See you then. Nice talking to you, Andy." And
Hallie Lawrence was off the phone.

Lisa came into his office. Her eyes were downcast and she seemed
aloof, in a self-protective way. She had done something earlier that
had annoyed Hallie. She had interrupted him during a call to tell
him his mother was on another line. He had almost barked at her
when he said "I'll call her back" and returned to his conversation.
Lisa was upset.

"Lisa, I'm not mad. It's just that my mother is not a call I consider
important enough for an interruption. Okay?"

"I just didn't want to take the chance, Hallie."

Lisa was taking the whole thing too hard, and Hallie was a little
surprised. She looked thoroughly miserable.

"Lisa, I'm not mad. I just thought I should mention it. My mom's
not an important call. Unless she can actually communicate to you
there is a life or death emergency—did you hear that? Life or

death—it's 'Gee, Mrs. Lawrence, I'm sure he'll get back to you as soon as he has a minute. Good-bye.' ''

When Hallie used a rather adorable falsetto voice with a Southern accent for this instruction on dialogue, it made Lisa laugh. That they were laughing made Lisa's heart soar.

"Here, these are your other calls," said Lisa, now feeling a little less miserable. "Oh, this Martha Housewright called twice, she said it was important."

"Why didn't you tell me that? Now, that's a call I would've taken!" said Hallie, immediately picking up the phone.

Now Lisa was really confused. When she had asked this Martha Housewright where she was from, meaning what organization, Martha had replied, "Darling, New York." "Aren't we all," Lisa had quipped, before remembering that Darling was a place, a place where the Lawrences had a country home. She must be from some local music group wanting a guest appearance for their local symphony. Hallie got a lot of those kinds of calls.

"Martha!" Hallie said to the telephone. "Hold on a minute . . . Lisa, don't worry about my mother, okay? She's a maniac."

Lisa gave him the half-smile as she left the office.

"Hi," said Hallie, back to the phone.

"I just felt like calling my boyfriend," said Martha.

"And what did you feel like calling him?"

"A total cornball turd," returned Martha. She laughed that girlish laugh that just killed him. She waited a beat and then asked, "Are you serious about going up to Darling this weekend? Because if you are, I want to call my mom and tell her."

"Absolutely. But don't tell her we're getting married. I should do that."

"What are you going to do, ask the coach for my hand in marriage?"

The coach. The very sound of the word and Hallie could smell the heavy, sweaty breathing of a large and furious bull.

"Of course I'm going to ask for your hand in marriage. In fact, I'm going to ask for the whole thing, hands, feet, breasts, lips, legs—"

"Hallie, could you be serious? I have to call my mom."

"Tell your mother we'll drive up on Saturday. Tell her I'm looking forward to meeting her—you know, kind of lather it on. Tell her you like me and everything, and—"

"You're such a cretin, I can't believe it sometimes! I told my mother I'm *crazy* about you! That I'm madly in love! You're such a nerd!"

"No, I'm not, actually."

"We'll have to stay in separate bedrooms, I'd better warn you now."

"But my intentions are clearly honorable!" Hallie said, horrified at the idea.

"Don't worry about it. My sisters and I worked that one out years ago. And you are a nerd and I can't stay on the phone with such a nerd any longer!"

And with that, followed by another laugh, she hung up.

What did she mean, she and her sisters had worked it out years ago? How many men had she brought home? Every time he brushed against the notion that there had ever been any other men, he felt feverish.

God, the sooner they were married, the better.

So Hallie called Lily.

"Darling!" she crooned softly.

"Mom, if Lisa tells you I'm on another line, don't ask to be put through."

"Oh, Hallie, darling, I am sorry. Don't be too hard on her, I'm afraid I did tell her to give it a try. Just in case you felt like talking to me."

"It's not that I didn't want to talk to you; I was on a business call."

"Well, there was always the possibility that you were just about to end your business call. I'm sorry, Hallie, I've just been dying to talk to you after what you told me the other night."

"Which part?"

"Unless of course it's no longer true."

Noting the ingenious way in which she avoided the word "marriage," Hallie felt like pretending he had no idea what she was talking about. But he decided against it.

"It's still true, Mom, I'm going to marry Martha. Come on, you can't say you didn't like her."

"I liked her, I didn't say that I didn't like her. Oh, Hallie, please come and have a drink with us tonight—no, on second thought, why don't you come for dinner? It's been ages since it was just the family, and we have absolutely no plans tonight except to lie around and watch TV. Boris made brisket."

Boris made brisket? Hallie's favorite dish cooked by the Lawrences' excellent cook/houseman?

"Great! I'll bring Martha. We can all sit around and get to know each other."

"Does she eat . . . brisket?" asked Lily gingerly. "I mean, it's not normally what I would serve for company."

"Mom! Martha's not company! She's going to be your daughter-in-law! Just think of her as mishpukha."

Using this Yiddish word for "family," one of the few Yiddish words he knew, he smiled to himself and swore he heard Lily thinking: no shiksa will ever mishpukh with me.

"Well, absolutely, bring Martha!" came Lily's cleverly calculated enthusiasm. "But maybe you could come early—like, say, right from work—and we could have a drink first. She won't mind meeting you here, will she?"

"No, I'm sure she won't," said Hallie. He was trapped. There was no way he could avoid talking to his parents about this marriage. The best he could do was postpone the conversation for a while, which would just make it worse, so he figured what the hell, go get it over with.

"I'll come over around six, and tell her to come at seven. How's that?"

"Heaven," said Lily, or as close to it as she was going to get for the time being. "Very casual, okay, darling? I mean, tell her she doesn't have to dress. I'm not in the mood to dress."

"Great! I'll tell her we're all going to sit around in the nude. She'll love it."

"So would your father. I'll see you later."

A little sarcasm, a little good-bye.

The rest of the afternoon was fairly uneventful. Hallie worked hard, and at twenty to six, as he was winding down from work and winding up for the evening ahead, Kip called.

Kip felt like talking.

"I can't right now," said Hallie. "I've got to go to the Maniacs' for dinner. Martha's coming, but I'm going early to have a drink with them. I have to teach them to deal with the fact that I'm going to marry her."

"What?" asked Kip in a low voice.

"Oh, yeah, I'm going to do it, Kipper. I'm going to marry Martha."

There was a pause.

"Fanfuckingtastic," said Kip.

As he left the office and took a full slam of frigid winter night right in the face, he was thinking about Kip—that something wasn't right with Kip. Even though the jokes were there, something in the tone of his voice sounded, well, kind of sad. And something in his gut told Hallie it had something to do with Kate.

He was right on the nose, but just off-center.

He buttoned up his coat.

* * *

"We're going to L.A. next week. They're giving Nikki a screen test."

Alfred, leaning forward in his chair, squinted one eye at Hallie and scrutinized him. Then he sat back and took a cigar from the pocket of his bagged-out cardigan sweater.

"A good move," said Alfred, striking a match. "She can never say you tried to stop her. In the beginning, you even encouraged her."

Alfred lit a match and held it to his cigar. As the puffs of white smoke were released from his lips, Lily went to the window and pulled it up a few inches.

"I'll have to open the window if you do that," she said.

"So open the window!" came the bellow from behind of what was now a cloud of smoke.

"I don't mind if you smoke cigars, Alfred. We'll just let in a little extra air, even though it's four degrees outside and we'll all catch pneumonia. I don't mind opening the window."

"That's right, Lil, live dangerously," he said. He grabbed her ass as she passed in an immaculately cut pair of gray flannel trousers. She ignored his gesture until she had retaken her seat on the sofa, moved a few of the many thousands of needlepoint pillows to support her back, pushed down the sleeves of her black cashmere sweater, and picked up her martini glass. Then she gave Alfred the old seductive but admonishing look Hallie had seen her give his father all his life. Subtle as it was, it was positively feline.

The family sat in the coziness of Lily's library, with a fire blazing, and the comfort of all the books. It really was Lily's library, not only because it was her little private room for entertaining, filled with fantastic puffy sofas and chairs in fabulous fabrics, but because the walls were lined with books, the famous first-edition library of Lily's venerated grandfather, who enjoyed collecting first editions. It was an entirely Jewish notion. A man of great scholarly passion comes to America and converts the passion into business. As a wealthy man he can think of no pleasure greater than to own a lot of rare books, and then pass them on to his offspring. For Hallie it was a pain in the ass, because his mother wouldn't let him take any books from the room. They had to be read in the library, all because once, one time only, he had spilled a bottle of Welch's grape juice all over a rare copy of *A Tale of Two Cities*.

"What's the big deal?" Hallie had yelped as Lily threw the ruined volume at him.

"What's the big deal?" screamed Lily, one of the rare times when Lily actually sounded like an ordinary person. "From now on you'll read cheap paperback editions! And maybe one day, and I'm only saying *maybe,* I'll let you read these books again, but only *in* the library.''

Now Lily sipped her martini and watched happily as Hallie reached for a smoked salmon hors d'oeuvre. Sometimes it broke her heart to pass the library and not see Hallie hanging upside down from the couch, lost in a book. It had been a long time since she'd had to warn him about his brains exploding if he stayed too long in that position. The terribly attractive young man helping himself to a smoked salmon hors d'oeuvre was who her son was now. It made her happy he had survived his habit of reading upside down.

Among other things.

"All right, that's enough business, my darlings, let's talk about Martha," Lily said with a pretty smile and a very soft manner. Lily was armed to the hilt.

"I'm crazy about her," said Hallie.

"Yes, so I've gathered. And you plan to marry her."

"Of course. She's the one, Mom. I'm telling you, she's the one. This is it.''

"How exactly—I'm curious—can you be so sure after, how long has it been? A few days?''

The fire spit and crackled. Hallie inhaled, Essence of Lily Library, always with a slight clove scent somewhere, and of course a trace of Jicky. He had to explain Martha to his mother. Use very few words, was his first thought. Be very accurate, and thus, very conclusive. Get in everything. The problem was, he had no idea how to do that.

"She's— From the first time I saw her, I could feel that something fit. She just moved right inside me and fit. I can't put it any other way. She's bright, she's funny, and she's gorgeous. And she's the most sensational fuck I've ever had.''

Lily's lips barely parted to allow the clear martini to be pulled into her mouth. She set the glass down on the coffee table. A smile had frozen on her lips, a smile that afforded her time to consider whether to react to his last description of Martha's talents or not. She wasn't in the least surprised by it. It had to be great sex. Actually, she felt a moment of pleasure that she had managed to raise such a thoroughly heterosexual son, thank God. By no means was she not grateful for that small blessing in these times. But sexual attraction can throw acid on all clarity.

"She fits. Are you sure about that?" asked Lily with a light emphasis on "fits." We're talking about a shiksa here, Hallie, is what she didn't say.

"A hundred percent sure."

Hallie noticed that Alfred was staring at him openmouthed, an expression that would have altered radically had Lily been seated near enough to kick him.

"The sex is great," said Alfred, with a shrug to Lily, as if Hallie weren't there, as if they were continuing a conversation they must have had previously.

"I heard him, Alfred," said Lily. A few sparks flew from the eyes, but nothing big yet. "Can I suggest a longish engagement?" she asked, maybe even a little coyly.

"How long did you have in mind?"

"Oh, well, maybe a year? You can live together, sort of see how it goes. That's what most people do these days."

"A year? Mother! The very idea. I thought maybe you'd say give it a couple of days—"

"When are you planning to get married, Hallie?"

"Tuesday. Well, I have to go to L.A. on Tuesday, so I thought maybe Monday would be good."

"*This* Monday?" said Alfred. He was always uncomfortable in these situations, but he knew instinctively he should fill the gap so Lily could hold on to her composure.

Hallie watched Lily reach for a cigarette.

"Except for the fact that I want to marry her instantly, and except for the fact that she's not Jewish, is there any other reason why you don't like Martha?"

"It's not a goddamn matter of me liking her; you don't get married to someone you've known for two and a half minutes. And her not being Jewish has nothing to do with it."

Lily's library had fallen silent, except for a spit from the logs and the soft ticking of the mantel clock. God, things were serious when the three of them sat in this room and all you could hear was the mantel clock. As a boy, anytime Hallie had to be spoken to about his behavior, he had found himself in one of these clock-ticking moments. He would put a soulful expression on his face for his parents' sake, while privately challenging himself to see how many book titles he could read from where he sat.

"I don't care in the least that she isn't Jewish," Lily said.

Eyes resting on *My Antonia* by Willa Cather, Hallie sighed. At last. Phew. The Jewish problem. It was out in the open.

"Of course you do," said Hallie. "You care a lot. You're going to give me the speech about old Carl Oppenheim—"

"My father was a religious man, and so was his father before him. No matter how wealthy they became, they refused to assimilate."

"And I wish I had had the opportunity to personally congratulate them both! But the point is, you do care and you should admit it."

"Don't tell me what I care about."

"We're not prejudiced," said Alfred, once again not comfortable with the situation.

"Of course we're not," said Lily. "I can assure you that even if this girl was Jewish, if you wanted to marry her after knowing her for no time at all, I would—I would help you question it. And, Hallie, without my grandfather, Temple Emanuel would have suffered a great deal."

"I know about his contributions to Temple Emanuel, Mother."

"They were not just financial."

"A major spiritual force! Maybe he'll find it in his heart, wherever he is now, to forgive me."

The truth was, Carl Oppenheim would have forgiven him and Lily knew this. He wouldn't have spoken to him for a year (the old boy had been kind of a son of a bitch) but he eventually would have forgiven him.

"Don't bet on it," came a whopper of deep-throated Lily information. "The issue is not religion. We are *not* bigots."

"I know you're not," said Hallie. "That's why you're going to like Martha. You're going to love her!"

There was more to say, but at that point they could all hear the quiet chime of the front doorbell. Hallie got up.

"Boris will get it," said Lily.

"It's Martha," said Hallie.

And he left the room.

"I'll tell you what you're going to do, Lil," said Alfred, looking at her with his own style of the reprimanding stare. A stare well known by any musician who had ever worked under him, but not so well known by his wife. As a result, she was always a little frightened by it. The fabulously self-contained Lily Lawrence could still be frightened by her own husband.

"You're going to like this girl. You're going to accept the fact that he's going to marry her and that's that. No trouble, Lil."

"Oh, Alfred," she pouted. "I'm just not ready yet."

"It's time, Lil."

"Then there'll be grandchildren, I'll be a grandmother. It all goes so fast. I mean, doesn't it seem like three minutes ago that you and I were dating?"

"No, actually it feels like about thirty-five years ago, thirty-five sensational years ago. We're having a great life, Lily. Don't start digging graves. Certainly don't start digging mine."

"I'll go way before you do, Alfred. An ego like yours they couldn't kill with a bomb."

They smiled at each other, and Alfred sent her a lascivious wink.

Hallie helped Martha with her coat while she looked around the immense foyer, her mouth open slightly.

"Jesus, Hallie," she said.

Hallie had told her not to dress, that it was just a family evening, so it could be really casual. As a result, Martha was wearing a pair of jeans, old but well-maintained brown cowboy boots, and a beautiful man's navy blazer over a man's white shirt.

"You look great!" said Hallie, taking her in his arms. He liked her in jeans, she gave jeans new meaning. "And what a great jacket!"

"The jacket is yours, dummy. Christ, Hallie, I shouldn't be wearing jeans, look at this place. This is like a palace." She actually whispered.

He had a good hold on her hand as they walked into the living room, which was the shortest way to get to the library. Martha looked around, wide-eyed. "Why did you tell me it was casual? This place is amazing."

Hallie laughed.

"Don't let the fancy furniture fool you. Relax. This is where I grew up. Believe it or not, this is home."

Martha felt like she was in a museum and that there should be ropes across the rooms. She couldn't imagine that people actually sat on the sofas, so fine were the fabrics.

When Hallie and Martha entered the library, Alfred and Lily greeted her with open arms and made her feel completely at ease. Lily and Alfred were social pros.

"Oh, you're wearing jeans, I think that's absolutely divine!" said Lily. In her obviously temporary beneficent state of mind, she rather liked that Martha had come dressed to make herself at home. She was a little sick of the women Hallie had brought around previously who always had dressed to please Lily, and not him.

"Are you sure it's all right?" asked Martha, rubbing her hands along her jean-covered thighs.

"It's perfect."

"What can I get you to drink?" bellowed Alfred, the host.

"Jack Daniels on the rocks," said Martha without pause.

Other girls had always coyly asked for a glass of white wine or a sherry. At most, a Scotch. Hallie thought that her request, said with a toss of the silk hair, made her holier than ever.

"What a beautiful house this is, Mrs. Lawrence."

"Call me Lily."

"I have to mention it, or it's going to look bad, the way I keep staring around at everything."

Lily gave her a real Lily whopper of a smile, accompanied by especially crinkled eyes.

"What would you like to look at?" asked Lily. "Come. I'll show you everything worth seeing."

Hallie almost fell off his chair. Maybe the President of the United States might get such an invitation in Lily's home, or maybe only God, but she was up on her feet taking Martha by the hand, and leading her out to see Her Things.

Alfred and Hallie exchanged glances.

"You see that? Your mother likes her."

"What's she up to, Alfred?" Hallie got up and added a bit more Jack Daniels to his glass, having of course decided to drink what Martha drank.

"What are you talking about, she likes Martha. What's not to like, she's charming. I would tell you if I didn't think she was any good."

"That's for sure," said Hallie.

"I like her."

Hallie realized that if Alfred did have a problem with Martha, the first thing he would say was that he liked her. Being in the middle of such an obvious example of Alfred's means and ways made Hallie feel a bit sad, even though Alfred was smiling. He changed the subject.

"By the way, Nikki is going to do the film."

"Then I wash my hands of it!" Alfred's rage was instant.

It was a pretty startling burst of anger and it was obvious that it had been lying only slightly beneath the surface all evening. Hallie was not about to summon the nerve to ask him what was really going on with Nikki, why was Alfred so concerned, when his father ended it.

"We are not going to discuss it. If you ever feel you have anything to tell me on the subject of this motion picture, you'll hold it in, unless you're going to tell me what I want to hear: that Nikki is not doing this!"

"There could always be some unforeseen circumstance." He just couldn't resist giving Alfred a little of what he wanted to hear. After all, they had a dinner to get through.

"Of course!" bellowed Alfred. Then he laughed appreciatively at what Hallie had said. "You hungry? I'm starving." And he slapped the arms of the chair before getting up.

Dinner went fairly well. Martha was just plain endearing; there was something about her that was hard to resist, something that was completely devoid of ulterior motive. Lily knew Martha was going to be a popular girl in New York. She brought up the wedding.

It would be small.

They all agreed on that.

Small meant soon.

Then Lily noted and complimented Martha's ring, with a perfectly poised expression that concealed relief for such tastefulness.

Alfred asked Martha about her father and made a joke about being something of a coach himself and embarked on a monologue about being at the helm of a great orchestra, thus spilling his engorged ego all over the dinner table.

And all the time, Martha became more and more relaxed with the Lawrences, laughing easily, asking Lily a flattering but guileless number of questions about all the beautiful things in the apartment.

They ate their fill of brisket (which Martha complimented as a delicious pot roast), buttered carrots, and salad. A wonderful '71 burgundy was the touch that, along with the use of an Important China, elevated the meal from the shtetle to the penthouse. The arugula and fresh-herb vinaigrette helped too.

All the while, Hallie observed his parents with his usual keen eye and easily realized that Lily had made a conscious decision to like Martha. And it had something to do with Alfred. He saw the look she gave him, a look in search of approval, when she was complimenting the ring. Although no one else in the world would have noticed it, it was a how-am-I-doing look. Hallie actually wanted to say, "Not bad," but he wasn't supposed to see the look, let alone understand its meaning. So he kept quiet, and simply speculated on how long it would last. He also thought it was an excellent card for Lily to choose.

As long as she pretended to like Martha, things would be easy.

There was only one awkward moment. It was when Martha asked who was Bartók, she always forgot, and Hallie had had to sort of mumble "Composer" and pretend his parents hadn't heard this. But he had seen Lily's spine get straighter.

10

THEY BORROWED THE LAWRENCES'
car, a '73 navy-blue perfectly maintained Mercedes, and headed for Darling on Saturday morning. Martha was
in an incredibly cheerful mood as she
sat in the passenger seat eating a corn
muffin and drinking coffee from a take-
out cup.

Hallie was feeling cheerful too,
but not nearly as cheerful as Martha.
For two reasons. First of all, on the
previous night, for the first time since
they met, now a week ago almost to
the hour, Hallie and Martha hadn't
had sex.

The second reason for his incapacita-
tion in the cheerfulness department
was anxiety about meeting Martha's
family. He kept thinking of the movie
Annie Hall, the scene where Woody
Allen is convinced that he is dressed
like an Orthodox rabbi, with long side

curls and a black felt hat, while sitting in the Halls' goyish dining room. Hallie found himself patting his hair where it grew just near his ear to make sure it hadn't suddenly had a growth spurt.

It wasn't Martha's fault that they hadn't had sex, even though it was she who had fallen asleep. Hallie had been on the phone with Kip, in the living room, while Martha had gone to bed to read. Once he was on the phone with Kip, brandy in hand, he had no concept of time, even with Martha in the next room. In fact, when he got off the phone, Hallie realized that he had had his mind off Martha for most of the conversation, something he hadn't even been able to do at work.

Kip's marriage was on the rocks.

Kate was giving him ultimatums about having children. And while Kate's instincts were to nest and breed, Kip wrestled with an instinct of his own—to escape and move on. In other words, they were no longer in the same solar system, and apparently Kate had no idea about this.

"Hallie? I can't stand the breathing," Kip had announced.

Hallie allowed an appropriate pause to recognize the solemnity of the statement. Not being able to stand the sound of the girl's breathing was terminal. Once the sound of the breathing got on your nerves, it meant you felt like killing her. It was over, you had to break up.

"Breathing, huh," Hallie said, with due respect.

"Hallie." Kip paused while ice hit the sides of a glass. Hallie knew Kip was drinking Scotch. He was sounding not a little drunk. "I'm running on empty."

"Is there anything I can do? Do you want me to meet you?"

"Is Martha there?"

"Yes."

"You're offering to meet me and leave Martha? Hal, what can I say. Are you nuts?"

"Don't start drinking, Kip."

"Don't start getting logical with me, asshole."

The two friends talked on and on, debating the Kate situation from all aspects. They resolved nothing, but decided that sometime soon Kip would come down to the city and stay with Hallie and Martha.

It was one-thirty when Hallie went into the bedroom. Martha was asleep, lit only by the glow from the television, where David Letterman was signing off. What a vision she was in her T-shirt with those breasts pointing to the ceiling and her long legs outstretched under the covers. How beautiful her face was suspended in sleep, with her lips parted slightly. He turned off the TV, brushed his teeth, threw off his clothes, and jumped into bed beside her. He began to kiss her shoulder, her neck, while he searched under the shirt for a handful of breast. But something was wrong.

There was no response. Nothing. Many times before he had awakened her during the night with the slightest coercion to find her eager and passionate. But now, she was comatose. In fact, at one point he put his head against her chest to check out the heartbeat, expecting to hear silence. But it was regular and peaceful. Then she sighed deeply and turned over. He tried kissing her, but her lips were totally passive. He pulled up her shirt and began sucking on her nipples, which even hardened in his mouth, but still she did not stir.

That's it, he thought. She's no longer attracted to me. It didn't even last a week!

Luckily, he didn't shake her violently into consciousness before realizing he was being a real jerk. She had had a lot to drink at dinner. She had announced that it was the best wine she had ever tasted and proved this by accepting all offers to refill her glass. So Hallie curled up behind her, like a spoon, and eventually fell asleep himself, although not until after thinking he felt as if he hadn't had sex in two years.

Now, in the '73 navy-blue Mercedes, Hallie reached over and put his hand on Martha's leg.

"You were asleep last night," he said.

"Hallie, that's the third time you've said that."

"Well, excuse me! I mean, a guy gets horny."

"We fucked yesterday morning!"

Something bothered him about her use of the word "fuck." He didn't like the way it sounded, and while he thought of himself as too cool to be bothered by something like that, he kind of disapproved of her language. Besides, they didn't "fuck," that was what he had been doing all his life before he met her. What they did was more of a religious ritual transcension, heretofore unknown except maybe in Tibet. How could she call it fucking?

"Kip might come down to New York soon. Would you mind if he slept on the couch?"

"Of course not. I thought Kip was a really great guy."

He was glad she liked Kip. It was as if she had told him she liked the way he dressed. There was no way he would alter his dressing or his friendship with Kip.

Hallie glanced out the window at the exit sign for Darling. He heard Kip recall for the four hundred millionth time that this was the spot where Hallie had talked him into going to Harvard. Kip had sounded so damned sad on the phone last night that Hallie had

left the Housewright phone number with his answering service, to
be given out only in an emergency, thinking maybe Kip might need
to talk. Of course it occurred to him that wanting to talk might
constitute an emergency for Lily, who might just decide to call. But
he had to overlook that because of Kip.

Martha became more and more animated as she began to give
him directions to her house. Along the way she pointed out her
high school, the diner where she and her friends used to hang out,
the house where the family doctor used to have his office before he
moved to the new medical complex. Hallie found it all absolutely
fascinating.

Then they turned into a long drive and faced a big white New
England house, with forest-green shutters and a friendly front
porch that ran the full length of the house. A pile of pumpkins sat
near the front door. Inside, behind parted country curtains, glowed
a warm yellow light that could only be called cozy. It was a perfect
TV commercial of a New England house. Except for one thing.

Parked in the drive, near a Volvo station wagon, a small Japa-
nese-looking thing with a hatchback, and a Jeep Wagoneer, stood
one of those cocklike, low-built, shiny black sports cars, the kind
you rarely ever see. Something with a name like Testosterone.

If it seemed odd to Hallie, it caused apoplexy in Martha. She
began screaming and jumping up and down, reaching over to
pound on the horn, to Hallie's horror.

"Oh my God, oh my God, oh my God! Stop! Stop! Just leave it
here!" And before he had turned off the motor, she had jumped
out of the car and was lifting her long gray flannel skirt above her
knees and running to the porch.

And then Hallie saw why.

Ham Housewright, pitcher, was coming down the porch steps
toward her.

Ham Housewright, pitcher, was lifting Hallie's own Martha into
his arms.

Ham Housewright was huge.

Hallie had to tell himself to get out of the car. It was an overcast
day and the air was frozen, smelling like compost, crispy apples, and
burning leaves. He walked across the graveled drive toward Martha and Ham. This is it, he thought. I am in the process of meeting
Martha's family. Here we go.

The sister and brother were so engrossed in each other that he
began to feel sheepish as he approached them, and he felt tingles
of nerves that he thought might be a sudden growth of wool.

This colossus wasn't only her brother, he was . . . *"And pitching
for the New York Mets today,* HAM HOUSEWRIGHT.*"* Hallie couldn't

get over it, it was so great to see Ham standing around in the driveway of the house in which he grew up. Hallie had met a lot of celebrities in his life, but none had ever given him the bang he was getting from this.

How many times had Hallie watched him on the mound, his face under scrutiny of the TV cameras, a study in placid venom. House-wright was known as someone who never smiled. Even when it all connected, the powerful expanse of shoulder, the mighty forearms at bat, the long legs, and he hit one of the many home runs that made his pitching even more of a miracle, Ham never smiled.

But he was smiling now, and the expanse of shoulder and the mighty forearms were wrapped around Martha. And Hallie stood there feeling sheepish.

Not for long. Martha broke from Ham's embrace and ran to bring Hallie's hand to meet her brother's.

"Ham Two, this is Hallie!" She said her brother's name as one word, as if it were Chinese or something. And she was beaming as the two men shook hands and exchanged smiles.

Hallie looked into the face of Ham Housewright, pitcher, and saw not only a broad grin, but something else the TV cameras couldn't capture. Without the cold concentration on the game, he had one of those faces that looked exactly as it had when he was five, kind of shy and innocent. The face of a five-year-old with the body of a six-foot-five man. A face that gave very little evidence that it ever had much need to be shaved. A face with a slightly upturned nose and blue eyes and a jaw almost exactly the same as Martha's. A face that gave new meaning to the word "handsome." But the face of a shy and gentle small boy. It took Hallie completely by surprise.

"It's great to meet you," said Hallie, unable to conceal his delight in the many reasons that this was true.

"Same here," said Ham, looking directly into Hallie's eyes, which was not an easy thing for someone so naturally shy to do. And he smiled even more, and he kind of nodded at Hallie as if to convey his good wishes, which were already so conveyed that the nod was, of course, superfluous. Then he looked at Martha.

"I think you better go in and see Mom. She's a little overexcited."

"Oh, great. Typical," said Martha to someone she had been exchanging intimate tones with since she was born. "My mom's all excited to meet you, Hallie. Just try and understand, she's just a little ditsy."

Ditsy? Interesting choice of word. There really is no such thing as a ditsy Jewish female. The neurosis is never quite that quaint. But at that moment, Ditsy Housewright appeared on the front porch and Hallie understood completely.

Martha's mother was untying the strings of a blue apron, an act she abandoned to throw her arms around Martha.

"Oh, you look wonderful, honey. Absolutely wonderful," said this woman with a truly beautiful, if aging, Nordic face. Here were the blue eyes that explained Ham's, the wide mouth that bloomed on Martha, and the jawline so fine it had reappeared in both off-spring. Her hair was arranged in a page boy and one side was held back in a tortoiseshell barrette. Just above and slightly below the hair clip was a smudge of flower on the graying blond hair. With her apron dangling untied and unnoticed, she kept her hands clasped neatly together. "And this must be your young man!"

"Mom, meet Hallie!"

Her whole face just lit up. She took both his hands in hers. She smiled at him through eyes that told him that Adie Housewright had concern for the well-being of every living creature on the planet.

"I'm Martha's mother!" She beamed. There was a pause. "Adie Housewright."

"It's so nice to meet you, Adie," said Hallie, yes, shyly. "How are you?"

"Oh, I'm just fine! I'm just fine!" Adie said, not a little ditsy, still beaming. "And have you met Ham Two? This is Ham Two—"

"Mom, I did that," said Martha.

"Oh, you've met! Ham Two was in town and he heard you were coming, so he ran right out here for lunch."

Hallie kept looking at her eyes. It wasn't often he ran into eyes like those. Eyes like those made sons like Ham Housewright.

"I think that's so cool," said Martha, clapping her hands together. "How long are you in New York?"

"Couple of days."

"Oh, Hammie, it's so good to see you!" said a delighted Martha.

"And look at what this naughty boy has bought himself. Just have a look!" said Ditsy, indicating the Testosterone.

"Oh, too bad!" said Martha with sisterly sarcasm. They all went over to peer into the black interior of this ramrod of an auto. Martha wanted to know if she could drive it and Ham assured her that she could, while Hallie wondered when these gentiles were going to notice that it was about ten degrees out.

And then his darling girl said, "Let's go in. It's freezing."

"Of course, let's go in. Hallie, you have to meet everyone else! Everyone's here except Glenn." And with a gesture reminiscent of a hen, Adie, her apron still dangling from her neck, moved them all toward the house.

As they passed the pumpkins near the door Hallie noticed a few brown leaves race across the wooden porch floor and rest against the pumpkins. He thought it was great. And when he entered the house, his eyes took in everything, but particularly how much family was to be found everywhere. This was the house of a family, with children who were born here and grew up here. No one entering the house where Hallie grew up could possibly tell who the hell lived there.

And then the smell hit him. A combination of roasting meat and potatoes, cloves, nutmeg, cinnamon, and apple pie. It rushed up to Hallie's nose and into his brain and sang the national anthem. Something told him this was how this house had always smelled while the family was growing up. It was absolutely patriotic.

Martha took his coat and kissed him, right in front of her mother and brother. Then she linked her arm in his and led him into a family room decorated in pleasing comfortable florals and plaids, on modest but comfortable furniture. The men in the room were all watching a college football game on TV while the women were chatting and two small children, a boy of six and a girl of two, played on the floor. But everyone looked up as Hallie and Martha, followed by Adie and Ham, came into the room.

From the corner of his eye, Hallie immediately found Martha's father. He was sitting in a well-worn leather club chair, a Scotch in hand, amply filling out a green-and-blue flannel shirt and corduroy pants. The others in the room all shouted greetings and came toward them when Hallie and Martha entered, but Hallie observed that Ham One watched for a pass to be completed on the screen. Then he got up too.

"How's my girl?" he said. And the others parted like the old Red Sea to let him get to Martha.

"Hi, Dad," she said as she received her father's hug. "Hallie, this is my dad, Ham One. Coach, this is Hallie Lawrence."

"How do you do, Mr. Housewright," said Hallie, choosing to avoid Dad, Ham One, or Coach.

"Ham, son. Just call me Ham and don't bother with any of that Ham One and Two nonsense. Anyway, that little son of a bitch isn't around often enough to get us confused." He indicated his name-sake son and laughed with great affection. Hallie didn't want to tell him that he doubted he'd ever get them confused.

Hallie noted that, as he had suspected, Ham Housewright was a large man, easily six three. What he looked like was an aging athlete. An athlete on the decline. But that was on the outside only. In his mind he ruled any playing field, anytime, anywhere. Hallie could see that in his eyes. This was the guy who, Martha had told him, once coached a jacks game she was playing with her sister.

Hallie saw challenge in Ham's eyes. They seemed to say, "Okay buddy, let's see your stuff. Starting lineup or bench warmer." There was something about his face that looked a little like a gentile version of Paul Newman.

Now came other introductions, all made over the sound of the college football game coming from the TV. He met Mimi, Martha's oldest sister, and her husband, Tim, managers of the Darling Inn. There was a rather harried quality to Mimi, as if even there, on a Saturday afternoon taken off to be with the family, she was still watching over things. She immediately asked Hallie if he'd like a drink. Tim was a bookish type (or was it just the horn-rimmed glasses?) and said "How do you do" as if Hallie were standing on the other side of a reception desk.

Or maybe it was just in Hallie's mind.

He met Virginia, Gin, as she seemed to be called, a senior in high school, a ripening but still gawky version of the beauty she promised to be. You could see from the way she composed herself that she was not comfortable in her paisley skirt and garnet-colored sweater, that she would rather be in jeans. But she looked like something from a Ralph Lauren sexual fantasy, right down to the graduated pearls she wore around her neck. This was what you had in mind, Ralph Lifshitz.

Or maybe it was just in Hallie's mind.

Then he met Calvin Wilmore Housewright, Martha's oldest brother, who was a doctor, specializing in, needless to say, sports medicine. Calvin was the oldest Housewright offspring, and Martha later explained that Calvin was really Calvin Two, but when Grandpa Calvin died, it wasn't necessary to say Two anymore. Calvin, or C.W., as everyone seemed to call him, had a pretty, dark-haired wife called Barbara, who was rather exotic-looking compared to the rest of the Rockwellesqueness of the family. C.W. and Barbara were the parents of the two children. The little boy extended his hand to Hallie, an act that required a great deal of bravery.

"How do you do?" he asked in his six-year-old voice. The resemblance to his uncle the pitcher was uncanny.

"Let me guess," said Hallie. "You must be Ham Three."

"Good guess," said Barbara. "But this is Bunker, and this is Little Martha." She indicated the two-year-old girl who had blond hair and sparkling brown eyes, not unlike his own Martha's.

Once the introductions were over, there followed several seconds where no one said a word and everyone appeared to be staring at Hallie. But after a few seconds, and it really was only was a few seconds, Ham One clapped his large hands together and spoke.

"Mims, get the young man a drink. What are you drinking, my boy?"

Who's drinking? thought Hallie. I'll just mainline some Demerol.

"Dad, I already asked him," said Mimi patiently. She headed for the bar in the corner. And a bar it was, not the collection of bottles kept in an eighteenth-century cabinet locked with a key for most of Hallie's adolescence. A real bar that you could go behind and fix drinks. And it was not only a bar, but some kind of sports altar because on the shelves were probably two hundred sports trophies and ribbons.

"Fill mine up too, as long as you're at it, Mim. Hal? Take a seat," said the coach.

Of course he called him Hal. Hallie was too faggy for a man like Ham One to take seriously. Or so Hallie thought.

"Try one of Mama's crab toasties," Mimi said. "They're so good."

So Hallie sat on the indicated plaid-covered sofa and tried one of Adie's crab toasties, which were a kind of crabmeat-and-mayonnaise concoction served on wedges of English muffin. Hallie thought they were delicious.

"These are great," Hallie said, munching away.

"Well, thank you," said Adie. "I bet they've gotten cold. They're not as good when they're cold."

"No, perfectly warm," Hallie said. "Absolutely superb."

"Superb" was not a Housewright word. Ham One never called out "Absolutely superb" to any of his players. Adie thought it sounded princely.

"I'm just going to check on my oven and I'll be right back," she announced, with a wink to Hallie for his compliment. She left the room. And then an odd thing happened. The women, all of them— Mimi, Martha, Virginia, and Barbara, C.W.'s wife—all went after her. The children settled back to their game of Leggo, or rather, Bunker returned to attempting to build some kind of rocket and preventing his sister from wrecking it.

This left the two Hams, C.W., Tim, and Hallie.

The men.

To watch the game.

"Oklahoma and Nebraska," said Hallie, quite proud of himself and grateful he had read the sports page that morning. He sipped his Jack Daniels.

"It's twenty-one to seven, Nebraska," said C.W., filling in the score for him as if Hallie had been dying to know all during the introductions but had been too polite to ask.

"Drop back, drop back, drop—" Ham One sat forward in his chair, screaming to the little players on the screen, but the quarterback was sacked. "The little bastard doesn't drop back!"

"Of course he does, Dad," said Ham Two, not without respect. "They're just not giving him any time."

"That's a goddamn piece of Swiss cheese, that's not a front line, you're right! But then you're the football man, aren't you."

With Ham Two being a Met and everything, his father's words were obviously loaded with sarcasm. There was a story behind it somewhere, but for Hallie, the most interesting story was the drill-sergeant sarcasm in Ham One's voice.

Ham Two looked over at Hallie, whose eyes must have revealed his empathy, and smiled.

"Football fan, Hal?" he asked.

"Actually, I prefer the Mets," he answered.

"Yeah, me too," said Ham Two, smiling.

"Martha tells us you went to Harvard," said Ham One. "Play any ball?"

"I played football at prep school. Exeter."

"No kidding! What did you play?"

"Quarterback," said Hallie. Ah, the fond memory of it all, that one glorious sports season of his life.

"Quarterback!" said Ham One, now totally interested in Hallie. The Michelob commercial helped.

"Well, JV."

"Why not Varsity? What happened, son?"

What happened was that Hallie had broken his collarbone, whereupon Lily had taken to her bed and threatened to die if he continued to play. He knew he would never have made Varsity anyway because while he was big for a tenth grader, he never really got much bigger. But how could he tell the coach that he stopped playing because his mother made him quit?

"I was injured," he said, tossing it off, like the romantic twang of it, figuring the subject was over.

"What happened?"

I broke my collarbone??? Suddenly, between Ham the coach and Ham the pitcher and C.W. the sports doctor, Hallie understood why Martha had pointed out the home of the family doctor. Her brothers must have lived there. A broken collarbone? These guys played with broken femurs.

But Hallie said, "I broke my collarbone."

There was silence.

He also thought of adding that he had a leg that had been so badly shattered, it had been amputated. But here he was, about to marry their Martha, and he couldn't very well tell them he only had one leg.

"I wouldn't have made Varsity, I'm too short. Who ever heard of a Jewish quarterback anyway?"

Yup, that's what Hallie said.

Ham Two was the one who laughed first and he gave Hallie a little nod. Then the others laughed, too; a laugh intending approval of Hallie's candid remark, but also a laugh of relief. The ice had been broken. The word "Jewish" had been spoken and not by one of them. Nope, it had been Hallie who now sat soaked in the spillage of his good old hysterical subconscious. Leave it to him to bring it to a head.

"So you're a lawyer, Hallie," said C.W.

Hallie regaled the men with his best law anecdotes and the whole atmosphere grew, he had to admit, increasingly easier, as the smells from the kitchen seemed to intensify.

Little did he know that the minute the Housewright men set eyes on him, they had no problem with his being a Jew. He didn't look Jewish. He was a good-looking guy. Now they could be glad he was rich.

In the kitchen, the women were standing around watching Adie remove a honey-shining glazed baked ham from her large oven.

"You're about done now, aren't you," mumbled Adie to the ham.

Mimi went to the oven. When she heard her mother's verdict about the ham, years of training and her current vocation sent her to raise the temperature so the sweet potatoes remaining inside the oven would get crisp. "He's so cute, Martha," she said.

"Isn't he?" said Martha. "God, I'm so in love with him!" She sat leaning against a kitchen stool and appeared to swoon. "Look at my ring. Look at this!"

The women stopped everything to gather around Martha.

"Lord, Marth," said Adie, taking her daughter's hand. Her Swedish blue eyes focused on the diamond. "That is one impressive ring."

"My, God!" said Virginia, looking worried. "Do you know what a ring like that costs?"

"Gin, that's rude," said Adie with swift maternal authority. She returned to her ham. "It's absolutely beautiful," she said about the ring, but to the ham.

"It is beautiful, mother," said Martha. She slipped from the kitchen stool and went to Adie and put her arms around her from behind. Ever since she became taller than her mother, this had been her favorite way to hug her. Adie patted Martha's arm, in recognition of the embrace, but continued to work on her meal. She began to lay little pieces of parsley between the diamond shapes created by the cloves. It was her theory of presentation: always use a little something green.

"God, that smells good!" said Martha.

Then the back door opened and they could see a young woman enter in a turquoise wool blanket of a coat. She tossed her long brown hair as she crossed the glassed-in vestibule where Adie kept her gardening things and the washer and dryer, and stepped into the kitchen.

"Martha, Martha, I'm so sorry I'm late!"

"Glenn!" shouted Martha with delight, and rushed to embrace the turquoise-colored wool. "Oh, honey, I was getting worried about you. God, this coat is heaven!"

"Do you like it really? I made it."

"You didn't!"

"I did."

"God, Glennie, you've gotten so good."

"I think the color's a little much, Martha, don't you?" said Virginia of the garnet sweater and paisley skirt.

"Are you crazy?" Martha exclaimed. "The color is what makes it."

Glenn took off the coat and hung it on a back-door peg. She went over to Adie and kissed her cheek. "Hi, Mama. I'm sorry I'm late."

"Well, you are," said Adie without compunction. "I'm glad you're here, but I did ask you not to be rude and come late."

"Oh, it's not rude," said Martha. "I'll take her to meet Hallie. Stop acting like he's the damned king of Europe. He's my Hallie. He's the guy I'm going to marry. He's totally cool."

Glenn looked at Martha strangely for a second. "I've got to meet this guy," she said. Then she added, "Let me see your ring. Oh, Marth, it's gorgeous! You can't walk around with that on! That's the kind of thing you put in a vault. It's huge! It's— I mean, it's not even the kind of thing you would want to wear every day."

"I haven't had any problems wearing it so far," said Martha.

"Let me meet him this minute. How's my hair? Should I comb it first?"

When Martha walked into the family room with Glenn, she found her two brothers and her father listening to Hallie telling a story. And, most important, with their backs to the game.

"Ham Two! Nobody told me you were here!" shrieked Glenn, rushing into her brother's arms.

"Didn't you see his car?" asked Martha.

"That's your car? Oh, Hammie! It thought you came in that,

Marth!" And now she looked at Hallie where he sat on the plaid sofa smiling at her. "I'm Glenn!"

"Well," said Hallie, "how do you do?" He rose to shake her hand. This sister was definitely the most like Martha. She was also a beautiful woman, with similar flare for original dress. She didn't quite measure up to Martha on either level, but she would certainly qualify as a yes to the question "Are there any more at home like you?"

"Hallie! It's so nice to meet you!" She shook his hand and then embraced him, wrapping both arms around him tightly. It wasn't exactly an unpleasant feeling for Hallie. "I have to hug you, I just do. You're going to be Martha's husband!"

Hallie thought it was a charming thing to say, but the closeness of the embrace had certainly been an additional statement.

"You happened to be interrupting us," said the coach, after receiving a hug of his own from Glenn.

"Oh, Daddy!" she said. Seeing Martha stroke Hallie's hair as they looked at each other, Glenn got her sister by her arm. "Let's go hang out alone and leave these jerks with their game."

In the front hall, Martha said to her sister, "Hallie's not a game jerk."

"I guess Jewish guys aren't too sportsy, are they?"

"Nice, Glenna. Don't start bringing it up about him being Jewish, okay?"

"Martha, it doesn't make any difference."

But once in the kitchen, Glenn took a look at the honey-glazed ham and couldn't contain herself.

"I thought Jewish people didn't eat ham," she said.

"Oh my Lord!" said Adie. "It never occurred to me, but I think you're right!" One hand slowly rose to her cheek as she stared at the ham like a sudden uninvited and gross guest.

"Don't be ridiculous. Hallie eats everything. He's not that kind of Jewish. I mean, I've made him pork chops for dinner and he ate them all up."

"Well, maybe he was just being polite," said Adie. "I think I've got a chicken casserole in the deep freeze."

"Mother! He wouldn't just be polite about eating pork chops! He would tell me. We're getting married."

"What did his mother serve, dear?" asked Adie.

"Pot roast," said Martha, recalling the brisket.

"That's sort of nondenominational, isn't it. Lord, I should have made pot roast!"

"Oh, Mom, you're being silly. Your ham's one of the great dishes of the Western world. He'll love it!"

"I suppose he would have said something to you about the pork chops if it went against his religion."

Martha looked at Glenna, who was helping herself to a corn muffin from a basket covered with a blue napkin. "Thanks a lot, Glenna."

"You shouldn't marry the guy if you're going to be sensitive about his being Jewish."

"Glenna, that's enough," said Adie. "You're already on my bad side for being late. We have no problem with Hallie not being a Christian." Adie stabbed a carving fork into the ham and guided it onto a blue-and-white serving platter. "I've heard it said that Jewish men are very good to their wives. Very kind and very generous."

"I didn't say anything! God!" said Glenna.

"Where's Lark?" asked Virginia.

Glenna turned on her younger sister.

"We had a fight, okay? We had a fight and I told him to go fuck himself, that I didn't want him to come with me today."

There was a silence. Adie glared the most no-nonsense reprimand ever glared.

"Let's set the table," said Mimi, the eldest, taking over.

Each girl busied herself with the impending service of the meal. The only sound was the tinkling of wineglasses, the clinking sound of serving silver being retrieved, the sounds of cupboards closing and drawers opening. They were respecting their mother's silence.

"If my daughter uses language like that," said Adie to the ham, "it makes me wonder where she grew up. I can't imagine it was in this house."

"Mom, you're talking to the ham," said Gin.

"That's Mom," said Martha brightly, eager to dispel the tension. "Too many Hams in her life. She can't tell them apart."

"We'll call this one Ham Three," said Adie, reassuring Martha that although Glenn had aroused her wrath, she had no intention of letting it spoil the meal for Martha and Hallie.

Martha set out the wineglasses and then went off to find Hallie. She met him leaving the den.

"Hey! I haven't seen you in twelve years," he said, taking Martha in his arms. "I'm looking for the bathroom."

"Oh, down here," said Martha, leading him to the guest bathroom behind the front stairs. "Isn't Ham Two the greatest?"

"He's such a nice guy. I mean, he's such a regular nice guy. I like him a lot."

"That means so much to me. We're the closest of anyone in the family. We're only thirteen months apart. When I was born, Mom says Ham Two somehow thought they had me for him. He used to play with me like a monkey plays with a rag doll."

"What, pick you up by the leg and throw you in the air?"

"*No!*" said Martha. "He just never minded playing with me, all through our childhood. Of course, we did make up the best games. No one else was on our wavelength. My father used to tease him about always playing with a girl."

"But what a girl."

He went into the bathroom with its old Victorian sink, wallpaper with little flowers and bunches of wheat, soaps carved to look like shells, and several yellowing prints of New England snow scenes. Martha followed him in and closed the door. She turned the lock.

"Alone at last," he said, taking the opportunity for a quick kiss.

"We didn't care what my father said," Martha whispered. "Ham was such a good athlete, my father couldn't exactly call him a sissy."

Hallie used and flushed the toilet. He was washing his hands when Martha kissed him on the ear, planting with the kiss a puff of her breath. Then they began kissing deeply, but Hallie stopped them.

"Martha, Martha, don't. How can I go out there and face your family with this?" He moved her hand over his pants. He didn't figure that she would go for the zipper, lower herself to her knees on the beige wool carpet and proceed to take him in her mouth.

Oh, Jesus, with all those gentiles in the next room?

"Martha, wait—oh, Martha." It was much too late. And what she was doing to him, despite the many times she had done it to him before, seemed a miracle. Those lips. That mouth. This angel kneeling on a beige carpet in a bathroom with little flowers and bunches of wheat.

Then he left the room completely, shot out into the space he was finding more familiar, and punched right through the cosmic lid. She slid her mouth from him and swallowed sensually, as if she were downing an oyster. Hallie leaned against the wall, breathing hard.

They heard Martha's name being called for dinner. She quickly got up and glanced in the mirror, tossing her hair into place and adjusting her shirt. Hallie was still on his knees, his trousers open, his cheeks flushed.

"I can't get up," he said. "I just died and went to heaven. Rigor mortis has set in. You'll have to carry me into dinner in this position."

Martha laughed. "Come on! I'll go out first. Oh! Hallie, tell my mom you love baked ham."

Before he knew it, she had opened the door just enough to slip out and then shut it. He struggled to his feet and leaned over the sink, gazing at his flaming cheeks and tousled hair. He splashed cold water on his face, dried his hands on a towel with satin swans on it, and did up his pants.

"That concludes our half-time entertainment, and now back to the game."

11

WITH EVERYONE GATHERED IN THE
dining room, the tantalizing smells
now revealed their sources in the
clove-encrusted ham, the steaming
sweet potatoes, the buttery muffins,
the big bowl of broccoli. Hallie listened to the animated conversation
going on all around him and he looked
at each family member and observed
their distinctive features and their
striking similarities.

What Hallie found to be most awesome was the idea that they had all
been around this table together
throughout their childhood. Eight of
them, at breakfast before school, at
dinner every night. His family had
dined together two nights a week, Sunday night at a restaurant, and one week
night at home. He had never had
breakfast with his parents on a school
day. He had breakfast with Boris.

Sitting in the dining room, hearing all the conversation, joining in it himself, Hallie felt a little ecstatic. Here was a perfect family and he had a right to be there.

Perfect family. Poor Hallie.

He did sense that the coach was a real tough number, but it didn't occur to him that this might breed heartlessness. It was possible not to notice it because Adie's saintliness seemed to remedy all.

Hallie told Adie that the ham was the finest ham he'd ever eaten and that he was crazy about ham. He thought it was cute the way she looked so relieved and started chatting away about how she hadn't been able to make up her mind, ham or lamb, but they always had lamb, so she had decided on ham. There was something about Adie that was not from this planet. She seemed to live elsewhere. She was a little bit like that actress who played Glinda, the good witch, in *The Wizard of Oz*. Billie Burke, that's who it was. That's who Adie reminded Hallie of.

He watched Ham the pitcher eating dinner with his family as if he were just a regular guy, son of the coach and Adie, brother to Martha, to whom he seemed to address anything he had to say.

And when Larken Presby arrived, the one they called Lark, the one who was married to Glenn, Hallie instantly thought he was an asshole, and a terrific snob.

"Forgive me," he said as he took his hastily assembled place at the table.

"It's perfectly all right, Lark. Help yourself, and Ham, cut Lark a slice of ham, won't you?" said Adie.

Hallie found that statement very amusing, but no one else did. Ham had been slicing ham for too long.

"Did you get all your work done?" said Glenna, pretending that's why he was late.

"My father's called a meeting for tomorrow, Sunday, which eats the royal wienie, but that's my dad."

Lark's referral to the consumption of an aristocratic body part shocked Hallie, who figured someone like Lark would know better than to use words like that in front of Glenna's mother. But he realized that it came from a deep-seated arrogance that Lark was all about. The funny thing about Lark was that he looked a lot like Kip. Maybe not as handsome, but similar. Except he was shorter, and, of course, an asshole.

"Lark's family company is Presby-Coleman," said Ham the coach, for Hallie's information.

"Really," Hallie said as his eyes met the young heir's head-on. Presby-Coleman Pharmaceuticals manufactured a lot of famous things like cough syrup and nose drops and disposable diapers and probably napalm and poison gas, things that weren't advertised with the Presby-Coleman jingle about keeping America healthy.

"Yeah, we do our best to keep America healthy," said Lark.

No, thought Hallie, he didn't really say that. He was quoting from his own family jingle? This was great. Kipper was going to love this.

Later, after the meal had been cleared and Hallie sat alone with Martha in the family room, she thought she had to tell him that Lark was pretty dumb. Hallie pretended he hadn't noticed. Lark was so dumb that in fact his father had put his two daughters on the board of directors and explained the omission of Lark by saying, "Lark, you're too dumb. You stay in the field a little longer."

Lark may have been dumb, but he wasn't happy.

"It's why Glenna is so unhappy. I don't know if you could tell, but Glenn is not having a good time married to Lark. I mean, Glenn's sort of an artist, she designs clothes and stuff, and she's married to a bozo."

"Why did she marry him?" asked Hallie naively.

"Why? Because he's Larken Presby!" answered Martha. "The Presby boys were the best catch around. I didn't happen to think so, but that was the general saying."

Hallie was too busy gazing into Martha's eyes and noticing how dark her eyelashes were, and how they touched her skin when she looked down. He was too filled with ham and sweet potatoes and broccoli, and the apple pie, ice cream, and coffee that had followed, to hear anything but a blur of Martha's sweet voice, familiarizing him with family gossip. The words weren't important. Just the sound of the sweet voice and the closeness of her and the remarkable apple pie he hoped they could get more of later, that was all he needed. Hallie began to feel sleep creeping up on him all the way from his feet.

"Ham Two really likes you," said Martha. That, Hallie heard.

"I don't think he liked it when Lark—is that his name?—when Lark asked him about the team."

"Hammie doesn't mind talking about the Mets, he just doesn't like talking to Lark. He thinks he's a real fucking jerk. I mean, all Lark really wants to do with his life is windsurf. Every day, all day long. But Hammie likes you, which is fucking amazing!" She hugged Hallie playfully.

Twice she had said "fucking" in the same breathy speech.

He thought he should maybe say something to her, but he knew there was no way he would.

"How do you know he likes me?" Hallie asked.

"He told me."

And Ham was about to tell Hallie.

The rest of the family gathered in the family room once again. The coach poured brandies and Adie brought out a dish of home-made fudge that was simply delicious. Mimi told Hallie they sold it by the box at the inn and people stopped in just to buy it. It was Adie's little industry. Adie laughed and said it was nothing of the kind, she just loved making fudge.

The fire in the brick fireplace was blazing, but the wood supply was low, so on his way out to get more wood, Ham asked Hallie to give him a hand.

The two men stepped out into the crispy frozen New England night air. A big icy white moon lit up the front drive. Ham had long, gangly strides, strides known to millions of baseball fans as the Housewright amble, filled with threatening animal grace when he was approaching a pitcher's mound. But now it was a walk in a pair of loafers, crunching across his parents' drive.

"My sister's crazy about you," said Ham shyly. "So that makes you, um, cool with me."

"You really think she is?" asked Hallie.

"Yup." Ham had led them to a shed and he opened the wooden door to reveal an impressive stash of logs. "I've seen the way she's acted around lots of different guys and she's different with you. Martha's happy. I hope we can be friends, Hallie."

Here was one of Hallie's private idols asking him if he wanted to be friends, but all Hallie heard was the part about lots of different guys.

"I guess she's always had lots of guys in her life."

"Yup," said Ham, piling wood into Hallie's arms. Couldn't he have just said, "Well, not that many"? "Everyone always wanted to go out with my sisters. All of them. But especially Moo. Hell, they still do. I never wanted anyone fucking around with her, if you know what I mean, but I always felt a little bit proud that they all wanted to. You got any sisters?"

"No, uh, no, I'm an only child."

"That must've been weird." He had piled an impressive armload of logs into Hallie's arms. "Can you handle that?"

"Sure. I can even take a few more," said Hallie, lying through his teeth as he tightened his biceps and hoped for the best. "Uh, Ham, I'm not fucking around with Martha."

"I know that, you're going to get married to her, aren't you?"

"Well, yes!"

"You're the first guy I've seen that Martha really wanted. She really wants you, Hallie. I never saw that in her face before with anyone else. She's yours." The small-boy grin came to his face

and his aquamarine eyes looked squarely at Hallie, with the
tease, but exactly the same tease, that Martha had. "A lot of guys
on the team are going to shoot themselves when they hear about
it. They're always saying 'When are you gonna bring your sister
around again, Ham?' "

The Mets?

A vision of Martha's loveliness naked on a locker-room bench,
receiving the first-rate goods of the likes of the New York Mets—
he flushed the image away.

"Most've them are married, aren't they?" asked Hallie, realizing
that he sounded like the most naive asshole of the twentieth century.

"A man can fantasize," said Ham, finding no naïveté in Hallie's
remark at all. "You better face it, Hallie. A lot of guys have the hots
for Martha. A lot of them always have. And they always will."

Yes, yes, thought Hallie, the nightmare has occurred to me, but
now it has to include the New York Mets?

"This is a very scary thought, Ham," said Hallie. He shifted his
weight, feeling his arms under the enormous pile of logs.

"I'm not telling you this to scare you, Hal. It's just a fact."

"The hell you're not, Ham," said Hallie with a particularly un-
nerving smile. It was one of Hallie's specialties, calling someone's
bluff while simultaneously endearing himself, particularly calling a
subconscious bluff.

"I guess, come to think of it, it is scary, but with a beautiful girl
like Moo, it kind of comes with the territory. I guess you just have
to stay on your toes. But she's crazy about you. She's yours." The
two men didn't speak for a moment. "I've been watching you, Hal.
You're a hitter all right. Anyone can see that."

I'm a hitter, thought Hallie. The logs were feeling suddenly
lighter. Hallie smiled at Ham Housewright, who smiled back. They
had a moment.

They left the shed with their arms full of logs and began to crunch
back across the drive.

"By the way, that's not my car," said Ham shyly. "It just drives
my dad nuts that I'm making so much money playing baseball. It
drives him nuts that I turned down the football draft." This was a
famous fact about Ham Housewright, that he could have played
either sport.

"I guess his being a football coach and everything, he wanted you
to play football."

"Yeah, that's pretty accurate. I borrowed the car from a friend.
I told Martha. She's always been in on my little jokes with Dad. He
can be the biggest son of a bitch in the world sometimes."

Worse than Alfred? What are you, nuts?

But later that evening, when everyone had departed—except for Hallie and Martha; Gin, who lived there; and Ham the pitcher, who was staying as well—Hallie sat alone with the coach, watching the eleven o'clock news.

"What does your father do?" asked Martha's father, lighting his pipe.

"He's a symphony conductor."

"Alfred Lawrence, huh," said Ham. He'd obviously been told. "Adie's a big fan of his. Has a lot of his records. She's the music fan in the family. Is he a nice guy?"

"My father?" asked Hallie with surprise. "A lot of people seem to like him, sure. He's a big football fan. New York Giants."

"Is that a fact!" said Ham with definite relief. "Imagine that." Then there was a huge pause. Ham puffed the pipe. "You're getting my best girl."

"Not only yours, sir, but maybe the whole world's."

"She's the pick of the litter. Not that I'm not very proud of them all."

"I think that's very justifiable. You have a remarkable family, sir."

The coach looked right into Hallie's eyes and sniffed around for bullshit. He found none, of course, because Hallie was much too good at it; besides, the basic sentiments were honest.

"Moo will probably tell you I was a tough father. I was. Spanked them all, including the girls, till senior year in high school. Took them right over my knee."

The image, Hallie thought, was astonishing.

"I guess you did what you had to do, Ham," said Hallie. He couldn't get over that Martha's father would even mention this. He was sitting there casually telling Hallie he was a sex pervert.

"Moo's a good girl; doesn't swear, doesn't drink. Not that she didn't have her wild days, but she seems to have come through."

What girl doesn't swear and doesn't drink? Martha? His Martha who always had some potent potable in hand after six, and who had only hours earlier said two "fucking"s in the same breath? Sure, Ham. You're right. Good observation.

"You a practicing Jew, Hallie?"

Whoa . . .

"No, sir, not really. My mother observes certain traditions out of respect for my grandfather—"

"Carl Oppenheim. He was the greatest Oppenheim of them all."

"He liked to think so," revealed Hallie cautiously.

"And it was *his* grandfather who started the investment firm, am I correct?"

"Uh, yes, he had made a lot of money during—"

"The Civil War!" The coach finished Hallie's sentence. "I was a history major, believe it or not, at Dartmouth."

"Oh, I believe it."

"Particularly twentieth-century America. Heck, I still enjoy a good history book better than anything else. Carl Oppenheim was an influential figure."

"Oh. Well, thank you," said Hallie, who was a little pleased that Ham knew who his grandfather was. This was one of the few times in his life he ever felt that way.

"What do you think he'd say about you marrying a Christian girl?"

"My grandfather died when I was ten," began Hallie. "But I think he would have understood. I think he would have seen what it is I love about Martha, sir. Plus, I also understand he appreciated beautiful women."

"But he married a fellow Jew."

"My grandmother was considered a great beauty who also happened to have been a Jew." Hallie said this in such a charming manner that Ham Housewright knew at once that Hallie was someone to be reckoned with. He was everything Ham feared about Jews, that they all sort of knew something he didn't. Hallie was a descendant of a venerated man of finance, who must have been as smart a Jew as they come. Sure, his father was a fruitcake musician, but Ham felt that Martha was in good hands. Besides, Ham Housewright hadn't been in a church since he got married.

"I just want you to know," said Ham, again striking a match to relight his pipe, "I think Martha's found herself a first-rate husband, period."

"Thank you, sir."

"Now that's out of the way, what makes you think you want to marry my daughter after knowing her for one week?"

"It's like receiving the perfect pass, and suddenly the whole field is open. You run with it, right?" God, how could he have turned it into a sports metaphor?

The coach puffed on his pipe and then his lips parted into a smile, while his teeth held the pipe. And from his throat came a sound of approval. A kind of spontaneous grunt. Finally he took the pipe from his teeth.

"I'd say that's exactly what you do, my boy." And Ham the coach laughed, but only in his eyes. "Run with it."

Finally alone in the guest bedroom, one of the most goyish rooms in which he had ever been, Hallie sat on the bed wanting Martha. She had said she could sneak down once her parents had gone to bed, which would be by eleven; once they had closed their door, they never came down until morning. That was a fact—tried and true, she'd said.

Tried and true? How many times had this been tried, to prove true? That's what he thought about as he sat on the bed, wanting Martha.

The room had a padded and silent feeling, what with all the curtains and tiny-patterned wallpaper, and wall-to-wall carpet, in rich shades of beige. He looked at the bed, with its bedspread printed with small clusters of nuts and leaves and flowers, in shades of brown, gold, and gray with a little yellow thrown in. This was the very bed in which the tried and true had no doubt been proved. Feeling decidedly nauseous at the idea, he decided to take a shower.

After he had showered and dried himself with a brown towel, he went back into the bedroom and got into bed. The sheets felt wonderful, as fresh sheets are wont to do when one has just had a shower. Hallie sat back propped against the fat pillows. He took off his watch, noting that it was eleven-fifteen, and put it on the night table. He picked up his book and clicked the switch on the bed lamp to see if the wattage increased. It didn't.

Any minute now, old tried and true Martha, old T and T herself, would sneak down.

Hallie opened his book and tried to read, but the unfamiliar surroundings, with which he so wanted to familarize himself, called his eyes from the page.

Martha grew up here. This is the house.

Hallie saw himself in a mirror with a pine frame, hanging on the wall over the chest of drawers. There he was, propped against the pillows, alone in the bed, book in hand, bare-chested. He flexed a bicep and realized he hadn't done that since Harvard and it amused him.

Then he began hallucinating.

He saw in that mirror a rearview of Martha, naked, and she was bent over him—and then the image was gone. But his heart palpitated, thinking that soon she would be in this room, in this bed, and he could watch everything they did in that same mirror. He got such a hard-on, it lifted the sheet like a circus tent.

Then came the knock at the door.

"Hallie?" whispered the voice.

Hallie hopped out of bed, hard-on first. He stood behind the door and opened it just enough to allow his whopper to do the greetings.

"I meessed you so much," he said, giving a French voice to his cock.

"Uh, Hallie, it's me, Adie."

Hallie slammed the door. Oh, sweet Jesus H. Christ on a raft, he thought. Oh no, God of Abraham, Buddha, Muhammad Ali. Please let that not have happened. Please. Take away my foot, but don't let that just have happened. Maybe she didn't see it! Hallie's thoughts went exploding. He threw on his pants and said, "Adie, come in!"

Adie Housewright entered with a steaming mug of something dark and chocolaty. She looked Hallie directly in the eye. Her serious look was not deadly, but lit by the tiniest hint of a smile. An admonishing smile, but the smile of a woman, and not a mother.

And maybe there was some distant possible chance that she hadn't seen it after all.

"I somehow get the feeling it wasn't me you were expecting, Hallie," she said sweetly, like Billie Burke. One hand drew the neckline of her pink wool robe closer together.

She saw it, all right!

"Uh, Adie," he began, about as awkwardly as anyone had ever begun anything.

"I made you some divine hot chocolate. It's my special recipe, made from dark cocoa powder and milk and sugar and Triple Sec. I thought you might like some before you went to sleep," she said, ignoring his awkwardness.

"Thanks! Uh, that's so nice of you. So thoughtful." He still could barely speak.

"Take it. Have a sip."

Hallie accepted the mug and gulped a hot mouthful, which was heavily spiked. Chocolaty and delicious, but definitely alcoholic. The warmth spread down his throat, scorched into his stomach, and reminded his heart to rewarm his veins. He found he could breathe again.

"There, isn't that better?" asked Adie. "I'm glad I added a little extra Triple Sec. I think it came in quite handy."

Again, the admonishing little smile.

There was nothing Hallie could say.

"Are you comfy in here?" asked Adie. "I hope so. It's a pretty room, isn't it? I always think a guest room should be one of the prettiest rooms in the house."

"It's a very pretty room. And comfortable! Great bed!" Great bed? Why did he have to mention the bed?

"It's new, yes. Mimi was after me for ages. She kept saying, 'Mama, you can't have such a pretty room with such an awful bed. If people can't sleep, they sure don't care about the wallpaper.' Mimi is a very sensible girl. We bought it last Christmas."

"I'm sure I'll sleep very well. That was a great dinner, Adie."

"Yes, Hallie, you told me three times." Adie smiled one of her sympathetic-with-every-living-creature smiles. "I'm very glad you're going to be Martha's husband. You see, Hallie, she's my artist. Martha loves beauty and color; it's so fitting that she is so beautiful, don't you think?"

"Oh, definitely," said Hallie, a little mesmerized. Adie had the habit of waving her hand as if she were patting bubbles in the air when she was making a point. She spoke with a dreamy quality.

"I always knew she would live a charmed life because she always saw so much beauty everywhere. And I think it's just wonderful that she found a magic prince like you."

"I love her very much," he said. It was the kind of thing you could just come out with and say to someone's mother, especially one who already thought he was a magic prince, even if she had seen his hard-on.

"Yes, I know you do, dear." Adie patted his arm and then kissed him on the cheek. "I'll say good night now. Oh, and by the way, I don't think there's a thing in the world wrong with marrying someone when it's love at first sight. I think that's just what it should be. I do hope she settles down, she's been such a wild thing. Good night, dear."

Adie closed the door behind her. For all the love, for all the lack of withholding, for all the gentleness that Adie Housewright had just expressed, there was now only one thing she had said that Hallie could remember: "wild thing." The most artistic of her children. Didn't gentiles often use the word "artistic" when they meant cheap slut? He took another sip of the powerful hot chocolate.

I do hope she settles down?

Not without trepidation, Hallie decided it might be safe to take off his pants again, and he got back into the bed. But he sat upright, not even leaning into the pillows. Suddenly, he began to think that he knew absolutely nothing about Martha, despite the fact that for an entire week he had grilled her nonstop for every detail about every day of her life as it had been before him. Now her own mother expressed hope that she would settle down. Settle down from what? Banging the entire New York Mets baseball club, including the management?

He had seen no indication so far of any wildness at all and she seemed more than delighted to be settling down. In fact, he found her delightfully homespun for a sex goddess. He hadn't detected any wildness in her, except, of course, in bed.

Except, of course, in bed?

Once again, Hallie told himself that he was obsessed, that no good comes of being obsessed, but never had he been obsessed like this before and something told him there was no way he could stop it. He picked up his book but stared again at his reflection in the mirror. The image of his cock greeting Adie at the door poked at him, but he tried to put it aside. His eyes studied the reflected mahogany headboard and footboard, and then Martha was with him again. He had an urge to tie her up, tie her to the bedposts and take her with terror in her eyes, not real terror, of course, just enough to make him feel like Attila the Hun.

Again came the circus-tent effect.

This time it was a little worse because it was the nagging kind of hard-on that had to be relieved. The threatening kind he always got that said, "Don't expect this to happen many more times in your lifetime, buddy, if you don't do something about it." The painful kind.

Then he heard someone in the bathroom.

"Hallie?" Again a whispered voice. He grabbed the covers closer around him, but soon saw Martha appear in the bathroom doorway.

"How'd you get in there?" he asked.

"Through the door. There's a door in there that leads to the pantry off the kitchen. Didn't you see it?"

"I thought it was a closet. Come over here right this second."

"A closet?" Martha laughed as she came toward him. She wore a big flannel plaid robe. "How dumb can you get? By the way, where did you get that?" she said, indicating the hard-on.

"Don't ask," said Hallie. "I've been lying here with it for days. It has a mind of its own. It answered the door to your mother!"

"What are you talking about?" She kissed his mouth, one of those unexpected French kisses.

"Well, your mother was kind enough to bring me some hot chocolate and it answered the door."

"I don't think I want to hear this." She preferred kissing him.

He undid the tie on her robe and reached in for a little exploring. His hands felt the exquisite skin that wrapped over her hips, and he reached down and kissed her right in the pubic hair. She broke from him and went to the door and turned the lock. Then she took off her robe and climbed on the bed. They sat kneeling, looking at each other for a moment.

"My parents love you. And Hammie loves you. Isn't that great?"

"Well, what's not to like? I fit right in. I guess your father and Hammie just recognize a fellow athlete when they meet him."

Martha fell over laughing.

"Wait, what are you laughing about? Huh? Why is that so funny?"

"Because you're such a good sport."

"Who's being a good sport? I happen to shoot a mean game of pool."

"Well, I could tell that by just looking at you."

"Are you trying to tell me something about my body? You don't think I have a great body?"

"Don't I?" she asked. She kissed him and Hallie watched their reflection in the mirror, real now, not a hallucination. But to be sure, he grabbed her ass with both hands and squeezed it.

It was remarkable, he thought, there's the reflection of her ass in the mirror. He had to get a mirror for their bedroom.

Life was perfect.

That was the last thing he thought before he reached the cosmic beach.

Then, as they lay together in the dark, on the tumbling verge of sleep, Hallie mumbled, "Who's your favorite Met, besides Ham?"

The next morning, everyone sat around eating pancakes, blueberry muffins, and tons of bacon.

Ham the Pitcher had to leave early because he was catching a flight to Florida. Hallie found it hard saying good-bye to him but Ham assured him he wouldn't miss the wedding for the world and that he might even bring a few of his buddies.

No, that's okay.

Glenna came by and had to talk to Martha desperately, so they went off to the family room. This gave Hallie a chance to talk to the coach and Adie, who he realized were intelligent people, once their initial nervousness had worn off.

Then the phone rang and Martha came to tell Hallie it was for him.

He followed Martha to the family room and took the call from the coach's worn leather club chair. Martha and Glenna sat off in a corner and resumed their intimate conversation. Hallie said "Hello" into the phone, expecting Lily, or maybe even Kip after all, but it was neither. That golden Russian accent of Nikki's greeted him wildly.

"Hallie Lawrence, where are you?"

"I'm not at home. Hi, Nikki, what's up?"

"Oh, Hallie, I'm so sorry to disturb you, but I've been thinking, why do I have to make a screen test?"

"They do it all the time. You've never been on film before."

"That's not true, they filmed us doing the Brahms in Vienna three years ago."

"It's not the same thing. They'll light you, they'll do your makeup, they'll take a look at your acting, and they'll know they're doing the right thing making the picture with you."

"You're sure they'll know that?"

"Aren't you?"

Hallie had slipped right into the real Hallie Lawrence with ease. He waited patiently as Nikki pondered his question.

"Of course, I'm sure! . . . Hallie?" Her voice got very soft and almost childlike. "I'm nervous. Why am I nervous? I have been performing all of my life."

"I don't know. Why are you nervous?"

"I already asked myself that question. Now I'm asking you why you think I'm nervous."

"Maybe because you think making the picture is a mistake?" Hallie was smiling.

"Oh, please!"

"Think about it."

"Never! *You* think it's a mistake? After everything you said to me? I'm talking to Alfred after all? Well, let me tell you something! I am not nervous, I am not in the least nervous, not anymore! I never felt more sure of doing anything in my life!"

"Way to go, Nikki!"

There was a pause as Nikki fell into the trap.

"You!" she said, and Hallie could tell she was smiling, too. "You are scumbag!"

"What's the Russian word for that, Nik? I'd like to retaliate."

For the life of him, Hallie could not figure out why he felt such goodwill for Nikki at that moment. Perhaps because he could be the Hallie Lawrence he was best at, right here in the Housewright family room, and it made him feel connected again. Maybe he was finding that he just plain liked Nikki. Genuinely liking people happened rarely to Hallie Lawrence.

"Was that the Russian violinist?" asked Martha as Hallie hung up the phone.

"Yes," said Hallie.

"I thought so."

"You should have told her it was you. You've met."

"I did," said Martha with a stunning smile that dashed across the room and hit Hallie in the heart. She tossed the silky hair, and still smiling, put her lips together and sent him a kiss. "I just wanted her to know who you were with, as long as she's calling you on a Sunday morning."

Such possession! How fabulous.

"That's a very sexy job you have, Hallie," said Glenna, "making actors feel better."

"She's not an actor, she's a violinist. But it is what I do for a living, you're right."

"I think that's very sexy, don't you, Moo?"

"Glenna, shut up," said Martha. "You want Hallie to think you're some kind of nympho?"

"I love a nympho," said Hallie diplomatically.

"Let's help clear breakfast," said Martha, getting up and swiftly leaving the room. "Then I think we should get going."

Glenna gave Hallie a look that was pure invitation. He pretended that she hadn't.

"What do you think of my parents?" asked Martha, dying to know. The navy-blue Mercedes was passing through the center of the town of Darling and was heading toward the Hudson River, toward the Lawrence house Martha had asked to see.

"Well, on what level? Your mother is from another planet—"

"Oh, God, that's so great! She is, she's completely from another planet."

"And I thought she was terrific. And your father is definitely . . . yes, he's—" Hallie found himself a little stymied.

"Oh, my father's a great guy. He's just an old pussy cat, really."

"He spanked you till you were a senior in high school? That's a pussy cat?"

"Oh, big deal, everybody gets spanked—there it is! I can't believe this is your house!"

"Uh, not everybody, Marth." If Alfred had tried to lay a hand on Hallie, Lily would have shot him. Lily herself had smacked Hallie a few times, and there was the throwing of the grape-juice-stained copy of *A Tale of Two Cities* at him, but actually spanked? No.

"Well, it didn't happen very often," said Martha. "I got very good at not getting caught. But Glenna sure didn't. She really deserved it every time, boy. She's still such a bitch, and Hallie, don't flirt back with her ever, and I mean it. She always flirted with my boyfriends."

"Flirting is okay. It's just flirting, Marth."

"No! You may not ever, ever, flirt with Glenna, do you hear me?" The honey-colored eyes glared at him. She was serious and Hallie thought it was adorable.

"Oh, yes sir, General, Captain, Emperor, Hitler." The car drove up the long circular drive and stopped under the carport. "Boy, you sure are jealous of Glenna."

"Fuck you!" said Martha, not a little angrily, and she got out of the car. Hallie watched her for a moment: the hair swaying down the back of a big blue sweater, those long legs in long jeans, the stride that knew exactly where she wanted to go. She was heading for the back of the house.

Hallie sighed and got out of the car.

He found her standing at the edge of the flagstone patio looking out over the lawn, down toward the pool and pool house. He came up to her and took her arm.

"Marth, what did you say to me?"

"Look, I'm sorry, okay? Glenn just pissed me off the whole weekend. She made my mom worry about making ham because you're Jewish, she flirted with you—"

"It doesn't matter. How could you say 'Fuck you' to me? How could you take a concept as wonderful as that and make it sound like a threat? Are you crazy?" Martha was staring out across the lawn, but her pout gave way to a smile. Hallie put his arms around her. "Is that a nice thing to do? Hmmm?"

"I'm sorry," she whispered as he kissed her neck. "Being with my family makes me a little crazy sometimes."

"Oh, I know that feeling." He turned Martha around so she could look out over the property and he hugged her from behind. "Down there, at the end of the lawn, is the river. There's a path to get down."

"I know. Sometimes I would sneak up that path, sometimes Hammie would come with me, and I would look at this house from right down there, just dying to know how it would feel to be up here, looking the other way. It makes me so happy."

"Well, here you are," said Hallie. He was tickled that this could make her so happy.

Martha was engrossed in the vista, taking it all in, with kind of a serious expression for someone who was pleased. She sighed. "This is where you grew up. You grew up in this house and in that apartment. You're so elegant."

"You really think so?"

"Yeah, right, really elegant. You're so goofy, that's what you are!" She had to tease him because she had given him a compliment. That was Martha's house rule.

"Um, Martha? Could you— Do you really think I'm . . . goofy? No, I mean it, don't laugh, do you think that, somewhere deep down inside?"

She was still laughing. "Yes, deep down inside, I think you're a total nerdy goofball, Hallie Lawrence. Yes. How did you guess!" She was really laughing now. It was horrible.

"If you don't stop laughing, Martha, I am going to torture you to death."

"Oh, really? How are you planning to do that?" She turned to him and put her arms around his waist. "I want to have your babies."

"I want to give them to you."

"I want lots and lots of goofy babies."

"That's it. I'm going to do it." He grabbed her to him and kissed her, and kept kissing her, and when she began kissing him back, it began to get a little desperate. Then Hallie heard a car door somewhere on the property and he stopped kissing Martha. There was always a chance it was an ax murderer. He looked up and suddenly, striding toward them, was none other than Kip.

"I thought you were an ax murderer! What are you doing here? How did you know I'd be here?" Hallie said, grinning at Kip, who wore a decrepit yellow mackintosh.

"Hey, Martha, how are you? I have the good manners to always address the lady first."

"Hi, Kip!" she said enthusiastically. She kissed him on both cheeks and told him it was great to see him again.

"Well, old boy, you told me you were going to be in Darling this weekend. I figured if I drove over, sooner or later I'd find you."

"Well, this is . . . great!" said Hallie. The ever-so-slight pause was not unnoticed by either of them.

"Isn't it?" Kip grinned at Hallie, but he looked pained, and not just from the pause, and Hallie was glad Kip had driven to Darling to find him.

They took Martha into the house and Kip conducted the grand tour of the ten bedrooms, the little studies and libraries and rooms for just chatting, the grand living room with the grand piano, and Martha just loved it all. "Oh my God," she kept saying. Hallie even got a little bang out of it and didn't feel embarrassed the way he had most of his life. Also, Kip did the tour so well, filling in little historical anecdotes, some about good old Carl Oppenheim, others about Kip and Hallie.

Then they sat around in the sun room, drinking a fine wine from Alfred's cellar, telling Martha more anecdotes about events that had happened in the house when Kip and Hallie would come down from Exeter or from Harvard. She couldn't believe that she had never met them; hadn't they ever gone out for pizza?

"I worked at Emilio's. You guys never came to Emilio's? It was the best pizza in town."

"Hallie, how come we never went out for pizza?"

"Too normal!" said Hallie. "If we wanted pizza, Lily had the cook make one. What was that cook's name?"

"It wasn't Emilio," said Kip.

"I think it was Bertha, that German woman."

"Actually, she made great pizza," said Kip.

At that moment Kip looked at Hallie and Hallie looked at Kip and Hallie could see in his best friend's eyes that something was really wrong.

They decided to have a late lunch before returning to the city, so they found themselves at the Darling Inn, where Mimi fussed over them and Kip told Hallie and Martha that he had left Kate for a few days. He had just gotten into his car and told her he would see her in a few days. Kate had cried and Kip hadn't looked back but it had damned nearly broken his heart. Martha cooed sympathetically and Hallie felt very glum. Here he was about to marry the best girl in the world and his best friend was in trouble with his wife. It would put a damper on things.

Kip came back to New York with them and spent the night on the sofa.

12

OBSESSION WITH MARTHA'S PAST
was beginning to influence Hallie's
forward motion, to say the least. He
tried to ask himself why it was happening, but before he could answer, he
forgot the question.

Around noon on the Monday after
the weekend at Martha's parents', he
received a call from Andy Werdlow
on the coast. The screen test had
been scheduled and Hallie and Nikki
would be flying out in the morning.
They'd all have dinner tomorrow
night on the coast. Sensational. Andy
might have a terrific announcement
to make then. Terrific. Hallie never
inquired what the nature of the announcement might be.

Andy noticed that Hallie didn't ask,
and it made ending the conversation a
little more nerve-racking for him. Not
that he would have told him. But at

least the guy could've asked what kind of announcement it was. Hallie Lawrence wasn't cool, the guy was an iceberg.

By the end of that conversation Hallie was already bored with Andy Werdlow and he hadn't met him yet.

Hallie called Martha, whom he had left at home with Kip.

"She's out shopping," said Kip. "I'm the houseman. Can I help you?"

"Want to have lunch?"

"Hobnobbing with the servants, Lawrence? I'd love it. But I can't. I'm going to visit Clara and Dickie."

"How exciting for you," Hallie said, smiling, easing back into his desk chair. Clara and Dickie were Kip's parents.

"Got to keep track of your parents, although it's pretty senseless since you lose them in the end anyway. They called. They're in town, old boy. Holed up at the Carlyle."

"How did they find out you were in New York?"

"Kate told them, which was a little much, don't you think?"

"Is that why they're here? To talk to you?"

"Are you nuts? My parents come to New York to talk to *me?* They're here anyway. They're here to Save Library Books From Getting Into the Hands of the Public, or something like that. Some benefit— Oh, look, Martha's just walked in. She just got back. Appreciate the invite to lunch, old boy. By the way, you're so˙ fucking lucky."

Hallie heard Kip's voice, muffled, calling Martha to the phone. It warmed his heart to think of those two together at his house. He wanted to be there too. Then Martha got on the phone.

"Hi! I went shopping and I got the greatest suit!"

"Oh, yeah?" He loved the enthusiasm in her voice. "You know what? Get over here around six o'clock. Just get dressed up and come over to my office. We'll go out and have a drink or some-thing."

"God, is that romantic or what."

Lisa looked up from her desk and felt her mouth slowly crank open as Martha came walking toward her. Who was this and how could she keep her from whatever appointment she had with Hallie?

"Who can I say is here to see him?" her red lips asked.

"Martha," answered this goddess with the warmest of smiles. But the warmest of smiles had no effect on certain kinds of women who met Martha, and Lisa was one of those women.

"Martha? Just a minute." Lisa efficiently picked up her phone, but her eyes followed the shoes, black suede, the dark stockings that had a sheen to them, the magnificent mink coat, the hands pulling off woolly gloves and thus revealing a magnificent diamond ring. "Oh dear, I see he's on a call, Martha. Can you wait just a minute?"

"Sure! No, wait a minute, he's on a call? That's so cute! I have to see this!"

Martha walked breezily toward Hallie's office door as Lisa jumped up from behind her desk.

"Excuse me, you can't just go in there."

"Shhhh!" she answered with a conspiratorial girl smile totally inappropriate in a place of business, and totally lost on Lisa.

Lisa knew one thing now: Martha was not a client.

"I'm not kidding, you can't just go in there," said Lisa, but her voice trailed off as Martha opened the door and walked right in. Lisa followed quickly and stood dumbfounded as she saw Hallie beam broadly at the sight of Martha, who went and sat in his welcoming lap. Lisa also saw that even as Hallie spoke on the phone, he pulled back Martha's dress and caressed the skin between her stocking and garter belt. Lisa quickly retreated.

To her desk.

To the ladies' room.

To a booth, where she could close herself off and curl up.

It's temporary, she told herself, before she started to feel the tears pouring out of her eyes onto her stunned, emotionless face. He met her somewhere and they're having a little affair. You don't get serious with bimbos like that, and she has to be a bimbo. Even Hallie Lawrence is entitled to have an affair with a bimbo, but God, it's so beneath him. Be steady, be Katharine Hepburn.

When she got back to her desk, Hallie's office door was closed. Pretending not to, she listened with all her might as she passed. She heard nothing, then a sound that, though muffled, was unmistakable. A male groan. A male, groaning, "Oh, Jesus."

She went to her desk and sat down and found herself looking at a legal pad and she began typing, without any idea what the words in front of her meant.

About five minutes later, Hallie and Martha came out. He was putting on his coat, while she held his scarf.

"Oh, Lisa, have you met Martha? I'm sure you two will be talking on the phone often enough. This is almost Mrs. Hallie Lawrence."

Hot needles sprayed against Lisa's forehead.

"You're kidding," Lisa managed to say. Then she reminded herself to smile. "This is sudden."

"That's what everybody says," laughed Martha with terrific congeniality.

Lisa nodded. She watched them leaving the office and called out a little weakly, "Congratulations."

Lisa sat very straight and hardly moved. She was stunned. Hit on the head. Out for the count. A total KO. Because Martha was exactly the sort of girl you were afraid might be with someone like Hallie Lawrence. That fabulous. Lisa was overtaken. A thoroughbred had hit the track and left Lisa in a puffy gust. There was no competition.

Martha did that to women.

Lisa wondered if she could work for Hallie any longer.

That night her best friend, Lori, came over, and Lisa cried while they ate M&Ms and frosted banana cake, about the most unthoroughbred thing a girl could have done.

Martha wanted to have a drink at a hotel cocktail bar, something she considered a very Manhattan thing to do. And she wanted the hotel to be The Plaza. As they walked along, Hallie suggested that maybe they go somewhere where they could get married on the spot, like Nevada. Martha asked him why he didn't want to have a wedding.

"God, what kind of wedding?"

"The kind where I can dress up like a bride."

"Is that what you want?"

"Yes! When I was a kid I used to put a half-slip on my head, you know, put the elastic around my head, and play bride. I always wanted to dress up like a bride when I got married. I wanted to have a real wedding."

How could he possibly explain to Martha what kind of nightmare a real wedding would be once Lily took control? He did it badly.

"Aw, Martha, we don't want to go through all that."

So Martha shrugged and terminated the conversation. She didn't exactly sulk, but Hallie thought she seemed a little less happy than usual. Once inside the Oak Room, with several martinis in him, Hallie thought a little wedding might be nice after all, and it had the desired affect. Martha was as happy as ever. They would just have to keep it small, that was all. She said they had to keep it small or her mother would invite her three hundred thousand aunts and cousins.

So they happily agreed to have a little wedding after all and Hallie noticed Martha had a way of getting what she wanted. They were just sitting in the Oak Room, thinking how beautiful everything in the whole world looked, when in came Alfred.

He came in with Ace Newbald, a highly regarded musicologist whom Hallie had known most of his life. Alfred loved old Ace, but of course he secretly thought he was full of shit.

"My son!" gasped Alfred as he approached the table, his camel coat a mantle on his shoulders, his scarf too long and too white.

Hallie rose because Alfred's arms were open and he had little choice. After the embrace, he shook hands with Ace and then introduced him to Martha, whose hand Alfred was kissing.

"You're getting married? Mazel tov!" Ace Newbald said, reverting from highly regarded musicologist to old Jewish person.

"Will you look at my daughter-in-law-to-be?" crooned Alfred. "Just take in the beauty of it. You are looking at a rhapsody."

"I'm looking," said Ace Newbald, and he too kissed Martha's hand. "What a pleasure, Martha. I've known Hallie all his life."

"Really," said Martha, entering in the spirit of things.

"Well, we're here on business, so we'll take leave," said Alfred. "Ace wants to pick my brain for a piece on the Beethoven Late Quartets."

"Well, Ace, you couldn't do better if you spoke to Beethoven himself," said Hallie. It seemed like a nice thing to say. He knew the truth was that if Alfred and Beethoven were in the same room being interviewed about the Late Quartets, Beethoven wouldn't get a word in.

"You're off to L.A. tomorrow?" said Alfred as an aside to Hallie.

"That's right; Nikki's doing the screen test," he said.

"Screen test, huh," Alfred said, giving Hallie a dark look. "Letting this go a little far, aren't you?"

In that moment, right there in the Oak Room, where everything had just looked so beautiful, Hallie realized the full extent of Alfred's expectations; he still wholeheartedly believed Hallie would put a stop to Nikki's film career. Just the other night he had said he wanted to hear nothing more about it, but now here he was, telling Hallie he was letting things go a little far. Hallie realized that Alfred was a crazy person. Hallie was looking into his father's face, aware of the Bay Rum after-shave, and had no desire to accommodate him. Alfred had lost his influence, and in that moment, right there in the Oak Room, it struck Hallie as monumentally pleasant.

"They want to do a screen test," said Hallie, with his best charming bad-boy smile, "but they assured me it was just a formality."

Alfred fixed his wild and hairy eyes on Hallie. "It's wrong!" he announced with conviction. Maybe the Huns had had conviction like Alfred's, but not too many modern people.

They said good-bye and Ace Newbald and Alfred Lawrence went off, following the genuflecting maître d', who had been hovering at a polite distance during this interval to table-hop.

"Your father's so great, isn't he," said Martha.

"So . . . great?" repeated Hallie. He studied her like a lab animal for a moment.

"I think he's so sweet and charming and he's kind of sexy, in a way." Her wide smile beamed at him, the honey eyes sparkled with innocence.

"No. You're wrong on every count, Marth. Please, he's not sweet." It took his breath away. "That is not what Alfred is. And God, he's not sexy, please don't say that."

"You're wrong. It's just because he's your father."

"Would you describe the coach as sweet?"

"Sure. I told you, he can be a real pussy cat."

How could Hallie be the one to inform her about the subconscious and its variety pack of manifestations, when she had done so gloriously well up to now without acknowledging it?

"Hmmm," was Hallie's only comment.

"You're pissed off at your father about the movie thing with Nikki. When you're not pissed off at him anymore, he won't bother you."

"Martha," he said gently, "it has nothing in the world to do with the movie and with Nikki. It goes back a little farther than that."

"You just don't want him telling you what to do. It's completely normal, Hallie. Let's have another drink. Let's have twenty more drinks!"

Well, so much for having to explain the subconscious to Martha. As long as you're accurate, who cares how you get that way? In time, Hallie would learn that accuracy was what Martha was all about.

13

WAKING UP IN HOTEL ROOMS NOR-
mally gave Hallie a certain sense of
anxiety at finding he wasn't at home,
but waking up in a hotel room with
Martha gave him palpitations. He surfaced from his sleep identifying at once
that he was in the Bel-Air Hotel, but
without rolling over to check, Hallie
knew instantly that Martha wasn't in
the bed.

That was it. She was gone. But then
he heard the toilet flush.

He figured the odds were that it
must be Martha, and probably not one
of those murderers who shoot people
on the freeways, so she was still real,
and had actually come with him to Los
Angeles.

Hallie noticed that there was too
much sunshine in the room. The early-
morning air was coming in warm and

heavy. It was the too-much sunshine that gave it away. He was definitely in L.A.

Hallie hugged a pillow to him as he lay covered only by a crisp sheet, and his mind wandered. He closed his eyes and saw the muddy black sky over L.A. at night and his heart palpitated again. Jesus, Martha.

He pushed away the image and thought about the airport, JFK, where Hallie and Martha had met up with Nikki in the Sky Club.

Nikki had looked so cool, like some modern-day white lady who sings the blues. She was all dressed in black, in a black suit with black Persian-lamb trim, black sunglasses, and an elegant Parisian black hat on top of the amazing curls of red hair. Next to her was her violin case and her hand left it only when she rose to kiss them each on both cheeks. She gave Martha a little hug as well.

"I hear you are getting married to Hallie. It's great news. Here, sit down next to me, we can talk and get acquainted. You must be very special if Hallie picked you."

What struck Hallie as odd was not only how gracious Nikki was, but how completely unfazed she seemed at his arriving with Martha. He hadn't told her he was bringing Martha. Maybe she had just assumed he would. She hadn't registered the least bit of surprise.

During the flight, Nikki sat with Martha, engaged by her as if Martha were a toy that had been brought along to keep her amused. And Nikki was amused by Martha's natural girlish intimacy, which made Nikki feel completely at ease. Hallie sat behind them, working, but occasionally he leaned forward and strained to listened to the intimate chatter.

"I took cello for six months," Martha was telling her. Oh, my. "It was really hard. Playing the violin must be even harder."

"Nah," said Nikki. "You're tall. Is it hard for you to be tall? It is no harder for me to play the violin."

"You're kidding! I never thought of it that way. God, Nikki, you're terrific! I'm so glad to know you."

"Likewise. Listen, we can go shopping in Los Angeles if we have time. You never know what we might find."

"Oh, definitely, if you're not busy all the time, that would be great!"

It warmed the cockles of his heart, which had probably never had that experience before. He was as glad that Martha was getting on with Nikki as he had been that Martha liked Kip.

A ridiculous limousine, courtesy of the studio, awaited their arrival, with a driver who was MTH, Much Too Handsome. But it was the driver stealing glances at the redheaded mad Russian, and

the girl with the twenty-five-mile-long legs, that made Hallie see
the odd image of it all. He was in Los Angeles, ludicrously hot for
late November, getting into a limousine with two gorgeous babes.
It was a male dream come true. Hallie almost felt embarrassed. But
"almost" is the key word. He was so fond of these women, he was
having a good time anyway.

Something had happened during that flight, during the ride in
the limousine, at Pink's the hot-dog stand, where the driver had
waited while they ate, during the nightcap they had back at the
hotel. Martha and Nikki had become very close. Buddies. And it
was a heady experience for Hallie.

"That's a scary face," Nikki had said as an incredibly made-up
ultra-blonde passed their table in the bar.

"These women wear so much makeup," said Martha. "Some of
them would be pretty without it."

"Incredibly Made-Up Ultra-Blondes," said Hallie. "IMUUB."

"Moob? Like a cow?" Nikki asked, laughing.

"Yes, kind of a cow, yes," said Hallie.

"I like cows," said Martha. "Don't talk of cows in a pejora-
tive way."

Hallie remembered saying good night to Nikki, and putting his
hand on the back of her head as she hugged him.

Then the dark sky over L.A., and Martha's gaspy breathing.

Now the room was filled with too much sun.

Somewhere outside the French doors, from way off in the thick-
air distance, came the sound of a buzz saw. Some landscaping was
going on somewhere out there, or else someone was being chopped
up, Hallie wasn't sure. Then the buzz saw stopped and the silence
returned.

He was glad they had come to the Bel-Air. It was a very pleasant
hotel. Usually Hallie stayed at the Beverly Wilshire because it was
in a tall building, and once inside, you could pretend that you
weren't in L.A. But a few times during his youth he had stayed at
the Bel-Air with his parents and had thought it was a very nice
hotel.

Holding his pillow, he closed his eyes against the sun-drenched
room and suddenly saw the dark sky, heard the sound of Martha's
breathing.

Mulholland Drive. That's where he had taken her.

After depositing Nikki in her room for the night, he and Martha
had taken a drive in the Mustang convertible Hallie had ordered
to be delivered to the hotel.

Once out of Bel-Air, they had turned up Beverly Glen and
driven out along Mulholland Drive. They had the top down and

God, the sight of her drove him crazy. With the wind blowing her hair high behind her and her sculpted profile outlined against the night, she looked like an ornament that should be sitting out on the hood.

Martha had loved it all, the wind, the few stars that managed to shine through the muddy air, the billions of stars that shone across the San Fernando Valley. And Hallie, cornball that he was, saw the stars in her eyes as Martha took it all in. She announced that Mulholland Drive was the only street in L.A. worth living on, if you could afford it. "This is truly gorgeous," she had said. Then she made him pull the car over onto the narrow shoulder of the road. When the engine stopped, a great stillness took over, far removed from the muffled sound of distant traffic.

"It's so beautiful, isn't it? This probably isn't true, but they say that Steven Spielberg stood on his head and looked out there and decided on the model for the spaceship in *Close Encounters,*" she said.

"You're kidding! What an asshole." Hallie didn't really mean that. He actually thought Steven Spielberg looked like someone who might be his friend. Standing on your head and looking at the Valley and deciding it looked like a spaceship was very much something Hallie would do, but only with Kip. Never in front of a girl. And God help him if it ever became a story people repeated in cars as they looked out over the Valley.

"Oh, I think that's kind of a nice story, if it's true," said Martha. "That's the kind of thing you would do, Hallie."

Wait a minute.

But suddenly Martha began unbuttoning her blouse. She opened it to her waist and sat there exposing those magnificent breasts in that cleavage machine of a bra. It took his breath away. Then she pulled her skirt up, exposing stockings, garter belt, the works, and removed her panties.

"I'm going to fuck your brains out," she said, coming at him with her mouth. Her lips brushed him.

"Should, um, should I put up the top?"

The only sound was the jangle of her two gold bracelets as her hand was undoing his belt, unzipping his pants, finding maybe the biggest hard-on he'd ever had in his life. The issue of putting the top up died. Her mouth was on him now. Hallie remembered opening his eyes on the verge of explosion, thinking this time would be it, this time he would actually leave the planet, shoot out there, and Martha would be left sitting in a Ford, alone. This was definitely the best.

And then she stopped. She straddled him and, semicomatose, he

watched her lift her skirt till it covered only her hips, as she lowered
herself onto him. Slowly. So slowly that no matter how hard he
tried to hold it in, he couldn't. He pulled her down hard and shot
beyond the muddy sky and way past the stars. He was so jolted
beyond anything resembling a familiar experience that he cried out,
"Jesus."

The Mustang fuck. That's what she had called it. It came to him
now and he pulled the sheet over his body and tried not to worry
about her choice of words.

The bathroom door opened and she came out, and for the first
time he saw Martha in a bathing suit. His eyes widened. When she
was nude she didn't look this naked. She wore a simple one-piece
black number, but cut so high up the sides that most of her ass was
revealed. The legs had picked up another ten miles. The small hips
made the broad shoulders even broader, and the breasts were two
ripe fruitful swellings, very revealed.

"What's that?" asked Hallie, slowly sitting up.

"This is a bathing suit, Hallie. You wear it to go swimming."

"Oh, swimming! Of course!" He got out of bed and came toward her.

"And that's what I'm going to do, go for a swim. We have time,
breakfast is at eight-thirty, right?"

"You have time, but isn't it chilly? It's November." He was
circling her, taking it all in.

"Are you kidding? It's seventy-five degrees out there."

"Well, seventy-five isn't hot, not really." He stopped circling and
simply stared. "Where do you get a thing like that? Is that Freder-
ick's of Hollywood or something?"

"I bought it in France, years ago. You like it?"

"Like it? Your whole body is hanging out, Marth." He ran his
hands over exposed parts.

She draped her arms around him and played with his hair. "You
put a suit on, too. A nice swim will put you in a good mood all day."

"There's really no need to improve my mood." He kissed her.
"I have to call my office. It's already ten-thirty in New York."

She put on a terry robe provided by the hotel and headed toward
the door.

"Good. Wearing the robe is a good idea. Maybe you should wear
it in the water. I don't think you want to take that off outside this
room."

"Call your office and come for a swim!"

He walked her to the door of the room, not at all sure he could
actually let go of her arm and let that body in that bathing suit go
out in public. He felt absolutely no sense of noblesse oblige when
it came to offering a display of Martha.

But he did let her go, with a silly grin, and ran to call his office. He would just make sure everybody was under control and quickly join her. Maybe there would be nobody up this early to see Martha.

He spoke to Lisa, feeling much goodwill toward her competence, and he said so. Lisa, having recovered from the news of Hallie's impending nuptials, had adopted a fresh point of view. She decided he was simply going through his first wife. When the marriage hit the rocks, Hallie would start spending long night hours at the office, and she would be there, dazzling him with competence.

Everything at the office was under control.

Abundant bougainvilleas spun fuchsia-colored petals into the morning breeze, Hallie thought, in a literary kind of mood as he walked toward the pool. The sweet, heavy air, fragrant with lush foliage maintained by warm Mexican hands and the warm California sun, kept people from realizing what they were actually breathing. The atmosphere of Eden is what you get when you stay at places like the Bel-Air Hotel, the impression that things are really, after all, not as bad as people are saying.

As Hallie walked, thinking about the foliage and how money bought deception, the pool came into view and with it Martha, pulling herself from the water in one fluid movement, wet and wearing that bathing suit. She didn't see him, but he watched those legs as she walked back toward the diving end. Those legs were poetry in motion.

My wife, thought Hallie. She's going to be my wife.

Martha passed by a young man smoking a cigar sitting in a pool chair, and she spoke to him. He laughed and said something back. She continued walking toward the edge of the pool.

My wife just talked to that schmuck with the cigar, thought Hallie.

So he walked past the man Martha had spoken to, to get a closer look. Hallie, with his inbred hotel-guest manners, nodded. The man, probably Hallie's age, with "Miami Vice"–style hair on his head and cheeks, puffed his cigar into the early-morning air.

"Hello," he said to Hallie.

"Morning," said Hallie, passing him. He noticed the man was reading a script and that the Hollywood trades were conspicuously laid out before him. Hallie walked on a little farther and chose a chair of his own. He looked over at Martha.

She was poised for a dive, which she executed with her inborn athletic ability. It was a marvel. Every muscle in her body had moved to one command, and with one graceful slice she entered the water. Not a ripple. Really, hardly a ripple at all. She surfaced and swam like something born in water. It was sensational. At the other end, she pulled herself from the pool as if this exit were just another fluid stroke.

As she walked toward him, Hallie knew the man with the cigar was watching that body.

"That was better," he said to her.

"Thanks, Steve," said Martha.

Steve? She knew him?

"Hallie!" she called, seeing him now for the first time. She came to him and draped her wet body on top of him. The shock of her cold wetness made him want to cry out, but he didn't feel like showing what a wimp he was in front of Steve. Besides, there was something fabulously exciting about it. He held her to him.

"Water cold?" he asked.

"Not if you just dive in. It's great!"

"Who's Steve?" he whispered, trying to sound nonchalant.

"Oh, just some guy who tried to pick me up. Wrap your robe around me," she whispered, enclosing herself in with him. "See, Hallie Lawrence? You can't leave me alone for one minute."

"That's nice." His consternation was blatant.

She wrinkled her nose at him. "You jerk. He was diving when I came out here and we started to talk about diving, that's all."

"You were talking about diving? He was definitely trying to pick you up."

"He was just a friendly guy. People in California are notoriously friendly. I was being friendly back."

"So you're saying that you're going to talk to every guy who tries to pick you up because you're just being friendly back? Interesting news, Marth."

"Only in California. I promise." Straddling him, she squeezed water from the ends of her hair onto his chest. "Will you get in the pool!" She kissed him and got up. "I'm going in to take a shower. Don't come back until you've taken a swim. Cool off, dearie."

Dearie? She said it just like Adie.

She put on her terry robe and walked off.

Steve watched her walk away and then he spoke to Hallie over the five lounge chairs that separated them.

"Jesus Christ," he said, indicating Martha. "What a piece of work!"

Hallie didn't know what else to say, so he thanked him.

"You in the biz?" asked Steve.

"Uh, I'm a lawyer," said Hallie.

"Show-biz lawyer?"

"Uh, no," said Hallie, with one of his amiable-enough smiles. He got up and took off his robe. Suddenly under the water was where he wanted to be.

"I'm looking for a good show-biz lawyer. Steve Gross. How do you do?"

"Nice to meet you, Steve," said Hallie and he dived into the pool without even testing the water with his foot.

Once back in the hotel room he heard Martha's words ringing in his ears, "You can't leave me alone for a minute." Knowing full well she had been teasing, Hallie was still hard-pressed to dismiss the idea. He was actually relieved to see her come from the bathroom, in a sheathlike short light-blue linen dress, alone. Hallie stared at her.

"You look great," he said, but with an undertone of despondency.

"Look what came for us."

On the coffee table was one of those baskets of fruit and fancy crackers and custom-size cheeses, all tied in cellophane. Hallie looked at the card with little interest.

"From the studio." He let it drop back to the table, and he slumped onto the sofa.

"What's wrong?"

"Me? No, everything's great!"

"You're such a liar."

"I just found out I have to hire armed security guards to keep men away from the woman I'm going to marry, but I'm getting used to the idea. It's nothing." He smiled a kind of manic little smile at her.

"Oh my God, you really can't take teasing at all, can you!" Martha said it as if it were the greatest piece of news she had ever heard. She laughed out loud. "That's so fabulous! You never had brothers and sisters. Mind you, you sure can dish it out."

"I can take teasing."

"God, is this going to be fun!"

"Martha, stop it!" implored Hallie. "It's not fun, okay? I have a problem; I have a feeling I'm maybe going to be a little psychotic when it comes to jealousy and you, but it's no big deal, I'll work on it."

"Oh, baby, I shouldn't have teased you." She was all over him, suppressing the giggles. "Hallie, listen to me, and I mean it. I'm crazy about you, nuts, out-of-my-mind crazy. This is mad love, Hallie. And there's no guy on the planet who could take me away from you, got that? There are no longer any other men in the world. There's you, and then there's all these other humans who wear trousers and shave. Got it?"

"This is fabulous news."

"I'll give you a little time to get used to it, but I've been with guys who were jealous before. Don't do it, Hallie. There's no reason. Not you."

"I'll never be jealous again." Hallie knew that was one of the biggest lies he had ever told. And he noticed that her little statement "I've been with guys who were jealous before" had a deeper sting than the jealousy he had felt about Steve, who was such an obvious asshole.

"You just can't get into a whole routine every time some guy talks to me."

"I'm a jerk."

"That's for sure."

There was a knock at the door.

Nikki stood looking at herself in the mirror. She was dressed in a French linen suit that was an old-fashioned cream color, the color people have always worn in the tropics, not white. She had bought the outfit in Paris the previous spring. It looked wonderful with her hair, and had become her favorite thing to wear in warm places. With it she wore shoes of cream-colored suede with a kicky old-fashioned shape to the low heel. But Nikki wasn't looking at her clothes.

Absently she ran her fingers over her hair, pulled it back, and held it for a moment. She was thinking. Then she picked up her violin case, opened it, and tuned the violin quickly. She played a short passage from a Bach sonata and then put the violin away. She locked up the case, took it with her, and left the room.

As Martha opened the door to admit a waiter with a trolley, she saw Nikki in the cream suit with her violin case.

"You look fabulous!" cooed Martha. "You look like a glamorous movie star. It's perfect!"

"Good. I'm glad you think so." Niki entered their hotel room.

"You do look great, Nik," said Hallie. He was looking her over, trying to decide what it was that made her look so special. Nikki looked timeless.

That was what he saw in her face, timelessness. Nikki's face could have been found in any century. Martha had said that about *him,* thought Hallie. He hadn't really thought much of the concept, but now he saw it in Nikki's face. She was a beauty in her own right.

"Well, thank you," Nikki teased. "I'm so glad you approve of me."

"I think you look perfect. Have some coffee. I wanted to have a few minutes with you before the meeting." Hallie was suddenly in a very good mood.

"Black with sugar, darling," Nikki said, settling on the sofa. The way she said "darling," the slight exhaustion in her term of endearment, reminded Hallie again of his Russian grandmother.

"I'll pour the coffee," said Martha. "You two go ahead and talk."

"Nik, there's a couple of things we should discuss before we meet with these guys. Now, whatever you hear me say, don't contradict me."

"Who contradicts you? When did I ever contradict you?"

"I may have to say some things that will appear that we are not completely sold on the idea of you doing the picture."

"I can't believe you're telling me this."

"I mean, basically let me do the talking at this meeting. You can talk about fiddle playing and stuff but not the film—"

"You're so funny," said Nikki, accepting her coffee. Martha sat down on the sofa and slipped off her shoes as if wearing them when it wasn't absolutely necessary was simply not something she did.

"Why am I funny, Nikki?"

"Because you think I'm an idiot. When have I ever contradicted you?"

"No, no, but if they're going to hire you to make a film, they must understand exactly who it is they're hiring. You can't appear too eager. Remember, without you there is no film worth making. They'll have to hire some actress who the whole world will know isn't really playing the violin, and it'll stink. With you, there's a possibility for them to do magic. Just remember that."

Nikki's forehead knitted into two lines as she thought it over. "Why do you think I don't know how to behave in negotiations? You're afraid if you pretend to the movie people that I'm not so interested, then I will think it's Alfred making you say it."

Of course, that was exactly what Hallie had been worrying about. It was too bad that Hallie Lawrence couldn't have been more direct about it, but that wasn't his way. Nikki didn't have that problem.

Nikki started laughing. "You are behind me a hundred percent, Hallie. I know that, now you get used to it. I will be perfect."

She was poking around in her cream-and-black pouch bag for something. A small bottle of elegant-looking scent.

"Martha, this is for you. It's the perfume you liked on the plane. I get this in Paris. I always buy a couple of bottles."

"God, Nikki, that's so nice!" Martha took the vial and sniffed at it. "Mmm, it's wonderful," she said, putting some on her wrist. "What do you think, Hallie?"

He thought it was an aroma that smelled clean, with just a hint of exotic Sahara nights.

"That's nice," he said confidently. He had smelled a lot of perfume in his time, including that one, on Nikki. He was still wondering how he could have been so transparent in Nikki's eyes.

Martha had gotten up and was hugging Nikki and they started talking about the shop where the perfume was sold, and Hallie was not surprised that Martha knew of it, she read a lot of magazines. He watched them as he sipped his coffee, occasionally interjecting his own comments, occasionally receiving reassuring looks from Nikki that he didn't quite understand.

Then he got up to get his briefcase. It was time for breakfast.

The hotel dining room was filled with breakfast-meeting people from the film business and rich-looking folks from Midwestern cities. Hallie politely walked a few steps behind Martha and Nikki as they approached the maître d', who was speaking with a man who wore black Weejuns and white socks. Hallie knew who it was at once.

"Andy Werdlow," Hallie said, extending his hand.

"Yes?" said the man, aloof as if he were the king of Europe.

"Hallie Lawrence! Andy! We meet at last."

"Hallie!" He took the extended hand and shook it, all best-buddies-for-life smiles now. "This is a pleasure! And Nikki Mikhailovitch. You look wonderful!" He offered Nikki a kiss. His eyes went next to Martha, and he couldn't quite control himself when he saw that face. For a flashing instant, his eyes widened. It was a little William Buckley-esque.

"This is Martha," Hallie said. Suddenly, he was incapable of announcing that her last name was not yet Lawrence.

Andy introduced his assistant, a young woman named Kimberly Cohen, who wore her hair in a high pony tail like Pebbles of "The Flintstones." She was really honored to meet them all. She looked like one of those women who try to seem very capable, very smart. But somehow the Pebbles hairdo, accompanied by the jangling of a lot of intentionally crappy jewelry, countered her intended impression.

"We got the booth, right over there," said Andy, hinting that the table at which they were about to be seated had some moronic significance.

As they walked through the dining room, Hallie looked Andy over. Black Weejuns and white socks. Khaki pants that were much too wide. A blazer cut in this year's cut, and a shirt that Hallie thought might be Polo. It was Misguided Preppy. Hallie stored the information for future reference. He also noted that Andy was the kind of person who practically had to kill himself to fend off a weight problem, because even though he was trim, he seemed fat.

His face had that pork-like look when he smiled. It was something about the cheeks.

They ordered coffee before ordering breakfast. Then Andy turned his attention to Nikki.

"Nikki, now that I'm sitting here with you, I have to tell you how exciting this is for me. You meet a lot of talented people in this business, but for me, meeting you is an event. It will go down in my life as one of the rare great things that ever happened to me."

"Well, thank you so much," she said, smiling a White Russian smile.

"I've been listening to your Prokofiev Violin Concerto. But I always go back to the Brahms. That's all I listen to on my Walkman when I jog, classical music, and, for a long time now, your tapes."

Nikki took this in for a beat, her eyes sparking mischief. A quick exchange of looks between Nikki and Hallie told them both they were seeing the same image: Andy Werdlow puffing along in jogging clothes, getting his dose of the classics at the same time.

"The Prokofiev is a better piece," Nikki finally said with a controlled smile.

"I think I know what you mean," said Andy. "The more I hear it, the more I'm beginning to think that." Andy opened his menu with an emphatic shake of his head. While reading it, he stole another glance at Martha.

Hallie was amused.

There was some chitchat about getting Nikki to the studio by ten, so they finally ordered breakfast. Martha and Kimberly Cohen both wanted the fresh fruit slices with yogurt. Martha helped herself to another whole grain roll from a small basket and announced that the rolls were delicious. Andy quickly agreed. Hallie ordered bacon and eggs, something he rarely ate, but, like French crullers, they made him feel loved. Andy wanted the same. Nikki ordered oatmeal. Nikki is hearty, thought Hallie.

"Now I can tell you the news," said Andy, finishing off his orange juice. "We've signed our director. We've known for some time he wanted to do it, we've had a lot of conversations, but we now have him signed. Malcolm Ferrari is directing this picture."

"Malcolm Ferrari?" repeated Martha.

"You don't know who he is?" asked Kimberly with a slight edge of condescension, which was a big mistake. "He did *Monopoly* and *Le Plage Bleu*. He's English, but he's done most of his work in France." And the ever clever Kimberly jangled her noisy jewelry as she reached for her coffee cup.

"I know who he is," Martha said with a perfectly charming smile.

"This is news?" said Nikki with a tart sweetness. "Andy, you told me this already. You told me this weeks ago."

"We've signed him, Nikki. He—"At that point Andy stumbled slightly. "Wasn't signed. Frankly, he was holding out to see if we could get you. He's a terrific guy, and a genius."

"And you have him signed! Congratulations!" Hallie said jovially, knowing that, ninety out of a hundred times, someone who is referred to as a genius is not. He was delighted to hear Andy admitting he had used Nikki as bait, before Nikki had formally agreed to do anything at all.

He now knew he could negotiate for Nikki anything he wanted. It was no longer a work trip.

"This is going to be Malcolm's first Hollywood picture. Every studio has been trying to get him. It's his first picture with a real budget, and we reckon this budget to be . . . well, frankly, anything we need it to be."

"Well, that sounds like a first. Great," Hallie said. He was enjoying the conversation, and he sounded as perfectly charming as he was sarcastic. It bothered Andy Werdlow, but he wasn't sure why.

"He's flown in from London to direct the test, Nikki. He's at the studio now."

"What a coup for you, Andy," said Hallie.

"Word gets out about this package and, well, suffice it to say, the phones have been ringing."

"How did word get out?" Hallie asked with a smile.

"People are watching me, Hal, what can I say? I'm a riser."

Phenomenal, thought Hallie with glee.

"Is that so? Well!"

Andy Werdlow was quick to explain with what speed he'd reached the level of executive vice-president. This level of rank in Hollywood was the military equivalent of sergeant in the Salvation Army, compared to some of the corporate twelve-star generals who could buy a whole studio tomorrow, if they didn't feel that show business was as risky as it was. But Andy wouldn't know that. So Hallie listened as Andy told the story of how he had been responsible for the biggest box-office hit of the previous summer.

Hallie found himself glancing at Martha, which he had been doing periodically because the truth was he couldn't go for very long without looking at her. She still dazzled him. He found himself studying her nose, the way it lifted up at the end as if held by an imaginary thread. Martha smiled at him as he looked at her. A very steady, unreadable, poised smile. It made him reach over and cover her hand with his own, a demonstration of affection that he felt was inappropriate at the moment. But he simply couldn't help it.

Was there something going on in her eyes that didn't match the poised smile? Some sort of worried look? He looked back at Andy Werdlow, an instinctively sound thing to do, before he could begin to imagine any one of a billion things that could be wrong with Martha.

"I'm not clear on something, Andy," Hallie said.

"What's that, Hal?"

"Did you tell Malcolm that you had signed Nikki, or that we were still having conversations?"

"I told him she was coming out for a screen test. It's more than a conversation we're having, Hal. I don't want you to worry about our offer. It's going to be something everyone will be happy with. We're in the ballpark already."

Hallie wanted to say you could be in the ballpark as often as you like, but the odds were you wouldn't be playing on the team. But he thought that as far as sports metaphors went, it was weak. What poor old Andy seemed to be disregarding was the fact that, screen test or not, Nikki could still turn down the picture. If Hallie was going to do what Alfred wanted, that certainly would have been the case. But Hallie was behind Nikki a hundred percent. Little did Andy Werdlow appreciate his luck.

"I can't imagine that there'll be a problem, Andy," said Hallie with a charming smile.

"Yes, I enjoyed very much the script, and I was happy to have an opportunity to read it," said Nikki, like someone returning a library book. The slightly dismissive tone, draped in that Slavic singsong, was perfect. It was gracious unavailability to die from. Nikki was really something. "And, Andy, I met Malcolm Ferrari one time before, he came backstage after a performance."

"Yes, Malcolm remembers meeting you," said Andy.

"I should hope so," said Nikki, all charming smiles.

"I think it's magic. I think the whole thing is going to be magic," said Andy, mopping up his remaining egg with a piece of bran muffin.

The conversation drifted around for a while and then Kimberly said to Martha, "That's the most gorgeous ring I've ever seen in my life, when are you getting married?" It was delivered as one run-on sentence.

"Oh, uh . . ." Martha, beaming, turned to Hallie. "When are we getting married, Hallie?" she asked. She had asked him in the private voice that they had come to use with each other, whispered, enthusiastic intimacy. As always, Hallie found her unbearably exciting when she used that voice.

"Very soon in the near future," Hallie said, smiling shyly, because it was still out of character for him to discuss personal things, not to mention something as personal as one's wedding. Andy was staring at Martha. Andy had a look that somehow combined dismay and awe.

"Oh, you should pick a date, you should pick a date," said Kimberly. "If you don't pick a date, years go by, and before you know it, you don't even feel like bothering anymore and the next thing—that's it. It's over." Kimberly Cohen must have known from experience, such was her pressing need to give the advice. She pushed up the sleeves of her oversized jacket and the jewelry jangled.

Good grief, thought Hallie and decided to give Lisa a raise.

Somehow or other the subject of New York came up and Andy announced it was where he grew up.

"You're kidding; where in New York?" Hallie asked, recalling his observation about Misguided Preppy.

"Manhattan. I went to Riverdale."

"No! Is that so," said Hallie. One of Hallie's special skills was working the old-boy network, which he could do like few people. He had an arsenal of tactics for the way people viewed their schooling. While Riverdale was a fine and respectable private day school, attended by JFK and all that, any boy who went to Collegiate and then Exeter, and then Harvard, as Hallie had done, had a kind of top-of-the-heap mentality, which, if you think about it, isn't his fault. Before revealing the facts of his education, Hallie tried to discover acquaintances he and Andy might have shared, once it was established that they had been in the same year. But, of course, they didn't know any of the same people. Hallie would act quite surprised when Andy said he didn't know someone, as if to imply: "What were you, a loser or something? I'm naming all the cool people." And when Andy started to look as if he were changing his formerly held opinion that he had been popular in school, Hallie recalled someone from dancing school or a similar campaign to encourage heterosexuality to provide a mutual acquaintance. It was usually some twerp whose mother ran every event in the independent-school circuit. Then came la piéce de résistance—to convince Andy in all charming sincerity that if they had know each other, Hallie was sure they would have hung out.

Not on a cold day in hell. Hallie Lawrence could be quite a little shit when it came to knocking people off guard.

Andy wasn't sure why, but he suddenly wanted to change the subject.

"Martha, I take it you model," he said.

"Oh, no!" she laughed.

"You've never considered it?" he asked in true amazement.

"Oh, I did some modeling when I lived in Paris, mostly runway, a few editorials, but I couldn't stand it. It's really boring, Andy."

"But the money!"

Hallie didn't hear the conversation continue. When the fuck had she lived in Paris? And been a model? He felt Martha's leg press against him. He tried to tune back in.

"Well, you could be making a fortune. You have a beautiful face. What about acting?"

"Acting? I don't think I could act my way out of a paper bag. That's a job for trained professionals. Or haven't you noticed?" This tease, delivered with Martha's sisterly affection, made Andy a little nervous.

"First picture I worked on was with Meryl Streep. I know good acting, Martha. Look, I see gorgeous women out here all the time trying to make it, but with that face you could have a real future."

"I have a future," said Martha, and she held up Hallie's hand for Andy to see. Then she gave him the most inconceivably gorgeous expression you could imagine. An expression you easily imagine on billboards everywhere you looked. The look that makes men drool.

Hallie was still wondering about Paris, but it struck him as a lot of nerve on Andy's part to be telling Martha how gorgeous she was and how she should be a model or an actress or whatever. When had she lived in Paris?

The breakfast meeting came to an end and they were all back out in the fragrant air and the sunshine. Hallie said he had to get something from his room, he'd meet them at the car in five minutes. He took Martha's hand and they walked off.

Once inside the room, Martha seemed a little nervous, but maybe that was only how she seemed whenever she smoked. And the first thing she did when they came in was find a cigarette. Hallie pretended to be looking for something in his briefcase.

"When did you live in Paris?" It just came out, no preamble or anything. He just looked at her dead-on and asked.

"Two years ago, why?"

"No, nothing, nothing. I just didn't remember you telling me anything about that."

"I did, silly. I told you I spent time in Paris that first day we talked for twenty million hours."

"Yeah, well, when you said you spent time there, I guess I figured a couple of weeks, a month maybe."

"Well, it was a little longer than that."

"Uh-huh. How long was it, actually?"

"Eighteen months."

"Eighteen months! That's a year and a half."

"Good boy, Hallie."

"That's worth mentioning, that's all."

"I was in Paris studying painting. Look, idiot brain, do you realize we haven't even known each other for two weeks? Now, as weird as it might seem, that's not very long. I'll get around to the details. Not all the details are interesting."

"Painting! You were studying painting? That's *completely* interesting to me, Martha. Everything you ever did is completely interesting to me, don't you understand that?"

"Well, that's what I was doing in Paris."

"Okay! Okay, now I know. It just came as a surprise, that's all."

"You're a lunatic."

"A lunatic? I just think if the girl I'm going to marry lived in Paris, spent time in Paris, doing things, it's something I want to know about."

"All right, I'm sorry, I should have told you." She looked at him for a moment and dragged on her cigarette. "Hallie, look, I don't want to come to the studio."

"Wait a minute, Martha—" That's it. She hates me, Hallie thought.

"I don't think it's fair to Nikki. I want you to give her all your attention. She needs you. I think she's nervous."

"You're suddenly the angel of mercy with my attention? Martha, of course you're coming. Nikki was delighted that you were coming."

"I just think it would be better if I didn't. Would you mind, Hallie? I'd just sort of be in the way, and I think it should be Nikki's day. I'd like to just get some sun, read, relax. That would be heaven for me."

She hated him. It was over.

"Well, maybe you'll come later. Maybe you can drive out and we'll all have dinner. You could take the car. Do you think you could find the studio?"

"What do you think I am, some kind of retard? Of course I can find it." She put out her cigarette and took him in her arms, pressing against him.

"Okay then. I'd better get going, everyone'll be waiting." Having her so close to him could lead to other things.

"I'll miss you, God knows why." She twisted a lock of Hallie's hair into place. Then her tone changed. "Hallie, call me, all right? Let me know what's happening."

That was when Hallie was sure there was something about her that was nervous. The hair twisting. The smoking. And now, something in her voice.

"Is something the matter?" he asked.

"No, not at all. Just because I want to stay here doesn't mean I won't be missing you like crazy and thinking up all kinds of dirty things to do when you get back."

"Let's pretend I just came back." They kissed. It was one of their better kisses, the ones that usually led to going all the way. But Hallie did have people waiting for him, including Nikki, so he became businesslike and forced his way deep into himself and away from Martha. In fact, as he closed his briefcase he couldn't even look at her or he would have lost his resolve.

He couldn't believe he had consented to let her stay on her own. As he walked along the path to meet the others, he thought about Steve, who probably had nothing better to do than pretend he was in the movie business and try to pick up girls. But Steve was an asshole and Martha knew it.

Still, how could he leave her alone?

In the limo with its pretentiously darkened windows Hallie sat next to Nikki, who sat with her legs crossed. The only thing that betrayed Nikki's nerves was the way her leg swung up and down to some distant but steady rhythm. It was a comforting motion, like a rocking chair, and Hallie could feel it as he sat next to her.

Was he nuts to leave Martha behind? Hallie whispered to Nikki.

Nikki said, "Definitely not." She said, "Martha would be bored to death at the studio. Hallie Lawrence, you did the right thing." She patted his hand.

There had been a touch of relief in Nikki's manner when Hallie told her that Martha wasn't coming. It was subtle, but Hallie picked it up. Martha had been right.

While they drove through Los Angeles Studioland USA, in that limo, hidden behind tinted windows, Andy and Kimberly filled them in on local gossip (about which neither Nikki or Hallie cared), mostly concerning malicious aggression on the road to success. All during the drive to the studio, Hallie kept thinking he must have been nuts to leave Martha behind. There was no expression on Nikki's face at all, which Hallie noticed was a first.

At the studio they walked through blazing, blinding sunlight, following Andy into one of the large sound stages. Then it was dark and the sound was all perfectly absorbed. Hallie liked sound stages. At a particularly high point in his egomaniacal life, Alfred had hosted a twelve-part television program on the history of music. A very classy production. It served to popularize further the notion that Alfred Lawrence was a genius, but it never fooled Hallie. While a lot of the series was filmed throughout Europe, some work was done on Hollywood sound stages, and when Hallie was brought to visit and was given a tour, he had thought movie studios were fun. He felt as if he had shrunk and were in an electric train set. The whole thing had reminded him of his trains. Sound stages still felt like train sets.

"Normally we use something smaller for a test, but this is all we had today. What the hell. It's a little like hiring a sedan and having them send you a stretch!"

It was more a statement about the studios having stages this large standing empty than it was about luck and limos, thought Hallie. He would have preferred it if Andy had acknowledged Hallie's intelligence. Andy was putting himself at a distinct disadvantage.

Nikki and Hallie followed Andy toward the brightly lit spot that was the setting for the test. A number of gaffers worked on the lights, taking orders from an elderly, interesting-looking man with a pipe, who spoke with an English accent. He was the lighting cameraman and he was happy to meet Nikki, and was especially delighted by the color of her hair. He mentioned something to his best boy when he saw that hair, and then said he was pleased to meet Hallie as well.

Malcolm Ferrari came up to them and they shook hands. He immediately brought up having met Nikki once backstage, did she remember? Hallie couldn't remember ever having met him at Lily's, now that Malcolm Ferrari stood there in the flesh. Malcolm had wild good looks. His features were rather aristocratic and he could have been an ad for Polo clothes, but his own choice of dress was jeans and a T-shirt with an old brown leather bomber jacket. He had longish blond hair, not unlike Kip's but a little thinner, and disheveled in a way that Kip's would never be. He also had a few days' worth of stubble on his cheeks. Still, he didn't really come off as being in any way self-conscious about either his wild good looks or his hip-director dressing. He wore it well, somehow.

"Nikki, did you memorize the dialogue?"

"Of course I did, silly."

"Good, well . . . actually that's good news–bad news. I wanted to discuss with you any lines you might feel awkward about, anything you want to change."

"I don't understand that. When someone gives me a piece of Beethoven to learn, I don't make changes in the awkward parts."

"Beethoven is dead," said Malcolm. "If he were alive, I'm sure he'd at least want to hear what you'd have to say."

"Well, well, aren't we flattering!" Nikki gave him one of her devilish smiles, which in turn made Malcolm smile. "Should I change?"

What was interesting about Malcolm, Hallie thought, as he listened to Malcolm listen to Nikki, was that Malcolm was a very good listener. He had a very direct manner, a way of looking you right in the eye when you were speaking, and listening very closely to what was being said. It was something Hallie himself had perfected, and he was always interested to see it in others.

Nikki went off to change and Malcolm told her he would see her in the makeup room. Then he and Hallie walked over cables to a table laden with somewhat sad-looking doughnuts, bagels, orange juice containers, and an urn of coffee.

"Coffee?" Malcolm asked, releasing something brown from the spigot.

"Please," said Hallie. At least it was brown.

"I've met your mother and father. Now there's a duo."

"Yes, indeed," Hallie said, his tone indicating that was the end of that subject.

"Your father's kind of a maniac."

"Well," said Hallie. "You're half-right there." He didn't feel the need to submit the missing word, ego: half ego, half maniac.

"There's one thing about Alfred Lawrence, though; he is very good at one thing—"

"Brahms," furnished Hallie.

"Brahms, absolutely," Malcolm repeated, pleased that Hallie had read his mind. And without thinking that Hallie had heard this maybe half a million times in his life, he added, "How did you know I was going to say that?"

"It's been said," Hallie said with a charming smile.

"I'm sorry, I guess you've heard that a million times before," said Malcolm, smiling. He had a very attractive smile.

"Don't be silly. Only maybe half a million." Hallie gave him a deadpan look, and Malcolm laughed. A big, wheezy laugh that erupted into a cough, a cough that took him over completely. Malcolm put his hand on Hallie's shoulder. It might have been construed as an endearing gesture, but Hallie felt Malcolm hold on for a moment, really hold on as if he were a little scared. And then, of course, as soon as Malcolm had finished coughing, as soon as he was fully recovered, he reached into the pocket of his bomber jacket and, finding a pack of Gauloises, he lit up.

And bingo, Hallie got Malcolm Ferrari.

Malcolm had the Degenerate Tortured Genius problem. The old DTGs. These people sit around self-destructing and you're supposed to want to take care of them because you're so in awe of their genius. You're supposed to convince them somehow that a shorter life wouldn't be a relief. Kip, it was long ago decided, didn't qualify as a DTG because there was no proof that he was a genius, although he was filled right up there with degenerate torture. The truth was,

Hallie did figure Kip to be a genius, but one who was so blocked it might never see daylight and thus it was a moot point.

Malcolm Ferrari, however, was a perfect DTG.

"Tell me about Nikki," Malcolm said, exhaling smoke, as he ran one hand through his hair, causing further disheveling. But he still remained undeniably handsome.

"She has a fairly comprehensive emotional range, you can tell that by simply talking to her. I guess someone like you could turn that into acting, what do I know about it?" Hallie gave him another one of his better charming smiles. "But, Malcolm, don't forget something. She's a world-class, maybe one of the best of our generation, violinist. That's what Nikki is. Because of that, there's a lot at stake."

"Hallie, I know that. I know what's at stake here. I can make it work. I have a point of view that will make it work. And, I realize she's not just an actress."

"Good to hear," said Hallie.

They kept doing the scene over and over. It didn't seem to bother Nikki. She would have little discussions with Malcolm and then everything would fall silent and the cameras would be rolling. It was a pretty good scene, one that started out on a comic note and ended on a sad one. That's all you could tell about it, out of context with the rest of the film, and that it took place in a dressing room, backstage after a concert. The Russian violinist, Nikki, is visited by another Russian who still lives in Russia. It could have been the corniest scene in the world, but Nikki was leading into it with a great sense of character, establishing that this was a person who is not the least bit sentimental, and if she did become sentimental, it would be a very big deal. Nikki was managing to do it. Nikki was good.

That's why Nikki didn't mind doing it so many times.

After a few hours, Hallie went off to stretch, to stroll around the sound stage, and to torture himself with thoughts about what Martha might be up to. He found a pay phone and decided to call her. She was so glad to hear his voice and wanted to know how Nikki was doing, and she told him that she hadn't spoken to a single person while she sat near the pool, except for this really amazing twelve-year-old girl. Hallie realized that Martha's telling him that she hadn't spoken to anyone made him feel good, and that this was a terrible thing. Martha was a gregarious girl, and he was making her feel that she couldn't talk to anybody. He would have to do something about this.

She was proud of the fact that she hadn't spoken to anyone.

Very bad.

He resolved to have a talk with her and apologize for being such an asshole.

"I'll send the car at eight for you and then you can go on and pick up Nikki," said Andy. "I'll get to the restaurant a few minutes early and arrange things."

"Good producer-like thoughts, Andy," Malcolm said. Hallie liked that. It had the right touch of irony. Malcolm was in very good spirits after his satisfying day directing Nikki. His good spirits were a little contagious.

"You sure you guys don't want to drive out with us?" Hallie asked.

"No. I'll want Nikki to myself," said Malcolm.

"We have to talk," said Nikki with mock seriousness.

Hallie liked this degenerate, Malcolm Ferrari.

Nikki and Hallie rode alone in the studio limousine. It was already dark, and Nikki put on the reading light while she poured herself a vodka from the car bar. "You never expected me to be so good." Nikki's eyes showered him with the old mischievous sparks.

"You were terrific. You were, Nik."

"I like Malcolm. He's very sexy, don't you think?"

"He's not my type," said Hallie.

"I like him. I was surprised." She dropped an ice cube into her drink and stirred it with her finger. "You don't like him, that's not surprising."

"I like him too, but you asked me if I thought he was sexy. I guess I can see it, how a woman might think he's sexy."

"Oh, you are nerve-racking," She smiled at him and it occurred to Hallie that it was a shy smile. He'd never quite seen it before. It was really pretty.

He took her hand. "You're going to be great, Nikki."

The car dropped them off at the hotel and then one of those absurd pieces of timing happened. Had it been five minutes later, he wouldn't have even seen Martha coming out of the hotel bar with a tanned, good-looking man in his late forties. They were laughing. Martha saw Hallie and lit up.

"Hallie! This is Alex Monchet, an old friend from Paris."

"It's a pleasure to meet you, Hallie," said the man with a thick French accent. "Martha tells me you are getting married. Congratulations."

"Oh, thank you very much," Hallie managed to say.

"Alex, I can't believe we ran into each other. It's been great seeing you. Thanks for the drink."

"It was a pleasure, Martha. You're looking so well, *chérie.*"

"Oh, Alex." Martha put her arms around him and hugged him good-bye.

"Nice to meet you, Hallie," said Alex as he walked off.

"How did it go?" asked Martha, slipping her arm around Hallie as they headed for their room.

"Very well. It went very well." He knew as well as anything he had ever known that he mustn't ask the next question. Everything in his adult brain told him to stay silent. Make a plan. Go into the room, go into the bathroom, take a shower. But don't ask about Alex. "Who is Alex?"

"Oh, he's an old friend from Paris. I couldn't believe running into him! I haven't seen him in so long."

"Old? I'll say. What was he, in his seventies?"

"Oh, that's mature," said Martha. She opened the door to their room.

Upon entering, the first thing Hallie noticed was an ashtray filled with cigarette butts. How could she have smoked all those cigarettes?

"You know, I think you're about to have one of your jealous attacks," said Martha. She was opening the basket of fruit, squeaking the cellophane as she rolled it into a ball.

"Jealous attacks? A jealous attack about some frog from your past?"

"That's *friend,* Hallie. A friend from my past." She picked up a peach.

"Friend! That's what I said! Don't eat anything now. We're going out."

Hello, Lily.

"I'm starving! Where are we having dinner?"

"Someplace out at the beach. We're meeting up with everyone— Nikki; the director, Malcolm Ferrari; Andy, whom you met this morning— What kind of friend?"

"Damn it, Hallie! I lived in Paris for eighteen months! I had friends when I lived there! Why are you so pathetic about my past?"

"I want to know, that's all!"

"I don't think you do!"

"What's that supposed to mean!"

"Look, I had a really nice day. I took the car and went driving all over the place—Melrose Avenue, Hollywood—it was great! I never got out of the car, I just drove around." She put the peach back. "Half the time I didn't even know where I was!"

She was changing the subject. Hallie, for a moment, regained his senses.

"You could have gotten out of the car. You don't have to be a prisoner in a car— Oh, Jesus, Martha. I'm doing terrible things to you, Marth. He took her hand and they sat on the sofa. "I'm acting like an idiot, and I know it, and I'm doing it anyway. You can't not talk to people, Martha. You can't not get out of the car. Talking to people comes naturally to you. I'll get used to it."

"You shouldn't be so insecure!"

"I tried it once, back in 'sixty-three. It didn't work."

"I really wanted Alex to meet you. I was hoping you'd get back in time. And then I could tell in one second by the look on your face that you wanted to kill him."

It was that obvious? That alarmed Hallie.

"I didn't want to kill him. I'm sure he's a great guy."

"He is! He's a photographer. He took pictures of me and that's how I got to do some modeling, Alex showed them around."

"Uh-huh." He was trying to sound casually interested, but the manic edge was in his voice. "What kind of pictures?"

"What kind of pictures? Fashion shots, Hallie— No. Wait. Lots of dirty, filthy porn—split beaver, whips and chains, the works. What do you think I am?"

"Agggggh!" was Hallie's only reply. Just hearing her describe the possibility that such pictures had been taken by any other photographer than him reduced him to a gagging, raging idiot. It was so out of character, he had to sit back.

"Any more questions, Hallie? Why not ask me what you really want to know? Did I sleep with him?"

"Did you sleep with him?" came Hallie's hoarse echo.

"Damn you, Hallie!" She looked at him for a moment. "Okay, okay, you want to hear it? We had been friends for a really long time and I mean friends, and then one weekend we went out of town together and somehow it happened. It didn't mean anything, it just happened. I was sorry it did because it sort of ruined our friendship, for me anyway. It didn't matter, because I was moving back to the States in three more weeks. Okay? Now you know the Alex story!"

She looked at him helplessly.

"I love you," came Hallie's whispered, desperate response. "Martha, I'm having a very hard time adjusting to the fact that you had a—that there have been guys like Alex. It brings out some kind of homicidal tendency I didn't know I had. I'll get over it. Give me time."

"Oh, Hallie—"

"Logically, I know it's crazy," he interrupted. Managing to confess this all to her, he was delivering to her on a platter all the vulnerability he had held on to for his whole life. In fact, he suddenly understood, all that talk about making yourself vulnerable in relationships. "I know there've been . . . other people."

"I wish I had never been with anyone before you. I wish I could do the old virgin-bride routine; honestly, as corny as that is, I wish it were true."

"You don't have to get extreme, Marth. Although it is an appealing thought."

"Hallie, listen to me. I can understand if you get jealous about me talking to some guy, or some guy flirting with me. I understand that. I can deal with that, I can make you believe, sooner or later, that I don't want anyone else but you. But your stupid hang-ups about the past are loony-toonsville."

These words were almost a comfort to him. He took her hand.

"I get these visions about you that make me nuts."

"What kind of visions?"

"Like you and the New York Mets."

"What? I never ever went out with any of Hammie's jock friends. Ever!"

"Really?" He might have started to recover at this point, but his eyes rested on the ashtray full of cigarette butts, more cigarettes than he had seen her smoke since he had met her. "You smoked a lot of cigarettes."

"I guess." She tossed this off.

"Did—um—now just say if I'm wrong—did Alex maybe come in here with you and smoke a lot of cigarettes?"

"Oh, Jesus H. Christ! You really are crazy! Damn it, Hallie. All right, here we go. I'll tell you something now. You're sitting around worrying because I once spent the night with Alex—"

"I have a problem with that! I can't help it!"

"Alex isn't the problem! Alex meant nothing! I lived with Malcolm Ferrari for a year!"

As layers of the consequences of this statement began to pile on top of each other like sheets of tissue in Hallie's brain, he found that he had become physically paralyzed. From somewhere far away he heard Martha ask him to say something, but he had completely forgotten how to speak. He was aware that she was leaving the room, but his eyes remained focused on the blush of a nectarine in the fruit basket, the exact place they had frozen when she had told him this news. The sound of a faucet running located Martha in the bathroom. The faucet shut off. He was aware that she had come back, was standing in the doorway to the bedroom, but he couldn't get his eyes to look in that directions. Force them, he told himself. Move your eyes. Start with the eyes. Miraculously he managed to move them from the nectarine to his arm. He tried to lift that arm but it wouldn't budge.

I'm a dead person, he thought. I think I'm legally dead.

Martha was coming toward him and somehow he managed to look at her. She carried a glass of water. He managed to open his mouth and indicate thirst.

"Want some?" she asked. He felt his head bounce up and down once, and then he sipped from the glass. "I didn't tell you about Malcolm because it was so awful." She found her pack of Camels and lit one up. "It was a really fucked-up relationship. Every time I wanted to leave him he threatened to kill himself. And the whole time"—she paused and dragged on the cigarette—"the whole time he was fucking somebody else. And I never knew."

"That son of a bitch," Hallie said, finding a small whisper of a voice.

"I couldn't believe it because we had this totally passionate thing. Did you ever see his film *Monopoly?*"

He made his head go up and down again.

"Well, you know how it's about all the things that happen after that girl is found dead? And how the film starts with the camera panning over the girl's dead body?"

"Vaguely."

"That was me."

"That was a naked body." That was a naked body people actually talked about after seeing that movie. Hallie recalled that now. Everyone went around wondering whose naked body it had been, because you never saw the face. People had conversations about it and decided that it could have qualified as one of the greatest bodies in the history of the world.

There was numbness in his legs. No movement.

"I didn't want to do it," continued Martha. "God, I didn't want to do it, but he had me all convinced that it was important to the personal statement he was making in the film, that the girl everyone was obsessed with and who was murdered was me."

"That's some personal statement!"

"I never told anyone it was me. I never told my parents or anyone. But I did it. That's the kind of control he had over me."

"I don't want to hear this."

"Why the fuck not?" she shouted. "He fucked me over, Hallie. Why can't I tell you about the first person who broke my heart? You're going to be my damned husband. I thought you wanted to know everything. Why can't I tell you, Hallie?" Martha started to cry. His heart went out to her. He wanted to take her in his arms.

But Malcolm Ferrari?

"How could you do this to me, Martha?"

For a moment, she just stared at him. "Is that all you can say?" She ran out of the room and he heard the bathroom door slam.

Then Hallie felt tears welling up in his eyes, something that hadn't happened to him in years. How could he have said something so completely insensitive? It was awful. But the tears seemed to shoot some lubricating agent into his whole body and soon he rediscovered the use of his limbs. He got up slowly and went to the bedroom.

I lived with Malcolm Ferrari for a year.

The words repeated themselves in his numb brain.

"Uh, Marth? You in there?" he pathetically asked the bathroom door. "I didn't mean how could you do this to me, I meant why didn't you tell me earlier, before I met him. Marth? . . . Don't hate me."

"I don't hate you," came the reply.

"It's just that, well, you should have told me sooner."

The bathroom door opened. Martha stood facing him, blowing her nose.

"I nearly freaked out at breakfast when Andy said that Malcolm was the director. I almost fainted."

Since Hallie had seen no such emotional reaction from her at breakfast, he realized the degree of shiksacity he was dealing with.

"I would have told you when we came back to the room, but you were throwing fits about not knowing I lived in Paris. I knew you'd completely freak out if I told you about Malcolm. I knew I'd better be cool and not say anything, for Nikki's sake. I thought you should meet him first. There's a lot of good things about Malcolm and he's really talented and I didn't want you to have bad feelings about him."

As opposed to the way he felt now?

"I spent the whole day worrying, actually hoping the whole deal would fall through and we could go back to New York and I would never have to mention it. But as long as we're all having dinner tonight— The thing is, Hallie"—she moved toward him and put her arms around his neck—"you could tell me about the first girl who broke your heart and I wouldn't say I don't want to hear about it."

He looked into that face, that beautiful face, with the honey-colored eyes now reddened, and the lips looking puffy and succulent. For the first time in his life, Hallie realized that no girl had ever really broken his heart, so to speak. Oh sure, there had been girls on whom he had had crushes and who never reciprocated, but no one had ever gotten close enough to the Hallie Lawrence heart to do any more than maybe leave a small scratch.

And in that moment he knew Martha was the only one who could, and why.

He could lose her and it was fear of that potential nightmare that was doing him in. The pain he felt on learning about her past was a kind of rehearsal, a training ground for potential future pain, should he ever wake up and find her gone. That's what was driving him crazy about her past. It was a place for familiarizing himself with pain for the future. There was nothing he could do about her past.

He realized that it was so neurotic that he would actually have to give it some thought.

It made him take Martha close to him and whisper how much he loved her and how he would handle it, the whole Malcolm situation, and how he wouldn't let it ruin anything. Martha sobbed. At least he understood what had been making her so nervous. He hugged her tightly.

I lived with Malcolm Ferrari for a year.

This time the words repeated themselves through a fog. This was it. It couldn't get any worse than that. Now he could get better.

Driving to the beach, he kept his hand on Martha's leg, on the silky stockinged thigh exposed by her short skirt. She looked magnificent, Hallie kept thinking.

"Does he know that you're here?"

"How could he know? I haven't spoken to Malcolm in over a year."

Hallie nodded.

There were a lot of people milling around outside the restaurant Andy had chosen, hoping to get in. Or perhaps they were hanging around outside the restaurant in hopes of seeing some celebrity, it was hard to tell. Inside, the bar made of stainless steel and pink marble was crowded with chatting patrons. The bar was the next area of waiting, on the road to actually being seated. It was very possible you could be asked to wait at the bar for your table and find the restaurant had closed before anyone spoke to you again. But at least you had gotten to the bar. At least you had gotten to pass by the ones who milled around outside for a living. It was a real asshole's paradise, Hallie thought.

The maître d', another MTH (Much Too Handsome), immediately escorted Hallie and Martha to the table. Hallie could see that Andy and Kimberly were already seated, and that Andy was sort of sucking on Kimberly's hand. Interesting. The hand was dropped the minute Andy spotted Martha and Hallie.

"Great," said Andy, rising. He took in the white Alaïa suit Martha wore and tried to pretend that he wasn't dazzled, nor concerned that it was more hip than anything even he was used to seeing. That was the effect it had on Kimberly, who was a little devastated. She wore a whole new bunch of nighttime junk jewelry, with equally noisy effect, and the same hairdo, revealing that it was not some quick way she had worn her hair to work that morning, but an actual free-willed choice. Scary.

Andy Werdlow, in typical Hollywood fashion, felt free to kiss Martha's cheek after having met her only once before. Martha stood taller than he, so he was forced to reach up. She was quite polite about it, though.

Hallie shook hands with Kimberly, who immediately told him that they could view the rushes from the test at ten in the morning. Martha ordered a Jack Daniels. Hallie decided that was a good idea. Any moment, Malcolm would come in with Nikki.

The thing to do was not watch the entrance. Never once look to see if they're coming in. Instead, Hallie would watch Martha's eyes.

Andy was glowing. He was aware of all the stares coming toward his table because people didn't know who Hallie Lawrence was and he definitely looked like someone they should know. And people were staring at Martha. Andy was doing the Hollywood Climb right in front of everyone's eyes, in this Members Only establishment. Andy the member was rising.

Hallie was pretending he was in a very good mood or he would have been embarrassed by the whole thing.

"Ah, here they are!" Andy announced.

He didn't have to. Hallie had seen it in Martha's eyes. They had frozen for a second, then sought out Hallie's. He held her hand.

Malcolm, having abandoned the bomber jacket but not the jeans, wore a nice-enough tweed jacket, probably Armani or something, and a shirt with the top button buttoned. He was smiling, as was Nikki, as he came to the table. And then he saw Martha.

"Martha?" His astonishment was clearly visible. There was a red glow flushing his pale face, which must've taken quite a burst of adrenaline, considering the probable state of his circulatory system.

"Malcolm," said Martha with a lovely smile. "Is this a coincidence, or what? Hallie Lawrence is my fiancé."

Not bad, Hallie thought. Not bad at all. She was just sort of breezing right along, unrattled, unperturbed, with, of course, the advantage of prior knowledge of this encounter. Malcolm, on the other hand, knocked clearly off guard, was grinning like a small boy, like a small boy who had been caught.

"I don't believe this, darling," he said, leaning to kiss her a little too automatically for Hallie's taste.

But Hallie had worked very hard to reach a plateau of detachment. Clearly he wanted nothing more than to kill Malcolm, but since this was out of the question, he would take the opposite track. He would be utterly carefree and charming. And, when a raging wave of jealously threatened to break over him and render him insane, he employed another kind of Hallie Lawrence trick.

He listened to opera.

Hallie loathed opera, but there were a few monumental tunes that he would play in his mind when terror threatened in one form or another. You could say he had an internal headphone, and by playing opera he could block out annoyances of all kinds, particularly ones that might render him homicidal. He listened to a few bars of Mario's lament from the last act of *Tosca. E lucean le stelle.* The irony amused him and he could eventually tune back into the conversation.

Malcolm was explaining to the inquisitive Andy how he and Martha knew each other.

"We were together for a while, in Paris." Malcolm gave Martha a look filled with intimate fondness, stayed with it, then looked over to Kimberly as he made his way to his seat. "How are you tonight, Kimberly?" Malcolm knew he had to make a hasty recovery. This guy was a scumbag, thought Hallie. He really is going to pretend he can handle the whole thing.

Martha and Malcolm were across the table from each other and Hallie waited for any looks they might exchange. He didn't have to wait long. As Malcolm ordered a whiskey, he spoke to the waiter, then stole a glance at Martha, who was leaning intimately toward Nikki.

"How did it go?"

"I was great," Nikki said, smiling mischievously.

"I'll bet you were!" Martha said.

"She was superb," said Malcolm.

Hallie observed that Malcolm was listening to Martha's every word, even from across the table where he was pretending to listen to Kimberly. And what did Hallie see in Malcolm's eyes as the Brit looked at Martha? A kind of gentleness. And how did Martha respond? With a smile.

Hallie figured if he really felt himself starting to freak out, he would go and call Kip. He might go and call Kip anyway. Only Kip could appreciate the monstrosity of the situation.

But Hallie did what he had planned to do, he became chatty and charming. He really didn't have to try very hard to become these things. Once he'd made the all-important decision to socialize, he could be pretty much at ease. It was making the decision that was difficult. But once done, he turned up his socializing juice (which did take effort that night) and soon everybody felt very good about everything.

He had a long and interesting conversation with Malcolm about English student art.

There was a little bit of conversation about the film. Andy had arranged for Hallie to meet with the business and legal people to finalize the deal, or so he hoped, the following morning, right after they'd all seen the screen test.

At one point, Hallie found himself staring at Malcolm's lips, aware they were lips that had been moistened once by Martha. A huge wave of rage peaked, but Hallie tuned up *Tosca* and focused on Martha. God, she's gorgeous, he thought. God, look at that face. He replayed her words about how crazy she was for him and the wave of rage dissipated.

"What are you having?" she asked, leaning on his shoulder to read from his menu.

"The liver," said Hallie. He placed his hand on her thigh. Malcolm had had his hand there . . . how many times?

"Gross," said Martha.

"You're not kidding," said Hallie.

"Then why are you having it?"

"Oh—I'm uh—I love liver."

Martha giggled and whispered an obscene thought into his ear. Hallie knew the display of intimacy was for Malcolm. He was delighted to oblige. This putz let Martha get away?

They talked about Hollywood, they talked about Russia, they talked about shooting in London. They talked about Andy, they talked about Malcolm, and Hallie took a cigar offered by the restaurant's owner at the end of the meal. As he lit it, puffing it into life, Malcolm spoke to Martha. Andy, Nikki, and Kimberly were chatting among themselves.

"How've you been? It's been ages, hasn't it?" asked Malcolm, acting very much the small boy again.

"It's been ages, Malcolm," said Martha. There was a directness to her that gave away a slight distaste. "I think this is an amazing coincidence."

"I don't know if I can handle it."

Martha gave him a warning look, a back-off-don't-even-think-of-getting-personal look. Then she smiled beautifully. "You can handle it. May I have a cigarette, Malcolm? I'm out."

That was probably the cue, the sign of nerves that alerted Hallie. He put his arm around her. He draped his arm around her shoulder. Hallie had never done this with a woman while at a business function. He had thought that putting his hands on hers, at breakfast, was a bit beyond decorum. But now he had his arm around her and across the table was a man who was after his woman. Hallie Lawrence felt like a riverboat gambler.

Putting his arm around Martha at that moment was just the right thing to do. It was exactly what Martha needed, an act of claiming, and it greatly comforted her. She leaned against him, anchoring herself there with solid assurance. It was a touching moment that they had, both aware of the solidity their bodies formed, leaning so closely together. His hand stroked her hair and, for a billionth of a second, there was no one else in the room.

In the car, on the way back to the hotel, Martha let him have it.
"I'm really mad, Hallie. I really am."
"Why?"
"You were so nice to Malcolm. You didn't have to act like he was your new best friend in the world. You're usually so standoffish, why did you have to pick Malcolm to strike up an instant friendship with?"
"Don't be nuts, Marth. He's directing Nikki's picture."
"Oh, bullshit!"
"When am I standoffish? I'm not standoffish."
By the time they got back to the hotel, Hallie was finally starting to lose it. The more Martha ranted on about how unnecessarily nice Hallie had been, the more Hallie himself wondered why he had chosen that form of behavior when the truth was he wanted to kill Malcolm.

Soon waves of hurricane proportion were slapping around inside him, wild jealousies he had never perceived possible. It was little things Martha was saying, little poison seeds she was leaving all over his brain. Little things like "Oh, Hallie, I love you so much and I love what we have together so much that now I know the only thing I ever had with Malcolm was great sex."

He watched her take off her shoes and collapse onto the sofa, back in the room. Great sex. She had great sex with Malcolm. That's nice.

"Malcolm can be terrific, he's smart and fun, but he's a real slimeball, Hallie! And I don't think you should forget that."
"Forget that? At any moment, at any given moment I was prepared to cut his heart out! Did you know that? Huh?"
Martha looked at him and smiled, rolling her honey eyes in a self-effacing gesture. Then she stopped smiling. "I'm being so dumb. I guess it was just seeing him again that made me so angry—

no. No, not angry, I just thought he seemed pathetic. I couldn't believe I was ever so crazy about him." Another seed, thank you very much. "I thought I could never sleep with anyone else again. I thought it could never be that good!"

"Do you have to keep mentioning how good the sex was, dammit, Martha?!"

Hallie opened the French door a few inches and got a whiff of eucalyptus. When he turned around, Martha stood up and whipped off her suit, not as a seductive act, but with annoyance, as if being dressed up for one more minute were intolerable. This left her standing in a white garter belt, stockings, and a white lace bra. Hallie saw that she had not been wearing underpants. She took off her bra and tossed it aside. She inspected the fruit basket and helped herself to a peach and moodily bit into it. The lips sucked into the peach juice and came up moist.

"I can't believe the things you choose to hear, Hallie. I'm in a bad-enough mood as it is, seeing Malcolm and everything; do you have to start one of your jealousy things?"

"Were you attracted to him? Is that the problem?"

"What?" It was amazing how she grabbed her surge of anger, gave it some kind of secret command, and turned it into a big teasing smile. "Uh-oh, I could nail you on that one, nerdo!" Her eyes telegraphed the upcoming tease. "I didn't know how to tell you this, Hallie, but I've decided to dump you and go back to Malcolm." Hallie's look of horror caused her to laugh out loud.

"That's not funny! That's your idea of funny?" Hallie yelled. The sight of her made his blood pressure soar. "Look at you, you're a fucking miracle."

Martha was smiling at him as she sucked out another mouthful of peach, letting the juice smear across her moist lips.

In the next second, Hallie's mouth was on hers, kissing, moistening his own mouth with that same peach juice. It sort of took Martha's breath away, but she responded almost savagely. And that did it. Hallie suddenly felt violent, felt the weirdest violence he had ever known. It was the kind that usually winds up in the groin, having wrecked havoc with every other body part, but now his groin was directly next to Martha's. He kept kissing her harder, as he reached for her hand and grabbed the peach. And then he took that peach and was rubbing it between her legs, smearing her with wet peach juice. Martha gasped, her legs parted with abandon, and Hallie rubbed that peach against her and she actually gasped out loud. Then his mouth was between her legs and he began to suck the peach juice, the bits of peach flesh, the warm cream of Martha, licking her, savoring this amazing taste treat.

"Oh, God, Hallie."

Then he stopped and turned her over so that her ass faced him and, spreading it, he began to rub the peach there as well, and he sucked off more peach juice. Martha's gasps were unlike anything he'd heard from her before, and somehow this made him feel even more violent. So he entered her from behind. Slowly. And she groaned. As he rhythmically moved in and out of her, the tight muscles of her ass jiggled. A horrid image of Malcolm raced across Hallie's brain, right in the middle of the frenzy that gripped both of them. He squeezed his eyes shut. Hallie's weird violence was keeping him erect for much longer than usual. Something was different. And when he came, finally, almost rabidly, it was more like breaking through a wall of glass than punching through the cosmos. It was dangerous.

Martha was still bent over the sofa and Hallie collapsed onto her, holding her from behind around the waist. Only the sound of their recovering breathing could be heard. They said nothing. Then Hallie heard the faint sound of violin music drifting out across the L.A. night. It was Nikki playing the Bach *Chaconne.* He would always remember that after the Peach Fuck had come the Bach *Chaconne.*

14

HALLIE WAS RELIEVED TO GET BACK to New York, where at least the weather made sense. Although it was the end of November, a series of days came that were clichés of autumnal delight: rich gold sunshine, deep-blue skies, longer and longer shadows, and the trees still had a few yellow and red leaves that clung on before joining their next life as compost. In a week they would all be gone.

He tried not to think about Malcolm Ferrari but it was useless, so he tried to limit thinking about him to maybe two or three times a day.

Nikki had been signed to do the picture. It had really been amazing, seeing Nikki up there on the screen, twenty million times larger than life. The screen test revealed something extraordinary. In the process of transference from the real Nikki to Nikki on film, you could somehow look right

into her and see her from behind. It was the weirdest thing, but she
looked exposed by the scrutiny of the camera, as if her face couldn't
keep in her soul and it spilled out of her eyes and radiated from her
skin. Hallie always saw that devilishness in her, but somehow,
transposed onto celluloid, something magical happened. She had
what you might call "enormous presence," even more so than in
real life, which in Nikki's case was a great deal of presence indeed.
She was superbly photogenic.

"Beautiful," he had said, his only comment on the entire test.
Nikki tried to shrug it off modestly, even giving him a little nudge
in the darkened screening room.

"Not so beautiful," she had whispered, but she was a little un-
nerved by how beautiful she looked. She saw so many things she
had never seen by looking in the mirror. The flaws were there still,
of course, vibrating off the screen, but there were other things that
made up the package with which she hadn't come to terms yet.

She knew she looked beautiful and Hallie had said it, so it must
be true.

Negotiations for Nikki's contract weren't negotiations at all; they
simply agreed to everything Hallie asked for. They needed Nikki
and they wanted Nikki to be happy, so he wrapped up the whole
thing in one afternoon. Andy suggested another dinner, but Hallie
told him they were booked to leave for New York on the red-eye.

"Got to get back for Thanksgiving tomorrow, eh?" Andy said.
"I tried to get back this year but no way, I'm swamped. I'll be lucky
to get out for some sushi."

"Well, if we weren't leaving, we would have loved to join you
for dinner tonight," Hallie said as he shook his hand.

By six o'clock on that night, Nikki, Martha, and Hallie were
dashing up the Pacific Coast Highway toward Big Sur. They all
agreed it was a great idea to spend Thanksgiving together. Nikki
had invitations to too many dinners, Martha's mother would have
so many people it wouldn't matter, and Lily would have to reach
a little. So there they were dashing along the coast that everyone
always said is so fantastic. Hallie thought it wasn't bad. Martha
thought they should all get houses and live there. Nikki thought it
was all very Bruckner.

Hallie was smiling. He said, "Copeland."

Nikki said, "Again an American composer? Are you nuts?"

Alfred heard that Hallie was back in town. For every hour that
went by and Alfred heard nothing, not a hello, from Hallie, Alfred's
mood grew menacingly dour. Finally, after three days, Lily called.

"Darling," came Lily's voice over his office phone. "You've

invited us to dinner. Martha says she's going to cook. I think that's divine." Despite Lily's treacle-covered words, Hallie knew something was up.

"She's a terrific cook."

"So you've said. I think it's wonderful that she's invited us."

"Well, good! When are you coming?"

"Tomorrow night. Now I'm going to let you get back to your work because I know you're much to busy to chat, so we'll do it tomorrow."

"Okay."

"And then you and Alfred can chat and everything will be just great." Such perfectly pronounced vowels covering such harpy-esque displeasure.

"Great! We'll chat all night long. All of us! It'll be great. Look forward to it, Lil."

"I think he's feeling ruffled that you haven't called him since you got back, Hallie, but I could be dead wrong. You know how sensitive he is, it could be any one of a number of things."

Sensitive like a nine-hundred-year-old sturgeon.

"You want me to call him?" Hallie said, trying to resign himself.

"What, now? Oh, I think he's at rehearsal now . . . But you could probably get through."

"I'll see him tomorrow night. I'll talk to him all night."

"Well, okay," came Lily's own brand of petulance, which was very sexual, both little-girlish and femme fatale.

"Come around seven-thirty," said Hallie.

"Okay."

"Say good night, Lily."

God, he hadn't said that in years. Weird. When he was a kid, really small, like six or seven, he thought it was the funniest, most side-splitting thing he'd ever heard, the old "Say good night, Gracie" Burns-and-Allen routine. Once he'd heard it, he adopted it as a routine of his own. It was a natural for him, as Lily had been setting it up for years, with her "Say good night, Hallie," whenever she wanted him off to bed. "Good night, Hallie," he began saying back, and exiting the room with great shrieks of laughter. God, kids are idiots.

Then he learned to reverse it, to say, "Say good night, Lily," when he thought Lily should be sent off to bed. It drove her crazy, she told him it was fresh, but he kept it up for a while, then dropped it out of boredom.

"Good night, Lily," said Lily with a little laugh that was quite genuine, because she remembered it, too.

He immediately called Martha.

"Brave girl!"

"Oh, hi, Hallie! Guess what?"

"You invited my parents for dinner."

"God, you know already? Your mother's great, she was so excited. You'd think they'd never come here for dinner before."

"They haven't."

"Are you kidding me?"

"Well, once. When I first moved in, eight years ago. I just wanted to tell you I think it was terrific of you."

"Well, thanks, Hallie Lawrence, soon to be husband of Martha Helen Housewright."

"Helen? Your middle name is Helen?"

"Oh, shove it up your ass, you turkey. I love you, bye."

She definitely had no problem with the vulgar, thought Hallie.

Inadvertently, Martha had set up the inevitable confrontation between Hallie and Alfred, but it was okay. Hallie was really glad she had invited his parents to dinner. He was looking forward to it.

However, the next day he did a strange thing. He was walking along Fifty-seventh Street, having just come from a meeting, thinking about his parents coming to dinner, when he hailed a cab and headed to Nikki's apartment on Riverside Drive. Arriving at her building, he found himself so stymied at being there that he could hardly remember how he'd arrived. He went to the corner to a pay phone and called her. She told him to come up right that minute.

Nikki's apartment was fabulous, the living room in particular. It was all white, with great moldings and carvings, and bare except for some carefully chosen antiques. The only place to sit was an enormous green velvet couch that Nikki told him was Russian. It looked very Czar-esque.

"This place is terrific," Hallie said, admiring the view of the Hudson River from the window.

"Max used to live here with me. That's why it has so little furniture. But these things are all mine."

"Max who?"

"Max Steinholdt."

"I didn't know you lived with him."

"Hallie, the whole world knows I lived with him. You never heard it?"

"Max Steinholdt is so old."

"He's sixty-seven now." She raised her glass of vodka after she had offered one to Hallie. "To forgotten times. They should stay forgotten."

Nikki gave him one of her radiant smiles and curled into the sofa.

She was wearing a long full skirt made of crinkled silk and she wrapped it around her knees and hugged them to her. Hallie could smell her perfume, which was something he'd never smelled on her before. It was wonderfully exotic.

"So, tell me, why are you here?"

"I just wanted to see you, Nik. I just stopped by for a drink."

"No news? No suddenly finding out the deal is no good and the picture is off?"

"You already signed the deal, Nikki."

"I still think it might happen . . . that at the last moment, you could come to me and tell me the offer is an insult!" She smiled and sipped her vodka. "I can't tell you how happy it makes me that you did this for me, Hallie."

"I'm very happy that you trusted me, Nikki. You had no reason to."

"That's for sure, no reason at all!" She narrowed her eyes and pointed a finger at him. "But there is something about you, Hallie, that told me to go ahead, to trust this one. And I'm very happy to find out I was right!"

"You actually had doubts?"

"I rehearsed today with Alfred. He is acting like a little sad dog."

"You talked to him about the film?"

"Sure. I tell him we start to make it in January. He said he will just have to get used to it, but it will take him a long time. I say, good! Take your time. You can do it! And he starts looking like a small dog. But this is Alfred when he's not getting his way. New?"

"Nothing under the sun." God, it was great talking to Nikki about his father. It was almost like talking to Kip. After all, Nikki had been close to Alfred for almost half her life. It was better than Kip. It was like having a sister.

"Alfred is like a father to me—"

"I was just thinking that!"

"But fortunately for me, I am, let's say, less emotionally involved with him because actually he just isn't my father. For you, let's see, for you he will be meaner, he'll try to make you feel bad because you didn't do what he wanted."

"That's what he'll try to do, Nik. I'll indulge him a little bit, but I know him too well to let him get away with it."

"Sure. You have been probably doing things he doesn't like for a long time."

"Most of my life. But this is the first time in a business transaction."

How could he admit that to her, when he was admitting it to himself for the very first time? The truth. He had always given in to Alfred over business matters. Any idea that he had ever done otherwise was in Hallie's mind and a complete hallucination. It was a lot to think about, this truth, and on top of that he had just told it to Nikki.

"The first time? And you did this for me? I drink a toast to you, Hallie Lawrence."

He couldn't believe he had told Nikki that. He couldn't believe it.

She leaned toward him and kissed his lips. It was a simple friendly kiss, but nonetheless, it had been on his lips. Close family members sometimes kiss on the lips, Hallie thought.

Lily just went completely overboard as she wandered around Hallie's apartment, astonished with all of Martha's little touches. She thought it was absolutely divine to use the pre-Columbian pots for flowers. She immediately called it Utilitarian Art and thus pronounced it a movement.

"You ought to do the entire place over, Martha." Lily was sitting elegantly on the sofa, a drink in hand. "Why is it that every boy on the planet eventually makes his apartment look like his dorm room at college?"

"I think you might find that every boy on the planet doesn't do that," said Hallie, bringing drinks for himself and Alfred.

"Well, I suppose there are some boys who have an inclination for fixing their places up, but I wasn't thinking about those kinds of boys." Lily smiled.

"Oh, Hammie, my brother, you should see the way he lives. He has this apartment that he never goes to, with everything in boxes. And he never went to college."

"Some boys didn't go to college, Lil," said Alfred. He hadn't spoken at all since coming in, but felt compelled to make his presence known.

"Are there boys like that?" asked Lily, lacing her words with apologetic self-mocking irony.

Alfred sat in Hallie's most comfortable reading chair, sunk in deeply, his legs outstretched in front of him, his hands placed delicately together as if in prayer. It was one of his more common poses.

Hallie had made a point of hugging Alfred first, a gesture that at least got Alfred to take off his coat. Then Alfred had poured himself a tumblerful of sherry and sunk into the chair, determined to make no cover for his bad feelings.

Goddamn it, thought Hallie. Why does he have to give a performance in front of Martha? He's a fucking guest; what about Martha?

"What's your schedule this month?" Hallie finally asked,

obliged, as he had been all his life, to bring Alfred into the conversation. You either couldn't get a word in edgewise, or you had to pull him in by the hair.

"I'm working," he answered with a shrug, pathetically pretending gratitude for small blessings.

Martha and Lily were off to the kitchen. When did this start, going off to leave the men to themselves? Did cave women do it? Yes, they must have, figuring it was a moment's respite from the constant fornicating that must've gone on. But it was time to drop the tradition or at least practice more refined timing. Hallie wished that Martha were in his lap lying against him rather than oven-gloved and dinner-checking in the kitchen.

"Martha's parents are very nice," said Hallie. He would keep trying to have a conversation with Alfred for a solid five minutes.

"That's nice, I hope we'll meet them soon. I look forward to it. I look forward to your wedding." He raised one eyebrow. "You're having a wedding?"

"Why don't we talk about it tonight?"

"You're not having a wedding." He closed his eyes and shrugged; even his lips shrugged, as if it would come as no surprise to him that Hallie would betray him like that and not invite his own father to his wedding.

"I didn't say that. I just want it to be a wedding and not a circus," said Hallie amiably. He decided he would play the part of Pal with his father. It usually worked.

"I won't let her turn it into a circus," Alfred grumbled. Conspiring against Lily came automatically, but it didn't change his mood.

"You have your work cut out," said Hallie, sipping his Jack Daniels.

Alfred looked at Hallie directly for several long seconds. He was preparing to speak. In fact, the stare and the pensive face were already part of whatever he was going to say.

"Are you proud of yourself, Hallie?"

A slammer. Alfred was not going to be petulant, as Hallie had assumed, he was going to be vicious. This called for a totally different set of armor and Hallie had to make a quick change.

"I'm not sure I understand the question."

"You think I'm a fool, giving the advice to you about Nikki that I did? The ravings of a maniac?"

Yes, thought Hallie. Bingo, old boy, that's it! "I understood your point of view. I understand all your thinking," Hallie said instead.

"Then you're the maniac, my son."

"Why, thank you very much," said Hallie, an old and tired standard reply for an Alfred insult. "Nikki's going to be great. This film will be special—" An image of Malcolm came before Hallie's eyes and caused tingles behind his forehead. Get away. "I think it will work out better than you might hope."

"Nikki's going to be great?" repeated Alfred a little contemptuously. "Nikki *is* great. Nikki's going to become a tabloid personality, and you did this to her, my boy. I haven't got much else to say on the subject. Can I smoke a cigar in here?"

"Sure. Nice of you to ask."

Tabloid personality. In Alfred's mind this was the lowest level to which a person could sink, worse than poverty, worse than ill health, worse than a concert that wasn't sold out. A tabloid personality meant filthy lies were told about you in trashy exploitation journals. It meant public shame. People in the arts who really counted for anything were *never* in the tabloids. What Alfred didn't get was the possibility that there were people who didn't give a shit about that kind of thing. But on the other hand, it was a pretty horrifying idea, Nikki in the tabloids.

Hallie immediately dismissed this prophecy and concentrated on the Maestro who could foresee such degradation, and the Maestro's motives. But all and all it was a well-delivered blow. The worst, Hallie figured, was over. Wrong.

"It's just that you're so goddamned irresponsible. You go to Harvard Law, you even manage to develop a first-rate reputation, but you're still an idiot. Only an idiot could do this to Nikki. You're going to destroy her."

"That's all in your mind," Hallie managed to say, but his voice quivered and he wanted to kill himself. He had long ago lost count of the number of times that Alfred had called him an idiot, and he never quite figured out why it bothered him so much. But it did. It used to be the one thing that would make Hallie cry when he was a kid, and scream back outraged denials.

"It's in my mind?" said Alfred, between puffs on his cigar. "Good! Maybe that's where it will stay. Who knows?" He threw Hallie the phoniest good-natured smile in the history of the world. Hallie thought about Nikki. He thought about telling Nikki every word Alfred had just said.

At dinner, Alfred was in much better spirits, as if his menacing words to Hallie had served him like a bowel movement. They dined on a beautiful rack of lamb, and the subject turned to the wedding.

It would be on the Saturday after next.

No, Jews don't get married on Saturday.

Only one of us is a Jew. The wedding is going to be on that Saturday night.

After sundown, that's a thought.

No, that's a decision.

They would invite Martha's immediate family, which was a total of ten people. Therefore, Lily could invite ten people, but she had to make sure she and Alfred were among the ten. So she could really only invite eight people. Lily looked pale.

"But Hallie, darling, there are so many people."

"I know. We don't want them."

"You don't have to put it like that, darling."

"Eight people, Mom."

"Well, let's see," said Lily. She would pretend to go along. "We'd have to have Dodo, and Babe, who's married again—"

"She doesn't have to come all the way from California."

"Oh, don't be so silly, of course she'll come! And we'd have to have Ace and Sylvia, but we'd have to have the Thalmans, and the Warfields and—"

"Don't forget Kip and Kate. Kip's going to be the best man."

"Well, of course! I was counting Kip!" She had totally forgotten about Kip. "Hallie, this is absurd, it can't be done. There will be too many people who will be crushed. Let me have just our very oldest friends, darling, I promise. Let me invite fifteen people."

"Eight."

"I might as well not invite anyone, that's the only diplomatic thing to do."

"You could do that. You could just have family. You could have Babe and Dodo and that's it."

"Well, then I'd have to have my dear Henry and Sasha—"

"Henry lives in Düsseldorf and you haven't seen him in ten years. You don't even know if he's still alive."

"He's *alive,* Hallie," said the throaty, threatening, honey-covered voice, and the deadly venomous glare. Lily straightened her shoulders and gained even more height to her regal posture. She reached for a cigarette from her alligator cigarette case, a gift from her eldest sister, Dodo, for her twenty-fourth birthday, which she had recently found and was using again. Her perfect red nails held the cigarette as Hallie lit it for her.

"God, you know so many people, it's hard, I understand," said Martha.

"Look, I'll give you an example." Lily exhaled smoke and sniffed slightly, and focused on Martha. "Noel Brandt is one of my oldest and dearest friends, and if he didn't get to do your dress, he'd be crushed. Irreparably crushed, darling. And if he did your dress, well, he'd just *have* to come to the wedding."

"Noel Brandt?" asked Martha, impressed. "I don't think I could ever afford anything of his, Lily."

Don't fall for it, Martha, baby, thought Hallie. But he actually smiled at Lily's brazen weapon. She's yanking out old Noel himself.

"Well, honey, why would you pay for it? I never pay for a thing!" She had made this announcement in a loud whisper, as if they were suddenly in the French Underground or something. "I just give him divine presents and invite him to a tiny, small, intimate wedding for my son and his beautiful bride, whenever such occasions come up. It means more to him than money, he's positively rich already." It was amazing how, once she got going, how many well-enunciated words in a row Lily could so lyrically string.

Hallie knew he was going to lose, and that Lily would be allowed to invite a few more people. He knew Martha would be spectacular in a Noel Brandt dress and he had a feeling that such a dress was very appealing to her.

"I guess you have to invite Noel," said Hallie.

Lily couldn't hide her astonishment. She had expected a major assembly of expletives from her son, not cooperation.

"Hallie, I'll tell you what. Let me invite a dozen people. I promise, I swear, I won't do more. That way I can say we kept it to a dozen people and it somehow—"

"Sounds acceptable. But, Lily—"

"No, no, don't say it, I promise. I absolutely promise, no more than a dozen. Now, Alfred, you'll have to give this a lot of— Alfred? Oh Christ, he's asleep. Can you stand it?"

Sure enough, Alfred sat in his chair at the table, his chin resting on his chest, napping away. It was perfect. It was as hostile a nap as anyone had ever taken.

So the wedding was arranged and Lily called Noel at home, right there on the spot. There was absolutely no time to come up with anything, but she knew he could do it. And Lily arranged to take Martha to meet Noel.

"What's going on?" said Alfred, pretending to return from his nap refreshed.

"The wedding is Saturday after next," said Lily. "Now, there's one other tiny little thing. What about a reception?"

Hallie smiled. He should have known. "After the little ceremony we can all have dinner."

"Yes, but do you mean just those few people who are going to be at the ceremony, or can we have—"

"Mother, it's one and the same, the ceremony and the reception and the hors d'oeuvres and the music—don't forget the music—it's all one and the same. There's no one else."

"Well, now that is totally unfair, Hallie. The least you could do is let me give you a party afterward. I know traditionally the bride's parents do it, but . . ."

"Yes?"

Boy, had Lily fallen into a hole. It was not like her to be caught in such flagrant disregard for protocol, and she rushed to cover herself.

"Well, darling, you've asked to get married at the house. I just sort of assumed we'd do a little party there, afterward. I'll call Martha's mother—Adie, isn't it?—and we'll have a long talk about it."

Adie Housewright and Lily Oppenheim Lawrence in the same phone conversation? One in which Lily was going to convince Adie that it was just fine for the Lawrences to give the wedding? God save the queen.

"I don't think this is going to be a problem for my mom. She's going to die when she sees your house. She's going to love it. She's so looking forward to meeting you, Lily. I've told her so much about you."

Lily actually arched her back under the stroke.

"Well, I'm looking forward to meeting her, too," she said, all charm and feigned humility. Lily did a very good ten-year-old girl.

"Martha?" Hallie looked right at his bride-to-be. "Do you want to have some kind of thing after the ceremony, some sort of party?"

Martha sat and thought about it. You could really see her mind working over it, the idea of a party, as well as the most diplomatic response.

"Maybe a small one."

"Lily, are you prepared to accept the word 'small' as having a meaning? For example, that two hundred people is not small?"

"No, actually, two hundred people is not small," said Lily, perking up and behaving herself.

"A hundred people is small," offered Alfred, taking off his glasses after returning his engagement book to his pocket.

"Well, we're very used to having a hundred people," said Lily.

"Wow. You are?" said Martha.

"But, darling, you can't invite a hundred people with a week's notice at this time of year. It's the Christmas season, for God's sake."

"Do your best, Lil," said Alfred. They all knew damned well that anyone receiving an invitation to the wedding of the son of Lily and Alfred Lawrence would cancel any other plans. Lily would have to phone them all, in order to apologize personally for the spur-of-the-moment madness of it all, but Lily would get no refusals.

Lily was happy.

Martha was happy.

Alfred, at the last minute, said wait, he might be performing that night, and then checked his diary (which he had already done) and announced with great pleasure that he was free.

Hallie was just okay. But Martha made love to him on and off all night, and then Hallie was just fine.

Martha then began a series of fittings with Noel Brandt that were to culminate in two things: a simply *fabulous* dress, and Noel's discovery that Martha might be the greatest model he had ever dressed. As long as he had her in his lavish atelier, he had her try on other creations he was preparing to throw out to the psychotic fashion world. And he couldn't believe how Martha looked in his clothes.

"It's her bones," said Lily at lunch with Noel one day. Noel had a wonderful little office that looked as if maybe Louis XIV had slept there. Near the window was a small important dining-room table that could be set for two. Tête-à-têtes were Noel's whole life, and having one with Lily, at his place, was tête-à-tête heaven.

"Fabulous bones. And not just the face," he said, pouring Lily some more crisp Chablis.

"No, not just the face—the shoulders, the legs—all her bones. She has a magnificent skeleton," said Lily.

Noel leaned intimately toward Lily, as if he could possibly be overheard in this inner sanctum.

"Lily, I want her to be my woman."

"But, darling," replied Lily as she slowly lit a cigarette. "She's going to marry Hallie."

"Curses!" said Noel, and he laughed. "No, I mean the Noel Brandt woman."

"You want her to be a model?" asked Lily, looking as if Noel had just proposed selling Martha's flesh on the local street corner.

"Good God, Lily, no. Just let me have her for the new perfume. Just one campaign."

"I wouldn't make that offer to Martha if I were you, Noel. I have a feeling she might take it. I don't think Hallie would like it."

"Someone would have to explain to Hallie that it isn't the same thing as being a model, it's a corporate image."

"Darling, no one has to explain anything to Hallie. A model is a model. Give it time, Noelie. Let's see how busy Martha keeps herself once she's the little wife at home."

And they both understood that by saying "Give it time" and "Let's see," Lily had given her approval, should the moment present itself. Expediting that moment was Noel's job. He would plant a few seeds.

That afternoon when Martha came to the showroom, most of the work on her dress was complete. It was simply a matter of finishing touches, perfecting the line of the cream satin silk as it clung to her hips like a glove. From the front, the dress appeared to be a simple silk satin column, allowing Martha's body to give it all the lines it needed. From behind, a train of soft tulle fabric gathered just at the bottom of the spine, splayed out like a gown in a fairy tale.

"Noel, it's so gorgeous I can't believe it," said Martha.

"Look at you, Martha. Look at the way *you* look in it." He leaned to her ear as he looked into the mirror over her shoulder. "I've never dressed anyone who looked as good as you do. You have magic."

"I feel like the queen of the world in it, Noel." Martha, it should be added, was in a state of utter dazzlement.

"As you should. Now, what shall we put on your head? What shall we do?"

"I know exactly what we should do!" exclaimed Martha, stepping down from the fitting platform and gathering an armful of tulle lying on a nearby worktable. "You make a little hat, very flat, sort of fifties-ish, and you attached this veil at the back of it, just the way the tulle is attached to the dress."

Noel sort of froze all movement. Nobody made suggestions to Noel Brandt. He hadn't actually been *asking* when he said, "What do we do with the head?" He'd only been thinking out loud. He certainly hadn't anticipated an answer. Yet, when he recovered from that experience, one that he hadn't had in years, he found he had sketched in his mind a hat very much based on Martha's idea, and no matter how he would try, he wasn't able to alter the concept. There was something about Martha.

"Leave it to me," he said quite sweetly. The Noel Brandt girl had style of her own. How absolutely dreamy.

While Martha was at the fitting, Hallie had decided to take the afternoon off and just bum around with Kip. It was important to have some kind of bachelor party, just the two of them, so Kip had come down to New York. He had gone back to Kate when Hallie and Martha went to L.A., and Hallie thought it might be time to ask how things were going. Kip replied in a monotone that they were "together," but he said it with a shrug in his voice. Jesus, thought Hallie, Kip wasn't with Kate at all. He saw in his friend the resignation that comes with reaching a dead end and realizing that you've lost.

They started their afternoon of bumming around with lunch at the Harvard Club, followed by a game of squash. The alcoholic consumption that had accompanied their meal destroyed all physical coordination and they just ended up laughing a lot.

They showered and decided to go to over to a particular filth emporium on Eighth Avenue where they had these booths you could go into and watch a girl take off her clothes and eventually bring herself off, if you put in enough coins. She would go just so far and a curtain would fall, and you had to put in more coins to see her go farther. For some reason, what he and Kip had really believed before (that she actually did bring herself off) seemed rather fishy now. There was no more magic left. The girl Hallie kept feeding coins to was pretty depressing, or at least that's how it struck Hallie. She had a hole in one of her fishnet stockings and she had drawn the missing pattern onto her leg with an eyebrow pencil. After a few coins, Hallie began to feel sick from the overwhelming odor of disinfectant that was mopped all over the floors every hour to clean up the layers of discarded semen.

It was dark when they came out of the filth emporium. Kip and Hallie walked along Eighth Avenue, Hallie with his coat open, Kip in a big green army trench coat.

"I didn't even get a hard-on," said Hallie. "What a gyp."

"Me neither. Do you think we're getting old?"

"That's it! We're getting old. I knew it. I knew it would happen sooner or later, and now it's happening. I feel like this is some kind of momentous moment for us, Kipper."

"God, you're such a corny bastard, you know that, Lawrence? It's the way you handle booze. Here, take some of this, because God help you when you hit empty." Kip took out his silver flask, a real beauty that had belonged to his non-teetotaling grandfather. He offered it to Hallie.

"Wait a minute, what do you mean, when I hit empty? When is that?"

"When the alcohol wears off. You're going to be sick, but not for a while, so keep the level up, man."

"To keeping up the level," toasted Hallie as he swigged from the flask. "I thought maybe you were talking about my life in general."

"Your life in general is okay, Hallie."

"You're sure?"

"Yup."

"Well, then, let's just make a pact. We'll never stop getting hard-ons no matter how old we get. We won't let it happen," Hallie said in all sincerity.

"Right! We'll get those little balloons put in, that you pump up before you get laid."

"What if you pump it up too far and blow your cock off?"

Kip laughed. Hallie laughed. Kip put his arm around Hallie and led him to the street to hail a cab. "What we need is another drink."

"Definitely! . . . Blowyourcockoff is actually a little-known modern Russian composer."

"Dimitri Blowyourcockoff? I've heard of him." Kip's arm tightened around Hallie's shoulder. "You son of a bitch, you're marrying Martha."

Hallie eventually hit empty and spent until four o'clock that morning throwing up. He had never in his life been so drunk. Kip was passed out on the living-room sofa. It was the end of a perfect bachelor party.

"You're a naughty boy, Hallie Lawrence," Martha said as she brought him some coffee and a cold cloth for his head. "I think Noel Brandt was coming on to me today," she mentioned, when Hallie seemed to feel better. Hallie assured her Noel Brandt was not coming on to her, and then barfed again. Why did he have to throw up? Why couldn't he just pass out, like a gentile?

Next year in Jerusalem, my ass, thought a miserably ill but happy Hallie.

15

TWO WEEKS IS NOT VERY LONG TO
have to wait for an event like a wedding. Some people plan it a year in
advance, guaranteeing that after the
event takes place, a depression will set
in equal only to those caused by post-
partum or Christmas. But two weeks
takes about five minutes, really, and
soon it was the night before the wedding. The Housewrights had come to
town and they were giving a dinner at
their favorite restaurant in New York
City, which luckily happened to be a
first-rate steak house.

The problem was, the Housewrights
were staying at the Plaza.

It wasn't a big problem, but Lily did
have to talk to Hallie about it. She
might not have said a thing, but the
Housewrights had invited the Lawrences to their rooms for a drink
before dinner. And Lily would not set

foot in the Plaza until that awful man and his awful wife sold it. They were the ultimate in tabloid-personality nausea. According to Lily, they were bad for the Jews, and when it was pointed out to her that neither the man nor his wife were, in fact, Jewish, Lily replied that whenever she heard his name mentioned, it was always followed by "And they're not even Jewish." This phrase, she maintained, was a Kristallnacht classic, and thus was bad for the Jews.

"Lily, there's no way the Housewrights could have known how you feel. The next thing you'll tell me is that they're being anti-Semitic just because they're staying there."

"I didn't say that. There are so many nicer hotels, Hallie—"

"Lily, come on."

"It's just my own particular feelings about the place. You have to have standards, Hallie."

"I'll give you standards, Lily. Rely on your manners. I'm not telling the Housewrights you're not coming."

"Well, all right. I just thought that maybe they'd like to come here first."

"The whole wedding is at your place, Lily. Give them some ground."

"What on earth are you talking about? I think it's absolutely charming that they've arranged a dinner. Don't make it sound like we're all going into battle. I'm sure Martha's parents are lovely people, Hallie. Martha is a lovely girl."

He should grab Martha, go to Las Vegas, get married, and send a postcard. Thank God, Kip would be at the dinner.

Lily was perfectly behaved at the Plaza.

Kip and Kate met them all at the restaurant. It took Hallie about three and a half seconds to see how wrong things were between them. One look at Kate's face told everything. She had always been a very pretty girl, in a perfectly ordinary sort of way, with her dark hair and light eyes. But Kate's prettiness had diminished. She had developed a sad look, a permanent furrowing of the brows, a look that made people wonder what was wrong. Even when she smiled, that expression didn't go away. It really killed Hallie, because he hadn't seen her in a while. But all the sad stories he had heard from Kip he could see were true by just looking at Kate's face.

Hallie chose to sit next to her, with Martha at his left.

The coach had a very take-charge manner about the whole evening, herding everyone from hotel to restaurant, herding them all around the table. He was wearing what was obviously a new suit and he looked handsome, in a rugged, former-athlete kind of way. Alfred warmed to his manner immediately because Alfred was a helpless slob when it came to the logistics of social evenings. Of course, once they were where they were supposed to be, Alfred held court and regaled the Housewrights with some of his best anecdotes, while Lily sat beaming a charming smile and pretending she hadn't heard the stories forty-five million times.

With so many people chatting gaily at the table, including Glenna and Lark, Gin, C.W. and Barbara, Mimi and Tim, not to mention the Lawrences and the coach and Adie, Hallie turned to Kate. They looked at each other. Then Kate looked past him to Martha, who was talking to Kip, and back to Hallie.

"Martha's beautiful, Hallie," said Kate, smiling but not losing her forehead furrows. "She's really lovely."

"Thanks, Katie."

"She's really first-rate beautiful. How old is she?

"Marth? She's almost thirty."

"That's young."

"It's not so young."

"I'll be thirty-four soon."

"We'll all be thirty-four soon, you, me, and Kip. That's not so old, Katie."

"It is if you want to have children that don't have little old gray-haired parents by the time they go to first grade."

"Wait a minute, hold on here; we won't be that, none of us, I promise." Then Hallie decided to be sensitive. "Look, Katie, Kip may not be ready to have kids yet, but he will, I'm sure. Give him another year."

"No, Hallie. Kip doesn't want to have kids with me. That's what he told me."

"People say things when they're mad. Did you have a fight?"

"No, he said it very calmly, the day before yesterday."

Kate picked up her fork and slipped it into the arm of a piece of broccoli she had ordered with her steak. She had just told him that the marriage was over, but Hallie couldn't quite deal with it.

"You know what I think?" he said. "I think it has to do with his painting. I think now that he's starting to sell, it could make a big difference in the way he feels about having a family. He's nervous about being a success right now. He's nervous because it will mean he has to grow up."

"Oh, Hallie, I wish that were true," said Kate, her eyes soulful as she looked right at him with a glimmer of hope. Then she said, "I'm having an affair."

"You are?" Hallie said, completely taken aback. "You're a survivor, Kate, I'll say that. You always were."

When Hallie tuned back to the table after his conversation with Kate, he heard Lily compliment Adie's new flowered silk dress, and Adie tell Lily that she just loved her darling earrings, which just happened to be eighteenth-century Russian. Alfred was telling the coach they were *both* coaches of sorts, and Martha laughed when Kip said he really was the best man, a far better man than Hallie.

That was the germination of the Best Man Routine, which was to dominate the evening.

Kip went overboard with it once he'd stumbled on the concept. He kept saying things like, "Well, as the best man, I'd like to say you're wrong, Hallie," as they discussed which port to have for dessert. Or the reverse: "I am the best man to service the mighty Hallie Lawrence at his nuptials. Think about it. There is no one else." When at the end of dessert he proposed his toast with port glass in hand, he announced how proud he was to be the best man, that he was so glad to have finally been given the correct title, because it had always been true, he was the better man of the two. Alfred immediately said, "Here, here!" and quickly downed another glass of champagne. He couldn't even wait till Kip had finished his toast. Then he made a big fuss apologizing and getting his glass refilled. Kip had made just about every better-man-of-the-two joke he could think of and it was getting on Hallie's nerves, but everyone else was laughing. Then, as Kip raised his glass, he called Hallie a lucky bastard. Hallie noted that Adie didn't mind the vulgarity and realized she'd been to too many sport events with the boys to notice. Everybody applauded Kip because he had made them all laugh. Hallie got up and hugged him and suddenly felt something like a lump in his throat.

As they left the restaurant, Martha once again voiced her disappointment that Ham Two couldn't make it to the dinner, and it took a lot of reassuring from her siblings and Adie to convince her that he would be at the wedding. He was on a plane returning from Japan as they spoke. He had committed to exhibition ball, Moo, now come on, you know about that.

Out in the street, under the restaurant's awning, Martha told Hallie that it would be bad luck if they spent the night together before the wedding, so she was spending it at the hotel with her family. Hallie was devastated. He particularly wanted her to be with him the night before the wedding because he was becoming very nervous about the whole thing. As the event approached, Hallie was beginning to realize how in his role as groom, he would be at the very center of things, and he remembered how much he hated that particular location. Then Glenna started butting into the conversation and agreeing that the bride and groom couldn't be together the night before. Adie just shook her head, because she had to pretend that Martha and Hallie hadn't been spending the night together now for some time, but Glenna went on and on about bad luck like some kind of harpy, and Hallie knew what Martha had meant about Glenna being a pest.

So Hallie went home.

As the wedding day for Hallie Lawrence and his beloved Martha dawned, Hallie woke up with a start. His eyes opened and he jumped out of bed almost in one move. Wearing nothing, he opened his curtains, folded his arms, and looked out on the street. There were no people. The morning sky was a heavy frosted violet color and the air was still and cold. Hallie's breath made foggy patches on the window glass. A young man came from one of the apartment buildings across the street, a real jock pulling on a crumpled Polo coat. He's leaving his girl before her parents wake up, Hallie thought. He had done it only half a million times at that age. By the time this particular day ended he would be with one woman forever.

But what if it wasn't going to be forever?

What if, even after they were married, he still felt the crazed pins dancing in his temples every time he thought about her having ever been with anyone else?

No. He was going to grow up and be a husband.

Husband.

Husband, husband. This is my husband, I'm her husband, I'm your husband, this is my wife—Hallie tried a crash course in the skills of marital nomenclature. Tomorrow morning at this time he would be waking up with Martha, and she would be his wife. It felt wonderful.

Hallie was suddenly extremely happy. No matter how much he dreaded the wedding itself, it would, like all things, conclude. He got back into bed and read until about seven-thirty. The doorbell rang. It was Kip. This was great.

Kip had guessed Hallie would be up, so he had decided they should get an early start at spending the day together until the wedding. They were due at Lily's at five. Kip was already smoking a cigar when he walked in with their wedding clothes and hung them in Hallie's bedroom closet. But something wasn't right with Kip. He was trying too hard. It was subtle, you would have had to know Kip a long time before you would notice it, but he was trying too hard to appear cheerful, as opposed to his normal ironic cheerful act.

They made breakfast and sat around leisurely eating it.

They took a walk. They went to a newsstand and read the mag headlines. They both had disgusting hamburgers at Jackson Hole.

They went back to Hallie's and poured themselves each a brandy. They sat around chewing the fat.

And all that time, Hallie couldn't help feeling that something was seriously wrong with Kip. Finally, he couldn't stand it any longer.

"You're bummed out. I can see it, you're bummed, so why don't you just talk to me?"

"I'm not, old sport! Look! This is you and me hanging out before your wedding. Don't mistake that for being bummed out."

"I don't know why you can't talk about it with me. Stop being such a gentile."

"All right, that's it. Let's go. Circumcise me. Right now. I'm willing to convert." Kip unzipped his jeans and let them drop.

"You're already circumcised, Kip. It wouldn't be any fun."

"What do you want me to tell you, Lawrence old sport, that I'm really feeling lousy?"

"Just don't be a damned phony, okay? Give me a little credit; I think I can understand what you're going through. I talked to Kate last night."

"She told me. She told you she was having an affair? You know whom she's having an affair with? A creepy local lawyer who's lost half his hair."

"And I don't suppose we hope that he finds it."

"Exactly, but that's not the problem. The problem is I can't get upset about it. I keep waiting for some kind of rage, but I can't find any—is this gentile enough for you? I just feel indifferent and kind of glad someone's making her happy."

"Well, don't you think there's a chance that I can understand how you're feeling?"

"Yeah, right."

Kip went and put on "Sweet Baby James" by James Taylor. Nothing held more nostalgic memories for them than that song and the old turnpike to Boston, and driving back to Cambridge together at 4 A.M.

They had decided to wear morning coats because it isn't too often in your life you have an occasion to wear them, unless you're some kind of British asshole. They both felt it was pretentious but still had fun putting everything on. It was like dressing for a military display. Hallie thought he looked pretty damned debonair, and much more at home in the tailcoat and dress shirt than Kip. Kip always seemed on the verge of loosening his tie anyway, and there was always a button that had only made it halfway into the button-hole. But he knew how to tie a perfect bow tie without even thinking about it.

"I'm having painter's block," Kip said out of the blue, as they were putting on their neckwear in front of the mirror in Hallie's bedroom.

"That's only because you sold your first fifteen-thousand dollar painting."

"It has nothing to do with that."

"You'll paint again. Stop it."

Hallie and Kip decided to walk to the Lawrences'. Kip had on a ratty green army jacket and his tails swung out beneath it, but neither of them noticed anything out of the ordinary. Hallie wore a dress coat.

Because it was the Christmas season, there were extra lights twinkling everywhere. Of course, the lights were going up as early as October these days, so it was beginning to look like the New York solution to the darkest days of the year instead of anything to do with a specific holiday. Normally, Christmas lights annoyed Hallie, but on that particular evening in early December he was on his way to marry Martha Housewright and it felt as if all the lights were for them.

Kip's mood seemed to darken further. He said he was pissed at all the cocksucking Christmas crap everywhere, and that Kate was annoyed that he wasn't picking her up from her sister's so they could go to the wedding together. Kip had told her that was a lot of bullshit, that they would be together at the wedding, that he was Hallie's best man, and he was going with Hallie.

"You could have picked her up. We could pick her up now."

As they walked, Kip lit up a cigarette and then said in his best Jack Nicholson voice, "Hallie, I'm sick of playing by the rules. Does that have any meaning for you?" He put his hand on Hallie's shoulder, a posture they so often fell into when they walked. "Kate and I have about five minutes left together. However, that's not the kind of thing I want to bring up on your wedding day, my man. Do you get it? Do you get it? Do you? Do you?"

"What a guy. Always the Humanitarian."

"A.T.H."

Hallie draped his arm around Kip.

Hallie Lawrence did not appreciate what would be forever called his wedding to Martha. He certainly would have agreed that the event that took place in Lily's apartment that evening was possibly the most spectacular, awe-striking display of taste in the history of weddings held at home. But there was a problem, and it all started when Nikki arrived for the reception accompanied by Malcolm Ferrari.

Before that, though, things had been pretty good.

When Kip and Hallie arrived at the Lawrences, they found Alfred, Ham, C.W., Tim, Lark, and, low and behold, Ham Two standing around in the living room. As Hallie and Kip entered, the pitcher came toward them, smiling his small-boy smile.

"Hallie, good to see you again." He shook Hallie's hand.

My hand is in the hand of the Met's number-one pitcher, thought Hallie. He just couldn't quite shake the novelty, pardon the pun.

"This is Kip Courtland. Kip, Hamilton Housewright."

"Wow," said Kip, nodding, "how do you do, Ham Housewright?" And Kip smiled and pumped his hand and they looked as if they were both six years old.

They greeted the others and Hallie had to accept an embrace from Alfred in front of the Housewright men. At least it was brief. Other guests began to arrive, people hand-chosen by Lily for this now famously intimate ceremony. Old family friends, like Ace Newbald and his wife, Clara. His Aunt Dodo, who smelled like old ladies' powder, and her companion, a prim woman named Lisle. Dodo was very white. Her skin was the same color as her snow-white hair, which was set in a severe bun, the way Lily wore hers. Dodo was fifteen years older than Lily. His Aunt Babe, who was five years older than Lily despite her name, was with some dude named Erich, who was her latest husband. She hugged Hallie to her Galanos. Babe was almost as good-looking as Lily, but had too much of their father's nose. Lily looked more like his grandmother, the bird.

"Well, I just can't believe any of this, I just can't believe little Hallie is getting married," said Babe. She had that liquid Lily Lawrence voice too, but the Babe version was even more gravelly, so that almost every other word she spoke cracked.

"You haven't met Martha," Hallie said to her in a nephewish voice.

He couldn't help looking at Dodo and thinking that she was no longer an elderly lady, she was a very old woman.

Hallie began to get a little nervous when Martha's mother and her sisters came into the living room. It reminded him of why everyone was gathering at the Lawrences'. They had been helping Martha to dress in the guest room Lily had assigned them, and they seemed to be in almost giddy spirits, even Mimi, innkeeper and professional worrier. Adie looked as if she might drop over backward in a dead faint any second.

"Hallie, dear, don't you look handsome! My word! I am just dying for a cigarette. Do you think it's allowed?"

"Of course, it's allowed. Lily smokes like a maniac."

"Oh, now dear, don't say that about your mother, she's the most

darling, warm, generous person I've ever met." Adie took a cigarette from her evening bag, which did not in the least match the
cornflower-blue dress and shoes she wore.

"Shouldn't you put a flower in your lapel, dear?"

"Should I?" asked Hallie.

"This is a job for the best man!" said Kip, springing to attention.
"Excuse us, we're off to be flowered."

They bounded up the stairs and met Lily in the upstairs hall.
Hallie had one of those rare moments when he was taken off guard
by how beautiful she could look, before he remembered she was
his mother.

She patted at the gray roses that were tucked into her bun at the
nape of her neck. She seemed to be miles away as she walked along
reviewing the strategy for the evening's maneuvers.

"Nice dress, Mom," said Hallie.

"Oh, Hallie! You came! Thank God."

"Yeah, well, you know, I wasn't going to, and then, at the last
minute, I decided what the hell, I know how much these things
mean to you."

"Don't start," said Lily, equally deadpan.

Then he smiled and repeated, "Nice dress, Mom," because it
really was. Noel had outdone himself with gray velvet and jet
beading and a full gray satin skirt. Hallie kissed her on the cheek.
Kip did the same, and also put one hand on her ass. He just loved
doing that to Lily Lawrence. She had never once let on that she
noticed it.

"Hello, Kip, my love. Let me see, what are you two wearing?"

"Oh, not this suit," said Hallie cheerfully. "I just came over here
in it. I brought along a clown costume. I'm going as a clown."

"Oh, you were always going as a clown. You would never be a
ghost or anything Halloweenie."

"He was always a wienie, Mrs. Lawrence," volunteered Kip.

"I once went as an accident, don't you remember?"

"Oh, I remember that, that was revolting. And, Kip, don't call
me Mrs. Lawrence."

"Lily! Forgive me! May I tell you what a vision of beauty you are
tonight? Surely, there is one fewer goddess in the heavens this
evening, you are here amongst us."

"You outdo yourself sometimes," said Lily. Years of enduring all
the phases of humor that these boys could dish out, including ironic
displays of great flattery, made Lily slightly sarcastic herself, but it
was loving enough. "Do you have the ring?"

"I'm the best man, aren't I?"

"I always thought so," said Lily, picking up on the joke.

"Hallie? May I have a word?" asked Lily somewhat petulantly. She indicated her bedroom door.

"I'll stand guard," said Kip. "By the way, we came up for a boutonniere."

"Oh, well, Alfred's got them."

"Say no more, I'll go find Alfred."

So Hallie went into his parents' bedroom with Lily.

"I want you to give this to Martha," said Lily, handing him a velvet box. Hallie opened it to reveal an exquisite necklace-and-earrings set, circa 1915. Seed pearls and diamonds. It had belonged to Lily's grandmother.

"You want me to give this to Martha?"

"Mmmm," purred Lily. "Do you think she'll like it?"

"This is very decent of you, Lily." Hallie made sure that his voice sounded more grateful than his words might indicate.

"I'm very fond of her, Hallie. I think she's very special."

Hallie didn't say anything. He kept rubbing his finger over the same spot on the velvet box.

"Well? Don't you think she'll like it? What's the matter with you?"

"I'm touched. I'm very touched, Lil, that's all." And he kissed her on the cheek, and added a hug.

But before it could get maudlin, Hallie went to find his bride-to-be, despite a lame protest on Lily's part that the groom is not supposed to see the bride before the ceremony. But Lily was not one to stand on ceremony, she told him (which was a colossal lie), and she let him go. Besides, Lily knew that the necklace was just the final touch Martha needed with that unbelievable Noel dress. Now everything that Lily could possibly control was perfect.

Hallie knocked on the door of the guest room that had been given over to the bride.

"Come in," he heard his own darling Martha say.

So in he went in and there she was, and she took his breath away. Adie was with her, and so was Glenna.

"Oh, dammit, Hallie! You're not supposed to see me now!"

"Get out! You're spoiling the whole wedding!" shouted Glenna.

"Hallie, dear—" began Adie.

"You ladies will have to excuse us for a moment—I can't believe the way you look, Marth—I have to have a word with my bride."

Something in the Hallie Lawrence manner told these ladies not to argue with him, so they left the room. But Glenna whispered it was bad luck as she was leaving.

Hallie lunged for Martha but she held him at bay.

"No! It took too long to get this way, you can't touch me until afterward. What do you think of my dress? Isn't it gorgeous? Damn! I didn't want you to see it until I came out.''

"Will you forget all that bullshit for two seconds? I have something for you."

And he gave her the velvet box.

"God!'' yelped Martha, staring at the necklace. Then she looked up at the ceiling.

"What?'' said Hallie, also looking up.

"No, no, I'm just trying not to cry! This is so— Oh, Hallie this is for a magic princess, not a regular girl.''

"Who's marrying a regular girl?''

"Don't let me cry! God, my mascara! Put it on me, quick! Put the necklace on me, I want to see it.'' She removed it from the box and handed it to him. She watched in the mirror as he draped it along her throat.

"Oh, Hallie Lawrence, will you just look at that!'' Martha was absolutely enchanted. Then, with total disregard for her bridal finery, Martha hugged Hallie, kissed him, and reached for him.

He stopped her and knelt down.

"What's under here?'' he asked, lifting up the cream satin skirt. And he saw it all—the white lace stockings, garter belt, white lace underpants. "No, no, we can't have these," he said, taking off the panties. He stood up and threw them across the room. The top edge of the bathroom door caught them and wore them proudly.

"Hallie, don't!'' squealed Martha, but she moved closer to him. "Oh, what do I care? So what if the bride is completely disheveled and looks like she just fucked her brains out? I like it.''

"It's a good look,'' said Hallie, before she silenced him with a kiss, unzipped his pants, and had him on the verge of serious trouble.

Verge? What verge? She had lifted the silk satin skirts of her dress, and now, pantyless by his own hand, moved herself on him. He didn't know quite how she had managed to do it (he was aware that he was somehow leaning against the wall now), but they were standing there in the guest room doing it, bride dress and all.

"I love you, Hallie. From this minute on, I'm your wife,'' whispered Martha between rapid little breaths.

"Me, too. I'm your husband—Jesus.'' Hallie held her tightly as he came. "I am so madly in love with you, Martha, I want to eat you up.''

They uncoupled and Hallie straightened himself out as he looked into her eyes. Look at that face, he thought. Just look at that face.

"Marth? I don't want you to put your panties back on, okay? It's just a small favor I'd like to ask.''

"What a pervert! Okay, I'll just go to the bathroom and wash up—"

"Don't." He took her hand. "I want to think about it dripping down your legs during the ceremony."

"But it'll drip all over my shoes, it'll ruin my beautiful satin shoes! This is such a gross conversation . . ." She burst out laughing. "All right, I won't do a thing! Now get out. I'll see you downstairs!"

At that point, Hallie was appreciating his wedding very much.

During the ceremony he noted that the flowers everywhere were even more beautiful than usual. Calla lilies. Cream-colored calla lilies, looking like frozen carved light in their fantastic Lily Lawrence vases. He appreciated the oddity of the two families behind him, the coach and Alfred, Adie and Lily, a pitcher for the New York Mets and his Aunt Dodo. He noticed what a gentile Adie's minister, Pastor Jennings, was, and what a phony, as usual, Rabbi Berg was. He had always thought he was a phony, ever since the guy had prepared him for his bar mitzvah. Rabbi Berg was always smiling and shaking people's hands who gave money to the synagogue. But he was really a mean bastard when it came to giving religious instruction. He had a habit of trying to make you feel like shit.

After the ceremony, and a lot of kissing and handshaking, more guests began to arrive for the reception, entailing more handshaking and kissing. Hallie was feeling pretty kissed out, so he broke up the receiving line at first sign that it was slowing down. He walked off with Kip and they headed for the bar.

"I think we're supposed to take glasses of champagne from the tray," said Kip, pretending there were rules.

"Right," said Hallie, finding a champagne bottle they could call their own and uncorking it masterfully. He poured them each a glass and, with the bottle under his arm, he headed with Kip for the most comfortable sofa in the room.

"Look at old Alfred talking with Ham Housewright, pitcher for the New York Mets. It's great!" said Kip.

"He's probably telling him how to improve his fast ball. Either that or he's giving him a critique of the national anthem."

Martha came and joined them, lowering herself carefully onto the sofa, not yet used to wearing such a magnificent creation.

"Where's mine?" she said, indicating Hallie's champagne glass.

"I'll get it, I'll fetch you a glass; I am, after all, the best man. I live to serve." And, with a flip of his blond hair, Kip was off.

Martha giggled, and after Hallie gave her a sip of champagne from his own glass, she said, "Oh, Hallie, it's so beautiful."

"I'm so glad you think so, Marth," he said. He was feeling kind of goofy.

The room had filled with glittering personages, the crème de la crème, who were feeling even crèmier because here they were at the wedding of the son of Lily and Alfred Lawrence to that gorgeous—did you have a look at her?—girl. Everyone seemed to be having a great time, from Lily's duchesses in designer dresses to Adie's ladies who shopped at Lord and Taylor's, from grand old Jews in the arts to woodsy WASPs looking as if they didn't get into town much anymore. Lily was in full command. Every group she joined seemed to shine as she beamed up on them with her touchless embraces. She was in full command.

"Hallie, have you seen Nikki yet? She's not here," said Martha. They held hands spontaneously.

"She'll be here. She's an artist, they make entrances. She should have been invited to the ceremony."

"She's coming with Malcolm, you know."

"No, I didn't know," said Hallie. At that point, his appreciation of the wedding began to wobble. He now realized he had managed to make it through the entire day without a thought about Malcolm. "He gets to come to your wedding, Marth? I don't think that's particularly fair."

"That's not the point—"

"What's the point, Marth?"

"I think Nikki is interested in Malcolm. I think something's going to happen there."

"Don't be ridiculous."

"I could be wrong. I was wrong once about Glenna and this guy she was going out with. I thought she was going to marry him, but she ended up marrying Lark, of course. But that was the only time I was ever wrong."

"Once? That's all?"

"Hallie, you can't let her fall for Malcolm. You can't let her do it. She'll be annihilated."

"Wait a minute here, my little sugar-coated shiksa, Nikki can do anything she wants. Déjà fucking vu, have you talked to my father?" said Hallie. "Don't worry about Nikki."

"What's a shiska?"

"Oh, a term of endearment." Hallie nuzzled his nose into her hair. "It's *shiksa.*

"Like a shiksabob?"

"Shiksabob? What do you mean?"

"You know, the thing you eat with all the peppers and steak bits and stuff."

Hallie laughed. "How much have you had to drink, Marth?"

"Us shiksabobs can hold our liquor, Mr. Smarty-Pants Hallie Lawrence."

"I love you so much, Martha. I love you so much, God! You are the most adorable delicious thing in the whole world, Martha, Martha Lawrence, Martha Housewright Fucking Lawrence."

"Don't be fresh. And don't change the subject. If you think Nikki can hold her own with Malcolm, okay." Martha was looking at him with adorable consternation, thinking things through. "Okay. You know her better than I do."

Of course, the truth was he didn't, but Hallie knew for certain that Nikki couldn't fall for Malcolm Ferrari in a million years. It was something he just knew.

At that moment, as Kip returned with the champagne for Martha, Nikki and Malcolm made their entrance. Malcolm had the decency to wear a suit and tie, although it was too obviously Armani, and Nikki looked divine. She wore a gray Armani dress.

"Is that the fiddle player?" asked Kip, filling Martha's glass.

"Yes. And with her is the DTG."

"No kidding, so that's Malcolm, huh," said Kip, sizing him up with a little more interest, as he watched him greeting Lily.

"What's a DTG?" asked Martha.

"Lily's going to love him. Degenerate Tortured Genius."

"Oh."

"Looks DTG. Maybe I can sell him a painting."

"He may be a degenerate and he may be a genius, but he's not tortured," said Martha, who had reviewed Hallie's facile summary with a bit too much seriousness. She polished off an entire glass of champagne as if it were a glass of water.

"Whoa," said Kip softly, to Martha. "You planning to do that again?" He refilled her glass.

"Don't worry, no, I just needed a little quick kickoff. Do you have a cigarette? Do you happen to have a cigarette?"

"One cigarette coming up!" Kip stood up, almost clicking his heels, for God's sake, and removed one from his breast pocket. "As long as I'm up, I guess I'd better check on Kate. I'll return shortly."

"God, he's really into this best-man thing," laughed Martha. "I like it. I think he makes a great servant to the king."

"I'm the king?"

"Who else?"

She sat on his lap, bride dress and all, with the trailing skirt covering Hallie. He reached his hand under the skirts and moved it between her legs.

"Hallie!" she gasped.

"Just checking. Just checking to see that you didn't cheat and put on some panties— Ham! It's good to see you, Ham!"

Hallie's hand beat a hasty retreat as Martha jumped off his lap to hug her brother. With Ham was another one of the famous Mets, whom Martha was hugging like a long-lost friend.

Hey, let go, will you buddy? thought Hallie as he stood there, helplessly grinning. Where the hell was Kip? Kip, look who's here, for Christ's sake. We can talk baseball until dawn, if the guy takes his hand off Martha, off my wife.

"Hey, that's my wife you're feeling up," said Hallie, and yes, there was a tiny note, a musky amber note, of genuine annoyance. The two Mets had certainly heard it and Hallie couldn't believe he'd said it. He had the horrifying image of himself with a giant screw springing right out of his head.

"I love to feel up people's wives, man. That's what I do for a living." And he grabbed Martha even closer.

Ham Two laughed. It was some kind of jock humor, Hallie could tell that much, but the image of it was not good. The Very Famous Met had teased him.

"All my brother's friends feel me up, Hallie. It's just something you're going to have to get used to."

"Oh, okay. I'll do that." Hallie immediately lapsed back into relaxed charm, even though he was embarrassed; it was one of his great talents, simply assuming exterior command.

"Congratulations, buddy," said the famous Met, thinking Hallie's charming smile showed he was an excellent sport after all. "You got yourself some heartbreaker here."

Just because Martha had told him she hadn't slept with the entire Mets baseball team didn't mean it was true. After all, she had only said she never went out with any of Ham's jock friends, but she had not specified the New York Mets!

Heartbreaker?

"Have a cigar," said Hallie jovially, although it seemed like the most idiotic thing anyone had ever said. Kip came over with Kate, thank God, and introductions were made. "Give the man a cigar," said Hallie to Kip, realizing that he had forgotten to stuff a few in his pocket.

"Right away. Have a cigar." Kip offered the famous Met and Ham each a beautiful Havana, and offered one to Hallie as well.

The four men lit cigars ceremoniously, all of them enjoying themselves for a moment. Then Hallie felt it, the piercing laser beam of Lily's stare coming from across the room. They were smoking cigars in the living room before dinner? Did he have any idea how he had just ruined the entire evening by allowing four people to light up smelly cigars, before dinner was served? And it was too late to do anything about it. No one was going to ask them to put out their cigars. Hallie realized that even now, on his own wedding day, he had to give Lily a little nudge. He threw her one of the smiles he knew she liked.

As everyone stood around talking about the New York Mets with two real-life New York Mets, Hallie couldn't help searching the room for Malcolm Ferrari and Nikki. He hadn't seen Malcolm since Los Angeles, since the dinner when Hallie had been so absurdly good-willed. The sight of Malcolm, who was now holding Nikki's hand right in front of everyone, was getting on his nerves.

The two were heading toward him.

Hallie tried to pretend he was completely absorbed in a baseball anecdote when Nikki dived into his arms.

"You should have been at the ceremony," Hallie whispered to her. "I told my mother that."

"No, no, don't worry." Nikki squeezed his hands and leaned toward him. "Alfred keeps calling me 'movie star.' As soon as I set foot in the door, he tells everybody, 'Look, it's the movie star.' This is the very thing he was so worried about, that people would think of me as a movie star, but he's the one going around planting the idea in everybody's mind!"

"That's my pop! Just your regular, down-to-earth, everyday son of a bitch. Have a drink, Nikki. Forget him."

It was at that moment that Malcolm Ferrari reached for Nikki's hand, even as she was having this little tête-à-tête with Hallie, while at the same time he kissed Martha and wished her happiness. It was an image Hallie didn't care for at all. At that moment Hallie's appreciation of his wedding vanished. Nikki didn't take Malcolm's hand, she sort of patted it away. But the same couldn't be said for Martha, she accepted his kiss. It was only a kiss on the cheek, but Malcolm's mouth on any part of Martha sprayed red lights in front of Hallie's eyes. He directed them quickly to Nikki. In her eyes he could see a touch of the familiar devilishness, the daring challenge. He felt better seeing that comforting display of fireworks.

Dinner was announced.

Hallie went over to Martha, took her in his arms, and French-kissed her right then and there, not caring a fig if it was in good taste or if it revealed how desparate he was feeling to everyone in the room. It was worth it to kiss her in front of Malcolm. Of course, it revealed only a handsome groom kissing his beautiful bride and was perfectly appropriate.

The Lawrence dining room was very large and beautiful. It had dark wood paneling and the Picasso collage, and it was definitely not one of those rooms that make you feel as if you're in a trompe l'oeil hell. Ten tables of ten could be accommodated nicely, and the room was lit only by candles, each table holding ten tall tapers in various Georgian candelabra. Everything seemed like a dream, like fairyland, because Lily had outdone herself with table linen in cream and gray and centerpieces of English ivy entwined with roses and plump black grapes. The room glittered as the candlelight bounced from the silver table service to Lily's most elaborately cut crystal. People's spirits soared.

It took Martha's breath away. Hallie could feel it as she grasped his arm when they made their entrance into the room.

A quartet played beautifully in one corner, and it was no ordinary quartet. Alfred had hand-picked each member from the Juilliard graduate school, somehow convincing them that playing at a wedding was an essential part of a musician's development, good for a musician's sense of humility. Brahms, he reminded them, had played in a brothel. A party given by his wife was the next-best thing.

Hallie immediately saw that Nikki and Malcolm had been placed at his table. It burned him up that Lily had been so stupid. But then again, it was the right thing to do with Nikki. The wedding really wasn't any fun anymore.

Martha and Hallie spent a lot of the time making their separate ways around the room visiting the other tables.

The food was superb, and most people thought the langoustines in cognac cream sauce was the best they had ever had. The dessert was a pear sorbet with crème fraîche that had been flown in that morning and hot chocolate sauce with fat raspberries on top. Hallie had found that he wasn't very hungry, but he managed to choke down two portions of dessert. He always loved it when Lily served the pear sorbet with the phenomenal cream and chocolate sauce.

At one moment during the feast, Kip and Hallie exchanged looks. Neither was completely sure of what the other was thinking, but they just looked at each other and then ended up grinning.

The entertainment was provided, of course, by Alfred. His performance began with a toast to the bride and groom that was so effective that he practically had the whole room in tears. As soon as he realized he had worked them to that point, he took out his handkerchief and wiped away a tear of his own. This was followed by nose blowing in frequent bursts from all over the room. Jesus, what a master. Through most of the speech, he tried hard to convey an expression of good wishes to the bride and groom, yet somehow he managed to include himself in just about every other sentence. Hallie and Kip exchanged knowing looks, very much enjoying this stupendous display of Alfred's Ego Mania. Then, before the coach could even think of getting up to make his toast, Alfred told his captive audience that he had several guests who would perform a little something.

A famous diva sang *"O Mio Babbino Caro"* from Puccini's *Gianni Schicchi.* Hallie saw Martha's eyes fill with wonderment. He took her hand and kissed it while he looked at that sensuous, beautiful profile. He touched her lip and she kissed his finger.

Next, the quartet played a movement from Schubert's *Trout.*

Nikki heard it from the living room, on her way back from the powder room. She was looking at the Léger over the mantel. Such a superb Léger. It seemed to encompass everything about Léger that she loved. If Léger were alive, she would seek him out in Paris, meet him in a café, and spend the night making love to him, surrounded by the heady scent of oil paint. But Léger was dead and it would never happen.

So, Hallie Lawrence was married now. She wondered if it would change anything. She wondered if she should change anything in her behavior. She decided against it. The movement from the *Trout* was coming to the conclusion.

As the quartet finished, Nikki went back into the dining room. She was heading for Alfred, who was making his little bow of gratitude to the quartet members for having given the Great Genius Himself such pleasure.

"He's guaranteeing them a place in heaven for actually moving the Maestro," Kip whispered to Hallie.

"It's bowel moving in general," Hallie whispered back, watching Nikki at Alfred's side.

"Wait a minute, you forgot to ask *me* to play something," she said to Alfred with a touch of defiance. She took a violin from a member of the quartet and played a movement of the Bach E Major *Partita.*

When she had finished, it was Alfred's performance that was truly remarkable. Certainly Nikki had held the room spellbound with her exquisite sound, but it was Alfred's reaction that was actually more entertaining. Kip and Hallie were exchanging glances like maniacs now, it was that good. They had lit up cigars. It was not only after dinner, it was Hallie's wedding. Alfred just sort of stood there, as Nikki acknowledged the applause with a little bow of her head. He just stood there, not clapping, but looking down, sheepish, and hurt. Then he raised his finger and gently shook it at her, while he collapsed into her arms in almost exactly the way he always collapsed into Hallie's, just too exhausted by the pain and greatness of it all.

Hallie and Kip could hardly contain themselves.

When the coach at last managed to get in a toast of his own, most of it was to Alfred and Lily for their terrific party, for their generosity of spirit, and for their ability to make everyone feel so at home. He said he was proud to welcome Hallie to the family because Hallie was a "true gentleman and a scholar," and immediately Hallie thought what he really meant was a "true gentleman and a Jew." Isn't "scholar" just another one of the carefully cloaked gentile expressions for a money-lending Hebe? But other than that, Hallie liked what the coach had to say and his heart went out to him for having to follow Alfred's performance. The coach seemed very nervous, despite a blood count of maybe four or five percent alcohol.

Then everyone went back to the living room again for brandy and coffee and ultimately the wedding cake. Hallie had to talk to a lot of people, which he did with and without Martha on his arm. Finally, as he was chatting with a particularly wonderful old Russian pianist, a man of whom he was quite fond, he saw it: Malcolm talking to Martha, just the two of them. It didn't last very long, but he had seen it and it gave him a fresh splash of red lights before his eyes and a feeling of suffocating anxiety.

Hallie returned from the bathroom at one point and saw across the crowded room that Kip was talking to Malcolm. Oh, boy.

"Cigar?" asked Kip as Hallie approached.

"Absolutely."

"Anything else? Brandy? Coffee? Heroin?"

That made Malcolm giggle. He actually put one hand near his mouth, a hand holding a Galoise, as if to cover the giggle. The gesture was decidedly girlish.

"I'll have a glass of heroin, on the rocks, please," Malcolm joked.

Oh, Jesus. A look passed between Kip and Hallie, communicating all they were thinking. What an asshole. What an asshole joke. And, what a first rate DTG thing to say.

"I'm fine for now," said Hallie. "You okay, Malcolm? Feel free to use my manservant here."

"Best man. I like best man. Manservant I can be any old time. But today I am the best man."

"Mazeltov," said Hallie.

Kip just loved it when Hallie said things like that.

"Ah, here's a waiter, let me grab another brandy," said Malcolm, following a passing tray.

"Grab me one, won't you?" said Hallie. "Shhh," he now said to Kip.

"The thirty-second rule, my good man. Can't violate that."

The thirty-second rule was simply that you never talk about people until they've been out of your presence for at least thirty seconds, in case they return too soon and overhear you.

"Well?" said Hallie.

"PPOS." said Kip.

"You think?"

"Totally."

So they agreed that Malcolm was nothing but a Pathetic Pile of Shit. Hallie was almost looking forward to Malcolm's return so he and Kip could amuse themselves at his expense, but Malcolm never returned. He ran into Nikki en route to the brandies and fell into conversation with her. Hallie found it repulsive, the whole idea of Nikki succumbing romantically to Malcolm Ferrari, but he also knew it could never happen.

And then it was time to go. Lilly mentioned to Hallie that the crowd would not begin to disperse until he and Martha had left, but by no means was she asking him to go. It was vintage Lily.

Hallie grabbed Martha's arm and whispered, "Let's go, Marth. We can go now."

"I'm supposed to change."

"There's no time."

"I love it! Let's go run around New York in our wedding clothes!"

Hallie was saying good-bye to Alfred when his father looked at him with the oddest smile. It was just a simple, unloaded smile. Remarkable.

"Thanks for all this," said Hallie, the good son, and because he didn't know what the hell to make of the smile.

Alfred put his arm around Hallie. He undid his tie and allowed it to lie around his neck like the scarf he was more used to.

"She'll kill me," he said, indicating his open tie.

"Not if you're having a good time."

"Nikki and the director, you know the car, what's his name, Ferrari?"

"Yes," said Hallie in a stern voice.

"Keep your eye on that."

Unloaded smile my ass, thought Hallie, and he cursed his own näiveté.

"I will," said Hallie.

Right in front of Alfred, and right in front of Kip, who was just standing there, not saying anything, Martha came up and, cupping her hand, whispered in Hallie's ear, "I can't wait to fuck you."

"Mmmm," said Hallie.

"Could you come and tell my mom and your mom that I'm not changing?"

Martha was allowed to make her exit in her wedding gown. She was saying good-byes in such a warm and girlish manner, and she looked so gorgeous, that you couldn't help hear people wondering if leaving the wedding in your wedding gown, and not some stupid suit, might become the new rage.

Hallie was saying his own good-byes when he picked up the oddest dialogue between Lily and her eldest sister, Dodo, speaking with the belief that they were beyond earshot.

"Looking the part is not enough," Dodo said in her elegant tones. "You were always fooled by that."

"Dodo, I was not. That's not fair." Lily spoke in a tensed, softened voice kept only for her sister.

"The redheaded one," said Dodo. "That was an oversight on your part."

"Don't bet on it."

When Hallie and Martha were saying their good-byes, Lily whispered to him that, as usual, Dodo was driving her crazy.

Hallie and Martha came out into a dazzling December night, clear and crisp, with the moon lighting the edges of the clouds. Martha was right, it was too beautiful not to walk the few blocks over to the Carlyle, so the Lawrences' car and driver, Victor, were sent on with their bags.

God, he hated asking Victor to do things like that.

In their suite, Hallie and Martha held another party, to which they had invited a few special people. Kip and Kate arrived; as did Malcolm and Nikki; Glenna and Lark, whom Hallie didn't remember seeing all evening, that's how exciting Lark was; Ham and the other famous Met, who had girls with them now. They all sat around having a great time, ordering chocolate soufflé and more brandies. They talked about baseball a lot, and Martha had a long talk with Kate. Later she told Hallie what an amazing coincidence it was that her sister Mim's roommate at Bryn Mawr had been Kate's older sister, Patty. Hallie didn't seem to think it was a coincidence at all.

Malcolm smoked about two hundred cigarettes and had several coughing fits while discussing French cinema with the famous Met.

Finally, when the newlyweds were alone, Hallie took his bride, in her wedding gown, which she soon relinquished ravenously.

The sex, frankly, was somehow short of the usual cosmic jolting Hallie had become used to. It was more that feeling of glass shattering than actual explosion. It started to worry him, but he blamed it on his drinking several bottles of champagne. At least he got it up.

They lay quietly together agreeing that the wedding had been just about as nice a wedding as you could have hoped for.

Hallie fell asleep thinking about his Aunt Dodo.

16

THE NEXT DAY, HALLIE AND MAR-
tha left for Europe. They first went to
London because Hallie had to go there
on business anyway, but even he didn't
want to know where they were going
after that lest anyone else find out.
They were going to ramble, as Martha
kept calling it.

And while they were in London,
Nikki was performing with the London Symphony Orchestra, so Martha
had an opportunity to hear Nikki play
again, now that she knew her so much
better. The concert had an odd affect
on Martha. She became very serious,
almost pensive, for a while afterward.
When Hallie noticed, he asked her
about it. She said that it must be really
something to be that brilliant, to be
that good at something as Nikki was
on the violin. And when they all went
out for dinner afterward, Martha kept

231

saying she was very tired. And Nikki clucked over her and ended the evening early.

They went to Italy and even to Paris, where Martha took him to places it never would have occurred to him to go. He bought her fine French underwear and dresses, shoes, hats, and an antique American Indian bracelet they found in a flea market. She said it was the best bracelet she had ever owned. Martha loved French rock 'n' roll and she bought CDs wherever they went. She knew all the French rock singers.

They had a fine time and the sex was absolutely everything Hallie had ever prayed for since the day he was born.

They returned home just before Christmas, and when Hallie came home from the office after his first day back, there were angels hanging everywhere in his apartment. Hallie had to pretend that Christmas didn't do to him what it did every year—help him toward a keener understanding of the concept of suicide. However, this first Christmas with Martha was kind of touching. It was so folksy. American folk art. She also made some amazing baked goods.

They spent Christmas Eve at the Lawrences' annual Christmas Eve party. Lily did her breathtaking tree, the most perfect *Nutcracker,* holiday-in-the-country tree in the world. Nothing arty-farty about it, no pink-and-silver themes for Lily. It was a tree lush with toy creatures, lights, and shiny balls. A tree that seemed honored and proud to have found itself into the lavish home of Lily Lawrence. A snob of a tree. And Martha said she had never seen a more perfect tree in her life. Martha had ideals.

Christmas Day was spent at the Housewrights', where, to put it in a nutshell, Hallie felt like Ben Gurion in the Norman Rockwell world of it all. He did get to talk to Ham the pitcher for hours and felt so good doing it that at the end of the day, when the knob of his Christmas depression had always been turned up to full blast, he found himself feeling almost content instead. Adie said it was important to sit quietly at the end of Christmas Day, so the Housewrights and Hallie were all seated in the living room, with only the light from the crackling fire to illuminate the relaxation. Hallie smoked the cigar Ham the coach had given him. He sat on the sofa with his arm around the curled-up Martha and watched the snow falling outside in the silent night. He felt he was in a card whose message read, "Chappy Cholidays."

Hallie was feeling no pain.

Yet.

After the holidays, as the month of January settled in beautifully cold and dark, Hallie and Martha settled down to married life, perfectly prepared to live happily ever after, if not longer. They decided to continue living in Hallie's apartment because at a time when a quarter of a million dollars bought the living space of a basketball player's shoe box, anything more spacious than Hallie's would have cost enough to finance the medical care of the entire Third World for the next ten years. Besides, Martha thought it was a terrific apartment and said she couldn't imagine wanting more. So it began to look less and less like a boy's dorm room and more and more like a cozy home, what with Martha's additions and arrangements. She had great instincts for the mission furniture.

And he loved everything she did.

It couldn't have been more than a few weeks after the wedding that Kip showed up. It was late at night, and he came in soaking wet because he had to park so far away. Standing in the foyer, where he was dripping uncontrollably all over the floor, he announced that he had come to New York to paint, which, he added, was a farce because he was so blocked. He and Kate were getting a divorce. She had said she would give up the local lawyer, but Kip told her it didn't make any difference whether she did or didn't. "I want babies," she had said, "and you don't." "No, not with you," he had said. He had been honest; he couldn't be faulted for anything more. Hallie was secretly thinking what mean bastards people became when they were honest. It reminded him of how he'd dealt honesty to Danny so many times and had felt like a mean bastard, too. The truth is, honesty is actually an awful thing and it's hard to understand why people are always striving to be so honest. In a way it's anti-Christian.

But Kip might have been exaggerating the brutality of his words because he was upset. Kate had agreed to the divorce. She said at least it was a decision made.

Then Kip began to sob.

He was embarrassed as hell to be sobbing in front of Martha; you could tell that because he would turn away from her when the sobs welled up. He hadn't expected Kate to be so agreeable. It had really made him feel sad about the whole thing. He said it was heartbreaking for him because there wasn't anything he could do about his feelings.

Hallie thought that Kip was doing the Sensitive Routine, which one usually did when there were girls around and you were upset and afraid you might make an asshole out of yourself. You went right for the Sensitive Routine because girls just love it. But Kip was doing it so well that it began to make Hallie empathetic, too. There was some real emotional disclosure going on. Kip's feelings were real and pouring all over the floor with the rain from his coat and shoes.

Martha told him he was a very good person, deep down, at heart, and very sensitive, which meant Hallie hadn't been totally wrong about his first impression of Kip's sobs. She fussed over him and helped Kip to rid himself of his wet parka. She seemed to know just what to say and Kip grew to be totally, but totally, at ease in front of her. He was really crying now. Hallie knew he should be feeling bad, but he was so struck by how well Martha fit in with the two old friends, that he missed sharing Kip's grief. But that was Hallie for you.

They decided that Kip could stay with them until he found a place. Martha had recently bought a folding screen and she showed him how they could put it in front of the couch so that he would have his own little room.

After Martha had gone to bed, Kip and Hallie sat together smoking cigars and talking about honesty as a concept.

"I couldn't take it anymore. It got to the point when every time I walked in the room she would start to cry. And I couldn't comfort her; I couldn't say to her, 'Look, things will get better,' or 'Things aren't so bad,' because things were getting worse every time she started to cry. People can't do that to each other."

"I feel bad about it, Kip," said Hallie. Then he decided to try and lighten things up. "By the way, did I detect a little of the old Kipper Sensitive Routine back there for Martha?"

"Hallie, don't do that now," said Kip.

Hallie instantly felt like a heel. What bothered him most about Kip's divorce was that Kate had never been the right woman for him in the first place. Kip and Kate had met at Harvard and fell in together almost automatically, as if they had been assigned to each other like a course. They had the kind of meaningful sex you first have in college, and they held hands everywhere they went. Two years after graduation, the heat was turned so high by both their families to cement this most acceptable union that Kip had no choice but to give in. In spite of his undeniable rantings that he wasn't ready to be married because there were just too many beautiful babes in the world, Kip had had no choice.

And now, finally, Kip had decided he did.

They sat together by the light of one low-burning lamp and the light from the fireplace. From the bedroom came the muffled sound of the Rolling Stones.

After a period of silence, Hallie finally spoke. "You tried, Kip. You tried."

"Thanks, Hal," said Kip quietly. "The truth is, I never really did."

It was a touching moment.

*   *   *

A few days after Kip's arrival, Hallie got a call from Nikki. They talked almost every other day, because the picture had started shooting and Nikki was staying at the St. James Club in L.A. She would call to talk to Hallie and she would call to talk to Martha and they were keeping in close touch. But this time Hallie was working late at the office. It was nearly nine-thirty when the phone rang. Nikki said she had just gotten back from the studio, and she needed to chat. So they chatted about Alfred, about the film, about someone they both knew whom Nikki had run into at a restaurant, and then she got to the point.

"Hallie, is there a possibility you could come to L.A.?" She paused. He could hear her breathe. Then the tough little Russian voice continued, "I know this is not the kind of thing you might normally expect me to ask, but I need someone from home, someone who reminds me what's real; do you know what I'm saying? There's so much bullshit here. Can you come for just two days, one day, half an hour? I don't know, this is stupid of me to ask you. Never mind."

"What's the matter? What's wrong?"

"No, nothing. I just don't know who are these people here! I don't know how to tell what they *are.*"

"It's okay, Nikki, it's only Los Angeles. You're in L.A.!"

"I'm telling you something serious and you're making a joke?" Her return was an instant endearing challenge.

"Actually, I wasn't."

"So, you can come?"

"You got it, Nikki," said Hallie without a second thought. "Nikki, by the way, let me ask you something. How are you getting along with Malcolm?"

"How do you mean?"

"Why? What do you think I mean? Do you think I mean it in any particular way?"

"What are you talking about, Hallie Lawrence?" There followed a delighted laugh.

"I mean, are you working well with him?"

"Yes, it's okay. He's a little bit of a crazy person, but it's okay."

"I'm leaving tomorrow," said Hallie.

Nikki hung up the phone. Somehow she had known it would be okay to to call him and that there was a good chance that he would do as she asked. It wasn't the kind of thing she had ever done before, calling someone to come and comfort her. Hallie was her friend. It would be interesting to see if he would be bringing Martha along. It would be nice to see Martha, too.

*   *   *

That night, after the call from Nikki, Hallie finally went home. He opened his door expecting the sound of French rock 'n' roll, of Kip and Martha laughing somewhere in the apartment, expecting to see them coming out to greet him. But instead, the apartment was dark.

Hallie turned on a few lights and found a note that said they had gone to a movie but would be back by ten for dinner. It made sense, as he had told them he'd be back around then. Going to a movie was a good idea.

In the bedroom, he took off his tie and coat, hung them up neatly, then removed his shirt. This he wadded into a ball and chucked into the hamper from behind his back. He made a clean shot. He put on a sweatshirt, went into the living room, and made himself a drink. In fact, he made a whole pitcherful of martinis. He knew the old Kipper loved his martinis.

He noticed the red light on the answering machine throbbing on and off, so he checked it out. There were two calls. The first call was from Martha, obviously in a street phone booth, saying she was just calling in case he'd come home early, but since he hadn't, she and Kip were seeing a film and would be back by ten.

What a girl. A note and a call.

The second message was from Malcolm Ferrari. The son of a bitch.

"Martha, baby, I just felt like chatting; sorry I didn't catch you in. Oh, well, try again soon. Say hello to Hallie for me."

It was mind-boggling. Say hello to Hallie for me? The nerve, the largeness of balls, leaving a message like that. The unspeakable heinousness of his calling Martha at all. Hallie took a big gulp of martini. Then he took another. The best thing to do was erase the tape. Don't even let Martha know Malcolm had called.

He erased the tape.

Oh, God! Had he learned nothing from seeing a President toppled over the erasing of a tape? His fingerprints, which would probably glow in the dark under the right powder, would let Martha discover what a psycho he was.

But wait a minute. Did that call sound as if Martha had spoken to Malcolm since the wedding, or what? Of course! If the son of a bitch felt free enough to call for a chat, they must have spoken since then.

He should have played the tape once more before he erased it. How could he have erased it?

At that moment, Martha and Kip returned.

"Is that a pitcher of Lawrence martinis I see?" Kip's voice preceded him into the room. He entered and headed for the bar, still wearing his army parka. "Ah, and it's young Master Lawrence himself, home from defending the meek and oppressed at the highest courts in the land."

Hallie had moved away from the phone machine like a cat burglar in a silent movie. Martha came in and bounded enthusiastically over to Hallie.

"Hi, Hallie, we just saw the best movie I've ever seen in my life!"

"What's that?" asked Hallie. He held her as she pressed against him with a hug. She smelled like powdered sugar and lilacs.

"Love and Death. Woody Allen."

"Sonya here had never seen it," said Kip. "Can you imagine that?"

"You never saw it? Well, did you like it?" Hallie refilled his martini glass. He felt his hands shaking and ordered a stop to that immediately. Although he did feel a little disappointed that he hadn't been the one to take her to see the film if she hadn't seen it before, his real concern was how he could confirm that Martha had spoken to Malcolm.

Over dinner of lamb chops, the most sensational mashed potatoes ever made, and a delicious salad, they talked about the movie *Love and Death.* Kip and Hallie got into an old debate about whether or not it was like a Bob Hope movie. Hallie said it was because the comic hero was a coward. Kip disagreed, and said with those glasses the hero was a Jew, and that made it much funnier. Martha agreed, with a lot of animation. Hallie wrote it off, figuring they were just having an anti-Semitic moment.

Later that evening, Lily called him and asked him to have lunch with her. He hated having lunch with his mother because she always wanted to go to one of those idiot places where certain kinds of ladies lunch. Hallie suggested drinks somewhere later instead. Lily suggested tea at the Mayfair Regent, but they could sit on the balcony and not at one of the sofa arrangements. Hallie agreed. Then he went to join Martha in the bedroom.

When he climbed into bed beside her she was reading a biography, wearing one of her trademark T-shirts. Martha was always reading biographies. She particularly favored the tell-all variety, as opposed to the Boswell's *Life of Samuel Johnson* sort. In the tape deck near her side of the bed she was playing some French rock 'n' roll.

Hallie snuggled next to her, playfully doing his best to distract her from the book.

"Don't, I'm reading," she said, but with a laugh.

Hallie rested his head on her chest for a moment and thought about the Malcolm message.

"Marth, Nikki asked me to come out to L.A."

"She did?" Martha put her book aside.

"Yeah, I think she's a little weirded out, surrounded by so many Hollywood assholes."

"Hollywood assholes and Malcolm." The fact that she had bothered to separate him from the category annoyed him.

"She's not falling for Malcolm, she told me she thinks he's a crazy person."

"God, I hope you're right. You should definitely go and maybe you can talk to her. Warn her about him, Hallie."

"Did you tell her about Malcolm and you?"

"No." Martha put her book away and turned out the light. She melted her body against him as only she could, wrapping him with one of her long legs.

"No? Isn't that a girl thing to do?" Hallie took her into his arms.

"What do you know about girls, Hallie Lawrence?" She giggled sweetly into his neck. But Hallie wasn't feeling good.

"Well, look, Martha, if you're so damned concerned about Nikki and Malcolm, why don't you warn her yourself? You're the one who knows him. You're the one with the experience, God knows."

"Hallie, that's a little mean, don't you think?" Her body hardened slightly.

"When you spoke to Malcolm, did he tell you he was putting the make on Nikki?"

"I could hear it in his voice, definitely."

"Excuse me," said Hallie and he sat up. "And when did you speak to him?"

"I spoke to him a couple of weeks ago. He called here. He wanted to talk."

"Well, of all the nerve—"

"It's a funny thing about Malcolm," Martha overrode. "It was always said of him that all his girlfriends remain friends afterward— Hallie, I'm ignoring your craziness! I'm telling you the truth, and if you have a brain, you'll listen. I realized when I spoke to him that he can be a very good friend, once you're not angry with him anymore. And I guess I love you so much, Hallie, that I'm not angry anymore."

"Well, that's timely, because I'm angry enough for the both of us! Good friend? Is that what you think he's trying to be? A friend? Come on, Marth!"

"What's the matter with you, Hallie?" Martha switched on the light, and, pretty angry herself, crossed her arms defiantly. "Why are you angry?"

"I'm angry, yes, but I'm going to stay calm, I promise. I'm angry at the colossal nerve of him calling my wife! Trying to get you away from me! That's what I'm angry about!"

"You're screaming, Hallie!"

"Okay. All right! I'm not screaming anymore, see? Just take into account reality, Martha. The guy is not out to become your friend."

"If you think Malcolm is trying to take me away from you, you are certifiable. Come on, you can't be serious! Jesus Christ, give me a fucking break!"

There was something in Martha's voice that he just couldn't stand. She was really angry.

"Martha, I'm sorry!" He grabbed her arms. "Please, forgive me! I don't know what happens to me!"

After a beat, she took his hand. "I forgive you, nerd. But it's taking you a really long time to quit being an asshole."

"I'm not an asshole!"

Martha turned out the light again.

"Do I have to come with you to L.A.?"

"No, you don't have to, of course not. I'll go tomorrow and be back by the end of the week. Will you be okay? Actually, the question is, will I be okay?"

"Let's make sure," whispered Martha into the darkness as she took off her T-shirt.

So Hallie went to L.A. and checked into the St. James Club, which he didn't particularly like, but recognized as expedient. He went immediately to Nikki's room to pick her up for dinner.

"Come in quickly. Quickly!" She grabbed his arm and pulled him into her suite and closed the door. "Where's Martha?"

"In New York. What is this? KGB? CIA?"

"Malcolm might come and we are going to pretend we're not here. He lives in this hotel too, you know. In fact, we are going right out. I don't want to see him."

"Why? What's going on, Nikki?"

"Every night, as soon as he is back from the studio, he comes to ask if I'll eat with him. He would see you and ask, 'Can I come along?' And we don't want that, believe me—Hallie, let me look at you! Let me see you!" She took him in with glittering eyes. "You look good! Talk to me, say smart things! Tell me about Alfred! Let's talk about the Brahms! The Prokofiev! No! First we go!"

"Nikki, do you have a fever? Are you sick? And, more important, is it contagious?"

"What, I'm sick because I'm happy to see you?" She clapped her hands together with delight, but she was disappointed that Martha hadn't come. "I didn't know *how* glad I would be to see you! I'm starving! What about you? Hungry?"

"Let's get out of here!"

They ate at a restaurant not frequented by members of the film community, somewhere downtown. With several vodkas put away, Hallie was enjoying Nikki's animated anecdotes immensely. Then, quite out of the blue, she lit a cigarette and grew serious.

"Malcolm says he is in love with me. All the time, anytime he comes near me, he says to me, 'Nikki, I love you.' " She was full of theatrical emphasis and irony. "When he is giving me direction, or even when he isn't, always he has to tell me about big feelings he has for me every time I come into the room. He is miserable, he says, he has nothing but the film to express what he is feeling for me. That's how he knows it will be a masterpiece. In your whole life, did you ever hear so much bullshit?"

Hallie felt the most exhilarating, uncanny sense of relief. Nikki could never fall for Malcolm. But he had always known that.

"So, you're not in love with him," Hallie said. "He'll live."

"I *like* him very much. When we're working together, he is good, Hallie. But always he starts in about love, and feelings, and I want to faint so I won't have to hear any more."

Hallie did not think it was possible that Malcolm had fallen in love with Nikki. He saw only the basest motive for his behavior: the son of a bitch was using her to get to Martha. It wasn't hard to see Hallie was beginning to play with fewer marbles every day.

He spent the next two days on the set watching the film being made. Hallie was struck anew by the DTG of Malcolm. He now found Malcolm's endearing manner with him, which once he had rather liked, to be assaholic. Malcolm was acting as if Hallie were his best friend. He even asked him if he wanted to go driving with him on Saturday, but Hallie said he'd be gone by then; but too bad, he added, it would have been fun.

Hallie was still being Hallie Lawrence, even in this awkward situation with the son of a bitch, even with fewer marbles.

Hallie focused on the relationship between Nikki and Malcolm as they worked together. He noticed that Malcolm was always touching her, but in Hallie's mind this had more to do with Malcolm's assaholia than his coming on to her, it was that pathetic. And as far as Nikki was concerned, Hallie saw nothing in her attitude toward Malcolm that could have been construed as her falling for him at all, so the deprecatory remarks she had made about him the previous evening were apparently not false cover.

Hallie definitely concluded that Malcolm's flirtations with both him and Nikki somehow had to do with his trying to get closer to Martha.

On his last night in L.A., Hallie woke in a cold sweat. He had been dreaming that he was watching a horror movie on TV and he went to get Martha from the kitchen to join him. But when he went back to open the bedroom door, he opened the linen closet instead and found that he had walked into the horror movie. He was trying to figure out how to get back out before things got too scary when a figure in a large black, hooded cloak came and grabbed him. "Get out of the film" came the most horrifying, throaty, preternatural whisper he'd ever heard, and when he turned around to see who was inside the black cloak, there was nothing in it but thick black smoke. It was the sound of the voice that had been so scary; it left him paralyzed to the point that he was afraid to look over the side of the bed. Finally he turned on the light and reached for the phone to call Martha.

For all he knew, Malcolm was sitting in his room, on the phone with Martha right at that moment. He was relieved when Martha answered.

"Are you on the other line?" he asked.

"No! Hi, Hallie! When are you coming home?"

He did feel relieved and proceeded to tell her he didn't think there was anything to worry about with Malcolm and Nikki. His fear vanished. They chatted, said a few obscene things to each other, and then Hallie had a word with Kip about the assaholia of Malcolm Ferrari. He felt even better knowing Kip was there, taking care of Martha. Kip could keep her from going out alone, being friendly with some guy at the grocery store, and running away to live in Tucson.

She was safe.

The next day, as he was leaving for the airport, he ran into Malcolm in the hotel lobby. Malcolm talked about how glad he would be when the company moved to London, where most of the shooting would take place. Hallie told him the film looked good so far, and to keep up the good work. He said he thought the film was better when Malcolm worked faster, that it had a more spontaneous creative flow. Malcolm seemed to take the advice seriously.

Then Malcolm said, in the act of shaking Hallie's hand, "I spoke to Martha a few weeks ago. She's very happy, Hallie, she really is. It makes me feel good." He gave Hallie a look of such sincerity that Hallie wanted to throw up. Or punch the guy.

"You English don't usually say things like that, do you," he said with a pleasant smile. "I'm glad it makes you feel good, Malcolm."

As the cab drove off, Hallie didn't wave.

*   *   *

On the plane back to New York, the only respite he got from the nonstop, stampeding, thunderclapping headache, caused by knowing that Malcolm and Martha were speaking God only knew how often, was remembering his tea with Lily, the day he left.

Some respite.

Lily had sat there, slicked and chic in a dark suit, actually suggesting that Martha model for Noel Brandt. It was unbelievable. Hallie told her it was the worst idea anyone had ever had in the history of the world. Lily had pouted and said that there had been worse ideas in the history of the world, and suggested that Hallie knew it.

Sitting on the plane, trying to read *Sports Illustrated,* he happened to glance at an add that featured a very attractive girl in a bathing suit. Imagine the idea of Martha being looked at, in a bathing suit, by guys on planes all over the world. The headache started again, the roaring pitch, going past the point where it should stop and level off into no-man's land. Hallie found himself pressing on his temples, trying to squeeze the pain into stopping.

Jesus, maybe he had a brain tumor.

In New York Hallie's return was greeted by an enthusiastic Martha, who had made delicious salmon croquettes for dinner and had baked a beautiful chocolate cake on which she had written "Welcome Home, Hallie" in butter-cream frosting. It was a terrific cake.

"You made this?" asked Hallie, never ceasing to be amazed.

"Oh, it's real easy. This isn't a difficult cake at all." He had hugged her and sniffed her neck, which was perfumed with something mysterious and compelling. One of the most irritating songs he had ever heard in his life was coming from the speakers—and worse, Martha knew the words.

"You smell good," said Hallie.

"Oh, do you like it? Noel gave it to me. It's a brand-new perfume he's bringing out." Martha was scraping carrots like an expert.

"It's very nice."

"Kipper?" Martha called out. "Dinner!"

Hallie just loved the way she called him Kipper.

"I'm starving," said Kip, coming in from the living room, shirt-tails out, no shoes or socks, carrying a book.

"And I've cooked a great fucking dinner, if I do say so." She beamed as she went to remove dinner from the oven, bending from the waist, which filled her short skirt with the outlines of her behind. How could she look so positively like a fantasy homemaker and still say "fucking"? It never ceased to kill Hallie.

At dinner, he watched her in the candlelight. Her hair shone brightly, it looked so touchable, and her eyes caught the light and sparkled. The soft, pink lips parted and moved as she spoke, then closed on the rim of her wineglass. She laughed and tossed back her hair.

As soon as they had finished dinner, Hallie left the table and went into the bedroom. He kept going in and coming out, hoping Martha would get the hint that he wanted to be alone with her. Actually, Kip got it long before Martha did. He got his jacket from the front hall and said he was going out to the newsstand to look at the mags. Hallie busied himself at the mail table in the hall, where the mail had piled up in his absence. Suddenly he froze.

While absently flipping through envelopes, he'd come upon a picture postcard of the beach in Santa Monica. On the reverse side was the inscription, "The Pacific Ocean," and Malcolm's signature.

"Why, here's a card from Malcolm," he said calmly, considering the tingles running across his forehead. "And what a message, 'The Pacific Ocean.' Gee, Malcolm, I couldn't tell that from the photograph."

"A card from Malcolm? I didn't see that. I guess I didn't go through the mail."

"And if you had, you would have thrown this out so I wouldn't have seen it?"

"Why would I do that?" said Martha. She was holding a plate with a large slice of chocolate cake and a large dollop of fresh whipped cream, and a glass of milk. "Let's see it."

"What does he mean about the Pacific Ocean; is that a code of some kind?"

She put down the milk and quickly scanned the card, holding it as if it were distasteful. "Look, you boob, it's not even addressed to me. It's addressed to Mr. and Mrs. Hallie Lawrence. Grow up, jerko! And don't you get the humor? It's just calling things what they are. It's a sort of understatement."

"That's a laugh riot!"

"Stop it. Let's go to bed," whispered Martha, and she took her milk and cake and went off to the bedroom. Hallie stood looking at the postcard, convincing himself that the "Mrs." on the address was actually written a little larger than the "Mr."

"Shit," said Hallie.

He found Martha dressed in a fantastic outfit, some kind of black leather corset with silk underpants, stockings and garters, and the tartest pair of red high-heeled shoes ever thought up. She had lit about thirty candles everywhere and some Chet Baker played softly from the speakers.

"Did you miss me?" she asked, coming toward him.

"What are you wearing? This is fabulous, Marth."

She was smiling that incredibly wanton smile, with the lips slightly parted as she came and put them on his. Then she turned her back to him, bent over from the waist and, indicating the black silk panties, whispered, "Help me take them off."

His heart was pounding. The image. The long legs, the panties, the garters holding up the stockings, the black leather thing stopping just at the waist. He took off her panties, then she turned to him suddenly and began to kiss him and remove his shirt. She was all over him, kissing his chest, his neck, and he caught her momentum and began to pull off his clothes himself. He grabbed her to him, or she grabbed him to her; it was hard to tell because things were getting pretty exciting. There was something wild going on between them.

Hallie threw Martha on the bed and removed the corset so he could watch those magnificent breasts. He tried to enter her, but she scrambled away from him, only to sit up and begin kissing him all over again. She kept up this avoidance play, which was turning Hallie into some kind of Mongolian warlord. Each time he came close to entering her she would scramble away until he was so provoked he used real strength to mount her. She shuddered and gasped and closed her legs around him. With his newfound strength, he scooped her up. She wrapped herself tightly around him, and he moved them around the room as their rhythms became more desperate. Then he slammed her against the wall while he danced against her and she held him with powerful arms and legs.

"Oh, Hallie."

"Oh, Martha."

They moved into the living room, where he sat her bare ass on the sofa arm and they continued this rapturous madness. They were both sweating now, which added the extra sensation of their bodies' sticking together, and it drove them on.

In the kitchen, he seated her on the counter. He fumbled for an ice cube, and as he entered her again, he took that ice cube and rubbed it on her nipple. She screamed out and he immediately warmed it with his mouth. He repeated this. Martha was simply moaning. She was totally abandoned to him.

Then somehow they were in the living room again and he had placed her on the rug and they were coming, more violently than ever before. He could feel her spasms grabbing him and milk his life juice right into her while her hands held tightly on to his ass.

They were really exhausted when it was finished. They fell asleep in front of three remaining red embers in the fireplace, with him still inside her.

At about two-thirty they woke up freezing and made a dash for the down-covered warmth of the bed. They hugged each other very tightly until morning.

Not more than two and a half, at most three weeks after Hallie's return from L.A., Andy Werdlow called from London, where the film company was now shooting.

It seemed that at four weeks into their schedule, the film was shooting a little slower than they had anticipated.

"How far behind are you?" asked Hallie in the nicest of voices.

"Well, we'll probably need the time at the end that we left sort of open."

"That's why we left it open," said Hallie.

"Yes, well, I'm sure that will be enough time."

"You don't sound sure at all, Andy."

"Hallie, those few days you spent in L.A., well, Malcolm was shooting a lot faster then. I don't know, maybe he was trying to impress you or something, maybe because you're a smart New York lawyer, maybe because of Martha, I don't know, but he moved things along much quicker. You don't suppose you might come over to London—I don't know, whenever it's convenient for you—and maybe visit the set?"

Things must be pretty bad, thought Hallie. Andy had been speaking in an extremely calm voice that belied a certain panic. Hallie was familiar with that tone people get when they are trying hard to cover hysteria. He also didn't appreciate the reference to Martha and Malcolm.

"No problem. I'll be there by the end of the week."

Kip announced that he had found a loft down in Tribeca that he liked, the perfect place for him to sit around and have his block. He also announced that he had sold another painting, this time for twenty-two thousand dollars, and at this rate all he had to do was sit back and sell off all the work he'd already done and not worry if he ever painted again. He figured if he never painted again, it would only raise the value of the existing work. This theory, Hallie pointed out, was a simple rationale for painter's block, and he told Kip not to worry, the block would end.

When Hallie got around to mentioning the trip to London, Martha smoked a cigarette.

"I'm glad you're going," she said. "I think Nikki is falling for Malcolm."

"Martha, please. Why are you still talking like that? She thinks he's an asshole."

"I don't think so," said Martha.

"Well, I know she does," said the ever-confident Hallie.

Then he thought he saw Martha give Kip a little look. He wasn't sure, but he thought that's what she did before she spoke.

"Malcolm told me he's madly in love with her."

"Uh-huh. When did you speak to Malcolm?" Here we go again, thought Hallie.

"I had lunch with him."

She had lunch with him.

Okay, thought Hallie, quick—think about something else. Watch Kip go to the bar, pick up the brandy bottle and three glasses, and bring them over to the coffee table. Have one immediately.

"He just wanted to talk to me," continued Martha, taking the brandy Kip offered her. "He sounded so desperate, I figured what the hell. I mean, you'd meet with any human being who sounded so desperate. That's when he told me how he felt about Nikki."

"If Adolf Hitler wanted to have lunch with you and he sounded desperate enough, you'd have lunch with him?"

"Hallie, don't be a douchebag, okay?" Martha gave him a look.

"Martha, my dear, let me explain something," Kip piped up, "Hallie is a certifiable lunatic. He thinks Malcolm Ferrari could steal you away from him. What other possible cause could there be for this ludicrous hallucination, other than his lunacy?" Kip was into the possibility of a drama. Hallie found it annoying. He wasn't too fond of revealing his psychotic jealous side in front of Kip.

"Okay, so you had lunch with Malcolm. No problem. What was he so desperate to talk about?" Hallie's eyes focused on Martha, trying to stay cool.

"Nikki is falling for his bullshit."

"I happen to know otherwise, but go on. By the way, those were his exact words? 'Nikki is falling for my bullshit'?" Hallie heard the hostility in his voice and it was directed at Martha. If he could hear it, he could imagine how well Kip and maybe even Martha could hear it.

"Hallie, he'll dump her the minute the picture's finished. That's the way he works."

"You're nuts, Martha, I spoke to Nikki yesterday. She's not falling for him, okay?"

"Did you ask her?"

"Let me ask you something. When did you have this lunch with Malcolm?"

"He was in New York for the day, looking at some location, and we had lunch. He's got it bad for Nikki. And believe me, it's not totally one-sided."

"What's the matter with you, man?" asked Kip.

Hallie looked over at him and realized his rage was leaking out all over.

"She doesn't get what's going on," said Hallie. "She doesn't get that the son of a bitch is just trying to make her jealous, to win her back. That's what Nikki's all about."

"Nikki kept calling him!" shouted Martha, her frustration with Hallie ever increasing.

"She kept calling him, at the restaurant?"

"We had lunch at his hotel."

In bed! thought Hallie. That's it! I knew it! His forehead prickled and his cheeks felt warm. He stared at Kip, hoping the sight of his friend would keep him from having one of his catatonic episodes. It worked, because he wanted to kill Kip for being there and it helped displace his anger.

"I went to his hotel because he had so little time. And Nikki called him twice. I could just see by the way he was talking to her that something was going on between them. It was a little bit familiar to me, Hallie."

"When was this?"

"I don't know when it was; let me think, it must have been last Saturday, because I know it was the day you went to that lunch."

So, last Saturday, while he sat at a business lunch at the Harvard Club, where thoughts of whipped cream and Martha had sustained his unbelievable boredom, Martha had been in a hotel room with Malcolm, who had chosen that exact time to sneak into New York with some pretense about location scouting. Jesus.

"He's a sleazedog," offered Kip. He took out a pack of Camels and offered Martha one. She was quick to accept.

"Well," said Hallie, not without a little laugh of astonishment, "I think luring you to his hotel room is the last straw!"

"Damn it, Hallie!"

"Come on, man."

"Don't 'man' me right now, okay?"

"Listen to Martha, she's telling you the truth, man."

"Will you please stop saying 'man'?"

"I don't know why I give a shit," said Martha, getting up from the table. She walked toward the bedroom. "I just care about Nikki, that's all. I just really like her." She went into the bedroom and closed the door.

There was a silence left behind by Martha's exit.

"You're being an asshole," Kip said quietly.

"I'm not the asshole here, asshole." They were reaching new heights of maturity.

"If you could think a little bit beyond Hallie Lawrence, you might be able to see that there's no way Martha is interested in that sleazedog when she has you—"

"What do you mean? She was once?"

"But now she's married to fucking Hallie Lawrence, for Christ's sake. She's married to you! You're in another league and she knows it. You know how boring your stupid neurosis is?"

"You're flattering me to keep me off guard."

"And you're a paranoid little shit! You don't even fucking deserve her!"

Oh boy, did there ever follow a deadly silence.

"Martha is only trying to protect Nikki," Kip said finally. His voice had a tone that said they should carry on and not acknowledge what had been said. It was part of the special nature of their friendship that they both knew how to stop a fight even after a shot had been fired.

Hallie, who at once accepted the diversion from what would have been the first fight they had in maybe fifteen years, sank slowly back into the sofa.

"I just don't want to see you blow it, Hallie. Giving Martha a hard time about Malcolm is pathetic. She was afraid even to tell you she had lunch with him."

"I don't deserve her," he said. "You're right."

On the night flight to London, Hallie sat staring out the window, something he hadn't done on a plane in a long time. The stewardess came over to care for him in a manner that implied her duties might be continued in London. But she depressed him. Her big smile, her pretty blond hair, her obviously cared-for body only made him realize the perfection of Martha.

So he sat staring out the window into the night. What he saw was actually pretty spectacular—a full moon lighting the thick field of clouds below with a blue, surreal glow. Seeing the millions of stars, Hallie wished the plane could go higher, straight up, in fact, until other stars and other planets were as close as the big full moon. He thought about making love to Martha journeying through outer space and wondered if you could get a hard-on when you were weightless. He wished that plane engines were silent.

Martha.

Before he had left, they had discussed Hallie's insanity over Malcolm, and she had told him quite calmly to stop bugging her about him all the time, but she denied that she was mad at him because of it.

"I'm not mad at you, Hallie, honestly, but it's a drag, you know?

It seems that except for maybe the first week of our relationship, you've been going nuts about someone being after me. I thought we had it all out in L.A. I thought when we were married you'd stop. But you just can't stop."

"Yes, I can!"

"It's okay, I understand."

They made love the night before he left, but he could swear to God something was wrong with her. She seemed a little withdrawn somehow. He was sorry he had agreed to go to London. What he should do was stay home and take care of her, take her out, show her a good time. Play with her. He had asked Kip not to move out until he got back. He wouldn't be gone long, he promised. Maybe a week, tops.

So he stared out at the big full moon lighting the frozen clouds that seemed to cover the whole earth. In a way, he wished he could live up there, alone, on the blue clouds. He could hunt stray birds.

In London, it was a gray, overcast day, and damp.

Nikki was sitting in her dressing room at the Twickenham Studios, waiting. Usually she practiced when she was waiting. But today she felt the need to be alone. She was smoking a cigarette. It was a Gauloise. Nikki didn't really smoke. It was just an affectation she was in the mood for these days. She was watching herself smoke the Gauloise, looking into the dressing-table mirror. She wanted to go home. She wanted to go home to New York, to her apartment on Riverside Drive, to sit cross-legged on the bare dark wood floor near the fireplace, and play her violin.

She didn't know Hallie was coming.

17

HALLIE TOOK A CAB TO CLARIDGE'S, checked in and telephoned Nikki.

"What do you mean, you're in London? Nobody told me you were coming! Come over right this minute!"

She told him she was staying in a little mews house in Chelsea that belonged to a girlfriend of hers who was somewhere in Germany singing opera. She gave him the address and repeated that he should come right over this minute. But first Hallie took a bath in the giant Claridge bathtub. Only in England could a grown man actually find a bathtub where his feet didn't touch the other end.

The diesel-chugging cab pulled up to a charming little house as the brakes squealed to a stop. Although the cab motor idled loudly as Hallie paid the driver, the distant sound of violin playing could be heard coming from the

house. It grew clearer as the cab pulled away and left Hallie standing in the quiet street. Hallie listened for a moment. Nikki was
playing a movement from the Tchaikovsky Concerto, a section he
particularly liked. He inhaled the English winter evening, the damp
air that was scented with deisel fumes. For some reason, he felt this
moment was going to be one of those odd times you never forget
for the rest of your life. The door was red, and the door knocker
was a lion's head holding a ring. Hallie knocked.

The playing stopped, and in seconds, Nikki had thrown the door
open and gasped with pleasure.

"What did I do to deserve this? Hallie Lawrence, Hallie Lawrence, Hallie Lawrence," she said, hugging him with all her might.
In fact, it was more than a hug, she was holding on to him. "God,
oh God, it's so good to see you!"

He felt her soft curls against his face and smelled her wonderful
clean smell. "Nobody told me you were are coming! I'll kill that
Andy Werdlow. Not to mention you! You could have telephoned
me! God, this lifts my spirits so much, I can't believe it."

"You look great" was all Hallie could say. She was wearing black
tights with socks and leg warmers and a big gray cashmere sweater.

"You think I look good? Then pour us drinks and we'll celebrate!
I just took a bottle out of the pathetic little English freezer. I mean,
what do the English know about freezers? It's the size of a match-
box— The bottle is there, you pour. I'll get the snacks." She went
out to the kitchen, saying, "I love that word, snacks. It sounds exactly
like what it is. What do you call that, onomatopoeia?"

"Yeah, but 'snacks' doesn't sound anything like what it is."

"Yes, it does," she called out. "Snacks! QUICK food. Little bites.
SnaCCCK! It does sound like what it is!"

Hallie smiled. He looked around the pretty room. One wall was
lined with books from floor to ceiling and the curtains were a
dark-maroon velvet. There was a fire in the fireplace, and comfortable, deep furniture. But it was all on a very small-scale, like a doll
house. Hallie poured out the frozen vodkas as Nikki returned with
a tray.

Her violin, in its opened case, lay on the sofa, and a music stand
facing a chair stood nearby. Amazing things, violins.

"All I have is cheese, okay? Lucky for you, I was making batter
for blinis when you called, so we are having blinis and caviar for
supper."

It was good to see Nikki. He settled down deep into the sofa and
accepted a water cracker with a spread of Stilton on it.

"So, tell me everything," said Hallie. "How's the picture going?
How far behind are you?"

"Who knows, who knows, we'll see when it's finished how it's going. How far behind? I'm worried, not a whole lot, but I'm worried." She sat on the floor polishing off a Stilton-layered cracker herself, washing it down with some vodka.

Hallie was contemplating Nikki more than actually listening to her, kind of taking her in, because he found that he felt incredibly good being with her in this familial way. Her intelligence was the thing that came across most, aside from the bad-girl daring. A preoccupation with some thought or other kept her often unaware of herself physically. She would run her hand through her hair with total disregard for the way it looked. This lack of self-awareness, and thus of her own sexuality, was very endearing. Hallie had never noticed it before.

"The last thing we must let happen, Hallie, is for me to run into trouble with my concert dates. Alfred would love that. And no matter how good the picture is, how necessary it is to shoot longer, we can't let it happen because of Alfred. It's that simple. We can't be reasonable and allow them more time."

"Right on the nose, Nik."

She made Hallie come into the kitchen and he watched her turn the smooth batter into blinis and then they sat down at the little dining table set up in the living room. Nikki's eyes were on fire, crackling along with every amusing anecdote she told. She was full of anecdotes, and the more she ate the faster they came, and the more exuberantly she told them. But none had, so far, involved Malcolm. So finally Hallie asked her:

"How's Malcolm?"

Nikki shrugged. She sighed. She poured Hallie a glass of wine. She said, "Who knows?"

It was a bit noncommittal for Hallie's taste.

"Has he still got the hots for you, my dear?" asked Hallie, not a little embarrassed by his use of jargon.

Nikki looked at Hallie for a moment and then decided to say, "All right, tell me. What is it about Malcolm you want to know? Why do you always ask me about him?"

"I don't know, Nik." He had been afraid that he would feel foolish telling Nikki of his suspicions about Malcolm and Martha, and foolish he felt.

"I've notice that you always ask me about him."

"He's the director of the picture!"

"But what is it you want to know?" Nikki was a very perceptive woman, and she saw at once that Hallie actually didn't seem to know what he wanted to ask her, so she said, "Tell me, how is Martha? Is it good being married? Hallie Lawrence, newlywed! Maybe you should go on the TV show."

"Thank you," said Hallie.

"I remember now how I love to tease you."

"It's great being married. She's great. It's just great, what can I tell you?"

"She's such a beauty."

"I know, it is extraordinary how beautiful she is."

They had for the moment avoided a discussion of Malcolm.

When they were almost sick from eating so many blinis, they moved from the table to the floor in front of the fire. Hallie took off his shoes. He had another drink but Nikki didn't because she said she had to pay attention to her face for the movie. Hallie wasn't sure why he continued talking about Martha, but he did. Maybe it was that he felt so supremely relaxed, well fed, and so content being with Nikki. But it was probably the vodka that made him say, "It's just that the sex is so unbelievable with her. She drives me wild. She's the sexiest woman I've ever met."

That's not the kind of thing a man should ever tell another woman, no matter what kind of relationship he has with her. Nor should a woman tell it to a man. It will always release something in the other person that is better not released.

Nikki smiled at him. She sighed and took Hallie's drink and helped herself to a slow swallow. If anything, she appeared amused.

"I have to tell you something," she said. "I went to bed with Malcolm."

And Hallie saw the image flash itself on a large screen inside his brain.

"You've got to be kidding."

"I wish."

There was no way he could display any kind of reaction to this, as he felt an immediate shot of novocaine right in this chest, numbing any feelings before they could make brain contact. There simply was no emotional reaction to this information.

"Uh, gee, Nik," he stammered.

"Only one time. Now you know."

"It's funny. Martha thought you might be falling for him."

"I'm not falling for him, Hallie. I'm not falling for him." She said this in a way that had Hallie totally convinced. "I know now that he lived with Martha."

"Did he talk about that?"

"Afterward, yes. God, Hallie, she should have told me this! I asked her on the phone why she didn't tell me. She said, 'Sorry Nikki, I should have.' What a shiksa you have there, if you don't mind me saying."

"Well, I think she was a little flabbergasted at the coincidence of Malcolm doing the picture."

"Hallie, she should have told me, but I think she's just embarrassed for anyone to know what a fleabag she lived with before you. I don't blame her."

"Nik—"

"What happened with me and Malcolm was one night of—I don't know, it just happened—passion. Just passion."

"That's nice," said Hallie with a smile so phony he could feel his cheeks defying it with all their might.

"We were working one night late on a scene. I was tired and he was gentle—"

"No, no. Excuse me, Nikki, I can't explain this, but could you please not tell me what it was like with Malcolm in bed?"

"What, you're jealous? Don't pretend you're jealous!"

"Does Malcolm talk about Martha?"

"No, not really." Nikki's eyes focused on Hallie.

"Let me know if he does. He may be using you to get to her."

"Don't tell me that's what you really think."

"It is. Kip thinks I'm nuts, but I think you might understand."

"Could you go home now, Hallie Lawrence? I have to get up early."

The actor who played the love interest in the film was supposed to take Nikki in his arms and lean down to kiss her. Nikki was supposed to smile, very slowly, walk about three feet away from him, then say, "I can't do this. You can't expect me to still love you."

It took the entire day to shoot one setup, for one line of one scene from one motion picture. Not exactly brisk, even by the most languid auteur standards.

Hallie sat in the director's chair provided him just behind the camera, and watched without a thought about how boring it was. It was absolutely fascinating for him to watch Malcolm work. As he worked, Malcolm went into trances of deep, concentrated thought, pacing off by himself. He spent hours fussing over the lighting for Nikki's close-up and then changed the camera position so they had to relight the whole thing. He sat at Nikki's feet and spoke to her for twenty minutes at a time, his hands painting pictures in the air with pained, artistic gestures. And sometimes he took her hand when he spoke and held it close to his face.

It was this last little habit that interested Hallie the most. She's thinks you're a fleabag, he kept telling himself to his amusement.

Andy Werdlow kept giving Hallie "See what I mean?" looks, as time ticked by.

At the end of the day, when only a few crew members remained and Malcolm had finished a conversation with the camera man, Hallie caught his attention.

"Malcolm, let's talk."

"Great idea, Hallie, great idea. Let's go somewhere and have a drink."

"No, let's talk here. Let's find a place to sit down."

"I need a drink, man. This was a tough day."

"We'll drink afterward."

So Hallie and Malcolm sat down together, and Hallie came right to the point. He asked Malcolm why he was falling so far behind the shooting schedule.

"I can't believe you're asking me that, you of all people." Malcolm dug around in his jacket pocket for his pack of Gauloises. "I figured you for having a notion about quality. Why are *you* asking me what all those Hollywood imbeciles are always asking me?"

"Oh, I see. It's about a notion of quality. Okay, now at least I understand."

"I don't appreciate the sarcasm."

"Sarcasm? I don't get why you take that to be sarcasm," said Hallie, pretending sarcasm was not intended.

"They want me to shoot this thing without a thought to what it looks like," said Malcolm, exhaling smoke. "All they care about is, get the fucking picture on the screen. They just want a product to distribute, quality has nothing to do with it. If it's a load of dog shit, they don't care as long as it was made cheap and sells at the box office. Just as long as the stock keeps going up on Wall Street."

"Malcolm, the entire state of the capitalist system is not exactly the issue. At the rate that you're shooting the picture, you'll lose Nikki to her concert dates that begin again in March. You're supposed to have the picture finished by mid-February. That was supposed to be the deadline. We can go over two weeks tops. While you're being concerned about quality—and please, what else do we all want?—just keep that in mind." Again Hallie smiled at him.

"I took you to be the sort who wouldn't hand me clichés."

"Well, cliché is just my middle name, Malcolm old boy. By the way, which cliché were you referring to?"

"You're going to risk the integrity of the picture by threatening me with a *deadline?*"

Hallie had never had to hold himself back so hard from laughing out loud. He was smiling like crazy, though.

"So, what you're saying is that you are actually functioning without the concept of a deadline? You really mean that, Malcolm?" Hallie's grin was almost unbearable.

"Are you accusing me of being unprofessional?"

"Well, no! Well, that's why I'm so shocked that you're offended just because I suggested that Nikki has a schedule to keep."

"I'm aware of that, Hallie—" said Malcolm

"Well, good!" said Hallie, appearing genuinely pleased to hear that Malcolm might not be an ambulatory psycho who didn't believe in deadlines. "I'm her lawyer, Malcolm, that's all. I just won't let her break contracts. It's a messy business when that happens. That's my only concern. I'm her lawyer," Hallie repeated in the most pleasant manner he could muster.

They were quiet for a moment.

The sound stage seemed eerily silent. Hallie took a look at Malcolm and indulged himself in a moment of homicidal contemplation. Yet there was something oddly exciting about sitting so close to the enemy.

"Hallie, I wouldn't do anything to prevent Nikki from keeping her commitments. Nikki has come to have great meaning in my life."

"And what meaning is that?" asked Hallie, thinking, boy, was this going to be good.

"She knocks me out, man." Malcolm broke into a ridiculous grin, a bad-boy grin that Hallie thought women might find attractive but that he thought was the schmuckiest expression he had ever seen. That may have been the reason Hallie thought Malcolm was lying.

"Nikki is a knockout," said Hallie, keeping in the spirit of things.

"Hopefully you are talking about me!" Nikki's voice called out as she came toward them wearing sweatpants and a baggy navy sweater. "I have been looking everywhere for you."

Malcolm and Hallie answered simultaneously.

"Just talking to Malcolm."

"I was having a word with Hallie."

"I see!" she laughed. "Well, I'm starving! Let's get out of here."

"Don't worry about Nikki," said Malcolm softly to Hallie.

They stepped out into the damp, chilled evening, where Malcolm put his arm around Nikki's shoulder.

"Tonight Hallie and I must have a business dinner together, Malcolm. I won't be needing a ride, okay?" She went to Malcolm and kissed him freely on the lips.

"Perhaps we'll all do something tomorrow night," offered Malcolm, looking directly at Nikki as he spoke.

"Fine!" Hallie said. He was feeling a little stab of victory to be the one going off with Nikki.

They got into Hallie's rented car and Nikki said she hoped he didn't mind her pretending they were going to have a business dinner, she just wanted to be alone with him.

"Well, let's have a wonderful time," Hallie said, and with a display of his British driving skills, they drove into the London evening.

"Yes," Nikki said quietly.

And a wonderful time they had. They went up to a little Italian restaurant in St. John's Wood, drank a lot of Chianti, and laughed almost the entire time. There was something different about Nikki that night, Hallie thought. She seemed more relaxed, less prone to exuberance. In fact, she seemed utterly content.

"The Italians are all hot grapes, I like to think. Vivaldi, Scarlatti. Verdi. You have to think a lot about grapes getting hot, lying in the sun."

"Hot grapes? Jesus, Nikki."

"Oh, don't you know what I mean? It's like Italian wine, fruitier. Dripping with angels and cornucopia—is that how you say it, those things with the fruit stuffed in them?"

"Yes," said Hallie. "And the Russians are what, freezing cold screamers?"

"Yes, exactly. Freezing cold hands grabbing molten hot rods. It's screaming intellect, as opposed to the Germans, who are dour and solemn intellects and who want everyone to jump into the abyss, especially Mahler."

"There's passion in inviting you to jump into the abyss. That's why the Germans are the greatest composers of all."

"Yes, there's no doubt about it, the Germans are great, but the Russians are . . . larger and more fragile."

"Tchaikovsky is fragile? No, Nikki."

"Of course you don't get it, Hallie. Don't worry, the Germans are great. The Germans and the Austrians are great. Beethoven was great."

"I don't know, this hasn't been their century, though. The twentieth century was not a high point for the Germans in general."

After dinner, they walked to their parking spot. That was when Nikki told him Malcolm was going to New York.

"We have the day off on Friday. That means this will be a three-day weekend."

"Oh? Why the day off?"

"Malcolm has to go to New York again to check some location problem."

Hallie was watching the little white puffs of his breath as it escaped him in rapid little pants.

"Something is wrong with you, you're breathing like a crazy person." Nikki looked at him, rather amused.

"No, I'm fine. I just needed to fill up on a little extra air." He was embarrassed when he thought about how stupid he must have looked. But he was not to be sidetracked. "Why— He's going for one day only?"

"Well, he flies Friday, does his work on Saturday, flies back Sunday."

"I see. Well, actually I'll probably head back on Friday myself."

"You just got here, Hallie. I like having you here. Why don't you have Martha come over?"

"I'm a busy man, Nik; I've got to get back."

"I don't want you to go." For a few moments they said nothing and only Nikki's heels against the pavement made any noise. "I guess we are good friends now, me and you, yes? Please, it's so much better when you're here. It helps me to keep Malcolm away. Bring Martha over and then I can be with the two of you."

"We are friends, Nik. We're like brother and sister. I don't want Martha anywhere near him."

Nikki slowly shook her head. It was a very regal gesture. "You're such a child. If you were my brother, you would be my younger, idiot brother, that's for sure. You are a complete idiot!"

They were standing under a lamppost and the pinkish glow highlighted Nikki's curls and reflected in her bright eyes. She began to smile at him, an exhilarating Russian smile, the smile of a young woman on horseback, in furs, pausing in the moonlight before racing across fields, daring him to ride with her. He almost felt her call, but racing across his brain, on fire-breathing stallions of their own, came the echoes; Malcolm was going to New York.

Malcolm was going to see Martha.

It was out of the question.

"Stay," said Nikki. "I'll tell you what. Have you ever been to Moscow?"

The next day on the set Malcolm was a different person. Instead of being broody and contemplative and constantly jerking himself off trying different creative ideas, he seemed to be speeding. He made decisions and elicited energy from everyone around him. He seemed to know just what he was doing.

"What did you say to him?" Andy Werdlow had asked Hallie rather meekly. "You have to stay at least part of next week."

"Come now, Andy. I had nothing to do with this."

But he did, and he knew it. And that night, when the three of them had dinner, Malcolm confirmed that his explosive display had been for Hallie's benefit. He got very drunk and horrifyingly chummy and admitted that he wanted to impress Martha's husband.

"You're a lucky man. I blew it completely with Martha."

"Yes, well, I intend to keep Martha. That's something I feel strongly about."

"Well, then you're not only lucky, you're smart."

Although a bit modern perhaps, it could have been a reasonable-enough conversation if one of the parties hadn't been internalizing a psychotic episode. For Hallie, it was an admission from Malcolm that he wanted Martha back; Malcolm had admitted that he had blown it. He was expressing remorse for his loss, and that was good enough for Hallie.

It was then that Hallie went beyond the point of no return. Once he heard Malcolm admitting regret for having lost Martha, he sort of began to leave the planet.

Nikki noticed the edge in Hallie's voice. This was not Hallie Lawrence as she had come to know him. There was something about him that told you his heart was beating very fast beneath his calm, composed exterior.

And that night, from his room at Claridge's, Hallie called Lily and told her that he wouldn't object if Martha did a little work for Noel; he would work out the terms of the contract, of course; but meanwhile it wasn't a bad idea for her to have something to do. He suggested that Lily arrange to have lunch with Martha and Noel on Saturday, just a social lunch, but a good first step. Then he asked Lily to invite Martha and Kip to Alfred's performance, whatever he was performing, it didn't matter, that Saturday night. Lily said she was delighted to and said she was glad that Hallie was thinking about Martha while he was in London.

He called Martha and Kip, but there was no answer. He left an amusing message.

The next day Andy Werdlow expressed his gratitude to Hallie for staying on a little longer. He confessed that he hadn't known what to say to Malcolm to get him to work faster.

"Andy, you're with the studio, threaten to fire him. Threaten to throw his ass out on the street, and tell him the whole town will know he's a bum."

"I didn't want to go that far, Hallie. I mean, shit, what if he walks off the picture? You can't really insult creative people too much."

"My dear boy, you've got that wrong. You can't insult them enough."

Andy Werdlow didn't know Hallie well enough to realize what an uncharacteristic remark that was. He listened carefully and thought maybe it was good advice.

Hallie had wondered why he had made such a revealing statement. It had to have something to do with Malcolm

"What is Malcolm doing in New York?"

"He's looking at a couple of locations."

"I want to know his schedule. I mean, how do we know when he's coming back?"

"Oh, well he's got a breakfast at nine on Saturday with Carnegie Hall people, then he's out in Connecticut somewhere, looking at houses for the last scene of the picture. If he can get a plane out on Saturday night, he will."

So Hallie decided he would remain in London for part of the following week. Thanks to Lily, Martha wouldn't be home when Malcolm called. He felt more at ease.

Nikki and Hallie took a plane to Moscow on Friday night. It was an insane thing to do, but Hallie couldn't resist the suggestion.

They stayed with an aunt of Nikki's who lived in an impressive part of town, considering how many depressing housing projects there were. It was an old building full of the Russia that belonged to Tolstoy. Hallie had been to Moscow before but never with Nikki. She had many little architectural surprises for him.

Late on Saturday afternoon, when it was already dark, they stood in Red Square and looked at the Kremlin and Hallie almost cried. But as always in the case of Hallie Lawrence, "almost" was the key word.

Nikki put her arm around him.

They went to a concert at Tchaikovsky Hall, and ate some pretty terrible food. On Sunday afternoon, they flew back to London. Of course they didn't have sex.

Hallie left London on Thursday and flew back to New York on the Concorde because he suddenly felt so desperate to be with Martha that any time he could save till he got there, he would at all costs.

He got back home around midday and Kip called and insisted they come down and see his place. It was not Hallie's first choice of what to do on that particular day, but they would come in the late afternoon and leave early. The loft was huge and hadn't been ruined with a lot of trendy design crap. Kip told them how he had blackmailed his trust officer to obtain financing. He knew who the guy was banging and he threatened to tip off Mrs. Trust Officer, but he'd done it in the nicest possible way. And sure enough, a way to get at some money was found. They laughed, but Hallie thought it was a little ruthless, really.

Near the huge two-story windows was a cozy sitting area that looked as if it had been there for a long time. The furniture looked nice and lived in. On the walls hung some old prints in worn frames, of hunting scenes and horses. It really is in the blood, thought Hallie. Jews are eaters, blacks have rhythm, and gentiles have hunt prints. It was amazing.

Hallie complimented Kip, telling him he was proud of him for fixing up his apartment so quickly. Kip asked how could Hallie possibly think *he* had actually fixed up his apartment? Without Martha's help, none of it would have been possible. Martha said it was nothing, that it all came together because they just picked up stuff everywhere they went. Hallie thought it was great that Martha had helped Kip. What a nice thing to do, he kept thinking. She was so precious.

From the corner of his eye, Hallie had noticed that Kip seemed to be working again. There was a large canvas on an easel at one end of the loft and the area around it was a mess. He stopped himself from asking Kip about it, figuring if it was true, it would be something Kip would rather volunteer.

Finally, after eating sandwiches and drinking a few beers, Kip took Hallie over to see the canvas on the easel. It was a work in good progress and it seemed definitely to be about the female form.

"Jesus, Kipper. This is great."

"You like it?" asked Kip.

"It's got some excellent Kip Courtland rage."

"Thank you," said Kip, using the appropriate droll response. "The Leonetti wants it for a group show. This one and a couple of others."

"You're kidding."

"Nope. If I can finish on time. The show's in a month. Someone else dropped out."

"Well, finish it, my man," said Hallie. "Blow their socks off."

"I will," said Kip.

"I liked helping Kip fix up his place," Martha said later that evening when the younger Lawrences were home and alone for the first time in quite a while. They were in the kitchen and she was making them hot chocolate with Cointreau. "It's mostly just old stuff we found in junk stores. And Kip had a few things of his own. Try this. Is that too much Cointreau?"

Hallie sipped carefully. It tasted of déjà vu, and less frantic times. Martha was leaning on the kitchen counter, also sipping hot chocolate.

"It's delicious," Hallie told her.

"Well, I certainly didn't mind helping Kip. It gave me something to do."

There was something about the way she was leaning on the

counter, a certain languidness, that made Hallie ask, "Marth, are you bored? Christ, I don't want you to be bored."

"Oh, I'm not. I'm really not, I like taking care of the house." Before sipping her cocoa, she blew upward and let her breath rearrange her bangs. "There's always something to do."

Hallie looked into her clear honeyed eyes. It hit him that if she wasn't bored, then she was going to get bored. And with a lot of time on her hands, she would be very available.

"Hey, did you have lunch with my mother and Noel?"

"Yeah, I did."

"So, do you think you want to work for him?"

"Hallie, he just wants me to model."

"So?" Hallie drank in the way her nose lifted just at the end, held in place by an imaginary thread. He watched her lips as her tongue brushed over them, licking dark chocolate and Cointreau. He wanted her badly.

"Well, Christ, if I wanted to be a model, I'd go be a model. I know I can do that. I'm not interested. I thought maybe he'd ask me to be a trainee—you know, an assistant designer or something. Really work for him. I told him that I'd been designing clothes, me and my sisters, all my life. He didn't seem too interested. I don't want to be a model. I'm going to tell him no. I just thought I should tell you first."

Oh, holy Martha, oh, holiness of a woman whose instincts were to protect him like that. Hallie only wished he had a recording of what she had just said to play for Lily. Of course, Lily would blame the whole thing on him. She would assume that Martha had picked up his feelings and rejected the notion without a thought of what she might want for herself. But not his Martha. He wanted so desperately, at that moment, to be able just to love her.

"Martha? What do you want to do? If there was anything in the world you could do, what would it be? Do you want to design clothes? Do you want to work in an art gallery, or maybe the Met? You could go back to school, if you aren't sure. Maybe you'd like to be a lawyer. You could join my firm."

"Okay, I pick lawyer," she said, throwing him a luscious smile.

"Seriously. Do you have any dream that started when you were really young and that you still have in your secret heart today?"

"Well . . ." She was shy about it, a shyness Hallie thought was sensational. "Really secret? I don't know, you might laugh."

"Laugh? Baby, don't be silly. Go on, you can tell me anything."

"Well, I'd like a dairy farm."

Hallie took this in. Then he laughed.

"A dairy farm? You mean a cow farm? A farm with milk cows?"

"That's exactly right. And all my cows would be black and white. No brown ones. Then I'd have a horse and I could ride out and see the black-and-white cows in the fields. I think that's one of the prettiest sights in the world, and I've thought that since I was a little girl."

"You're not kidding, are you?"

"No! God, I'm not kidding! You think I'd make something like that up?"

"No, no, of course not." The truth was, it was exactly the kind of thing someone would make up. Who the hell wanted a dairy farm, for real?

"Hhmmm," said Hallie. "Well, that's certainly a thought. I don't think it's the kind of thing you can do in the middle of Manhattan. Maybe my mother could make a few calls and they'd let you keep some cows in Central Park. In fact, there's an old dairy in Central Park, maybe we could get it restored. We'll put up a big sign, 'Martha's Milk.' "

"Well, obviously you can't do it in Manhattan, you geek. And if you really want to get decent acreage at a good price, you'd have to go to someplace like Wisconsin, you couldn't really do it in New York State. Land's gotten too expensive."

Oh my God, she actually knew things like the value of dairy acreage in Wisconsin?

"A dairy farm." All Hallie could do was repeat the concept. The vision of Martha the Milkmaid was, while certainly provocative, a little perplexing, to say the least.

"Now you think I'm a jerk." Martha smiled.

"No, no, not at all. I'll try and think about dairy farming. I'll give it some thought." He wondered if there were Jews living anywhere in Wisconsin, let alone running dairy farms.

And then, because he was losing his mind, Hallie thought that putting Martha on a dairy farm in Wisconsin might be just the thing to keep Malcolm away.

"So, go study dairy farming. Go to Columbia, take a course in cow management, whatever you need."

"Oh, Hallie, really?"

"Sure. I'm not saying we'll be selling milk tomorrow morning, but maybe someday—"

"Oh, you're so good when you're like this!" She threw her arms around him in a rush of joy.

"I happen to be crazy about you," Hallie said calmly, while he reached to brush her bangs from her eyes.

"I was getting pretty worried about you and all that stupid jealousy you were having about Malcolm. You're over that now, aren't you?'' She was playing with his hair, kind of winding a curl around her finger.

"Oh, Malcolm? God, yes.''

"I saw him on Saturday and he's really becoming so drippy. And you were right about Nikki, I don't think she's in the least bit interested in him. He said she hardly pays any attention to him.''

Of course, Hallie heard nothing after she said, "I saw him on Saturday.''

"You had lunch with my mother and Noel, didn't you? And then you went to Alfred's concert?'' When had she seen him?

"Yes,'' said Martha.

It was obvious to him that the two things he figured would keep her occupied had fallen pathetically short of the mark. Pathetic. It's what he got for trying to manipulate things in the first place. Manipulation had always been so easy for him, he hadn't ever given a thought to failing at it.

A fresh wave of confusion swept his brain. She hadn't gone to the concert. She had been with Malcolm, and, without a doubt, in bed.

"By the way, how was Alfred's concert?''

"It was wonderful! I really enjoyed it. Kip is great to go to concerts with. He really explained things. He sort of told me what to listen for.''

"What did they perform? Tell me what they played.'' This had the lunatic quality of an terror-striking exam question.

Martha stiffened. She spoke in a quiet, angry voice. "The *Tragic* Overture, by Johannes Brahms, and the Rachmaninoff Piano Concerto Number Three, with a soloist whose name I can't pronounce. And then the Tchaikovsky *Pathétique* Symphony, which Kip kept calling the 'Pathetic'. After the Brahms, Alfred put his hands over his heart, and Kip pointed it out to me and said, 'Alfred always puts the old hand on his heart after he conducts Brahms.' You think I'm stupid about music, don't you. You don't think I know one piece from another—but that isn't even what it is, is it, Hallie?'' Tears started coming from her eyes. "What you really want to know is, did I even go to the concert? Did I go, or was I with Malcolm? Ask Kip if I went to the concert, Hallie. I saw Malcolm for a drink, met him at The Gingerman for forty-five minutes, then met Kip and your mom at Lincoln Center. And, Hallie, fuck you.''

This last suggestion she made with the most indifferent expression he had ever seen, even though tears were pouring down her face and she sniffled. She got up and went to the bedroom. She closed the door and Hallie heard the lock turn. He ran over and, sure enough, it was indeed locked.

"Come on, Marth. Let me in."

"Go away, Hallie. I don't want to see you for the rest of the night."

"But, Martha, I just got back! I—I really want to be with you tonight. Could you maybe not see me for the rest of tomorrow night?"

"No! Don't be stupid now, okay?"

"I was just trying to be funny and adorable, not stupid. Come on, Marth."

"Go fuck yourself, Hallie."

Why did she have to talk like that, a nice girl like Martha? He paced for several moments.

"I don't know why you even told me you saw him. I think you like to see me get crazy."

There was no response. Then her voice came back quietly.

"I think you need professional help."

He ended up sleeping on the sofa.

The next morning, just before he was about to walk out the door for the office, they made up. But she didn't want to make love.

18

THE ACTUAL HEAD OF PRODUCTION
of the studio, a very important man in
the eyes of many people, himself included, asked Hallie to lunch at the
Russian Tea Room. It seems that as
soon as Hallie had left London, Malcolm had returned to new heights of
the DTGs and had reverted to crawling along, savoring every tortured, degenerate, genius moment. The studio
head, an amiable-enough guy whose
name was Josh Birdsong, had a propo-
sition for Hallie. He wanted him to
become the executive producer of the
movie for a fee, and stay with the filming until it was over.

Hallie smiled. "I'm not interested in
titles, Lance."

"Josh."

Josh Birdsong wasn't an idiot, even
though it wouldn't have been especially surprising if he had been. He was

266

a calm, measured, understated guy, not unlike the persona Hallie presented. He had, in fact, also gone to Harvard. He was the Harvard man in Hollywood, he told Hallie without enough irony. Because he knew Hallie was an alumnus as well, he acted as if they were two Chosen Ones, meeting instantly on even ground.

Hallie asked him if he realized how big an asshole Malcolm was. Josh said he met too many assholes to notice exact sizes, which kind of won Hallie over a little bit.

"All I know is there's money to be lost if Malcolm doesn't get the film in on time. You seem to have some kind of effect on the situation. Besides, the affair between Malcolm and Nikki is becoming well known, and studios don't take well to sex being the cause for fucking up a production."

"I see," said Hallie quite calmly. He would withhold denial of said affair for the moment.

"Now, we'll deny all rumors that they were involved in a relationship provided he becomes reasonable and gets the goddamn thing in fast. But if he fucks up the picture, if he continues behind schedule, then his reputation will be shit and he can go back to London and direct dog-food commercials for the rest of his life."

Hallie was wondering why Josh thought he gave a damn about Malcolm's reputation. Hallie took out his date book and began leafing through it. He wasn't checking his calendar, however, he was thinking about buying Martha a nice present. He noticed in his date book it was the night Kip was taking them to dinner. By then it was time to reenter the conversation.

"Josh, why are you threatening Nikki?" He took out a pen and then found himself drawing a series of straight lines, giving each three strokes of his pen, then moving on to form a new one. "There's no fault with Nikki here, she's not delaying anything, she has behaved like a consummate professional; why would you threaten her reputation as well?"

"I'm not threatening Nikki." Josh's eyes hardened a little.

"Well, she would be the one he had screwed up the picture *for*. That doesn't sound like a particularly pristine position for Nikki, if—and this does remain a factor—there is any affair at all." There was a diamond necklace he had seen in the window of a Madison Avenue jewelry shop. It was a circle of emerald-cut diamonds. That was what he would buy Martha. "But what you're really doing is blackmailing me. You're joshing, aren't you, Josh?"

Josh didn't appreciate the pun.

"Well, blackmail is a little strong."

"You're talking about a potential libel case for my client." Hallie paused to smile, allowing for the illusion that he might be kidding.

"Libel cases are tough to win. I'd have to kill you." Hallie smiled a little more.

"Hallie," said Josh. "I'm not here to threaten anybody. It doesn't seem so unusual to me to put someone on a picture who seems to have some kind of psychological authority. The picture is sensational. It has the potential to be a critical success. That's a rare thing. You could add a lot at this point."

"I'm a lawyer. I have a career, Josh, with other clients and a firm to look after. I'm not in the film business. And what I'll add at this point is that Malcolm and Nikki are not having an affair."

"What makes you think that?"

"Well, what makes you think they are?"

"Smells like it to me. I can smell an affair a mile away."

"I think you may be wrong, Josh. I think maybe your nose needs a hearing aid, or a smelling aid, or whatever you use if your nose isn't too accurate."

"Of course, you never know what's really going on between two people," said Josh, suddenly the personification of intimacy. "He's never actually spent the night with her."

"What do you people have, movie-studio gestapo keeping an eye on things?"

This amused Josh and he smiled. "Look, go to London. He should be finished there in a couple of weeks. Then you can come back and there's what—a week of shooting here in New York? Just get the picture in, in three weeks. I think Nikki has a stake in this, Hallie."

It was not the first time Hallie had heard that the film company would be coming to New York; after all, it had been to see a location that Malcolm had come to New York on those two occasions. But shooting in New York, coupled with the word "week," somehow made it sink in. Malcolm would be in New York for an entire week. Maybe Martha would like to go to the Bahamas.

"A week in New York," Hallie said absently. "And you want me to take charge?"

When word got to Alfred that Hallie was now in the picture business, he called him up to see if maybe he should be getting another lawyer.

"Columbia University is not exactly the agricultural study center of the United States," teased Kip. Martha had found a few courses, one in agriculture and one in management, and had immediately enrolled at Columbia. As a matter of fact, Hallie was astonished to see how quickly she was able to announce that she was off to dairy school, as he called it.

"It's a start," said Martha with laughing eyes. It was just so wonderful the way Martha could combat Kip's teasing. So many women Hallie had been with had found Kip mean.

The three were dining at a trendy downtown eatery, an attractive restaurant not far from Kip's loft. Everyone in the place was dressed in black except Martha, who looked particularly glamorous that night, in a red crepe suit with jet beading in off-beat places. Hallie felt so good being with Martha and Kip that he wasn't saying very much.

Then he remembered Malcolm. It was too bad.

"Martha, I have to go to London again. This time I want you to go with me." Even as Hallie said the words, he knew it was a lie. He wanted to put her in a box somewhere, asleep, until the entire picture was over.

"Shit, Hallie, why didn't you say so before I enrolled in my courses? I had to talk my way in as it is. Classes have already started."

"I have to go. I'm working on the film now, I've agreed to become the executive producer."

"Mr. Ziegfeld!" said Kip. "Alfred must be delighted!"

Hallie gave him a look.

"Why did you agree to do that?" asked Martha, sitting there with a forkful of sweetbread hovering over her plate. Then she turned to Kip. "Kipper, could you go to the men's room or something for a minute?"

"Sure." Kip wiped his mouth on his napkin and took a long drink of water. He discreetly left them.

"Why are you getting even more involved with the whole thing? I just don't get it." Her eyes were wide and looking right at him, almost helplessly. God, she was gorgeous.

"To help get it finished on time. They're convinced I have an effect on that."

"But, Hallie, why are you spending more time on something that's been making you so crazy? Why do you want to work with Malcolm?"

The question was far too logical to mean anything to Hallie. "Martha," he sighed, "I have got to get Nikki through this picture and back to the fiddle without any snags."

"We've been married for six weeks and you've been away for almost three of them."

"That's not true; and Martha, I told you I travel, it's part of my work. I'm always working on things all over the country and in Europe. I take my clients seriously."

"Why don't you take your wife seriously? What's the matter with you, Hallie, don't you like me anymore?"

"Oh, Martha."

"I thought we were going to have fun all the time. I thought we would always be doing fun things."

"You could have come with me to London, you could have come with me to L.A."

"And watch you turn into some mad lunatic from outer space every time Malcolm spoke to me? Right, Hallie."

Martha was pissed off at him and Hallie found it to be the single most uncomfortable feeling he had ever experienced. He sat without speaking, holding her hand.

"You're . . . angry at me," he said meekly.

"Yeah, sort of, as much as I can be with a guy who's such a natural geek, you really should just feel sorry for him."

"I'll make it up to you, Martha, I promise. It's only for a few weeks."

Kip came back to the table because he couldn't stay away for the rest of the night. He tried to cheer things up by teasing Hallie about becoming a Hollywood mogul. Martha cheered up and said it was actually kind of neat. Hallie didn't feel cheered up at all.

Later that night Hallie lay on the bed, watching the eleven o'clock news. Martha came to the bed looking her usual scrubbed and edible self.

"Hallie, you want to know the real reason I mind that you're working on the film? I mean, I can tell you, can't I? You're my husband, I'm supposed to tell you when something is upsetting me, right?" She sat on the bed facing him. He automatically reached out to touch her thigh.

"Of course, Martha. You shouldn't be upset about any of it. Are you getting your period?"

"No, I'm not getting my period— God, are boys dumb or what?" She reached for a cigarette. "You're spending an awful lot of time with Nikki."

"Nikki's the client! Come on, Martha, don't smoke, for God's sake."

She lit the cigarette, exhaled and placed it in an ashtray while she shed her robe and, naked, went to get a shirt to sleep in.

"I don't smoke that much."

"Do you think I want to leave you for one minute?"

"Then, Hallie, what's going on with you and Nikki?"

"Are you serious?"

"Look, I would never have brought it up, but after everything you said tonight, telling us that now you're actually working on the movie? Well, I have to talk about it."

"Talk about what?"

"You and Nikki. There's something going on, isn't there?"

"Martha, my dear, have you completely lost your mind?" Hallie was really astonished. He even managed a little astonished laugh.

"Tell me if I'm crazy, okay? It's just something Malcolm said, that he had a feeling that there was something between you."

"MALCOLM SAID THAT?" You probably could have heard Hallie from ten floors below. "That total piece-of-shit bastard??? He told you there was something going on with me and Nikki?"

"Hallie, don't scream."

"That's it! He's dead. It's very simple, I'm going to kill him! Why would he do that to you, huh? Huh? You want to tell me why he would make up a *lie* like that?"

"Because he's a drip and—"

"I'll tell you why! Because he's after you, like I've said all along! Make up a totally insane *lie* about me, and the next thing you know, he gets you back!"

"Oh, Hallie, shut up! He's in love with Nikki, that's why he's pissed off. And he thinks she's in love with you! It's just that simple."

"Simple? This soap opera? I'm suddenly one of those stupid idiots on a soap opera."

"It's not my fault, Hallie." Martha began to cry.

"All right, listen. There is nothing going on between Nikki and me. Nikki thinks I'm kind of a jerk, kind of an immature asshole, that's what Nikki thinks. Sure, we've become closer than we might have had she not become my client, and we're fond of each other, but, Martha, she always thinks of me as Alfred's asshole son and for me—Martha, I have you. I don't even notice anyone else."

"She thinks you're nothing like Alfred!" Martha blew her nose into a blue Kleenex. Her eyes were still spilling tears. "When we heard her play in London, I realized that she's so special, and even though I like her, I'm a little jealous, I have to admit it."

"Martha! I'm obsessed with you! I can't believe you would think there's anything between me and Nikki!"

"I don't, really. I certainly don't want to."

"That SON OF A BITCH did this to you! Listen to me. I love you. I adore you. You're everything on the planet to me—"

"Well then, could you please stop acting the way you're acting about Malcolm?"

"I would die without you, I can't breathe without you, I'm—"

"Stop it, Hallie. Stop being like that, it just makes you pathetic."

"It's pathetic to be crazy about someone?"

"That's just what you are, you know. You're crazy about me. That's not the same as loving someone."

"That's priceless, Marth. You really had to dig in for that one, didn't you." It was awful. It was the cruellest thing Hallie had ever said to her. "I didn't mean that," he said. And the way he said it was so unlike himself, so utterly caught-off-guard sincere, that Martha believed him.

"This is getting a little out of hand, isn't it," she said softly.

"That's a looming possibility."

"We're always fighting, Hallie. It's dumb."

"We're a couple of idiots."

"I just can't believe the timing. I mean, if only Malcolm hadn't come into our lives. If only there had never been any movie, if only Nikki wasn't your client."

"This is completely my father's fault. But you can't say 'If only there was no Alfred,' because then there would be no me. Believe me, I've often thought it might be worth it."

"You don't know how many times I've said what bad luck the whole thing has been."

"But we have each other, that's what counts! Isn't it?"

Martha began to cry all over again.

"Come on, Marth, don't." He put his arm around her and pulled her close to him. He noticed she hesitated before moving. "You know, I was going to buy you a present today."

"You were?"

"Yup. I just ran out of time, but you are soon going to be the receiver of a terrific present."

"Hallie," whispered the sniffling Martha, "let's just go to bed."

And they did, and she sent him to the cosmic beach, and he realized he hadn't been there in quite a while.

19

BECAUSE HALLIE LAWRENCE WAS who he was, he took anything he decided to work on very seriously. He was incapable of doing anything but his best, and of course this took a lot of concentration and made him relentless because he was competing against himself. So once he was back in London, he went to the set every morning and sat by himself and watched and studied everything that happened, looking for ways to make it happen faster. Speed was the thing primarily on Hallie's mind. Speed to see this thing finished and out of all their lives.

He really should have been a little more calm and steady.

But he made Malcolm feel the need for speed and he had egged him into a match that Malcolm had unconsciously entered. Every time he moved on to another camera setup, Malcolm would send him a certain sly little smile, half affection, half fuck you. All Hallie noticed was Malcolm working faster. Malcolm was rising to the challenge, because he, Hallie Lawrence, had determined that he would. Malcolm had definitely picked up a snappy momentum. In light of that, Hallie's behavior seemed almost too modest.

One night in a pub, Andy Werdlow confessed to Hallie that the picture was ruining his career. The film would now probably come in on time, and more than likely be a critical success, but Andy knew he hadn't been in control. And Andy knew that Josh Birdsong knew, and Josh was the head of the studio.

Hallie felt sorry for the guy.

One Saturday morning from his room at Claridge's, Hallie telephoned his Aunt Sasha and went to have tea with her at the house she and his Uncle Henry kept in Belgrave Square. She said they were planning to close their house in Düsseldorf and take up full-time residence in London, especially with Germany reunified. Henry felt so strongly about it, he was there now, arranging to sell the house. It was too bad, it was a beautiful house. Did Hallie remember the house?

Oh Jesus, what made him think he should visit a relative? It was certainly a bad idea for someone wanting to pass time as quickly as possible.

Hallie sipped his tea and ate a cucumber sandwich, which wasn't very good. Sasha was pretending to be mortified about having been unable to attend Hallie's wedding because of the short notice, and Hallie had to sit there for a long time and listen to her being devastated, or at least pretend he was listening instead of trying to glance at his watch without being obvious. It was a challenge.

Finally, Hallie said good-bye to Sasha, youngest of the Oppenheim sisters, and walked back to Claridge's. He had noticed she, too, was beginning to smell like old ladies' powder, and he realized that Lily never would.

The minute he returned to his room, he knew he wanted to have a nice little dinner with Nikki somewhere. In fact, the more he thought about it, as he eased into the steaming, preciously long bathtub, Nikki was the closest thing to a relative he needed.

He called the hotel desk and ordered two dozen roses to be delivered to Martha. He dictated a message for the card to the operator: "I miss you STOP I think I'm coming down with something horrible because you're not next to me STOP I want to lick your face and various other body parts STOP—that's body *parts,* yes, operator—I am a miserable wretch STOP Come over and let me feel your body against mine, naked and pink and warm—no, make that hot—make that feel your body next to mine, naked and pink and hot and sweaty and—"

"Excuse me, sir," came the officious male British twang of the snotbag hotel operator.

"Yes?" said Hallie.

"I'm not sure what direction you're going with this, but in England we have rules about pornographic messages in the post, or on fax machines."

"What? Who the hell said anything pornographic? These flowers are for my wife and I can put anything on the message that I want."

"Ah yes, you Americans; your independence is always an inspiration."

Hallie immediately hung up the phone, had a word with the hotel manager, who knew his family well, and was assured that any notes he wanted communicated to Martha, with or without flowers, would be taken care of by the hotel manager's secretary. Hallie thanked him and, after hanging up the phone, he looked around the superb art deco suite and felt like a cross between Fred Astaire and a Nazi.

Hallie wished Kip would call him so he could tell him about the pornography charges he had just narrowly escaped. But Kip was out; Hallie had tried him earlier. He remembered he wanted to have dinner with Nikki, so he called her instead.

"Hey, Nik."

"What are you doing?" said the Russian voice.

"No plans."

"Then what you are doing is coming with me to hear Perlman play the Brahms tonight."

"Sure."

Nikki picked him up in a cab and they headed across the river to the Royal Festival Hall, which, like Lincoln Center, is another one of those generic performing-arts centers from the sixties that add nothing to the landscape.

When the house lights went down, he remembered how Martha had initially called Alfred's concert a "show." She was safe, he told himself. Only ten more days.

Afterward, Nikki said she hated to admit it, but Perlman was good. Hallie asked her if she wanted to go back and see him, but she said she wasn't ready to admit it to him yet.

They left Festival Hall and came out to a rare thing: an incredibly foggy London night.

"Oh, Hallie, this must have been what it was like in the old days, when London always had so many fogs. Let's walk in it. Maybe we'll come out in another century."

"Great."

Everything felt muffled. Car headlights were beams that kept disappearing. It was kind of fabulous, and Hallie was glad they were doing it, except he kept thinking, if they did come out in another century somehow, would Martha be there and where would he find her?

Walking across Waterloo Bridge, Nikki brought up the four Bs.

"First of all, I hate that argument because there are only three Bs. There's Bach, Brahms, and Beethoven. There's no need for a fourth B," she said.

"Obviously," said Hallie, who was relaxing a bit but also thinking about Jack the Ripper, and he wondered if it was actually true that they had caught him.

"Good, we agree on that. How I hate it when someone says Berlioz is the fourth B. Of course he would be, but he has nothing to do with Bach, Beethoven, and Brahms."

"Well, it wouldn't be Berlioz. If we were going to consider another B, it would be Bartók, but I agree, why do people do that, add on another B for the sake of enlarging the group? It's pointless."

"Bartók? What? *Bartók?* I didn't know you had such a handicap! You're deaf! Do you think Bartók and Berlioz are even in the same league?" Nikki clapped her gloved hands together in exasperation.

The trouble was, Hallie was looking at her and thinking: Lily and Alfred. How many of these conversations had he listened to between his parents? Poor Nikki. The last thing she would have wanted was to remind him of his mother.

"I'm sorry," she said, observing the sudden gloomy look on Hallie's face. "You're not so handicapped. Look back, you can't see the other side anymore. We're in the fog right in the middle of the river! I'd call it a Mussorgsky moment."

Hallie laughed. It was true. Identifying things by what they would be if they were a composer had became their daily game. They decided that if Malcolm were a composer, he would be Gilbert and Sullivan, mainly because he would have been so insulted by the comparison to an operetta.

They had left Waterloo Bridge behind and were crossing the Strand, heading for a little restaurant they both liked near Covent Garden.

"So," said Nikki, taking Hallie's arm as they walked. "Finally, tell me. Who would I be if I were a composer?"

"Tchaikovsky—"

"Don't answer so fast! Think. Give it thought. I am too heterosexual to be Tchaikovsky!"

"Well, who would I be?"

"Schubert."

"Schubert? . . . Really?"

"You don't think so?"

"He's so depressing."

"No, he can be brilliant. But who am *I?* I certainly know."

"Who are you?"

"Rachmaninoff."

"No, you're not Rachmaninoff."

"Do you want to bet?"

"Well, you've got the passion but you're smarter. I think Scriabin. That's who you are, Scriabin."

"Ha? You think that Rachmaninoff was stupid? Is that what you think?"

"Well, he was a conservative—"

"Who would you rather be on a desert island with, Rachmaninoff or Scriabin? Take the music for what it is, and decide if it's been done with greatness. That's the test. It could be an organ-grinder tune, but if it's a great organ-grinder tune that says all there is to say about organ grinding, then we like it."

"Nikki, please, don't talk to me as if I didn't know anything about music."

As much as it reminded him of Lily and Alfred, he actually liked talking about music with Nikki. They always ended up doing it.

Nikki was looking at Hallie from across the sound stage. She was sitting near the camera, and Hallie was in his regular seat off to the side, alone. He was reading something and seemed absorbed by it. Malcolm came over to her and rubbed her shoulders. It felt incredibly good. It gave her a shiver. Hallie caused her so much tension. He was talking more and more to her about Malcolm pursuing Martha. It was hard for her to comprehend his insanity, to fathom where it was coming from. It made her tense. He never noticed that she didn't say much when he spoke about Malcolm and Martha.

Actually, that wasn't true. He did notice and she sensed that he thought she knew something and wasn't telling him, but he couldn't get himself to ask her what it was she knew. But Nikki would never have let him ask. She would have instinctively changed the subject and diverted him from the brink.

There was Hallie, sitting off in his chair, alone, absorbed. Nikki couldn't divert him for much longer and for some reason it made her tense and gave her a shiver when Malcolm massaged her.

For the last few days in London, Hallie watched Malcolm direct Nikki's scenes and noticed the intimacy between them seemed a little stronger than what it had been when he first came to London.

Malcolm was touching Nikki, as he always did, but she was touching him back, laying her hand on his arm, putting her arm around his waist when he put his around hers. Hallie kept wondering how she could stand it.

As each day moved closer to the return to New York, Hallie communicated to Martha with increasing hysteria. He sent roses on a daily basis now. He had dinners ordered from New York restaurants and sent to their apartment and then they would talk on the phone while she ate.

Then late one night, he returned to Claridge's to find five messages from Martha. He immediately called her.

"Hallie? And just where have you been?"

"We were at dinner, a group of us from the film. What's wrong?"

"I can't keep this! It's out of the question!"

"Yes, you can. It's for putting up with these weeks apart."

"Hallie, this necklace must've cost two hundred million dollars."

"Oh, not even half that. I saw it a while ago and that was the present I wanted to give you. Unfortunately, it means I'll have to take you to places where you can wear it, but life isn't perfect."

"Geek."

"You still think I'm a geek?"

"I can't wear anything that costs this much money, don't you get it?"

"Put it on and sleep in it tonight. Sleep in the nude except for the necklace. Tomorrow, take it off. Just sleep in it. I'll be home in three days."

20

THEY WERE STANDING IN THE doorway of the apartment: Martha in socks, a T-shirt, and the diamond necklace, Hallie in his business suit, saying good-bye as Hallie left for the office. They had just spent the first night of Hallie's return together and he was feeling like the King of the Universe. The elevator arrived but he came back to Martha for one more kiss.

She didn't wrap her leg around him as she always did when he kissed her.

"I won't be here tonight, remember?"

"Marth, that's not something I could forget." He kissed her nose and then put his head under her T-shirt and licked her breast. She giggled and told him he was tickling her. He re-emerged from the shirt. "But far be it from me to stop you. You wouldn't want me to stop you. I trust you—"

"Hallie, I'm going to a fucking farm in New Jersey, with the biggest bunch of nerds you've ever seen from my class. It's a stupid field trip."

"I'm jealous of the field, I'm jealous of the cows, I'm jealous of the nerds."

Martha laughed and said she was wrong, she wasn't going with a bunch of nerds, they were football heroes compared to Hallie. And she told him he shouldn't make jokes about jealousy.

Lisa opened the curtains behind Hallie. It was that time of day.

When he'd hung up the phone, Hallie swiveled his chair to face the twilight. It was a particularly dramatic night, with a few clouds taking the last scorch of orange sun. Everything else was violet.

"It's amazing when you think that a lot of people in New York don't know about the sunsets," said Lisa.

"True," said Hallie.

Lisa had begun to get on his nerves. Her efforts to be efficient had a maniacal intimacy about them; she had assumed some kind of conspiracy à deux. Just because he had inquired about Malcolm's daily schedule a few times didn't mean she had to keep him abreast of the guy's every move. He explained to Lisa that he was simply concerned about the completion of the movie, and it didn't matter what time Malcolm left the set and where he went, unless, of course, he was supposed to be shooting. But Lisa chose to fill him in anyway. She was trying to win him over, Hallie recognized it, and it got on his nerves.

Of course, he ate up the information.

Hallie picked up the phone and called Kip. If Martha was going to be out of town that night, Kip would be his date.

"Can't, old sport."

"What do you mean, you can't?"

"Got to finish the painting. *M Times Fifteen Number One.* That's what it's called."

"Oh, I like that. Sounds so pretentious."

"I'm glad you appreciate that, old sport." Kip paused. "I'd like to see you, Hal, but I've got to work."

But Hallie wasn't to remain dateless for long. Somehow Lily smelled an available night on the wind and called him. Would he have dinner with her? Just the two of them, because Alfred was in Houston.

He accepted.

One good thing about dining out with Lily was that she never made him come to the house to pick her up. She was always content to meet him at the restaurant. The one thing understood, however, was that Hallie would arrive there before she did. Lily didn't like to find herself caught waiting for anyone. Because he had spent a long time on the phone with Nikki, Hallie arrived at the designated restaurant just as the Lawrence car was delivering Lily.

Thus they met on the street.

"Darling! You were almost late," said Lily, allowing him to kiss her cheek and smell the Jicky.

"Just think, two more minutes and I could have done it. I could have been late. Damn." He held the door for Lily as she entered the restaurant. For some odd reason, Hallie was glad he was having dinner with his mother.

"This is my most favorite restaurant," said Lily as they took their table, a beauty of a table well located in this dark-damasked, pathetically expensive eatery. She allowed Hallie to light her cigarette and exhaled gently through barely parted lips, and sipped her martini, which arrived just as they were seated. "Look at that floral arrangement. It's exquisite. Now, who does their floral arrangements? Damn, I used to know. It's someone old, someone who's been doing it for years. Just marvelous."

When Lily admired something, which was rare, it was laced with the conviction that her opinion was a pronouncement, which it really was. Hallie studied her as she sipped her drink. She sat so erect in her gray cashmere dress and her seriously important gray pearls. She seemed, thought Hallie, to be floating in space, not actually sitting at a table. Lily would float until the first kick from the martini placed her in her chair. A lot of people were still looking over at them, at Lily Lawrence. The martini would make them all go away.

"It was terribly decent of you to visit Sasha. If it's a toss-up when it's time for you to enter heaven, and I'm practically certain it will be, that might be the very action that will gain you admittance."

That's my mom, thought Hallie. That's my mom.

"Now, tell me," said Lily with an intimate incline of her head, "all about this film business."

"What exactly do you want to know? I don't want to bore you with details you're not interested in hearing."

"You're edgy, Hallie." Lily gave him a calming glance, which was about as calming as waking up and finding a big fat tarantula staring at you on your pillow. "I want to hear everything. The details aren't boring."

"Well, it's a stupid, boring business, with a lot of assholes who take themselves very seriously."

"So I've heard," said Lily.

"The film itself seems to be pretty good, but I wouldn't really know about that at this point."

"Why?"

"Why?"

"Yes, why? Haven't you seen any of it?"

"Of course, in dailies, but I can't tell."

"What can't you tell?"

"If the film is any good. That's what you asked." He would often have to do that with his mother, when she was in the middle of asking a lot of indirect questions. He would have to answer them until she broke down and asked what she really wanted to know. God, it was dull.

"Well, I was just wondering what it was, at this point, that might be keeping you from knowing if the film is any good?" Lily, erect as ever, looked right at him.

"Well, Mother dear, what is it *you* think might be keeping me from knowing if the film is any good?" Answering a difficult question with a difficult question is one of the arts of being a Jew.

"That's something you'd have to tell *me,* Hallie," said Lily, and although this was not phrased as such technically, it was just a question with good manners, but still a question, and let me tell you, Jews can do this for hours.

"The only reason I don't know if the film is any good," said Hallie, "is because I'm too familiar with it." Hallie threw in his cards, gave an answer, and prepared to change the subject. It almost worked, but not quite. He lost the entire round to Lily. He added, "I'm not too crazy about this Malcolm Ferrari asshole. I can't be objective about his work."

"Ah," said Lily. "Let's order. The lobster ravioli is heaven."

Lily wasn't wrong about the lobster ravioli. Claudio, the waiter, brought them their steaming plates and it was a real taste sensation. Hallie found it so delicious and creamy, it reminded him of Martha.

Maybe Lily saw the image of Martha float across his mind, because in the next sentence she was bringing up Martha, on a heretofore non-Martha night.

"Martha's been going everywhere with Kip," said Lily, blotting a dot of lobster cream from her lip before adding, "while you were away."

"Thank God for Kip."

"Yes," said Lily. "By the way, she told Noel she wasn't interested in being a model. It was interesting, the way she did it. Not at all rude; she handled it very well. Noel was positively shocked. He just couldn't believe that a beautiful girl would turn down the opportunity to represent anything he stands for." Lily paused for an elegant little laugh. "I found the whole thing so amusing."

"Really?"

"Poor Noel. And bravo for Martha. My God, she's a strong girl."

"Yes, she is."

And then Lily got to the point.

"I'm not amused, Hallie, to have people mentioning to me every other day that they saw my son's beautiful new bride here and there and everywhere with that attractive young friend of his, Kip Courtland, the one whose paintings are becoming so interesting."

"Why do you let other people make things an issue for you, Mother?"

"It's an issue, Hallie, whether other people discuss it or not." Lily's posture was making her look like the Grand Duchess of the Milky Way. It meant that Hallie had to be very careful, she was building up to something.

A busboy cleared Lily's place, and only when he had done so did she reach into her dinner purse for a cigarette. When the waiter had cleared Hallie's place, they resumed their conversation.

"There's nothing really to discuss about Kip and Martha being seen together, because I'm back," he said.

"Thank God for that," said Lily, completely dismissing this as if entirely irrelevant. "What is it you understand to be the nature of their relationship?"

"They're fucking, Mother. Is that what you want to know?"

Even though Hallie had said this in a very low tone of voice, Lily froze. Her eyes blazed momentarily with a look suggesting she was on the verge of infanticide. Hallie decided to ignore it. He asked what was good for dessert.

"Have the chocolate raspberry soufflé. It's worth it."

"Okay, sounds good." Hallie suddenly decided that the best way to handle Lily was to be nice to her, so he changed his tone. "Mom, Kip and Martha have become good friends. Do you think you could set aside all the phony bullshit about how things look to other people and try and understand that? Christ, here I am feeling relieved that I didn't have to leave Martha behind alone, and you're worrying about gossip? Come on, Lily."

"Martha should have gone with you. But then there's all that craziness and bad luck about Malcolm."

The words "bad luck" told him that Martha and Lily had had a conversation. Bad luck was how Martha had described the appearance of Malcolm in their lives. Perhaps they had been Lily's words in the first place.

What had Martha told her?

"What did Martha tell you?"

"Only about, well, you know, that they had a relationship and everything. That definitely explains why she didn't exactly want to be around the movie. But I'm not so sure, Hallie, why *you* had to be there?" Lily finished the remains of her wineglass and glossed her lips with her tongue. "Why did you get so involved with the film?"

"Nikki."

"Yes, but, darling . . . " Lily's expression simply dismissed Nikki as a logical-enough reason. "I mean, from what I understand, you never had to do that. You only had to do her contracts."

Paolo Mancini, owner of the restaurant, appeared at the table briefly with a complimentary Courvoisier for Hallie and a Calvados for Lily. The Lily Lawrence radiance was so powerful you'd think she had just knighted him as she thanked Paolo in her mellifluous best for remembering her taste in after-dinner drinks. Beaming with the false impression that he had just done mankind some kind of great service, Paolo politely left them alone.

"He's a dear man," said Lily. "I hope this place never becomes trendy. I would hate to think I couldn't just come at the drop of a hat." As if it weren't already trendy and Lily even needed a hat to drop to be instantly welcomed.

"Alfred wanted me to look after Nikki," said Hallie.

"Don't blame your father. He didn't want her to do it."

"He asked me to look after Nikki and I took him at his word. I've been involved with the film because I couldn't let Nikki become part of a disaster. I couldn't do that for Alfred, no matter what he wanted—"

"Well, now, Hallie, now that's unfair, he never wanted it to be a disaster. I mean, once she had committed—"

"Malcolm was being an incredible pain in the ass, running way behind schedule, so I stepped in to help out a little."

Lily looked at him hard and long, with an odd expression. It was almost a little sad. She sipped Calvados. "I observed Martha and Kip at the concert. They certainly have become very good friends. They seem to have an awful lot in common."

"Yeah, me."

Lily smiled at him, a full, all-out Lily Lawrence smile—broad glossed lips, squinted eyes. "In so many ways you're like your father. There's only you in the whole world. You've been told there are other people out there, but you're not quite sure you buy that yet."

Hallie wanted to kill her.

"Martha and Kip are very comfortable together, Hallie."

"Wouldn't you love it if I could just off-load Martha?"

"May I ask," she began slowly, "how on earth you could dare even think such a thing? I've never been anything but gracious toward Martha. I've accepted her from the very first time, and I've never been anything but gracious."

"You're gracious for a living, Mother. Except with me. Why on earth would you sit there and try to tell me there's something going on between Kip and Martha, when you don't know anything about what's going on at all? Why? Where's the graciousness in that?"

Lily was horrified that their lovely meal had turned into such an unleashing of bile from her son. But she had no consciousness of the effect of her insinuation.

"I could be wrong," she said, giving him her self-effacing phony smile.

"Malcolm is after Martha, Mother."

"No, Malcolm is after Nikki, son." Her smile broadened.

A slow, deep whistle began to build in Hallie's brain, coming from the back and making its way forward. He sat very still, pleading with himself not to get up, pick up the table, and throw it across the room. His mother had had that effect on him before, but this time the inclination to act on it was overpowering.

Oddly, any further hostility toward his mother dissipated as soon as he put her in her car. He walked home from the restaurant enjoying the cold night air, scarf around his neck, coat unbuttoned. And he thought about the fact that the film would be ending within the week and everything could return to normal.

He stopped at the phone booth on the corner of his block.

"Nikki, what're you doing?" he asked, the way he had so many times during their days in London. The stench of urine reached up from the ground near the phone.

She laughed. "You don't say hello anymore?"

"Hello, hello. What are you doing?"

"I'm watching the TV." She put the accent on the *t,* instead of the *v.*

"Want to have a drink?"

"No, I can't do that. I have to get up early."

"Ah, come on, one drink? It's only nine-thirty."

"Actually, Malcolm is here. We are working a little, then I must go to bed."

"Oh. Okay. I thought you said you were watching TV?"

"I just put it on. Malcolm is leaving."

"Okay, well then, I'll talk to you tomorrow."

He walked away from the phone, relieved to lose the smell of the urine, and disturbed that the son of a bitch was with Nikki. It was early enough for them to have had a quick drink, but no, the son of a bitch had to be there. The son of a bitch who thought he was going to try and get if off with Nikki, on top of everything else.

The next day, Hallie went to Carnegie Hall to watch the filming of the big scene where Nikki's character plays with an orchestra for the first time in the United States. Nikki would be playing the Tchaikovsky Concerto. There had been some discussion of her playing the Tchaikovsky. Malcolm felt it was too typical for a Russian émigre to perform a Russian work. He wanted the Beethoven. But the studio thought the Tchaikovsky was more accessible. Malcolm lost.

Carnegie Hall had been turned into a Hollywood set and the old dame of a hall seemed aloof and withdrawn, what with all the chaos a Hollywood filming brings. The mob of extras, hired to fill up the seats, were milling around, drinking fruit drinks, picking their way over acres of electric cables on the floors. The crews worked on five different cameras set up to record simultaneously five different angles while Nikki was playing. A full orchestra had begun to assemble in the orchestra pit. Lighting men called information to each other from great heights near the ceiling, while oboes rippled practice runs and violin passages twittered like birds.

Maybe it was the sound of an orchestra tuning up that did it, but to Hallie it made perfect sense when he saw Alfred coming toward him. As soon as his father was about ten feet away, he stopped. It was up to Hallie now to come to him.

"Glad you could make it," Hallie said. He stopped, refusing to close the ten-foot gap.

Alfred had told Hallie on the phone that he was too busy to come to watch the filming, but otherwise he would have loved to. He had been about as "busy" as a man in solitary confinement in a Latin American prison.

"Nikki herself called and invited me; I had to come!" he bellowed. His coat was draped over his shoulders like a cape, indicating that he really couldn't stay. Alfred opened his arms for Hallie's embrace. Right on the goddamn set, Alfred wanted to hug him. Hallie walked the ten feet and got it over with quickly.

"I'm glad you're here," said Hallie. He was trying his best to be polite. He thought he was coming off like some cheap politician, all smiles and frozen eyes, but Alfred seemed to interpret it as warmth.

"Nikki looks stunning, did you see her? Can I get you a little something?" Hallie asked. "Tea, maybe? With lemon?"

"Sure!"

Hallie stopped one of the young girls with shredded-up hair

and black clothes whom he recognized as an errand runner and asked her if his father could get some tea. She was delighted to get it for him.

"So, why the Tchaikovsky?" Alfred asked as he walked with Hallie toward the proscenium.

"It works for the story."

"But it's the Tchaikovsky."

"What's wrong with the Tchaikovsky?" asked Hallie, annoyed.

"It isn't the Brahms! Nikki should be playing the Brahms in this picture, I guarantee you. Nobody plays the Brahms like Nikki."

"I'm not having one of those conversations. Here. Sit down here, right on the aisle." He parked Alfred in one of the seats. "Some people would disagree with you, you know."

"What are you talking about, most people would disagree with me? Who the hell cares?"

Hallie had to smile. "Exactly. She's playing the Tchaikovsky, Alfred."

He had been unobtrusively trying to locate Malcolm during the conversation with his father, but couldn't see him anywhere. And now he did, and he lost his smile.

Malcolm was behind a camera located in a first-tier box, and with him, standing right beside him—and now, wait, now looking through the camera as Malcolm explained something—was his own Martha.

He begged the Forces for the ability to transport himself through space just once, just in order to get him into that box, and he'd never ask for anything again. But Hallie remained riveted in the aisle, next to Alfred sitting grandly in his seat.

"I heard you were here," said Nikki, coming down the aisle. Her face glowed with nervous excitement and her hair had been prodded and fluffed into a mane of red splendor. Hallie could see her, he could hear her voice, but it all seemed like a dream somehow. He saw that she was hugging Alfred, who had stood up and taken her close to his bosom. They embraced for several seconds, a long embrace, an embrace that was obviously saying something that was just between the two of them. Somewhere in him Hallie felt this was a touching moment, but all he could think of was the blatancy of what was occurring in the first-tier box.

The girl with the shredded hair brought Alfred his tea and Nikki emptied the two packets of sugar into the Styrofoam cup for him.

"So? Who's conducting?" Alfred asked Nikki.

Alfred sounded far away.

"Lowenstein. It'll be okay, because we shoot only certain bars of the piece, and it will be fine."

Nikki sounded far away.

"He's a bum," Alfred was saying.

"So? You conduct. Come, be in the movie, Alfred! That, I would love."

While the conversation between Nikki and Alfred had seemed muffled and incomprehensible, this request of Nikki's came in loud and clear. What had she just proposed? Was she out of her mind?

"Are you crazy?" said Alfred. "The girl is crazy out of her mind."

"Yes, this girl is crazy out of her mind," Hallie repeated, giving Nikki a look.

Nikki's eyes filled with sparkles as Hallie reacted to the way she had teased Alfred. What Hallie knew was, tease him too much and he'll accept. God, she didn't know that.

At that moment Nikki's name rang out and she was called to replace her stand-in for a moment on the stage.

"He would never," whispered Nikki as she passed Hallie and went toward the stage.

"Don't bet on it," Hallie called after her. She turned back and laughed at him.

"I'm not even staying, tell her, let alone be in a motion picture," said Alfred. But Hallie was looking up and observing that Malcolm and Martha were no longer in the first-tier box. If he hadn't seen her coming toward him now, he would have been certain that Martha and Malcolm had run off to Istanbul.

"Hi, Hallie," said Martha, kissing him, hugging him to her. "Did you just get here?"

"Yeah, a minute ago. You look great." Her figure was outlined in a white wool dress that emphasized her small waist, and she wore tan suede boots. "You didn't have to get so dressed up."

"Of course I did. We're going over to Kip's opening after this, remember? Everyone's coming. It's a real big-deal event. What did you do, forget?" She played with a strand of his hair.

"Of course I didn't forget. I sent him a bottle of port." It seemed to Hallie it had been a while since she had done something like that, played with his hair.

"Alfred! I didn't see you!" Martha bent down and draped Alfred with an affectionate hug, her silken hair falling against his coat. Alfred wiggled with glee under her attention.

"Hello, my dear," he said, patting her back.

"God, everyone is going to be so nervous with you here," said Martha with her charming accuracy.

"We'll see how much of a circus this really is," said Alfred.

"Hallie, can I talk to you for a minute?" Martha asked.

"Sure. We'll be back, Dad."

Martha slipped her arm through his and they walked up the aisle, cautiously avoiding the cables. "I already spoke to Malcolm, so I got that over with. I mean, I had to talk to him sooner or later, as long as I'm here, so I went up and talked to him." She was smiling at him as if she expected Hallie to be proud of her.

"Good. That's good, Marth."

"I pretended I was interested in the camera angle, so he let me look through the camera; we chatted for a minute and we came back down."

"That's good, Marth." Poor Hallie, he really was trying to act normal. He felt totally confused. Why did she always tell him whenever she had an encounter with Malcolm? What was the reason?

"I just hope I can show you that Malcolm means nothing to me, Hallie. I'll tell you everything that happens."

"Martha, don't—"

"Deal?"

"What deal? There's no need for any deals. Everything is fine."

They had stopped walking and were looking back down toward the stage. Hallie saw Malcolm talking to Nikki. He had an image of a sandbag falling from its ropes and slamming Malcolm in the head.

"God, look at him, he's all over her, for God's sake," said Martha.

"He's giving her direction. He's telling her what he's going to be shooting."

"Give me a break," said Martha with an enormous grin. "Can I smoke in here?"

"This is Carnegie Hall, for Christ's sake. You can't smoke in here."

"I'll go out to the lobby. By the way, I invited Kip to come by. Is that all right?"

"Of course!"

The next thing he knew, Hallie was introducing Josh Birdsong to Martha. Josh had been in New York and he'd dropped by to see the shooting. Martha said she'd be right back, she was going to smoke a cigarette.

A few minutes later, Hallie saw Martha came back to the hall with Kip. Kip would keep her from talking to Malcolm for the rest of the day. What a relief. So Hallie continued his conversation with Josh, whom he almost liked.

After a few hours, everything was ready to begin. The extras filled the seats, the orchestra was tuned and wardrobed in appropriate clothing, and Nikki, in her black velvet dress, was preparing to play. The hush that filled Carnegie Hall seemed greater than normal, because everyone knew the house had to be completely silent before the cameras rolled. Malcolm himself called for quiet.

Kip leaned over to Hallie and whispered, "DTG in a big way."

Hallie smiled, but he was more interested in stealing little looks at Martha, to see if there was any kind of reaction as she focused on Malcolm. All he saw was the honey-colored eyes looking expectant.

"Action."

The orchestra began to play the Tchaikovsky Concerto, not from the beginning but from somewhere in the first movement. After the appropriate number of bars, Nikki lifted her violin and the magic of her playing filled the room. Hundreds of people were mesmerized by it, and drawn to it. Gaffers. Extras. Teamsters. Guests. And there was Nikki's smile as she let the gift simply display itself. She was not acting anymore, so she just smiled.

"She's so good," whispered Martha with a dreamy expression on her face.

And then it happened. He waited for a particularly pianissimo moment in the music, then Alfred said, "Arghhrmmm." He cleared his throat audibly enough to be heard across the street. It sounded like a very sick bull, a bull with bad diarrhea.

"What was that?" came Malcolm's voice. *"Cut!"*

The music slowly came to a halt, as the sound of *"Cut!"* echoed around to the five camera operators all over the theater.

Nikki burst out laughing.

Hallie could feel tingles run across his forehead, sharp razor pricks that were his normal reaction when his father's egomania actually stopped traffic, as it had just done.

Malcolm was staring over at Hallie, who had jumped up from his seat and gone over to him. People began chatting and the silence was over.

"Don't do that," said Hallie. "Don't stop because of him. Just go on, you're dubbing in the sound anyway; just ignore him."

"No way, man. I don't want it. It breaks all the fucking concentration. Tell him, please, Hallie, not to make any noise."

"It doesn't break Nikki's concentration, and that's all that counts."

"How do you know?"

"What do you mean, how do I know? Nikki knows how to ignore Alfred!"

Malcolm looked as if he wanted to say more, but better judgment took hold of him. "Just tell him to shut up," he said arrogantly. "Okay, let's go again, everyone!"

And once again the silence came, *"Action"* was called, the orchestra played, and Nikki's violin filled everyone's soul with pure beauty. Until, once again, came the bellowing bull-like throat clearing. Hallie was still standing near Malcolm, and they glared at each other before, once again, Malcolm yelled, *"Cut!"*

"You're making a mistake, Malcolm. Keep shooting."

"Don't tell me when to shoot and when not to shoot; I'm the bloody director. Now, get him out of here."

Dying, absolutely dying inside, Hallie made his way back up the aisle to where Alfred sat holding his temple as if someone had fired a shot through his brain.

It was a strange moment.

It might have been one of the top ten most embarrassing moments Alfred had caused Hallie over the course of a lifetime, and yet embarrassed was not what Hallie felt. Sure, he was furious about the Ego Mania of it, but instead of telling Alfred he had to shut up or go, he said, "What's wrong? What the hell is bothering you?"

Martha was averting her eyes from Hallie and Alfred, looking nervously over at Kip. Hallie saw Kip pat her knee.

"Come on, you guys," said Martha.

"What are you hearing, Alfred?" asked Hallie. "Because it doesn't matter. What you're hearing her play now is not the music that will be heard with the film. So relax. It doesn't matter what you're hearing."

"What's bothering me? I'm glad you asked. *Nikki!"* he called out, getting up and walking toward the stage. "Excuse me, I won't take a minute of your time," Alfred said to Malcolm, passing him like a weed on the roadside. Nikki came to the edge of the stage and knelt down.

"Since when—" he began.

"I know! I just wanted to see if you were listening." She giggled.

Alfred's graceful hand tapped the air a few times, dismissing her words. Hallie watched them. Malcolm watched them. They exchanged a few intimate sentences.

"Good," said Alfred, and he turned from Nikki to go back to his seat.

"Excuse me, Mr. Lawrence," began Malcolm, "but we're making a film here. Whatever you just told Nikki, please tell me. I'm the director."

"Very nice to meet you, Mr. Director," said Alfred. "What I told Nikki has nothing to do with the picture business. Trust me!"

"Mr. Lawrence? We worked out Nikki's performance already. If you changed it to *your* opinion of what her performance should be, I want to know." Alfred was really pissing Malcolm off.

Hallie was loving it.

"What, mine? It's Tchaikovsky, you nincompoop." Alfred immediately gave Malcolm one of his devilish smiles to lighten the weight of the insult.

"Well, thank you, we appreciate that very much, but you see, we have to keep going. We can't stop. We have to complete the entire musical passage we're filming here."

"So? Shoot it. Now it will be good."

Nikki's movie was simply a chocolate cake into which Alfred had to insert his thumb, if only on the side, for just a little taste. He would shut up now, he had been indulged. Hallie had dealt with his pop.

But Hallie was feeling increasingly sick. Once again people seemed to be talking from a distance, people who were standing but a few feet away. Malcolm was at the edge of the stage now, Nikki bending down toward him, her face looking grave, her red curls catching the light. Malcolm hoisted himself up and joined her. He put his arm around her and held her as he spoke intimately to her. Hallie felt even sicker. Maybe he really was coming down with something this time.

Through space he saw Nikki signaling to him from the stage. He walked over and she bent toward him.

"Don't worry," she said reassuringly, despite the funny half-smile.

She must've been watching me, thought Hallie as he looked into Nikki's eyes.

"Oh, God, I was so terrified you and Alfred were going to get into a fight," exclaimed Martha as Hallie came out of Carnegie Hall to join them on the sidewalk, where Martha and Kip were standing and smoking cigarettes.

"It was excellent Alfred, wasn't it?" Hallie said to Kip.

"It was absolutely first-rate," said Kip. "Really. As good as it gets and you handled it very well, old sport."

"Oh yeah? In what way?"

"You didn't give a shit. You just let him do what he had to do. I'll catch up with you later," said Kip, stepping into the street to hail a cab.

"You're leaving?" asked Hallie with a note of panic.

"Yeah, I have to get over to the gallery for some press stuff. I'll see you guys later. Come over as soon as you're done here, and we'll get something to eat after the opening. You're doing great, Hallie."

Why was Kip leaving, didn't he understand the situation? He was leaving and there would be no one to talk to Martha, to pro-

tect Martha. It was thoughts like these that were sure signs that
Hallie had traveled into an aspect of himself with which he was
not well acquainted. He managed to say, "Good luck with the
show," anyway.

"Thanks, dude," said Kip.

Later in the afternoon, Lily dropped by the set. She came alone,
without Noel or one of her women friends with whom she had
lunched. She wore an incredibly smart suit under one of her dress-
ier furs. Hallie watched the girl with the shredded hair escorting
Lily to Alfred, who rose and helped her to glide from her coat
before she accepted his kiss.

Hallie was watching all this from above, from a first-tier box.
Martha sat beside him, chatting to him and leaning toward him
frequently.

"Look, there's your mom. Doesn't she look great? God, she
always looks so elegant. Isn't it a neat view from up here? One of
the cameras is right in the next box. You'll always know, when you
see the finished film, that the shots from this angle were from where
you were sitting while the film was being made. I like things like
that, don't you?"

What was that all about? thought Hallie. She was nervous as hell.
She sat very erect and stared down at the stage. Hallie followed her
eyes and, lo and behold, there was Malcolm, blatantly looking up
at Martha. He wasn't looking toward the camera in the next box,
he was looking at Martha, as if Hallie weren't sitting there, right
next to her. Malcolm smiled, he shaded his eyes with his hand
against the strong klieg light, and then he touched two fingers to
his lips and made a subtle saluting gesture.

Subtle like an avalanche, while you're on the slopes and you
never heard it coming, and the run was difficult to start with.

Martha turned back to Hallie. "You know why I wanted to sit
up here? Because Malcolm asked me to. He said to me, 'Martha,
I just want to see you for a few minutes while I'm directing. I want
you in my eye's view. I want to be able to look at you. You're
always so lucky for me.' And he asked if I'd sit up here."

"That's nice," said Hallie quite calmly.

"So I told him no, I couldn't. Because I was thinking, God,
Hallie's going to see me talking to you, Malcolm, and have another
shit fit. So I started backing away, and acting like a total weirdo, and
I suddenly thought to myself, this is nuts. You're not getting me
in this with you, Hallie. You go through it. I'm going to talk to
Malcolm, I'm going to sit up here for a minute if Malcolm thinks
it gives him luck, and you will just have to freak out until someone
spanks you!"

"Martha, I thought you were having a good time!"

"What a fucking lunatic you are."

"And you believe him? He just wants you as a kind of rabbit's foot?"

"Yeah, I do. I believe certain things like that. He said this was a very nerve-racking shoot day, what with the five cameras and everything—"

"I'm going to kill him."

"No, Hallie, you're going to kill me." Not a bad comeback, for a shiksa. A slight squeak in her voice gave away how she suddenly had to fight back tears. "He just asked me if I'd sit up here, for just a few minutes, because he needs some extra luck. He's going to ask Nikki to marry him." She looked at him for a moment blankly, and then with concern.

"God!" said Hallie, his head slumping forward into his hand. "Martha, I love you."

"Are you all right? Hallie, look at me."

"I can't."

"Why?"

"I'm crying."

"Oh, don't cry, come on."

"No, it's hopeless. I think I'll kill myself; I'll let you and Malcolm live, why not, you believe in things like luck."

"We make our own luck, Hallie, don't you know that?"

Hallie could only hear that there was not a bit of irony in Martha's delivery. She thought it was an intelligent statement. And worse, as he sat there with his head in his hand, she didn't even put her arms around him.

By the time the filming ended for the day, Hallie was feeling pretty bad. He and Martha had rejoined his parents in the orchestra seats and only once did he think he felt Martha's leg press against his.

Lily and Alfred left to go to Kip's opening. Hallie offered Martha the chance to go with his parents (he had to talk to Josh again), but both Martha and Lily insisted the younger Lawrences arrive together. Lily's insistence came in a simple scathing glance.

So eventually Martha and Hallie rode over to the gallery on Madison Avenue in a cab. He had really wanted to be alone with Martha, but they sat in the cab not saying very much. Hallie held her hand.

The cabdriver was a really hip-looking black dude, and Martha leaned over to him and told him she loved the song on his tape deck, could he turn it up? Clarence Clemons was singing "Savin' Up," by Bruce Springsteen. Hallie even recognized it, Martha played it so much at home.

"I like this song," Hallie said. It was pathetic.

"I wonder if Nikki's going to marry him. I wonder if she's going to say yes."

Hallie looked at the honey eyes, half hidden by the silky bangs. He looked at the lovely nose, the succulent lips, parted now in a smile, his smile, the smile Martha gave only to him. How could she be so perfect and yet so incredibly stupid?

In his mind, he replayed the way Malcolm had touched his fingers to his lips and sent the salute. Maybe you had to be there to see that it could easily have been the most intimate, tender, passionate gesture a man could give a woman, looking up at her from below. It was so good, that for all of Hallie's insights to the Degenerate Tortured Genius syndrome of Malcolm, he couldn't see it as just another performance. He saw only that this was a male who was staking a claim. If he could have grown antlers, Hallie would have run them head-on into Malcolm's chest.

"Martha," he said quietly. In fact, he was using the voice of a Hallie Lawrence who hadn't been around for some time, the controlled and elegant one. "Malcolm wants you to think he's going to ask Nikki to marry him. He wants you, Martha. Stop refusing to see this, or we're in big trouble." The voice was the old Hallie voice, but the sentiments were insane.

"Then we're in trouble, Hallie." Martha couldn't look at him.

The cab pulled up to the gallery, which was not only crowded but had attracted paparazzi like flies to manure. Hallie got out of the cab and took Martha's hand to assist her. Martha was smiling, but Hallie couldn't figure out what kind of smile it was. She pulled him playfully to her. "I'm really sorry that you don't believe that I love you. I really am."

Flashbulbs went off. Martha had taken Hallie's arm as they passed the gauntlet of photographers, and he was watching her face through the flashing lights. She still wore the funny smile and looked down modestly.

Things were beginning to appear surreal to Hallie, and the flashing lights didn't help.

Once they were in the gallery, as soon as they had joined Lily and Alfred, who were in conversation with Kip, Martha dropped Hallie's arm.

For some reason, the opening had become an "event," and Hallie was puzzled. The people milling around were almost Lily-esque in their social prominence. Somehow, the word had gotten out that the artists assembled for this show were on the absolute verge of Importance In The Near Future, which meant high prices could be charged for the art and they would still be considered bargains.

And, of course, still higher prices could be charged in the future. It wasn't bad for the artists, either.

Lily must've got the word out that drew the crowd. It made sense. She must have told someone well-placed that she wouldn't miss the show for all the world. She'd probably even mentioned Kip's name to more than a few Art Supporters. And now Lily was telling Kip that she was very proud of him, and Alfred was bellowing in agreement. They were grouped near a free-standing wall set in front of the window of the gallery, on which the painting *M* × *15 #1* was hung.

"Now, what exactly does that mean, Kip?" asked Lily. She had taken out a pair of tortoiseshell reading glasses and peered at the painting.

"What does it mean?" asked Kip. He and Hallie exchanged glances. "It means 'Starry Night.' "

"Oh, it does not," said Lily. "Besides, there already is a *Starry Night,* the Van Gogh; you can't call it that."

"I didn't," said Kip. "I called it *M Times Fifteen Number One.*"

Hallie really liked the painting and he wanted to tell Kip, but he was looking out the window, at Malcolm and Nikki lit by flashbulbs as they came toward the gallery.

"It means whatever you want it to mean," said Kip to Lily, but he was looking at Hallie. He moved closer to him. "You okay?"

"Kipper, it's a damned fine painting. I think it's the best thing you've ever done."

"It is not," said Kip.

There were far too many people in the gallery, Hallie kept thinking. It was too crowded.

It was hard to keep his eye on things. He kept trying to locate Malcolm and was aware that Martha had taken protective action by staying close to Kip. Then he saw Malcolm come to them, shake Kip's hand, and kiss Martha on the cheek.

The air was getting thick, Hallie kept thinking. Nikki, he observed, was talking to Alfred. Her arm was draped over his shoulder.

Flashbulbs went off sporadically throughout the gallery.

Hallie helped himself to a glass of champagne. Then to another.

What happened next takes a certain understanding of the physical positioning of everybody. Lily and Alfred had just left, and Kip, Martha, and Hallie were standing together near the door. Malcolm and Nikki joined them. The conversation was general. Hallie noticed Malcolm slip his hand around Martha's waist. A few of the roving photographers stationed near the door began to take shots, and as this happened, Malcolm removed his hand from Martha and put it around Nikki's shoulders. Nikki happened to look at Hallie at that moment, and the look triggered it.

Hallie took Nikki's arm and said, "Come on, we should be going. We're going to dinner."

Hallie saw Malcolm's arm tighten around Nikki's shoulders, and he saw Malcolm bend over to Nikki, and he saw Malcolm's lips touch Nikki's, and while flashbulbs were popping all around them, Hallie suddenly shoved Malcolm with all his might, knocking him off balance, and he grabbed Nikki's arm even tighter.

The whole thing took about ten seconds.

21

THERE WERE NO TWO WAYS TO IN-terpret the photograph.

With one hand Hallie had Nikki by the arm, and with the other he was shoving Malcolm away with all his might. The expression on Hallie's face showed unmistakable rage. It was on the front page of the *New York Post* the next day.

When Hallie saw it, he realized that the calls he hadn't taken all afternoon had been people calling to talk about the photograph. He had gotten more work done than he had in weeks by not taking those calls, but now he knew why Alfred had called three times.

Hallie stood in front of the news-stand in the lobby of his office building and stared blankly at the caption under the photo. It identified the photo as a romantic skirmish, an "International

Love Triangle." The glibness was unbelievable. The revulsion Hallie felt was primitive.

He grabbed the paper, with intention to buy it, but when he lifted a copy from the stack, he saw that underneath was the same picture yet again, and again under the next one, and so on. He put the newspaper back and headed across the lobby, crowded with ordinary people going home. Not only had he done to Nikki exactly what Alfred had predicted, but he had managed to become a "Tabloid Personality" himself. He headed out through the revolving door.

The air was wet with the relentless cold that comes in late February and makes people want to kill themselves. Hallie walked very carefully, a little slowly but very evenly. On the corner was another newsstand, and as he passed it, his eyes went right to the *Post*. There it was, and with the same picture. There was no chance it had been a freak printing that had arrived only at the newsstand in Hallie's building, perhaps arranged for by Lily, to teach him a lesson. It was on the *Post* all over New York. What *was* he to do about it?

There was no way he could escape the call from Alfred that would get through no matter how it was screened. There was no way he could escape the call from Kip that would be loaded with wisecracks.

The picture in that evening tabloid Nazi rag paper was very annoying. Annoying? Hallie knew it was more than annoying. He was trying to stay calm, but something in him was fizzing, as if his blood were carbonated. He thought about Lily. He stopped at a pay phone on Madison Avenue and called his mother. She wasn't home. He'd never felt so relieved in his life.

Hallie entered his building only vaguely aware of the lobby smell. He wanted Martha to be home. He wanted to talk to her about the paper. With a little luck, she wouldn't have seen the paper.

To his horror, the first thing Hallie saw when he walked into the apartment was the *Post* lying open on the living-room sofa, next to a large pile of soggy tissues and the telephone.

Martha called out from the bedroom, "God, have you seen the fucking paper?"

"Uh, yes, as a matter of fact," Hallie said.

"Have you seen it?" She came into the living room in a black sheath dress that fit like a glove. It made her dark-blond hair look lighter. She had been crying, her eyes were red-rimmed and bloodshot, but of course she still looked enormously appealing. "It's just awful, Hallie. I tell you, it's just awful!"

"Don't pay any attention to the paper, Marth."

"How could you do that, Hallie? Hammie Two called me up to see if I'm okay."

"Oh, Christ, well, did you explain it to him?"

"Explain what? How do I explain it?"

"I'm very upset about this," said Hallie.

She went over and got the paper and read from it: " 'Hallie Lawrence, brilliant lawyer, son of Alfred and Lily Lawrence, is rumored to be having more than a legal relationship with client Nikki Mikhailovitch. He got a little miffed when director Malcolm Ferrari showed affection toward Ms. Mikhailovitch. All this took place right in front of Lawrence's wife of three months, the beautiful Martha Housewright Lawrence.' How do I explain that you attacked Malcolm because he was kissing Nikki?"

"They got one thing right, 'the beautiful Martha Lawrence.' " He instantly regretted his words. "All right, I'm a jerk; I won't joke about it."

Martha gave him a blank look that told him it didn't even matter if he was a jerk. It didn't matter one bit.

He reached in for the Hallie Lawrence who used to be so good at things like making people brush off the occasional negative press. "Come on, Martha, you know that's a stack of bullshit. It'll be off the stands tomorrow, it will be forgotten, it's not even worth thinking about—" Even he could hear how much he sounded like a fool.

"Well, maybe it's nothing to you, Hallie, but to me it's just gross. The whole thing is just gross." She pulled a Kleenex from her wrist and wiped away the tears that had started to come again.

"I know how gross it is, Martha," said Hallie, finally sounding defeated.

"I'm leaving you." She turned and went into the bedroom.

"Because of one picture in the paper? Because one pimp columnist decides what a picture means?" He took off and followed her into the bedroom. "Oh, Marth, it's garbage—what's this?" He saw that on the bed was a suitcase, which she was filling with a few of her favorite things.

"You're the stupidest smart person I've ever met," she informed him.

"Stop that! Stop that packing!"

"I mean, here you are, Mr. Most Sophisticated Person in the World, Mr. Big-Time Lawyer, and you're stupider than I am!"

"You're not stupid! I don't think you're stupid, Martha! Look, will you just stop that? Why are you packing?"

"You're stupid because you can't see what that picture represents."

"What does it represent? You want to tell me?"

"It represents how stupid you are!"

"This is a brilliant conversation, Martha. Can't we have a conversation—stop packing!—that tells me a little more? What does the damn picture represent? Huh?"

"Everything, Hallie. Everything I've been going through with you since we met."

"What are you talking about—Martha, come on! You can't just pack and leave without having a conversation."

"We can have a conversation."

"If you stop packing! I'm not talking to someone who is standing there packing for some stupid-ass reason. Unpacking is another story."

She continued folding things for a few moments and then she stopped. "We can have a conversation. But I'm not unpacking."

"Jesus, I thought we had this whole thing straightened out last night."

"You got a little on the drunk side as soon as we got home; I don't think you would remember if we got anything straightened out or not. You weren't really there. Nikki called and you wouldn't talk to her. I talked to her. She said the idea of marrying Malcolm was completely and utterly out of the question. She said you were a crazy person."

"That's nice."

"I mean, we sat here, your best friend and your wife, and we told you what an asshole you are."

"Gee, sorry I missed that," he said.

"Me, too. We talked about everything. We talked about Nikki—oh, never mind, Hallie. I can't believe you don't remember any of it. Fuck, I knew at the time you wouldn't remember, so why am I surprised?"

Then all he wanted to do was grab her and say, "Enough." He wanted to hold her close to him. He wanted the balmy relief of reconciliation. But there was something equally strong that told him not even to try it; Martha didn't exactly seem receptive. He felt the beginning of some serious panic.

"You still think there's something going on between me and Nikki? Is that it?" Her honey-colored eyes looked into his and she gave him a look that told him she wasn't going to say anything. "Oh, but you're leaving me just in case. Is that it?"

"Oh, Hallie, no." She said this in a small, girlish voice and was coming toward him, to snuggle against him after all, or so it seemed. But she didn't. She passed him by and left the room.

He followed her to the kitchen, where she found a previously opened bottle of red wine and pulled out the cork.

"You want some?" she asked, again in that small girlish voice that verged on tears. She looked so sad that he reached out and took her hand. He held it for a moment, but then she withdrew it, flipped her hair back over her shoulder, and poured herself some wine.

"Oh, God, Martha—look. The film's over. We can get back to where we left off."

"It seems to me that as long as we've been together, this has been going on. I can't imagine you any other way anymore."

"What are you talking about?"

"You turned into a raving jealous maniac as soon as we got together. What if I had freaked out about that ballet dancer who showed up here that night? What if I treated you the way you've treated me about Malcolm? We had each other, Hallie, and no one who came before ever mattered. I could do it; why couldn't you?"

"Why are you so coherent?"

"Hallie, please, don't get weird. I don't think I've cried as much in ten years as I have lately."

"Well, just you wait and see how great it's going to be!" It was a line he'd been selling for too long. He suddenly felt like a phony. "Martha, I had an obligation to get involved with the film that started before I ever met you. The fact that it became such a preoccupation was more than I anticipated." That, too, he had hawked on so many previous occasions. He was no longer feeling like a phony, he was no longer feeling like himself at all.

"I think you revealed too much."

He did what?

"What did I reveal?" he asked calmly, desperately telling himself this wasn't the worst thing anyone had ever accused him of having done.

Martha sipped her wine. She turned her gaze away from him and looked off to the left somewhere, as if she were looking for the right words in the pots of ivy growing in the window.

"What happened yesterday—I could have predicted that something like that would happen, even though I really didn't think you were the type to get physically violent—was actually impressive. In a certain way, I have to tell you, I'm impressed. There have been a lot of guys who have been crazy about me, Hallie, and I mean crazy, but you really take the cake. You get the prize."

"Well? What's the prize? Another chance? It's got to be another chance!" He gave her a look that was so imploring that it caused tears to come to Martha's eyes again.

"Oh, Hallie, don't say it like that. It's too late. Get mad at me, or something. Blame me for quitting too soon. This is a real chance for you to get mad at me, Hallie."

"Martha, I'm not mad at you, I understand. I'm not letting you quit."

"Oh, dear!" said Martha, staving off a wave of sympathy for Hallie's deep brown eyes, which were looking at her with the expression of helplessness that had roped her in in the first place. She finished off her wine and rinsed her glass in the sink. Hallie stood blankly watching what she was doing, trying to think of something to say. After she had washed the glass she dried it carefully and put it back on the shelf, closing the cupboard door with a certain finality. Then she started to leave the kitchen.

"That's it? That's the end of the conversation?" He stopped her with a hand on either shoulder.

"No. There's more. But I have to pack." She walked out of the kitchen, leaving Hallie alone. He stood riveted on the spot, staring at the black-and-white floor, feeling that fizzing sensation again. His blood definitely felt carbonated.

She couldn't possibly be leaving him.

This couldn't really be happening.

He had to come up with something that would make her stay. He tried to scan an analysis of the situation, take in the whole, come up with a logical solution that would be unbeatable. But he couldn't scan a thing. All his brain had for him, even when he closed his eyes, was a soggy, gray, humid darkness. He defied it. He forced open his eyes and went to the bedroom.

Martha was really crying now, as she clicked the suitcase shut. And from time to time, she came up with a tiny, subdued sob. Hallie took all this the wrong way; he figured she was ready to melt down.

"Finished!? You packed a suitcase? Feel better? Good. I see your point of view about the whole situation. You're right, I have never behaved so badly in my life, and, believe me, I would like to tell you how embarrassed I am."

"Hallie, do you know how many times you've said that? And now you tell me you're embarrassed? I wish you didn't have to be embarrassed. It's not attractive. You shouldn't have been such an asshole in the first place."

"I'll get over being embarrassed! I'll get over being an asshole! I know I've said it before, but Christ! We were in the middle of the whole thing. Now it's over."

"You're right. It's over," said Martha, and she blew her nose into a fresh blue Kleenex.

"What are you talking about? Are you serious, Martha?" Hallie's panic was really growing now. "What about the dairy farm? You're gonna leave me to open a dairy farm on my own? Cows—suddenly cows have become my whole life! I've been secretly reading about cows myself—"

"Stop it," said Martha. "I'm in love with Kip."

The words hung around for a while, bouncing off walls, playing in the curtains, muffling in the bedclothes, dying on the rug, while neither of them moved.

"What?" Hallie asked softly, as if someone had just explained to him the theory of inverted time in a black hole.

"It just happened. I didn't want it to, God, he didn't want it to, but it just happened. We spent so much time together, Hallie, Christ!"

"What?" repeated Hallie, in the same confounded soft voice.

What Martha was telling him might have been in Cantonese; he could make absolutely no sense of her words.

"Oh, Hallie, I'm sorry. Maybe if we hadn't gotten off to such a bad start, maybe it all happened too fast— We didn't know each other, Hallie. I mean, you just swept me off my feet, but then you like threw me back down so hard, and I guess all during that time, Kip was there—"

"Kip Courtland? My friend Kip? The same Kip? You're going to try and make me think there's some kind of thing between you?"

Martha's face assumed a cold expression he had seen only a few times before. It was the kind of look you'd expect a woman as beautiful as Martha to have up her sleeve when she needed it. It was a look that shattered any previous notions you might have about your right to existence.

"Hallie," she began. Even her voice had changed slightly. "We could stand here and talk about all the things that didn't work for hours. But it's—it really boils down to three things. Number one, your insane, lunatic jealousy, and, um, number two is hard for me to say, but, well, the sex side of things wasn't—well, for me . . . God! This is hard to say—it wasn't what it should be."

"What?" Same quiet voice, but perhaps more cosmic bewilderment.

"I really loved making love to you, Hallie, I really did, I thought it was great how excited you got and everything, but I didn't— God, can you understand what I'm trying to say?"

"What's the third thing?" asked Hallie in a whispered monotone.

"Well, the third thing, and this is even harder than the second thing—which was really hard—the third thing is . . . Kip."

And then it hit Hallie Lawrence what this girl was telling him. It hit him hard.

Maybe it was the combination punch, the sex issue and the Kip issue placed next to each other that connected them into one seismic jolt that cracked his heart.

"You sle— You slept with Kip?" He hardly had any voice behind the question. "Don't answer that, please, don't answer that, please, don't answer that."

Martha didn't. She simply stared at him, her eyes wide and focused on his, her lips revealing nothing but their own beauty. Neither of them moved or made any noise. They were so quiet that Hallie could hear the refrigerator charge up out in the kitchen. He heard a siren somewhere outside and he wondered if it was a cop car or an ambulance, and where it was going. That was probably the last rational thought he was to have for the day.

He walked out of the bedroom somehow and went to the living room. He picked up the copy of the *Post,* carefully folded it, and picked up the wastepaper basket. He stuffed the newspaper into it, and then threw the basket at the wall. It crashed into a bookshelf, sending several volumes flying to the floor and breaking two pre-Columbian pots.

"Hallie, what are you doing? Hallie, don't those are good pots. They're very expensive. Don't break things up, Hallie, please."

Break things up? Had he broken anything? No, he had simply put the wastepaper basket down. What, was she crazy?

"Don't exaggerate things, Marth!"

"Hal, you look terrible. Let me get you some water."

Martha recognized the expression that clouded Hallie's face when he was about to become catatonic, which was the front he had always given her when he was really falling backward. He was now, however, falling backward at such a speed that he was forced to pay very close attention. There would be no catatonia today.

Martha came to him with a glass of water, which he took from her and gulped down, spilling most of it on his shirt, like a total spaz.

"God, you're spilling it everywhere," said Martha.

He suddenly pulled her close to him and kissed her hard. For a second he thought she might not pull away, but she did. Hallie felt a new boiling tributary join the raging river already in progress and rushing toward his brain.

"Don't, Hallie, I don't want to get turned on."

"Hey, I thought it wasn't any good for you!"

"Well, sometimes it was."

"You can't change your mind, Martha! It was either lousy or there was something going on, and I can remember a few times when I distinctly observed something going on."

"You mean the peach? I thought that was very hot. And that night when we went sort of mad and fucked all over the house."

"Well, exactly! I'm glad you noticed some of the highlights!"

"Hallie, stop it." She turned to go back into the bedroom. "I noticed a lot of the highlights."

"Martha, don't do this—" A large and scary gasp for breath came from Hallie. The fact that he held the water glass in his hand slipped his mind, as did the glass from his hand. He walked away as if he had put it on a table or something.

"You're not going. You're not leaving. You're not going anywhere. Please, Martha, don't go. Please, Martha, don't leave me, please, please, oh God! Please."

She was taking her coat out of the closet. She was putting it on. She picked up her purse and hauled the suitcase off the bed.

"No! Wait! Okay, but do you have to go now? Right this minute? You can't stay for another hour?"

"Hallie, I've told you everything. There's no point in dragging things out. I mean, when you know something hasn't worked out, there's no point trying to stick around and hope things will change."

"That's pathetic, you know that?" He saw her pick up the suitcase, drape her purse over her shoulder. "All right, all right, so go away for a couple of days. Go up to Darling. Isn't that where you're going?"

"No, it's not where I'm going, Hallie." She spoke softly and sadly, but with conviction. "I love Kip. That's where I'm going."

"You love Kip," said Hallie, slowly rolling the words over his tongue, discovering a maggot-like aftertaste. "Too bad. Because I'm going to kill him."

"I'll call you." She started for the door as tears filled her eyes.

"No! Martha, no!" And the door closed, and Martha was gone.

Suddenly, there were about three hundred feet between where Hallie stood in the foyer and the front door. He was panting as if he were running toward it, down three hundred feet of corridor, when, in fact, he was paralyzed and couldn't move at all. Martha was gone.

He had to kill Kip. It was the only thing to do.

He went into the kitchen and dialed the phone, but he got Kip's machine. He realized it would be stupid to leave a message telling Kip he was going to kill him, because it would be incriminating evidence that could be held against him when the whole fucking world was trying to figure out who killed Kip Courtland.

What about a weapon? Weapon? He would use his bare hands. He wanted them around Kip's throat. He wanted to see Kip's glasses hanging broken and smashed from one ear only.

He dropped the receiver, which fell floorward, but was jerked to a halt by the limitations of its length of cord.

He wandered into the living room. His shirt was damp from the cold spilled water, but it was only as repulsive as everything else.

Hallie sat down on the sofa and then immediately got up again. He poured himself a brandy and left the bottle open on the bar. Then he sat down on the sofa again.

Murder, he kept thinking. Murder.

After a while, this one-word thought dissolved into visions of Martha. He focused on one particular night, the first time he took her to Alfred's concert, the night he asked her to marry him, and a certain look she had given him that night. The look that had been only for him.

Now she was giving it to Kip?

The doorbell rang.

She's back. Oh, God, she's back.

But it wasn't Martha, it was Kip.

Kip was saying something to him, Kip was entering the apartment, Kip stood there talking to him. Hallie hauled off and punched him in the face with all his might, which turned out to be more might than Hallie Lawrence or Kip ever knew he had.

Kip reeled backward, his hands grabbing for his glasses, blood coming from his lip. He looked at Hallie, who was motionless, staring at him, while his hitting hand trembled.

"You asshole, you just broke your hand," said Kip. He took out a handkerchief and mopped blood coming from his badly cut lip. "You broke your hand, Hallie."

"Shut up, you pile of pigshit."

"Let me see it," said Kip, taking Hallie's hand in his.

"Fuck off!" said Hallie, backing away.

"I know you, Lawrence, you just broke your fucking hand. I heard it."

"I'm touched by your concern for my hand, scumbag!"

Kip looked at him blankly, sadly, really, but he was trying not to show it. "I want to talk to you. I've been sitting down in the car with Martha, and I just want to talk to you, Hallie."

"What do you want to talk about, Kipper? Huh? What are we ever going to talk about again? Nothing! We have *nothing* ever to talk about again. It's all gone. A lifetime of having someone to talk to, gone. You did it. You really fucked up." All things considered, this was fairly rational, coming from Hallie at that minute.

"It was a no-win situation for me, Hal."

"Oh, really?" The only thing that kept Hallie from punching Kip again was the outrageous pain beginning in his hand. He tried to move it but it was out of the question.

Hallie walked away, into the living room. He figured that if he walked a little, the pain might stop or at least reach an ebb he could cope with. But the pain was soaring, screeching, with no end in sight. He saw Kip coming into the room and realized that a lot of blood had come out of Kip's lip and even some from his nose, and there was blood all over his jacket and shirt. It made Hallie feel delirious.

"Why are you still in my house?"

"I want to talk to you."

"Forget it, and fuck off!"

Hallie checked out his hand again, surreptitiously, and noted that a definite blue color was showing through the puffing flesh, and that the skin was swelling on his finger joints, that his wedding ring was being smothered. He tried to get it off but it was out of the question.

"You broke your hand, didn't you, you asshole. You better ice it."

"You better go fuck yourself."

There was a moment of silence. Kip sat down in the club chair.

"I would never have gone after Martha, you know that—"

"I don't know anything of the kind, you son of a bitch!"

"She was just trying to understand what you were all about and I really tried to explain—"

"I bet you did, you shithead!"

"Hallie, you got completely out of hand over that pathetic asshole, Malcolm. I tried to tell you, you were making Martha nuts. If you'd seen all along what she was telling you about Malcolm and Nikki, which we now all know is a fact—"

"A fact, you fuckbrain? She turned him down!"

"He got close enough to ask!"

Hallie wanted to come up with a good retaliation, but the pain in his hand was screeching onto its plateau and it was a horrifying one. Hallie grimaced. "Get out, Kip."

"No," said Kip, taking out his handkerchief again and dabbing at the blood, which was subsiding, but still bad. "You're missing something. You're missing the most obvious part here. You shoved Malcolm yesterday because you didn't want him near Nikki, not Martha."

"Is that so?" The urge to punch Kip again welled up in his arm but stopped abruptly when it reached his hand. "You wouldn't happen to be one of the people who helped Martha think there was something going on between me and Nikki, were you?"

"Hallie, it was obvious to both of us how you felt! I explained to her that it was subconscious on your part, that you were probably not aware of your attraction to Nikki."

"That's what you explained to Martha? That's how you explained things? Agggghhh!"

Pain or no, Hallie lunged again for Kip, taking him unawares as he dived onto him, knocking them both back to the floor as the chair Kip sat in went over.

"You're a dead man!" screamed Hallie as he straddled him and began to put his hands around Kip's throat. But the mere effort of moving his left hand at all, not to mention with the force of a strangler, made him yelp and withdraw it reflexively.

"You finished?" asked Kip, pinned under Hallie on the floor. "Will you put some ice on your hand?"

Hallie began to sob uncontrollably, like a kid. He had heard Kip's caretaking words, words that Hallie had relied on for so many years, in case he did have an accident. And Kip had taught him how not to have accidents. Hallie just sobbed.

"Get out of my house, you son of a bitch," he said, crawling off Kip and climbing to his feet and going out to the kitchen.

"Hallie, I'm sorry," Kip called out, still lying on the floor, with his eyes shut. Two seconds later, Kip was on his feet and in the kitchen. And he was angry.

"Listen to me! No, you just fucking listen. I'm going to tell you the fucking truth."

"I'm not interested, Kip, don't you get it?"

"The minute I laid eyes on Martha, it was all over for me. Every time I saw her, every time I was with you two, I went nuts! And I swear to you, Hallie, she was yours, and out of the question, no way was I ever going to do anything about it. I left Kate because I knew that I had never been in love with her and I decided I would just eventually die, knowing there was no possibility that I would ever have Martha."

"So, what went wrong? Why didn't you just die?"

"Hallie—"

"I'll tell you why! Because people like you don't let themselves die, Kipper, they just go right out and get what they need to keep going! You wouldn't have died, you asshole; who the fuck are you kidding?"

"It's why I couldn't paint."

"And now you're painting up a storm! You've got Martha, is that what you're telling me?" A blistering image of Martha in Kip's arms, Kip able now to paint, fried a section of his brain. "Well, let me tell you something—your work sucks."

This created a momentary silence.

"Thank you," said Kip, with the same irony he had always used when Hallie criticized him. There was something about this response that really got to them both. Hallie sobbed. Kip began to cry, which was only the second time Hallie had ever seen him cry.

"What am I supposed to do? You did to Martha the one thing she can't deal with. You made her feel guilty. A girl like Martha doesn't know how to deal with something like guilt, especially when she didn't do anything. A girl like that just turns and walks away from it. You lost her."

The pain in Hallie's hand was taking momentary runs up and down his arm. The pain was so bad he was feeling cold. He needed a sweater. He didn't want Kip to see that he needed a sweater; yet, on the other hand, all that was over.

"Get out. I don't want to stand around here discussing this with you. You make me want to puke, Kip."

Tears were coming down Kip's cheeks, but other than that, you couldn't really see any other emotion. He took off his glasses and cleaned them badly on the least-soiled corner of his bloody hand-kerchief. "I guess you want me to say that I won't be with her."

"I want you to get out of here."

"I guess you want me to just give her up, and let her go back to Darling."

"You did it with her, didn't you. You already fucked her!" Hallie's voice raised in pitch, fired by the rage that accompanied the realization. And Hallie found that somehow screaming was a small relief from the pain in his hand. That cracking, throbbing, icy pain. So he screamed some more. "Okay, Kip, big shot, give her up! I'll give her up and you'll give her up, understand? How's that for a deal? Huh? What do you say to that?"

"I can't."

And Hallie hauled off and punched Kip again, with his broken hand, and this time he screamed from the pain. This time he broke Kip's badly cleaned glasses. For a split second, he worried that maybe the glass had gone into Kip's eyes and he would be blind, but the lenses were, of course, plastic and shatterproof, and remembering this, Hallie was enraged that he hadn't blinded the bastard.

And he was further enraged because he had now really done something terrible to his hand. The blistering plateau was left behind and the pain lifted up, exploring new heights. Yet, for all of that, he was readying to land another punch to Kip's face. Kip grabbed his arm and yelled, "What are you doing, man? Are you out of your mind? Come on, Hallie!" This last sentence actually came out as a sob. It was a terrible sound that neither of them had ever heard before, and it somehow seemed to make the true misery of the situation even worse.

Kip went to the refrigerator and took out some ice. He put it in a Baggie, added a little water, and sealed the bag. He then wrapped it in a dish towel and offered it to Hallie. "Take this and put it on your hand. You've got to go to a hospital. Do you want me to take you?"

And that did it. That was what finally did it. Kip didn't say, "I'm taking you to the hospital," which is what he would have said before; he asked, "Do you want me to take you?" He *asked* him. He had to ask. Because Kip had something better to do and they both knew what it was: be with Martha.

"There's only one thing I want from you, Kip. I never want to see you again. You're a shit-filled sleazebag. And your work sucks." The pain was making him incoherent. It was staggering how wrecked he felt, seething with rage coupled with this screaming pain.

"Go to a hospital," said Kip. Then he left the apartment, bloody lip and all.

When he was alone, Hallie began pacing, not up and down in one spot, but all over the apartment. He seemed to be trying to walk away from the shattering throb in his hand. He even, at one point, gingerly put the ice bag on it, but the pain only felt worse. He was shivering even without the ice. He was shivering and everything he saw seemed to be glowing red, and yet at the same time he felt blinded.

Lenox Hill was the closest hospital, he would go to Lenox Hill.

He went over and filled his brandy glass and forced himself to drink large gulps because it was what people did in the Old West when they had a bullet that had to be taken out, or a leg to be sawed off. For a moment, the brandy did actually work, and the level of pain became only excruciating. But the momentary clearance only made room for thoughts of Martha. The image of her with Kip, doing it. It knocked him back in his seat, right into the cushions, as he stared at the image, now playing on some vague spot on the ceiling. He watched them from a lot of different angles, on the sofa in Kip's loft—his Martha, doing it, with Kip.

He began to cry in retching, uncontrolled heaves. The cry was of almost preternatural outrage, the kind of cry that might come from having seen all of civilization from the beginning deteriorate to what it is today. He cried like that for a long time, occasionally getting up and making some kind of hopeless gesture to the air, and then collapsing back onto the sofa. He buried his head on his arm and cried, he sat back and cried wantonly.

When he finally couldn't cry anymore, he realized he only felt worse, which fired up the image of Kip and Martha again and severed a few more of the precariously few remaining cords that connected him to the rational world. He had to get out of his house.

He did it badly. Any piece of furniture in his way he kicked aside, breaking a lot of things. He put on a coat, flinched as he failed to pick up his keys with his broken hand. Some small voice told him he was going to the hospital to have his hand fixed. No, it was not so much to have his hand fixed as it was to get someone to stop the pain.

He ignored his doorman. He hated the way the guy was always asking how the fuck people were, tonight, anyway. And Hallie wasn't about to tell him.

It was unbelievably cold out now, maybe ten degrees, and fierce gusts of wind slashed into Hallie's face. But he stood there on the sidewalk, in front of his building, unable to move. Across the street was a row of town houses, with lights on in the windows. He had forgotten where he was supposed to be going. He was staring at those town houses with their lights on inside and thinking about the day at Carnegie Hall, when Martha had been sitting next to him in the first-tier box and Malcolm had smiled at her and Hallie had been shocked by the guy's audacity. Meanwhile, Martha had been banging Kip, who had been sitting with his parents, chatting amiably. A wave of sweaty dizziness defied even the briskness of the cold air. He felt both sweaty and cold at the same time. The cold was making his pain simply stunning. His hand was throbbing in steady icy jabs. He remembered that he was going to get it stopped.

He staggered over to Madison Avenue, which was the wrong way to get to Lenox Hill hospital.

Martha was with Kip.

They were driving in the car.

The same old Wagoneer that had been taking Hallie and Kip to Darling for years. She was sitting in Hallie's passenger seat. She probably had her hand on Kip's thigh.

He passed a wire garbage receptacle on the corner. Unable to use his hand, Hallie kicked it with all his might and it flew into Madison Avenue and rolled back to the curb. He kicked it again.

A stiff-assed couple about Hallie's age drew closer to each other as Hallie passed them.

"What are you looking at, cocksuckers?" he shouted.

"Alan!" screamed the woman, while Alan rushed ahead.

Hallie kept going. There were hardly any people on the street; the cold was keeping them indoors. Hallie began to feel waves of nausea and blamed it on too many colors everywhere, coming from overlit shops and galleries. Too many colors and too much bright light. He howled, a terrible animal sound, trying to release some of the pain. He didn't even have gloves. He had left in such disorder, he had forgotten gloves. He slipped the injured hand gingerly into his pocket. Even the soft lining caused agony.

Martha would probably cry for a while, then Kip would comfort her, then they would *make love.*

Kip was lousy in bed. Hallie had always pictured Kip being kind of lousy at sex. Then he remembered Martha's scathing words about the sex not being what it *should be* with him, and thought it must be better with Kip or none of this would be happening. He thought about blowing up a church.

Hallie sobbed and screamed "Goddamn it!" into the frozen night. No one came to a window or anything, because in New York it's not such an unusual sound. And it was eerie how there was no one on the street. Hallie noticed also that he was not headed toward Lenox Hill Hospital at all, and that he had to get there so somebody could give him a shot of something and he could be rendered unconscious, which seemed increasingly appealing. God, his hand was by far in the worst pain he had ever known.

He asked himself why he had to go and break his hand tonight, when the pain of Martha was all the pain he needed in the world, and then he realized the two events did have something to do with each other. He wished he hadn't hit Kip. He wished he had just stabbed him or kicked him in the balls. In the balls. He would have broken his foot if he had kicked Kip in the balls.

And then he was in front of an art gallery.

And there, in the window, was $M \times 15 \#1$.

And he realized the M stood for Martha.

He backed away, staring at the painting, and he backed into another wire garbage receptacle. And knowing no pain worse than the vision of that painting, he picked up the heavy container and hurled it with all his might through the window. Not only did it smash the shatterproof glass, triggering the shrillest alarm ever made, it went through and knocked the painting off its wall, tumbling it onto a large shard of glass that tore into the canvas.

It all happened in a matter of seconds, but to Hallie it was slow, poured motion, and it seemed he stood there for an hour before he began to run. But the minute he released the garbage container he was poised for flight and the minute he saw the painting penetrated by the glass he was gone. Flying. Running with a speed Hallie Lawrence had never known in his life. In fact, as he ran he wasn't too sure that if he flapped his arms he might not take flight and rise up over the city and be able to land on a window ledge somewhere very high up.

Fortunately, it was so cold that there were no people on the street, but as he fled Madison Avenue and flew down a side street, he heard voices shouting things like "I saw him," and "Which way did he go?" even over the shrill alarm. As he ran, coat flying out behind him, Hallie turned his head back to see if anyone was coming after him. He realized that you're never supposed to look back if you expect to outrun anybody, and then he remembered it was Kip who had told him that. He tore across Fifth Avenue and didn't stop running until he was over the wall and into Central Park. Cautiously, panting heavily, he peered back over it.

The streets were empty. The alarm was still shrieking, and a police-car siren seemed to be coming from somewhere, but no mob with a hangman's rope was riding after him.

Jesus, what had he done?

He recalled shattering the window, but it was Kip's painting with the shard of glass tearing through it that stayed in his mind.

He crouched down, trying to catch his breath. Each inhalation seemed to be directly connected to the shrill throb. All he wanted to do now was cut off his hand. He wanted to find an ax and get rid of it. Maybe he could gnaw it off, like an animal on the verge of becoming a coat. Staying crouched was no good. He had to keep moving. He set off into the park, and began sobbing again as he walked in the dark.

No one in his right mind goes into Central Park at night and expects to live. But Hallie was perfectly safe, because, of course, he wasn't in his right mind and that actually was his guardian angel. The psychos waiting for their evening slaughter wouldn't have touched the sobbing Hallie Lawrence. Too weird. But he would have killed anyone who came near him. It was really sad.

Eventually, when he was deep in the middle of the park, he stopped moving and looked up at the frozen sky. It occurred to him that all things beautiful were no longer the same. There was no more Martha. There was no more Kip. He sat on a rock in the dark, with the skyline twinkling around him. If Martha and Kip had been killed in a car crash, he knew he wouldn't have felt this bad. He cried again with big choking sobs. It was terrible.

His hand was killing him.

Looking around, he realized he was sitting near one of the park's baseball diamonds, and it came to him: no more New York Mets. He was forced to resign himself; he would have to become a Yankee fan. The horror. He thought about the night that he and Ham the pitcher had gone out to get logs, up in Darling. Ham had told him exactly what to do with Martha, and Hallie had completely blown it. He had gotten the word from the All-American himself, and Hallie hadn't heard it. He tried to console himself by thinking that Yankee colors were better anyway, but the truth was, it was no consolation. Oh, Martha.

He got up and started to run toward the West Side.

As he was mounting an incline with the ferocity of a battle horse, he slipped and found his face in wet, composting leaves. It stunned him, and he wondered if he was dead. He noticed he wasn't moving. He just lay face-down in earth-smelling, frozen leaves, which began slowly to defrost against his face and release the more pungent smell of mud. The fact that he could smell it gave him a pretty good clue that he wasn't dead at all, just catatonic. Could it be? Was he leveling off to simply catatonic?

Was this any place to have a catatonic episode, the middle of Central Park at night? He heard his mother calling, "Get out of that park now!" But Hallie couldn't move.

Voices. Youngish-sounding voices. The words were vague, but the intonation was youthful and urging. It was a teenage couple. They weren't in Hallie's mind. The girl was sounding cautious, the boy was trying to reassure her, telling her it was too cold for anyone else to be in the park. What an asshole, thought Hallie. In fact, what assholes they both were, on principle.

No more Kip. No more telling Kip about some asshole he'd seen last week. No more telling Kip about Alfred's latest World-Class EgoMania display. He should have killed Kip when he had the chance.

Hallie got up and didn't bother to brush the leaves from his hair or his coat, let alone deal with the mud on his face. He just got up and started to walk. The couple, leaning against a tree and kissing, broke apart as the girl saw Hallie and started screaming, "There's a man over there! God, he's going to kill us!" To which the boyfriend replied, "Run!" and off they went. They were good runners, thought Hallie as he watched them tear off into the darkness. Probably both Varsity something or other. If he ever had a daughter and found out that she was going into Central Park at night to make out with boys, he would move the family to northern Canada.

For one inexplicable moment, Hallie Lawrence had thought about having a daughter and the idea seemed totally normal, totally something that was meant to be. It was the damnedest thing.

The pain in his hand had reached a level by no means tolerable, but at least it wasn't going anywhere. He was beginning to incorporate it into his current vision of reality and he thought about it less constantly. It's already starting to heal, he told himself.

Hallie came out of the park and headed up West Sixty-fourth Street. He passed The Gingerman restaurant and he remembered how insane he'd felt when Martha told him she had met Malcolm there for a drink. Meanwhile, she had left Malcolm and gone to the concert with *Kip.*

He stood outside The Gingerman, staring in, looking for Martha, but he didn't know it.

When he got to Broadway, there it was, Lincoln Center. Hallie stood on the corner leaning against a lamppost, and stared at it. The performances were just over, and people were crowding out into the streets from the Philharmonic and the opera in search of refreshment, or a way to get home. A lot of people threw suspicious looks at Hallie, in his condition. But Hallie didn't notice. He just stood staring at Lincoln Center. Alfred was in there, in the Green Room.

A MIG fighter plane was launched somewhere and went screaming into the night, destination: Avery Fisher Hall. It was a kamikaze MIG, as it turned out, and it circled once and did a nose dive into the roof of the giant concert hall. The nose of the plane pierced through the roof and continued till it impaled itself in Alfred, as he stood pretending that he really wasn't a much bigger genius than Brahms. The Brahms Deferential Shuffle.

The Brahms Deferential Shuffle wasn't bad. Hallie left Alfred, MIG-impaled in the Green Room, and thought about the Brahms Deferential Shuffle as a concept, the BDS, and wondered why he and Kip and never thought of it before. A tear that Hallie wasn't even aware of slid down his cheek, making a track through the mud on his face. His nose was running and the only tissue he had was shredded past use. He wiped the tear away with his hand and thought he was pathetic, really pathetic for even thinking of Kip at all.

He stood on that corner for a long time, just staring at Lincoln Center, while his muscles were spasmodically twitching, trying to do for themselves what the idiot Hallie wouldn't do for them: move. Among the throngs on Broadway, Hallie saw a group of black teenage boys with snappy high-top sneakers and big black down-filled coats, huddled shoulder to shoulder as they walked to the beat of a radio the size of Cleveland. Hallie thought the music coming from it was very appropriate. It sounded like end-of-the-world music.

Eventually Hallie crossed the street. Lincoln Center had cleared out considerably and a only a few stragglers were making their way across the plaza, past the fountain, down the stairs, to waiting taxis, to limousines, toward subways. He stopped on the island between Broadway and Ninth Avenue and was waiting for the light to change, when he saw the Whooping Crane Lady. He recognized her at once: same old ladies' shoes, beige down coat, handbag, woolly hat with angora trim. She was waiting to cross too, or so it seemed, but she stepped off the curb and did it: "Whoop! Whoop! Whoop!" More shrill than the last time. More anguish. So much anguish that it made perfect sense to Hallie. She was screaming out against disintegration as a concept. "Whoop! Whoop! Whoop!" she repeated, this time looking right into Hallie's eyes. He did the logical thing. He stepped off the curb and screamed, "Whoop! Whoop! Whoop!" right back. Just the way she did it, like a big fat whooping crane.

"Whoop! Whoop! Whoop!" Hallie screamed again.

"Whaddya, crazy or something?" screamed the woman. And she walked off in a royal huff.

"Whoop! Whoop! Whoop!" Hallie cawed.

"*Crazy!*" screamed the woman at the top of her voice as she bustled across the street. "I can't take it anymore in this city."

The last series of whoops convinced Lily Lawrence that oh, my God, it was Hallie. She and Alfred were leaving Lincoln Center. She was poised to get into their limousine, which their driver had had to park outside tonight, when she heard the woman, then the man, whooping back. There was something oddly familiar about the man, although even from her vantage point, across the street, he did look like a bum.

"Get in, Lil," said Alfred.

"Alfred, wait a minute," she said. Lily lay her hand on his arm as she squinted to see the young man who was across the street. "Oh my God."

"What?"

"Is that Hallie?"

Alfred looked out to the young man. "What's the matter with you, Lil? He couldn't become a bum that fast."

"It is, it's Hallie."

"Get in the car."

"I've got to know."

"Get in the car, I'll find out. Take an aspirin."

Alfred went around the car and toward the street. When he got to the corner, across the street from where the young man stood, he called out, "Hallie?"

Hallie heard his name being called and saw that it was coming from the man across the street with the shock of white hair and the theatrical-looking coat worn like a cape over his shoulders. That man is my father, thought Hallie.

He simply turned and walked in the opposite direction, joining the crowd moving up Broadway.

"Of course it wasn't Hallie. What the hell makes you think it was Hallie?" Alfred asked Lily as he settled deep into the backseat next to her.

"A mother knows these things."

"That screaming lunatic in a filthy coat was your son?"

"That's true." Lily gazed out the window, but sat back only slightly.

Hallie went into a drugstore and wandered over to the prescription department. A small pharmacist stared at him from behind thick glasses. The pharmacist had three dyed hairs, grown very long from the side of his head, and brushed sideways over the gleaming-clean bald orb. The pharmacist was frowning.

"Good evening. I'd like to get a prescription filled for Demerol—"

"Well, let me have your prescription" came the squeaky, wheezy voice from below the three dyed hairs. At once Hallie realized that what the pharmacist had speculated was true: Hallie had no prescription.

"Ah, I don't actually have one on me, but if I call my doctor, he can phone one in."

"We don't accept phoned-in narcotics prescriptions."

"What are you talking about? That's not even legal."

"Legal? It's our policy, sir, that's as legal as it has to get. Not unless you have a charge account with us do we accept phoned-in narcotics prescriptions."

"So I'll open a charge account!"

The little man's lips pursed together and his shoulders shook. It was his idea of a laugh.

"Go ahead and apply. It takes two weeks before it can become active."

At that moment, Hallie understood the whole underlying cause for crime in the world today. There were people out there just asking to become sliced-up victims. The problem was, criminals, confused by nature, couldn't always recognize them, and innocent people got hurt. In a better world, criminals could be used to get rid of all the assholes. Criminals could go to asshole school and learn to recognize them. Hallie thought maybe he'd go into politics after all. He considered going around the counter and simply helping himself to a Demerol, and if this weasely little dork tried to stop him, he would knock him out. A very primal need was at issue here, the need to stop pain. And this pharmocology-nerd was standing in his way. Criminals were people who were confused, and desperate to stop the pain. That's all. Very simple. Something you've known all along. But in that moment, Hallie got closer to it.

"You have a wife?" said Hallie, leaning closer to the jerky dwarf.

"As a matter of fact, I do," said the putz, receding from Hallie as he had learned to do from watching his hairline.

"Good," said Hallie. "I just might look her up." He gave the man a regular John Garfield look, then a smile, and he walked away.

"Just exactly what do you mean by that, young man?" The squawks were supposed to sound bold, but the guy couldn't hack anything near bold because of the silliness of his voice.

On his way out of the drugstore, Hallie stole a pack of gum.

He continued walking west until he came to the Hudson River. The mighty Hudson, where, only eighty miles or so upriver, sat the town of Darling. The Lawrence house. Going to Darling would never be the same again. How could it be that Martha was gone? How did he know it was final? There were no desperate fantasies about getting her back. It hadn't even occurred to him. He just knew it was over.

The marriage to Martha was over.

Hallie almost threw up. It was pretty disgusting, the way he heaved. Actually, it had a lot more to do with the pain in his hand than it did with the horror of his loss. He was beginning to feel that it was imperative that he do something about the hand, if nothing more than lie down somewhere.

And that's how he found himself at Nikki's building on Riverside Drive, being announced by Nikki's doorman, riding up in Nikki's elevator. He rang the bell. She opened the door almost instantly, and realized Hallie was in some kind of big trouble.

"My God, what happened to you?" Her anguish was acute. "Come in, come in!"

"Are you alone?" he mumbled.

"Yes, of course, come in!"

Hallie stumbled through the door, more dazed than anything else at feeling the warmth of being indoors. "Thanks," he said quietly.

"Sit, sit down near the fire, quick, you're frozen. God, you're like ice cubes!"

"I'm freezing, Nikki," said Hallie, quietly following her orders. He moved into the living room and toward the fireplace. At first the heat felt almost painful as his veins thawed and his blood began to fill them. Hallie knelt down with both hands in front of him, warming them in front of the fire. It felt so good he began to wipe tears from his eyes onto his coat sleeve. His broken hand looked terrible. It was blue and fat.

"What's this?" came Nikki's voice, with an incredible sweetness. "What happened to your hand, Hallie? My God."

"I punched Kip," said Hallie.

"Kip? Now you're beating up Kip? What's the matter, you're not happy with hitting Malcolm anymore? Look at this hand; you're lucky you don't play the violin."

"Well, now there you go. And I thought I didn't have any luck at all," he said quietly.

The sound of Nikki's voice, teasing him even now in his hour of need, was good. That's all he could think about.

"Why are you so dirty?"

"I don't know."

Hallie just looked at her with his pitiful brown eyes. Nikki knelt down beside him. He noticed she was wearing a white robe, a satiny, smooth-looking white robe, with matching pajamas underneath.

"Martha left me. She left me for— I can't actually say it. . . . "

"You had a fight, you and Martha? This happens—"

"She left me for Kip."

Nikki said nothing. Her eyes grew subtly larger as the shock set in. They reflected light from the fire and Hallie looked into them as they sat together silently for a few moments.

"You must go to the hospital for your hand. I'll put on clothes and take you." Nikki got up and went to a silver tea service on a silver tray and poured Hallie a cup of tea. "It's still hot. You drink this while I change."

"Nikki? Is it all right that I came here?"

"Where else should you go?" She threw him a little of her daredevil sparkle. The familiarity of it felt good. "She left you? For Kip?" Nikki made a face that indicated she was, indeed, genuinely surprised.

Nikki went into her bedroom, took off her robe and pajamas, then just stared at herself in the mirror. Hallie's marriage was over. For some reason she totally believed there was no possibility of reconciliation. It was really over.

She shouldn't tell him yet, though. She should wait.

Hallie got up and went to the window. There was the Hudson River again, cold and black and shiny. A boat moved through the water, a tugboat. Was it warm in the cabin on the tugboat for the tugboaters? Nikki's house was so warm.

She had music playing. It was Rachmaninoff, the Third Piano Concerto. Hallie had always liked the piece, even though there was so much overblown sentimentality in the third movement. Nonetheless, it had always been one of Hallie's favorite pieces.

The same Rachmaninoff Concerto had been playing in the tape deck in Kip's car the day they went to Darling, the day he met Martha. Hallie's sadness was enormous, but somehow his rage was quieted.

The pain intensified as his hand began to warm. He thought about the fact that they had hammered nails through Christ's hands when they attached him to the cross and Hallie now knew how that must have felt. From now on, he would have some idea how it felt to be crucified. Jesus Christ. It left him feeling tragic.

Nikki came back dressed, carrying a warm washcloth and a towel.

"Here, let me wash off your face, you look like a homeless person."

Nikki, like a regular Mary Magdalene, gently stroked him with the hot washcloth and Hallie simply stood there gratefully. He studied Nikki's face, intent on cleaning him up, filled with more compassion than he thought he had ever seen in his life.

"This is terrible, Hallie Lawrence, I feel so bad for you." She rubbed a little harder at his cheekbone, but still with the touch of an angel of mercy. "What did you do, fight with him in the street? How did you get like this?"

"No, I hit him at my place. I guess this is from being in the park."

"You went in the park? At night? All alone? Why didn't you just walk in front of a car, instead!" Ah, the cry of the shtetl.

"Is Malcolm here?"

"No. Malcolm is gone, Hallie. He isn't here and he isn't coming here and you know I wouldn't marry Malcolm."

"Why did you let him kiss you?" Hallie asked.

Nikki then experienced something he had never seen in her before, a loss for words. She smiled, embarrassed, then the smile faded and she looked into Hallie's face nervously. "I can't tell you."

"Thanks," said Hallie.

"I can't tell you because it's the wrong time," she whispered.

"Nikki, don't do that, just tell me."

"We should go to the hospital, come on. The pain must be terrible, how can you stand the pain?"

"Nikki, why did you kiss him?"

"You're so dumb I'm not sure I even want to tell you. You probably won't even get it."

"Tell me!"

"It's the most embarrassing thing you've ever heard!"

"What?"

"I love you."

"I don't get it."

"See? I told you you wouldn't get it! Didn't I tell you? Put your coat back on—"

"I don't get why if you love me, you kissed Malcolm, that's what I don't get."

"I wanted to make you jealous, you idiot. See how embarrassing? The whole thing with Malcolm, I realized one night, I was doing to make you jealous. I knew you were married to Martha, whom you adored, and I don't know why I did it. You wouldn't even take it seriously that Malcolm was interested in me. I wanted to kill you! But I kept thinking what's wrong with this picture? Why is this man

with the wrong woman? Why is this man, this Hallie Lawrence"—
she looked down—"not with me? I wanted to be able to accept it,
but I couldn't. It's just that simple. Some part of me wouldn't accept
it at all. I tried to call you up last night to apologize. I was horrified
at what you did. I guess I just no longer expected you to respond
to my little flirtations. Finally, when you did, it made the front page.
I'm sorry Martha left you. I'm sorry she went with Kip. But I'm not
killing myself, you understand? Because . . . I love you."

Something deep in the center of the entire Hallie Lawrence
being began to make its way through ruins left by recent events.
A small and rubble-strewn passage had opened and something deep
inside him was being released, a twisting, crawling vapor, so sweet,
so all-encompassing in the comfort it afforded every cell of his
body, every cell of his mind, that it left Hallie in a state of amazement. He just looked at Nikki and she just looked at him back. The
longer they stood like that, with the Rachmaninoff still playing in
the background, the more nervous Nikki became. She rubbed her
hands together, seemed to be thinking about something, and then
she spoke.

"I was so used to having what I wanted all my life. When I spoke
to you that night at Lily and Alfred's, on the terrace, I thought,
bang! This is the man for me. I wasn't wrong when I had a crush
on you such a long time ago. I made up my mind, that night. I saw
it in your eyes and I was so sure you saw it in mine. But what
happens, before I have a chance? You go away for two days and
come back with some shiksa, some beautiful-beyond-belief woman,
who is also terrific." Nikki shrugged a little, a shrug of acknowledg-
ment. It was adorable. She even smiled. "The more time I spend
with you, the more I think there's been a mistake. God was out
getting a snack when this happened. If He would come back already, He would change things, I'm sure."

He took her in his arms and held her, probably tighter than he
had ever held anyone, until he felt as if everything in him had
flowed into Nikki, as if everything that was Nikki had flowed
into him.

"Nikki," he whispered into the fragrant curls. "I can't stand the
pain."

"Come. Don't worry about it, Hallie, they can fix it."

"You love me, Nikki? You don't really love me."

She put on her coat. "Sure I do. But don't ever bring it up again."

And then he kissed her, to the final unbearably corny, sentimental, heart-ripped-open-to-the-sky finale of the Rachmaninoff Third
Piano Concerto. He couldn't figure out why, with the pain in his
hand, with the devastating loss of Martha, he could possibly find a

kiss for this woman right now. It was as if he had momentarily been taken out of his body, his soma having evaporated, and had fallen into the music, and from the music came the kiss. And once it started, he felt so soothed, so deeply comforted somehow that he knew he was probably in love with Nikki—or else, soon would be.

Rock 'n' roll.

They didn't speak. They went out into the night and got into a taxi. The taxi took them to St. Luke's Hospital. Hallie kept thinking that John Lennon had died there. The doctors fixed his hand. Nikki and Hallie had still not spoken very much.

She took him back to her house because he said he didn't want to go home. He just wanted to hold her. His exhaustion was profound. His hand had stopped hurting, thanks to some pills. She told him he could sleep in the spare room. He said no way. They slept in her bed and he held her close to him all night.

And they slept happily ever after.

Epilogue

THAT'S THE HALLIE LAWRENCE story, everything that actually happened. One good thing to come of it was that with his union to Nikki, Hallie became a lot nicer, which is the moral of the story. Hallie Lawrence now considered it an honor when anyone showed interest in him, and he damn well meant it. He stopped calculating things.

He got a lot nicer because he realized that the worst things in life can happen, and you'll live. It made him cherish Nikki.

But the moral was lost on most people.

Most people believed that Hallie had been having an affair with Nikki all along, even though he had just married the beautiful Martha. Go figure. They were the least informed.

Some people thought that to lose

something as perfect as Martha Housewright Lawrence made Hallie a sad figure of a man. That he lost her to his best friend made him a tragic hero.

And some people realized what Nikki really meant to him.

But people sensed that the Hallie Lawrence story could happen to anybody and that's when the shudders crept in.

The most exclusive information about the story, that Hallie had in fact been obsessed with a nightmare of his own invention, stayed with the principals, and a very few others. Some people glibly said that it was obvious he hated Malcolm because he was really in love with Nikki all along, but it wasn't that easy. Hallie really did believe Malcolm was after Martha. But maybe he had to invent a catastrophe to prove to himself that he could survive, in which case he did a first-rate job.

The divorce was very simple. Martha got nothing, which is what she asked for. Throughout the whole proceeding, she was very sweet. She asked Lily please to take back the necklace that had belonged to Lily's grandmother, or she would give it to Nikki herself. Lily thought that was incredibly well-mannered. Hallie found the diamond necklace in a jar in the refrigerator. Martha married Kip immediately. They went to live in upstate New York, on land that had been in Kip's family since before the Revolution and—you guessed it—started a dairy farm. Kip had a whole barn to paint in.

On the subject of the damage done to $M \times 15$ #1, Hallie called the gallery and said he wanted to buy it, damage and all, and paid the asking price of thirty thousand dollars. Now Kip could say he had sold his first thirty-thousand-dollar painting and Hallie felt that was all he owed him, in light of having said his work sucked, in light of having punched him in the mouth. Kip called him, when the gallery stupidly told him who the buyer had been, but Hallie told him to fuck off, and call him maybe in ten years. In ten years, to the day, Kip would call him.

On the night the film opened, the Lawrences joined Hallie and Nikki for a viewing. The film wasn't bad. In fact, it got excellent reviews, especially from *The New Yorker*, which Lily said mattered most. It didn't do too much at the box office, broke even and made a bit, because basically nobody wanted to see a film about classical music. Andy Werdlow, who claimed to have said this all along, got a promotion, albeit at another studio.

Before going to the movie theater, Lily had given Nikki a present. It was the pair of fabulously important White Russian earrings with diamonds. They were Lily's favorite pair.

Needless to say, Alfred was so pleased at the union of Nikki and

Hallie that he sobbed unconrollably all during the wedding ceremony, and had to be helped to a chair right in the middle.

Nikki and Hallie lived happily ever after and spent the rest of
their lives arguing about music. After many years Nikki promoted
him from Schubert to Beethoven. But she remained Rachmaninoff,
especially the solo piano works. Nikki's career remained intact,
contrary to Alfred's predictions, and she continued to be considered one of the greatest violinists of her generation until the day
she would die, at eighty-seven.

Hallie would die three days later.

Their four daughters, their husbands, and all the grandchildren
mourned elegantly.